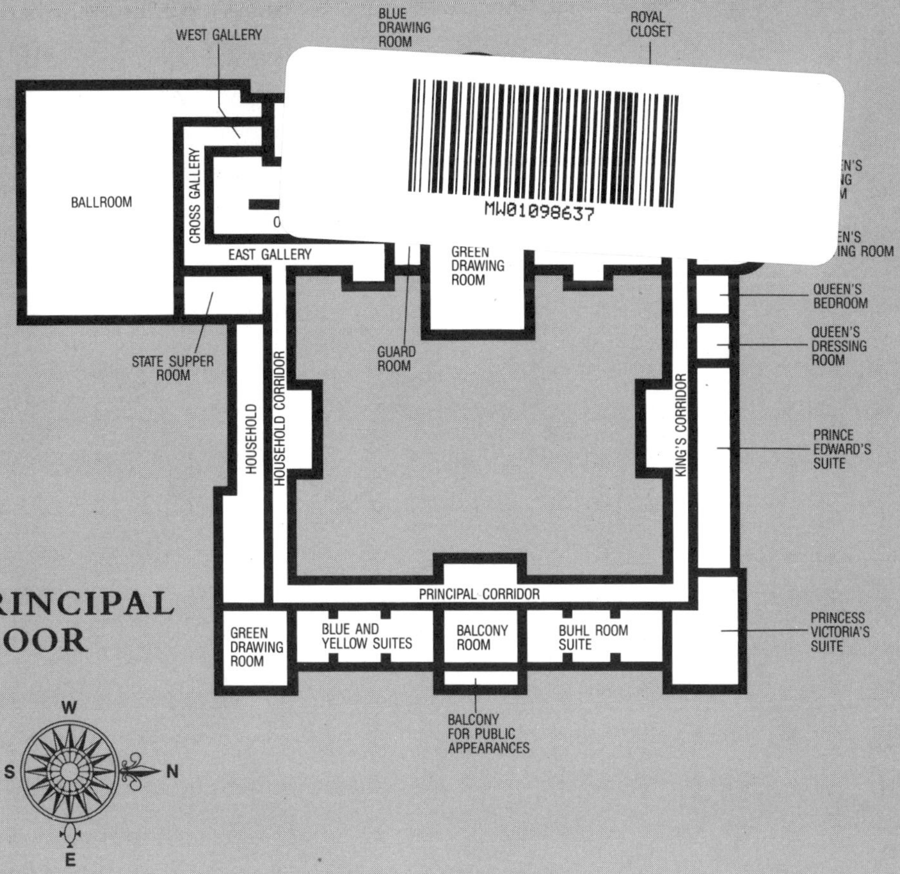

WEST GALLERY
BLUE DRAWING ROOM
ROYAL CLOSET
BALLROOM
CROSS GALLERY
EAST GALLERY
GREEN DRAWING ROOM
STATE SUPPER ROOM
GUARD ROOM
QUEEN'S BEDROOM
QUEEN'S DRESSING ROOM
HOUSEHOLD
HOUSEHOLD CORRIDOR
KING'S CORRIDOR
PRINCE EDWARD'S SUITE
PRINCIPAL CORRIDOR
GREEN DRAWING ROOM
BLUE AND YELLOW SUITES
BALCONY ROOM
BUHL ROOM SUITE
PRINCESS VICTORIA'S SUITE
BALCONY FOR PUBLIC APPEARANCES
W
S
N
E

PRINCIPAL FLOOR

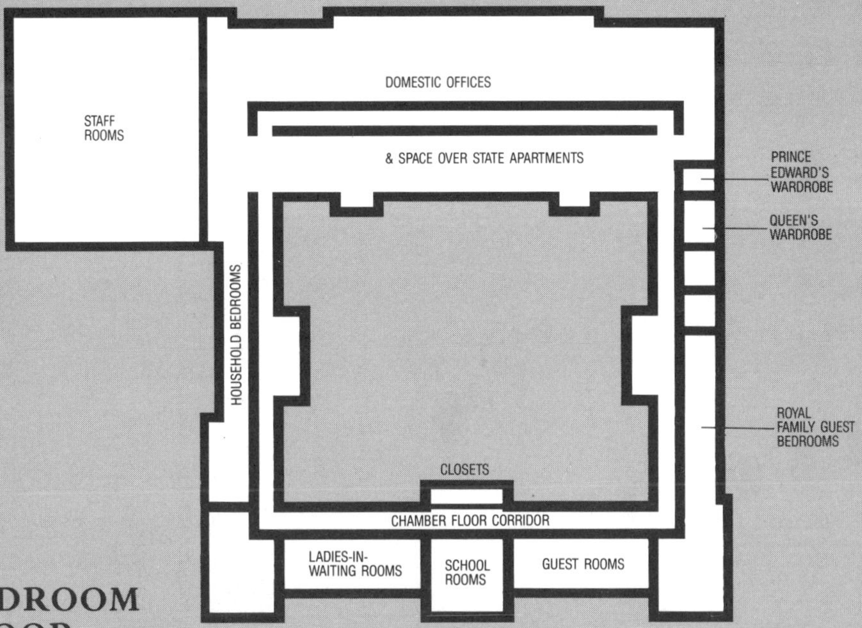

STAFF ROOMS
DOMESTIC OFFICES
& SPACE OVER STATE APARTMENTS
PRINCE EDWARD'S WARDROBE
QUEEN'S WARDROBE
HOUSEHOLD BEDROOMS
ROYAL FAMILY GUEST BEDROOMS
CLOSETS
CHAMBER FLOOR CORRIDOR
LADIES-IN-WAITING ROOMS
SCHOOL ROOMS
GUEST ROOMS

BEDROOM FLOOR

THE QUEEN'S SECRET

BOOKS BY CHARLES TEMPLETON

The Queen's Secret (1986)
An Anecdotal Memoir (1983)
The Third Temptation (1980)
Act of God (1977)
The Kidnapping of the President (1975)
Jesus: His Life (1973)

Evangelism for Tomorrow (1957)
Life Looks Up (1955)

THE

QUEEN'S SECRET

A novel by

CHARLES TEMPLETON

McClelland and Stewart

Copyright © 1986 by Charles Templeton

All rights reserved. The use of any part of this publication reproduced, transmitted in any form or by any means, electronic, mechanical, photocopying, recording, or otherwise, or stored in a retrieval system, without the prior consent of the publisher is an infringement of the copyright law.

The principal characters in this book are fictitious and are not derivative of anyone living or dead. Some of the people and organizations referred to exist, but any words, actions or attitudes attributed to them are entirely the product of the author's imagination.

McClelland and Stewart Limited
The Canadian Publishers
481 University Avenue
Toronto, Ontario
M5G 2E9

Canadian Cataloguing in Publication Data

Templeton, Charles, 1915–
    The Queen's secret

ISBN 0-7710-8451-X

I. Title.

PS8589.E46Q44 1986   C813'.54   C86-094163-9
PR9199.3.T42Q44 1986

Endpaper drawings: James Loates *Illustrating*

Printed and bound in Canada by John Deyell Printing Co.

To be a Queen and wear a crown,
is a thing more glorious to them that see it
than it is pleasant to them that bear it.
  ELIZABETH I

I would not be a Queen for all the world.
  WILLIAM SHAKESPEARE *King Henry the Eighth*

To Madeleine
. . . *again*

What follows is fiction.
It is a story of things that might have been
were they not as they are.

♕ PROLOGUE

BUCKINGHAM PALACE IS ONE OF THE TWO most celebrated dwelling places on earth, the other being the White House in Washington – although it should be noted that no tenant occupies the White House for more than eight years. Each British monarch since Victoria has lived in the palace, most of them disliking it, some expressing their dissatisfaction openly.

The public commonly thinks of Buckingham Palace as home to the royal family but it is unlikely that they regard it as such. It is, rather, the family's place of business, the head office in which The Firm – as one of its members once described themselves – does its work.

It is hardly a cosy place. There are almost six hundred rooms, with more than three hundred full-time and one hundred and twenty-five part-time employees, many of whom live in. Although each member of the royal family has spacious quarters, most of the palace is taken up by rooms of state – many of them breathtakingly opulent – business offices, service areas, and living quarters for staff.

The palace kitchens are larger than those in most hotels. Unfortunately, they are situated at the southwest corner, and if the Queen is entertaining in, say the Chinese Room – or simply having a private supper in her own dining-room –

the meals must be loaded onto large electrically heated trolleys which are then taken to the basement on a service lift, rushed along corridors to a lift on the other side of the building and finally taken up to their destination, as much as a quarter of a mile away. It hardly makes for *cordon bleu* cooking.

Among various exotica, the palace has: a private cinema, two art galleries, two "secret" doors, three hundred clocks (with two men employed full-time to wind and set them), a small emergency surgery theater, hundreds of fireplaces (only two of which work), a post office, an enclosed swimming pool, indoor squash courts, a covered riding school, and a switchboard connecting three hundred telephones and extensions. Anyone can call Buckingham Palace; the number is listed in the London directory. It is 930-4832.

There are a dozen chauffeurs, forty grooms and coachmen, ten gardeners, and a hundred or so maintenance workers. Among the twenty cars are six Rolls-Royces, each especially designed with oversize windows and raised seats to provide a better view of the passengers.

When the sovereign gives a garden party, there may be as many as eight thousand guests. The palace gardens easily accommodate them; they encompass some thirty-nine acres and include a large lake. Running through the gardens are two and a half miles of gravel pathways. There are also indoor tennis courts, a summer house, and a helicopter landing pad.

The palace might be described as a great fortress, surrounded by a thick brick wall ranging in height from eight to ten feet and surmounted by electrified barbed wire and metal spikes. At dozens of vantage points there are hooded television monitors, sirens, and auxiliary lights. The royal family is "guarded" by a number of military and semi-military forces but, most importantly, by the palace police, some two dozen officers and constables, all members of the Metropolitan Police.

For all this, there have been intruders: three teenage French girls who crashed a garden party in July 1980 simply by walking through a defective gate; three German hikers who scaled the wall in the summer of 1981 and spent the night in the garden, thinking they were camping in Hyde Park; and most notably, in 1982, a man by the name of Michael Fagan who twice broke into the palace, once to steal a half bottle of wine, and the second time to penetrate to the Queen's apartment while she was sleeping, having planned to slash his wrists in her presence.

Part 1

♔ ONE

MARY ALEXANDRA ELIZABETH ANN, Mary the Third by the Grace of God of the United Kingdom of Great Britain and Northern Ireland and of her other realms and territories, Queen, Head of the Commonwealth and Defender of the Faith, replaced the ivory and gold-plated telephone on its gilded cradle and said, "Bloody hell!"

She was in her sitting-room at Buckingham Palace and not, as she planned to be each Friday afternoon at this time, en route to Windsor Castle for the weekend. A woman of regular habits, it displeased her when the normal pattern of her life was disrupted. The delay had been occasioned by two telephone calls from the Prime Minister's office, the first, relayed half an hour earlier by her Private Secretary, informing her that the Deputy Prime Minister had called to request that she postpone her departure until the Prime Minister could himself come on the line. Mr. Forster was, the caller emphasized, unable to leave the House at the moment. Fifteen minutes later there was a further message: "The Prime Minister regrets to inform you that he will be delayed by as much as half an hour, but begging your indulgence, it is imperative that he see you this afternoon on a matter of the most urgent importance."

The Queen's pique was tempered somewhat by the

knowledge that her first minister would not have made the request unless the matter was, indeed, important. Hugh Forster was often oblique and sometimes infuriatingly noncommittal but he was unfailingly courteous and acutely conscious of the special nature of his relationship to the Queen. Knowing her fondness for the weekends at Windsor, he would not have interrupted her plans had he not thought it imperative to do so.

Moving to one of the tall casement windows, she drew aside the sheer silk curtain and pushed the window open. A rush of soft, spring air caught the curtain and billowed it behind her. The flow of traffic on Constitution Hill sounded like a distant surf. Below, a crew of gardeners was overturning the fragrant, loamy earth and snatches of their muted conversation rose to her ears. A flight of tufted ducks swept in over the north wall of the palace grounds and flurried to a raucous landing on the lake. Nearby in an Indian chestnut tree a mockingbird rehearsed. Overhead, no higher than the treetops, flat, sullen clouds scudded by. Frowning, Mary turned back to her sitting-room, leaving the window ajar.

"What ever could be on the Prime Minister's mind?"

Hugh Forster, Member of Parliament for Southwark and Bermondsey, Leader of the Conservative party and consequently Her Majesty's first minister, was also suffering from pique. As his gleaming black Bentley moved past the police barricade at Whitehall and eased to a stop at No. 10 Downing Street, he pushed open the limousine door himself and, not troubling to acknowledge the crisp salute of the duty-policeman, strode head down and face grim through the open door. On his heels, in that ungainly, arm-flapping half-run that led some political cartoonists to depict him as an ostrich, came his deputy, Owen "Chips" Chippendale.

It had not been a good day. It had begun to go wrong at 6:15 when the chiming of his bedside clock had stirred him into the head-throbbing realization that he was hung over. Nor had he anyone to blame but himself. The night before, he had dropped in late at the Canadian embassy at a reception for the new High Commissioner and had stayed on too long. The High Commissioner was an engaging, gregarious man, the heir to an enormous distillery fortune, who had been rewarded with the coveted London posting by a government grateful for his years as the party's bagman. A corpulent man in his fifties with a bibulous pixie face, he was a superb raconteur given to the telling of hilarious and raunchy anecdotes, and the two men had struck an immediate friendship. The crowd thinning, they had settled into deep, overstuffed chairs in the library, alone except for a houseman who hovered at a respectful distance, emerging from the shadows only often enough to refill their glasses.

Hugh Forster was a prepossessing man, although time had thinned and grayed his hair and gravity had tugged at his jowls. In his earlier years he had been exceptionally handsome, so much so that his political seniors were certain it would be an insuperable disadvantage. And in his first venture into the political arena their judgement seemed vindicated – the newspapers dubbed him "Pretty Boy Forster" – and it was only after he had made it into the House of Commons and had bloodied a few hard-nosed Labor backbenchers in debate that the image began to change.

Then, of course, there was the phenomenal Forster luck.

Hugh Anthony Forster had been born to privilege, the eldest son of one of the wealthiest men in England. Enrolled at Eton the day of his birth, he had not distinguished himself as a student. During the Battle of Britain he had gone straight from the classroom to the Royal Air Force and directly into Fighter Command. There, he quickly ran up a dozen kills and five probables, managing to get shot down twice, once behind enemy lines, from where he made his way to the coast and, in a makeshift, bedsheet-rigged sailboat, crossed the Channel to England.

After the war, restless, he had wandered the world, usually in the company of a roistering, one-eyed Australian adventurer whose capacity for liquor, blasphemy, and wenching had made him something of a legend. Forster named him Cy (for Cyclops) and the two of them raised various kinds of hell from the Mediterranean to Cuba to the Far East. All this came to an abrupt end when Cy fell hopelessly in love with an exquisitely beautiful Eurasian girl not five feet tall and weighing no more than ninety pounds and had been reformed with the suddenness of a convert to fundamentalism.

Back in London, Forster had joined the family firm but was soon restless behind a desk. Approached by a delegation from the Conservative riding association in Southwark and Bermondsey, asking him to stand in the next general election, he had consented, even though the seat was traditionally a Labor stronghold. On the eve of the election, with the public opinion polls forecasting almost certain defeat for the Tories, the sitting Labor member was charged with buggering a thirteen-year-old boy and Forster had won handily.

Now, in his private office at No. 10 Downing Street on a day that had gone downhill from a bad beginning, he was listening intently to the gravelly voice of Chips Chippendale, his Deputy Prime Minister. Earlier, even as his government was taking a drubbing in Question Time, Chips had slipped in beside him on the government front bench and whispered briefly in his ear. Eyes crinkled in disbelief, Forster had turned to his seatmate, his lips forming the words, "You're not serious?" and had been answered by the slightest nodding of Chippendale's gleaming bald head.

Ducking in and out of his bathroom, busy changing his shirt, he was glowering at his deputy as though holding him responsible for the bad news he had brought. "So she's having an affair," he said. "She *is* twenty, for god's sake! But marriage?. . . And to an American? Who's your source?"

Chippendale, clearly unhappy in the role of tale-bearer, grimaced and said, "Fellow by the name of Will Harrington. Absolutely trustworthy. Known him for years. He frequents a pub in your riding where Victoria and the American have been seen taking dinner. I gather there's a small, curtained-off alcove where they can be private. Will chanced to overhear them."

"Discussing marriage?"

"Marriage."

When Forster said nothing but continued occasionally to glare at him even as he knotted his tie, Chips added, "Hugh, look, I'm no happier about this than you are. I wouldn't have mentioned it if I hadn't satisfied myself that it was so."

Forster was shrugging into his jacket. "Who else knows about it?" Chippendale turned out his palms and shrugged in a gesture of futility. "And there's no question in your mind but that it's true?" He raised a hand to forestall a reply. "Never mind. I heard it myself last week and dismissed it as tittle-tattle."

He went to the telephone on his desk. "Martin, will you ring up Assistant Commissioner Benbough at New Scotland Yard. I'll hold. And, Martin, will you check that my car's standing by. I'll be going to the palace directly."

As the Prime Minister's Bentley passed through the North Gates at Buckingham Palace and moved slowly across the forecourt, another car, a sleek, bottle-green Jaguar, emerged from the Royal Mews, turned left onto Buckingham Palace Road and, tires rippling on the pebbled pavement, headed east. It had been a chill, louring March day, made miserable by an intermittent drizzly rain. With night falling, the streets glistened in the headlights of the homeward-bound traffic.

As the car paused for a red light at the entrance to Birdcage Walk, a close observer might have seen two occupants in the front seat: a bulking, balding man bent in concentration over the steering wheel and, in the passenger seat beside him, a slight young woman. It was not possible to identify her; a paisley scarf knotted beneath her chin covered her head and oversize sunglasses covered her eyes. Nonetheless, two women tourists, having seen the car exit from the Mews, ran a few steps in half-pursuit, craning their necks and chattering in magpie excitement.

The car made its surefooted way past the Parliament buildings onto the Victoria Embankment and, having followed the north bank of the Thames, crossed the river at Tower Bridge. In Bermondsey, it nosed through the heavy rush-hour traffic on Jamaica Road, passing long rows of drab, look-alike apartment buildings. The passenger had been silent through most of the journey, gazing vacantly out of the windows, but now she turned to the driver.

"You don't approve," she said, a slight smile curling the corners of her lips.

The driver was slow to respond. He was in his mid-fifties, the hair graying, the eyes deep-set beneath wiry, tufted eyebrows. "Begging your pardon, Ma'am," he said, "it's not for me to approve or disapprove."

"It's because he's an American, isn't it?"

"No, Ma'am."

"It would be all right if he were British. Billy Carnarvon, perhaps? You like him."

The driver was weighing his words. "If you'll permit me, Ma'am," he said, his tone respectful, "I'd be grateful if you didn't put such questions to me."

"Very well, then," she persisted, "tell me what your friends have to say when you're out together having a pint?"

"Ma'am?"

"Tell me. What do they say?"

"About what, Ma'am?"

"All that rubbish in the press about when I'll get married and to whom."

"It's not a subject I discuss, Ma'am."

"Discretion, thy name is MacIntyre," she said, suddenly wearying of the subject. She pulled down the visor and began to examine her face in the mirror.

The driver jogged onto a street named Paradise and then turned left, drawing up before a narrow, rectangular four-story building not thirty feet wide edging on the south bank of the Thames. The walls on either side revealed that the building had once been an integral part of a row of identical tenements, the others having long since been demolished, leaving only the vestigial memory of their rooms and halls and stairways, even their fireplaces and chimneys, imprinted on the red brick. The driver pulled up alongside a vivid green door boasting a massive brass knocker, released the lid of the trunk, lifted out a half-dozen small cardboard boxes bound together with string and, as the woman turned a key in the door, passed them to her.

"Midnight, I would think," she said and closed the door behind her.

In the dark, narrow hallway she called out, "Jeremy? . . ." There was no response. She put her parcels on the kitchen counter and went down the hallway to the living-room.

"Jeremy? . . ."

There being no reply, she crossed to the window that constituted the entire far wall and formed a frame for a dazzling view of the Thames and the city beyond. Almost beneath her feet the river slipped silently by, heavy with silt and bearing on its somber surface occasional tangles of debris. At the center of the river, a massive barge bulled its way upstream past smaller craft, all buttoned-up and moored in rows for the winter. Off to the left, beyond Tower Bridge, the illuminated cupola of St. Paul's glowed atop the ragged silhouette of the city.

The living-room was dramatic, rearing two stories high on the river side. On the near side, at the second-floor level, an open, cantilevered balcony ran the full width of the room. It was accessible only by a spiral staircase and comprised the bedroom and the bathroom areas. Even abed, one was granted a view of the river, privacy being achieved by the drawing of curtains. The walls and ceilings of the living-room had been painted moss green and trimmed with cream and gold, the dominant color having been chosen in part to camouflage the plumbing which ran the length of the ceiling and turned downward in a corner. An eclectic collection of pictures hung on every wall: oils and water-colors, prints and posters, some of them unframed. A Himalayan cat lay at the very center of the room. Having raised her head to see who had intruded, she rose, stretched, yawned, and then sauntered toward the woman, tail high in greeting.

The woman turned on a lamp and, before a mirror, removed the scarf and sunglasses and shook out her hair. Victoria Mary Elizabeth Ann, The Princess of Wales, only child of Mary III and heiress presumptive to Britain's throne, was not beautiful by the standards of the film and fashion magazines. The face was slightly asymmetrical, the nose a trifle long. The hair was its natural dark auburn and, in the dampness of the evening, beginning to draw into minuscule curls. But all of this was more than redeemed by deep-blue eyes shading toward violet, flawless skin flushed with that unique English pinkness, now heightened by her excitement. And when, in the tiny kitchen, she began to lay out the contents of the cardboard cartons, her smile of anticipation was, quite simply, dazzling.

On a tiny table, not quite square on its feet, she set out an assortment of food – finger sandwiches, roast beef sliced so thin as to be almost transparent, spears of carrots and celery, bundles of asparagus bound with strands of red and green peppers, and bowls of endive salad. Two strawberry tarts went into the refrigerator.

As she struggled to draw the cork from a bottle of red wine, there was the sound of a key in the front door. "Jeremy!" she cried, and ran into the hallway. First there was the smothering strength of his arms about her, and then a long, devouring kiss that dizzied her and made her push away to catch her breath.

The royal apartments at Buckingham Palace are on the second or Principal Floor, as it is called, and range along the entire north wing. The Queen's study is a high-ceilinged room, the most impressive of those occupied by the royal family, and features a bow window with French doors opening onto a small balustered balcony. It is more a sitting-room than a study; rich with polished woods and gold-leaf ornamentation and with oil paintings ranged around the walls. There is a settee with matching armchairs, various small tables, a balding but valuable oriental carpet and a marble fireplace. Her desk, a commodious piece with a matching lyre-back chair, is set near the windows and is surprisingly cluttered. There are heaped-up papers and books, a framed display of family photographs, an ornamented silver inkstand, an adjustable brass lamp and two overflowing *In* and *Out* wicker baskets. Near her left elbow, as she sits at the desk, is a small clock, and behind it a bouquet of cut flowers, one of a number placed about the room. There are two telephones, one equipped with a scrambler device. On a small adjoining table are the government dispatch boxes, each with a brass handle and bound in red morocco leather, delivered each day from No. 10 Downing Street and the government offices in Whitehall to wherever the Queen happens to be.

Every Tuesday evening at five o'clock (unless one or the other is out of the city, or Parliament has risen) the Prime Minister has an audience with the Queen in which he informs her about affairs of consequence in Britain and around the world. The meeting is more than a formality: Mary, as have been all of Britain's queens, was zealous at "doing her boxes," and Hugh Forster had learned early on to do his homework lest he be made to feel, in the words of one of his predecessors, "like an unprepared schoolboy."

Normally, on arrival at the palace, the Prime Minister is given a cup of tea and taken up to the monarch's sitting-room on her private lift. But on this Friday there was no time for tea, and when Forster entered and the Queen extended a hand – which he took with the slightest bow – the two of them moved immediately to armchairs on each side of the fireplace. Mary, prepared for the drive to Windsor, was wearing a tweed pantsuit with a mauve cashmere sweater and pearls. The Prime Minister was in the wrinkled oxford-gray jacket and striped trousers he had worn that afternoon in the House.

Forster noted the slight vertical frown at the center of the Queen's brow and hastened to offer his regrets. "I really must apologize for insisting on seeing you today," he said, "but I'll be away as of tomorrow for the better part of a week and. . . ." A boyish smile came to his face, and when he continued, he did so in a tone of deliberate formality. "Forgive me; it is my humble duty to beg Your Majesty's permission to leave the country."

Mary inclined her head. "Granted."

Forster pressed on. "As I was saying, I'll be gone for most of next week – "

"In Brussels and Marseilles."

"Exactly. For the Common Market sessions and on to a meeting with the NATO people."

"Then," Mary said pointedly, "perhaps we should get on with what Mr. Chippendale described as a matter of the most urgent importance."

"Indeed. Yes, indeed."

Forster shifted in his chair, casting about for the best way to introduce the subject. A fine dew of perspiration was beginning to form on his brow and he wondered momentarily whether he hadn't been precipitate in broaching the matter so soon. But clearly the story already had some currency and might well break in the newspapers during his absence. Heaven knew he already had enough on his plate without a constitutional debate in which everyone from parliamentarians to editorialists to dustmen would be putting in his penny's worth.

"I'm sorry, Ma'am," he began, his uneasiness betraying itself in an overconcern to brush away a piece of fluff on his trousers. "I'm somewhat at a loss as to how to begin."

She smiled at him, an open, easy smile. "Perhaps then, Hugh, the best course is to plunge right in."

"Indeed," he said. "Indeed. I wonder, Ma'am, if I might ask if you know a Mr. Jeremy Walsh?"

"Jeremy Walsh."

"The London correspondent for the *New York Times*."

The smile had lost something. "Yes, of course," she said. "I met him some weeks back at a dinner party here at the palace. Victoria presented him."

"He was Victoria's guest?"

"There were a dozen or so young people in. They went off afterward to the premiere of some film, as I remember. I had only a word with him." The frown was back. "I'm not quite sure I follow...."

He made a small cough behind a hand. "I believe you have known me long enough, Your Majesty, to know that I am usually direct in our conversations. My hesitation now stems from the fact that the matter is a rather delicate one and – "

She smiled at him again. "I must say, Hugh, that I've never known you to mince about so."

"Sorry," he said with a rueful look. "It's simply that I'm reluctant to presume in a family matter."

"Then let's take that as a given and get on with it." The smile was gone.

"Good enough. In a word, it has to do with Victoria and the young man I mentioned, Jeremy Walsh."

"Yes?"

"With the fact that she and Walsh have been seeing each other on a regular basis, and with what would appear to be reliable reports that they are planning to ... perhaps I might better say, talking about getting married."

Mary's face had grown flushed. In the silence, an impatient honking of horns could be heard from Constitution Hill. "I understand now why you were slow in coming to the point," she said. Her manner was offhand but there was steel in her voice. "I hope you have good grounds for your .... Forgive me, I almost said accusation."

"Yes, Ma'am, or I would not have spoken to you. I had a conversation on the subject with Assistant Commissioner Benbough at Scotland Yard not half an hour ago."

"Really, Prime Minister?" she said sharply, her eyes flashing. "I mean, *really*! Am I to take it that the personal activities of members of the royal family are now under surveillance?"

"Of course not, Ma'am. I – "

"Then surely I'm due some kind of explanation."

"Of course. As I was about to say, I'd received the report on Walsh from someone I regard as eminently trustworthy – and, I might add, the soul of discretion. He was quite certain of his facts. Consequently, there seemed no option but to look into it – believe me, solely to stop the story in its tracks. I think you'll agree it could make for a great deal of mischief. I could hardly raise it with Victoria or with you – certainly not on the grounds of rumor – and, inasmuch as the Yard is responsible for her safety and the officer assigned as her bodyguard is required to file daily reports on anything that might pose a potential danger, Mr. Benbough could not but be aware that she and Walsh are seeing each other."

Her voice had an edge to it. "Victoria has been perfectly open about it. There's been nothing clandestine."

The Prime Minister was looking at his hands, touching each fingertip to its opposite with slow deliberation. He sighed heavily. "If Your Majesty will permit me, it's been much more than that. Enough to say that I felt it sufficiently urgent to draw it to your attention. I take no pleasure in being the bearer of ill tidings, believe me."

There was a silence between them which, having begun, extended, and which neither seemed prepared to break. The Queen rose from her chair and Forster followed. He went to her, taking her proffered hand in his two hands. "I'm sure I needn't tell you how painful this has been for me. I wouldn't have come if I didn't feel it was my duty. It would be rather awkward if the press were to come upon it and begin speculating. Especially now."

"Why especially now?"

"When I return, I'm planning to table in the House a bill proclaiming Princess Victoria Day, a celebration of her reaching her majority." He smiled. "I've had a look at the preliminary planning. It's going to be a banner occasion."

Mary's voice was cool. "Yes, well, perhaps we can discuss that on your return. Good evening, Prime Minister."

In his car, insulated from the home-bound commuter traffic, Hugh Forster reached into the compact built-in bar, removed a bottle of Chivas Regal and splashed a generous amount of the tawny liquid into a glass. Drink in hand, he sat back in the seat, put his feet up, and seized the first quiet moment of the day to take stock.

The prospect did not please. His mind, trained in swift analysis, quickly laid before him the dimensions of the problem. He was confronted by a double jeopardy: if Victoria persevered in what seemed to be her intention, to marry Jeremy Walsh – and on more than one occasion Forster had had experience of the sinewy quality of her resolve – that intention might well precipitate a crisis that could result in the end of the monarchy. Of more personal concern was the fact that the white heat of such a debate might consume his government.

Hugh Forster's Conservative government was nearing the end of its second term and, as the public opinion polls agreed, was in considerable trouble. His first term had been an almost euphoric passage. He had been one of three candidates for the leadership of the party when, out of the blue, there had been an attempt on his life. Returning home late one evening, he had been ambushed by a disgruntled lorry-driver who had fired two shots at him from behind a hedge. When the driver of the car in which the would-be assassin was to make his escape panicked and drove off, the gunman was left to flee on foot. Forster took after him. Both shots had struck him: one in the upper right arm, inflicting a flesh wound, the other in the ribs, ricocheting downward through his left lung and lodging in his liver. Despite the wounds, Forster had cornered his assailant in a cul-de-sac, knocked him to the ground, and pinioned him until the police arrived. Whereupon, Forster had lost consciousness and was rushed to hospital where he hovered near death for the better part of a week.

The press, hungry for heroes in the dog days of summer, had exploited the story to the limit. The tabloids dug up and reprinted in florid detail some of Forster's exploits when he and his Australian friend, "Cy," had been adventuring around the world, made much of his record in the Royal Air Force, and raised a clamor that he be awarded the George Medal for bravery. When he had arrived at the Conservative Party leadership conference, an arm in a sling and pale from his ordeal, he had been given a tumultuous ovation. The vote was an anti-climax and, when not three months later the Labor party had been caught napping on a no-confidence vote in the Commons, the subsequent election returned the Tories with a comfortable margin.

But the United Kingdom had fallen on hard times, and after a prolonged period during which the pound sank and unemployment rose, the Conservatives were reelected by only a slim majority. Over the next four years a series of minor but meaty scandals and the loss of three by-elections in a row reduced them to a minority in the Commons. Forster had clung to power only by making concessions to a small rump in the House, a perilously unstable coalition of ultraconservatives and independents. An election in the near offing, it had been his hope to turn things around by mounting a massive celebration of Victoria's twenty-first birthday, counting on the fact that nothing so engrossed or distracted the British public as a major royal occasion.

But, as Forster knew full well, there was another side to the coin: nothing so divided Britons as the kind of controversy that had erupted when, in 1936, Edward VIII had sought to marry the American divorcée, Wallis Warfield Simpson, and when, some twenty years later, Princess Margaret had set her heart on the divorced group captain, Peter Townsend. The one had led to virtual exile and the other to an ultimatum that Margaret forgo Townsend or surrender any claim she or her children might have to the throne. And Forster knew that if Victoria persisted in her intention to marry Jeremy Walsh it would lead, almost inevitably, to the end of the monarchy. Walsh was unsuitable, not because he was an American, although that would not sit well with many, but because he was divorced and a Roman Catholic as well. Nor would the dilemma be resolved if Victoria were to abdicate. She was an only child, and the next in line of succession to the throne was a first cousin, Prince George, the Duke of Gloucester, a fatuous alcoholic who had been in innumerable scrapes since his teens and had come, in middle age, to near incompetence.

His Royal Highness, Edward, Duke of Connaught, Earl of Doncaster, Baron Montague, Consort to the Queen, was on the long distance telephone with his wife from his suite of rooms atop the Grand Hotel in Brighton where he was attending the opening session of The World Congress on Unidentified Flying Objects of which he was Honorary Chairman. For the previous three minutes he had been trying to explain why he was reluctant to return to London that evening.

"Of course I could, May darling," he was saying, "if it's really urgent, but it would be damned inconvenient. I'm to preside at the installation of the new board of directors tomorrow morning, and it's been laid-on for Nikki Fodo-rovich to drop by my digs after tonight's session. It was Nikki who made that simply marvelous sighting at Kiev. He's an amazing fellow; bright, outspoken, it's a wonder the Soviets let him come to the conference."

Although it was played down by some at the palace and was the source of occasional jibes in the press, Edward was a convinced believer in UFO's. Had he not himself, while piloting an Andover of the Queen's Flight near Lochnaga in the Scottish highlands, seen what he later described as an object "roughly the shape of a discus, with rotating lights at the circumference" which, he said, flew alongside for at least two minutes and then suddenly veered off? In his study at Buckingham Palace he maintained a large Mercator projection world map on which he pin-pointed all, as he termed them, "reputable sightings" (red for Confirmed, blue for Probables), adding to their number as reports were channeled to him.

"But, Edward," Mary was saying, concern evident in her voice, "you don't seem to grasp what I'm telling you. I'm not on the scrambler and you're on the hotel telephone so I can't go into detail."

"Tomorrow noon won't do? They're counting on me here."

"Surely it's enough to tell you that Hugh was here himself not an hour ago." Mary was losing her patience. "It affects Vicky .... All of us." She broke off. When she resumed, her tone was firm. "I'll say no more. Do as you wish."

Which was why the Duke, having tendered his regrets, was driven to the airport and within the hour was at the controls of the Royal "Wessex" helicopter on his way to London.

♛ TWO

THE BRITISH MONARCHY is the oldest secular institution in history. In over twelve centuries its continuity has been interrupted only once – for eleven years in the seventeenth century when Cromwell instituted a republic.

While dozens of kings and hundreds of pretenders in a variety of kingdoms have been either deposed, imprisoned, executed, or driven into exile, the British Crown has not only survived but has flourished. It has endured usurpers, internecine strife, abdications, assassination attempts, and republicanism. And today, perhaps more than at any time in its history, it reflects in a quite extraordinary way the diverse characteristics of the British people. In the face of the dissolution of the empire and a diminution in international status, the monarchy has demonstrated an astonishing resiliency and, although now virtually bereft of power, it is probably more beloved than at any time in its history.

Nor has the history of British royals always been admirable. Members of the royal family have been involved in murder, infanticide, fratricide, suicide, adultery, incest, bigamy, buggery, beheadings, arson, pillage, treason, and conspiracy. They have waged war and razed cities on every continent. They have also been responsible for countless acts of charity and compassion. They have endowed hospitals, museums, schools, and art galleries. Though they have slaughtered game in astounding numbers (one weekend's shoot at Sandringham bagging 3,600 birds), they have also expended money, time, and influence to preserve wildlife around the world. Some members of the royal family have been exemplars in personal morality, their marriages models of loving commitment; others have been licentious, concupiscent, and grossly self-indulgent. A number have suffered from and some have died from venereal disease. A few have been wise, gifted, and judicious; others have been simple-minded or insane. One, Prince Albert Victor, a grandson of Victoria I, was, some eminent criminologists have concluded, if not the notorious Jack the Ripper himself, at least associated with him in his crimes. Had he not died of pneumonia, complicated by syphilis, at the age of twenty-eight, he would have ascended to the throne.

Much of the success of the British monarchy derives from a commitment to an inflexible law of hereditary succession – you are *born* to the throne. And although there were departures from this precept before George I, the principle has been preserved. The crown goes from father to sons beginning with the eldest and, in the absence of sons, to daughters in order of seniority. If the sovereign has no children, his next youngest brother becomes the heir, and if there is no brother, the eldest sister, and so on. The system is, of course, sexist, which is why a male heir is referred to as "the heir apparent" while a female is usually called "the heiress presumptive": a son born after her would move her to second place in the line of succession. Even sons born to her younger brother would take precedence over her.

There is another inflexible law: the heir to the throne must be Protestant. One of the sovereign's titles is Defender of the Faith, and that faith is Church of England. And because the Church does not sanction divorce, it is unthinkable that the titular head of the Church might be divorced or marry someone who is divorced.

The stricture extends even further: brothers and sisters of the sovereign under the age of twenty-five may not, without the sovereign's consent, divorce or marry someone who is divorced. To proceed otherwise would mean the surrender of their right to the throne and the loss of their livelihood granted by Parliament.

Much of this was on Mary's mind as she awaited the arrival of her husband.

The *New York Times'* London Bureau offices are on the fifteenth floor of the International Press Center at 76 Shoe Lane, sharing the floor with the Kuwait News Agency and the CIPCO Petroleum Company Limited. The Press Center stands at the intersection of St. Bride and Stone Cutter streets, kitty-corner from the *Daily Telegraph* and one short block from Fleet Street, the heart of British journalism.

On this Thursday morning in March, Jeremy Walsh, the *Times'* chief correspondent, got off the lift at the tenth floor and, as was his daily custom, went up the stairs of the remaining five floors two at a time, congratulating himself that he was hardly winded upon reaching the top. Not bad, he thought, especially after a too-late evening the night before and much too much wine.

He was verging on being late. At 9:30 he had an appointment to interview Hugh Forster in his office at the Parliament buildings but needed first to make some notes by way of preparation and to check the teletype for queries from New York. It was early for him. His workday usually began at 10:30 and ended around 7:30 in the evening. As he liked to put it, he "enjoyed the luxury of the time difference" and tried to match as much as possible New York's hours.

There was a request on the teleprinter from Bernie Abrahams, the Foreign Desk editor: *Pls file soonest backgrounder Brussels talks*. He fired off an acknowledgment and buried his nose in the Forster clipping file for ten minutes, scribbling in furious shorthand on a wad of copy paper. Then, on the run, shrugging into his topcoat as he went, he called out to his secretary, Janice, telling her to inform Jedd Brownlee that he would have to cover Question Time in the House. Not trusting the building's notoriously temperamental elevator, he went down the fifteen floors in breakneck bounds. At the door, his chauffeured car was waiting.

At twenty-eight, Jeremy Walsh was the youngest chief correspondent in the history of the *Times'* London Bureau. He had won the coveted posting because of his imaginative and workaholic commitment to his assignments, his fascination with and expertise in European politics, and his spare but graceful reportorial style. He thought of himself not as a bureau chief but as a reporter and doubted that there was any worthier vocation. In an era of electronic journalism, when television anchormen call themselves reporters, he took an almost stubborn pride in the fact that he was a graduate of a system that required you to serve an apprenticeship in some of journalism's joe-jobs before you could think of, much less call yourself, a reporter.

And he had ascended by that route. Fresh from high school and dizzied by glamorous fantasies, he had been hired as a copy boy by the *Chicago Tribune*. On his first day as a journalist, he had (a) gone for coffee and/or food a dozen or more times, (b) extinguished a cigarette fire in a wastebasket, (c) fetched bundles of inky newspapers at the beginning of each new press run, distributing them through the editorial department, and (d) kept an ailing teleprinter in service by acting as the replacement part on a malfunctioning platen. None of which discouraged him one whit: he had attained to the presence of the legendary and would assuredly become a crime-busting reporter or a suave foreign correspondent before you could say Walter Lippmann.

Which in fact did happen, although not until, studying nights and weekends, he had earned a bachelor and master's degree at Northwestern University, with a major in journalism and a minor in European political history. As a consequence of which he had won a Rhodes scholarship to Oxford. From there it was on to the *Wall Street Journal* and finally the *Times*.

Leaning back in his leather chair, puffing on his pipe, Hugh Forster studied the reporter across the desk from him, at the moment scribbling notes on a wad of folded copy paper. What he saw was a man a little more than six feet tall, square through the shoulders but a bit on the lean side, with a mound of tightly curled brown hair worn close to his head and forward on the brow. Now, as he looked up to put another question, the eyes were seen to be almost startlingly blue under jet-black eyebrows. Broad cheekbones and a square jaw hinted at a Slavic ancestry. Good looking chap, Forster thought. I can see why Victoria is attracted to him.

It was Forster's custom from time to time to give half an hour or so to the senior reporter on the most important foreign newspapers, and the session with the *Times* had been laid on for some weeks. As late as an hour earlier, Forster had been tempted to postpone the meeting, giving as the reason the pressures prior to leaving for Brussels. But the opportunity to take the measure of young Jeremy Walsh was not one to be missed. He had decided to go ahead.

The questioning was informed, acute and at times, pressing. In other circumstances, Forster might have liked this man, but the circumstances were not other and there could be no doubt that the man sitting opposite could pose a potentially serious problem to his government.

With a part of his mind Forster had been debating whether to introduce the subject of Jeremy's relationship with Victoria, and now decided to do so. He would be oblique. Leaning forward in his chair, interlacing his fingers, he rested his forearms on the desk.

"Just before we finish up here," he said, thus effectively ending the interview, "tell me a little about yourself. I knew your predecessor quite well. You've been here now how long? Just over a year, isn't it?"

"A little longer, actually," Jeremy said. "It will be two years come October."

"Not as exciting as New York, I don't suppose?"

"No, no. I like it here," Jeremy said, anxious to get back to the interview.

"You're all settled in?"

"Yes, sir. I found a place – 'down by the pool,' as they say. On Rotherhithe Street in Bermondsey."

"In my riding, for goodness sake! There's only one building there as I remember – other than the pub. You're right on the river."

"Yes."

"The former Member and the city managed to put together a small park there. Fascinating area that, when the river was alive with trade from all over the world."

"Yes, sir. I wonder if I might ask you one fur-ther – "

"Pleasant place on a summer's day. Romantic at night."

"Yes, sir."

"You're married?"

"Divorced."

"Sorry."

Jeremy shrugged noncommittally. He was about to try for a final question when Forster began to tap his pipe on a massive crystal ashtray, emptying the ashes from the bowl. Looking up with a small, friendly smile, he said, "I hope you won't be taking one of our pretty London lasses with you when you go back home."

"No, sir," Jeremy said ingenuously. "Wouldn't want to interfere with the balance of trade."

Forster had been ready to pursue the matter further but now thought better of it. He glanced at his watch and rose from his chair. "I'm afraid I've got a meeting with my caucus." He shook hands at the door and said, "I've enjoyed our chat. We'll have to do it again soon."

Victoria and her parents were finishing a late supper in the Queen's private dining-room. Such had been the pressures of the day that it was their first opportunity to meet. The footman had brought coffee and a liqueur, and when finally they were alone, the Queen recounted the details of the previous afternoon and of the Prime Minister's unexpected visit. She told the story poorly, obviously ill at ease, frequently searching for the right word, and finished lamely. In the ensuing silence, when it seemed that Victoria was not going to respond, Edward broke in.

"Vicky, darling. . . ." He flashed a glance at his wife. "The last thing your mother and I want to do is pry, but we need to know if there's any truth in it. What I'm getting at is, are you in love with this American chap?"

Mary interjected. "More to the point, are you thinking of marrying him?"

Victoria had been toying with the bit of pastry on her plate. Now she raised her head and looked from one to the other of her parents. "I am sorry," she said. "I mean,

I'm sorry to have you learn about it this way. I intended to talk to you as soon as I'd sorted it out, but...." She gave a small shrug of futility.

"Then you are in love with him?" her mother asked.

Victoria drew a deep breath. "Oh, yes, Mother, I am."

"And you intend to marry him?"

Victoria smiled ruefully. "The question is, will he marry me? Truth to tell, I'm not at all sure he will."

"I'm afraid that's not quite the point," Mary said, rising from the table and going to the window to draw aside the curtain.

Edward cleared his throat noisily. "What your mother is saying –"

Mary turned back into the room. There was an edge to her voice. "What I'm saying is that – as I'm sure you know, Vicky – it's not a simple matter of falling in love and getting married. One doesn't do what one wants, not if it's in conflict with one's duty."

Victoria rose and remained standing, a hand on the back of her chair. "But, Mother, that's really not fair. I've done my duty. Ever since I could walk. I've gone where I've been told. I've done what's been asked. I've shaken god knows how many hands. I've smiled till my cheeks were sore. I've cut ribbons and visited coal mines and launched ships and made small talk with strangers. . . . At times I've been so bored I couldn't spit." She broke off, managing a woebegone smile. "I don't want to sound put-upon, but having lived most of my life for others I've decided that at this point I'm going to do what *I* want."

The Queen went to her and put her arms about her and the two of them stood silently holding each other. After a moment she held her daughter at arm's length. There were tears in her eyes.

"My darling," she said, "you *have* done all that's been asked of you. And the people love you for it. But you can't, you simply can't now just turn it off as though it were ... as though it were a tap. We – you, your father and I – we don't belong to ourselves. People may look at us and say, how lucky they are. To live in a palace. Money. Jewels. Servants. The best of everything." She turned to Edward, regarding him affectionately. "Your father ... spending much of his life following his wife around, careful to walk a step behind, guarding what he says."

Now she turned to Victoria. "That's what it means to be a royal. You *aren't* your own. You belong to the people. I know that sounds trite but it's true."

"It is, Vicky," Edward said.

Victoria took her coffee and joined her mother who had moved to sit in one of a grouping of chairs in a corner. "But surely," she said, "we've come to the point where some of the old ways can change."

"Some of them have," Mary said. "Can you imagine the woman you were named for doing a walkabout in Soho, as I did this morning?"

"But I'm talking about some of the sillier rules. All that nonsense about divorce, for instance. Mother, the divorce courts are full. Dozens of our friends – scads of our relatives, for goodness sake! – are divorced, and nobody gives a fig. It's just plain silly."

One of the Queen's cats leaped onto her lap and absently she began to stroke its head. "You forget, darling, that, among other things, your mother is head of the Church of England." She glanced up. "As you will be one day."

"But it's all so archaic. Nobody goes to church nowadays."

"We do."

"But that's different. We have our own chapel. But hardly anybody *does*, certainly none of my friends, except at Easter or Christmas or if someone's getting married. And rafts of Anglicans are divorced. The point is, it doesn't mean anything. It's just fusty old bores like the Archbishop, clinging to his job by hanging onto a bunch of rules as dated as the dodo."

"Your father happens to believe in those fusty old rules," Edward said, joining them. "So does your mother. You mustn't think that because something is traditional it's outdated."

"And you must remember," Mary added, "that you are who you are *because* of tradition. And I think it's fair to say that tradition, at least in part, is what held things together back in the bad times." She smiled. "And we're part of it."

Victoria shook her head in a gesture of impatience. "Oh, Mummy, that was ages ago."

There was a touch of asperity in Mary's tone. "We're going round in circles. Let's look at the realities. If you're serious about Mr. Walsh, there are three questions you'll have to deal with, *he'll* have to deal with: will he be willing to give up his American citizenship and become a British subject? Will he leave the Catholic church – "

"He's not really a Catholic. It's his family."

"Then there's the matter of his divorce. . . . By the way, where does his wife live?"

"In New York."

"Did they have children?"

"One. She's six."

A little-girl-lost look had come over Victoria's face. She smiled ruefully. "I *do* have problems, don't I?" She suddenly took heart. "But they aren't real problems. I refuse to believe that the GBP won't agree with me. That's what Jeremy calls them – the Great British Public. The world has changed. It has. I see it every day." She reached out and touched her mother's hand. "I'm not being critical of the way things have been, it's just that I believe it's time the monarchy was brought up to date."

She was suddenly elated, got to her feet and did a pirouette before her parents, ending with her hands outflung in a theatrical gesture. "Who knows," she said gaily, "but that I have come to the kingdom for such a time as this!"

Edward had gone to the parking area in the Mews to see Victoria to her car. Back in his study he extracted a book from the shelves and sat down to read. An hour later he went slowly down the corridor to the Queen's dining-room, tapped lightly on the door, and entered. Mary was in the chair in which he had left her. Some *petit point* lay in her lap untended. He went to the bar and took down a bottle of brandy. A glance at his wife brought a shake of her head. Snifter in hand, swirling the pungent liquid in the bowl, he sat down in an armchair across from her.

"You're sure you won't have a nightcap?" he asked. "A glass of warm milk, perhaps?" She shook her head again. "Then you'll excuse me," he said, taking a sip of the brandy.

There was an awkward silence. Essaying a laugh, Edward said, "This is one of those times when I wish I were a smoker. I think part of the whole smoking thing is that it gives you something to do."

Mary yielded a small smile and picked up the needlework. "Perhaps that's why I do these things," she said. She worked quietly for a moment. "Vicky got away all right?"

"Fine. Fine."

"It's none of my business, but she didn't mention where she was off to?" He shook his head. "I think I will have that brandy," she said.

As she watched her husband take down the bottle and pour the drink, Mary's frown was replaced with an affectionate smile. They had been married twenty-two years, and in that time their admiration and respect for each other had deepened. The consensus on Edward by those who knew him was an ungrudging and nearly unanimous, "Absolutely first-rate chap." He was the ideal Queen's consort. Tall. Handsome. Black of hair and dark of eye. Flat-bellied and energetic at forty-eight. Skilled at casual conversation. A bit vain, perhaps, a bit stuffy, a bit eccentric, but altogether, "Quite a decent fellow. And perfect for Mary."

Equally important, Edward was happy in his role. He enjoyed being in the public eye, liked the perks that his position yielded, and actually exulted in "spiffing up" in the various beribboned and bemedaled uniforms he was required to wear on state or ceremonial occasions. (There were three enormous walk-in closets filled with them.) The more pomp and pageantry, the more at ease he seemed, even during the elaborate and ponderously formal Opening of Parliament, an occasion that made the Queen fidgety for days before and visibly nervous during the reading of the Speech from the Throne.

At first he had not seemed the ideal candidate for husband of the young woman who would one day be Queen. There were questions about his royal lineage. He was the only son of an obscure and penniless Spanish Duke who had moved to England shortly after Edward was born and who had subsequently abandoned him to an aunt, never to reappear. There were doubts in some quarters about the legitimacy of a grandfather. But he *was* a direct descendant of Queen Victoria, and that, after some nit-picking at the College of Heralds, had led to the man baptised Prince Eduardo Alfonso Filipe becoming a naturalized British citizen, Edward Phillip Montrose, and some weeks later, (by a special act of Parliament on the eve of his marriage) Edward, Duke of Connaught, Earl of Doncaster, Baron Montague.

As he returned with Mary's brandy he said, "I've been

doing a bit of reading – that Princess Margaret-Peter Townsend business."

"And?"

"I was out of the country at the time and I hadn't realized there'd been such an unholy row."

"It was such a dreadful time for Lilibet," Mary said. "There she was, happily married, with a young family, and here was her only sister, very much in love and being flat-out forbidden to marry. I've often wondered how I would have behaved in the circumstances. Think of having to say no to your sister in a matter like that. Not simply telling her that she can't marry the man she loves but that she may not even see him any more."

"But did she have any other choice? Not really."

"Of course not. Churchill was opposed. The Cabinet was unanimous. A few of them threatened to resign if the marriage went ahead. The ridiculous thing about *that* was that three of them were divorced themselves. The clergy were on their high horse. The *Times* was thundering. The only advocates she had, poor child, were that scruffy lot who publish the tabloids. And the public, I suppose – at least that's what the polls showed." She sniffed. "Precious lot of good it did her."

A silence descended. It was Edward who broke it. "Which brings us full circle to Vicky."

"I've been telling myself that it's a bad dream," Mary said, "and that tomorrow it will all be gone." She stared at the brandy in her glass. "The terrifying thing is that the situation is even more impossible than it was for Margaret. She was only third in the line of succession – not a chance she'd ever be Queen. And Townsend. . . . A first-rate chap. Decorated in the war. Equerry to the King. Lived here in the palace for a time. The one mark against him was that he was divorced, and the innocent party at that. Poor darling Vicky, she has no idea what she's in for."

"But she could be right. Maybe the times *have* changed."

Mary was shaking her head slowly. When she responded, her voice was unsure. "They'll break her heart. They will. You'll see."

Victoria and Jeremy had decided not to have dinner in and, as darkness fell, had made their way hand in hand along the embankment to *The Famous Angel*. "The Angel," as its habitués refer to it, is a typical English public house, the name emblazoned on a wooden panel across the front of the building and repeated on the leaded-glass window panes in archaic gold-leaf lettering. It is a warm, welcoming place, redolent of the pungent, yeasty scent of draft beer, its walls decorated with a variety of ships' gear, including a bronze diver's helmet. By the main entrance is a fading replica of a ship's bowsprit in the form of the head and torso of a naked angel, hands clasped chastely before her breasts. At the center of the main room is a four-sided bar, its form repeated overhead in rows of gleaming glasses suspended upside-down. A broad staircase leads to a glass-enclosed dining-room overlooking the Thames and offering – as is proudly proclaimed – "The Best View of London Anywhere."

It was not Victoria and Jeremy's first time in the pub; they had dared it twice before; she incognito in a headscarf and dark glasses. The publican, a gregarious, neighborly man, had recognized her immediately and had ushered them up the staircase to a secluded alcove to one side of the dining-room, attending to their needs himself.

It was a Saturday night and the pub was jammed. The tumult of conversation, the boisterous laughter and occasional burst of community singing was such that Jeremy had to shout their orders for corned beef and cabbage into the cupped ear of the owner. He had brought them each a pint "on the house," but after a few sips they went to a bottle of wine, and after that, to a second. Jeremy sampled the steaming brisket, pronounced it good and wolfed down most of his portion. Victoria did little more than move hers about on the plate with her fork. They felt cocooned in a haze of happiness, unaffected even by the need to half-shout their conversation.

Afterward they strolled to Jeremy's flat, Victoria with her head against his shoulder and hugging his arm, he with his cheek against the top of her head, both of them aglow with a quiet exultancy. The wind that had blustered all day had gone off to bully elsewhere and a heavy fog had crept up the Thames, obscuring everything but the isolated areas below the street lights. Even the sounds of the city had been silenced, and the sense of isolation silenced them as well.

They'd met at one of the Queen's garden parties, mandatory ordeals at which a mixed bag of as many as eight thousand guests milled about on the lawn behind the palace, forming up in lines to be greeted by members of the royal family. This particular day had been hot and sticky and, having done her duty, Victoria was hoping to depart in all decorous haste for a dip in the swimming pool. As she mounted the steps to the terrace, heading for the sanctuary of the palace, suddenly, there before her was this man, top hat in hand, smiling in a friendly, relaxed way, impressively handsome in his swallowtail coat and striped trousers. "Hello," he'd said. "You won't remember, but I was introduced to you at the Odeon at the reception after the premiere of *The Tiger Moth*. I'm part of that necessary evil, the press. Jeremy Walsh of the *New York Times*."

She'd nodded, extended a hand, and was about to pass on when, for reasons she had not been able to recollect afterward, she had allowed herself to be drawn into a conversation. Then, again not really considering it, she'd told him that a dozen or so of the young people were going to remain behind for a swim and had invited him to join them.

"Skinny-dipping?" he'd asked banteringly. "I'm afraid I didn't bring a suit."

She felt herself color slightly. "They'll find you one," she said, turning to her private secretary who had been riding herd on her all afternoon. "Gordon will take care of it."

He'd stayed on after the swim for an informal supper, mingling easily with the group, and she'd found the opportunity for a chat. Later, abed, she found herself thinking about him. Unaccountably, she'd had a sense that their meeting was inevitable and had smiled that such a nonsensical notion had entered her mind. He'd telephoned twice the following day and left his number, but she hadn't been in and hadn't returned his calls. She had, however, left word with the switchboard that if he called again he was to be put through.

Now, back at his flat, Victoria, having eaten little, was suddenly ravenous. Jeremy busied himself, poaching two eggs and toasting muffin halves, simultaneously setting out dishes and hustling up coffee, while Victoria made that difficult by kissing the back of his neck and questing in his clothing with her hands until he was twisting and evading and squirming. Nonetheless, he persisted in getting the eggs to the right consistency and the warmed plates onto the tiny kitchen table.

Later, in his great bed, they lost themselves in their loving, the first time it had happened to both of them: there was no thought of what they were doing, no conscious giving or receiving or sharing, only an existing at the center of a sustained glow of total sensation, from which Jeremy emerged – he had no idea how much later on – to find Victoria, half uncovered, asleep.

He roused her gently. There was the pervasive knowledge that her detective was waiting at the wheel of her car somewhere in the outer darkness. She was slow to stir, but suddenly started into wakefulness with a frightened cry. While she dressed, he put on his robe and went down the spiral staircase to stand looking out of the living-room window, listening to the sound of the hooters on the shipping passing by. Of a sudden he was overtaken by a sense of foreboding that he couldn't shake, not even when Victoria came soundlessly in the near darkness to whisper that she was ready to leave. She too seemed somber, and their embrace in the hallway was awkward and oddly touched with alienation. As the door closed behind her and he watched her get into the car, he glanced at his watch. 2:35. It would be a long, dark drive back to the palace.

If Ossie Docherty had a particular talent, it was for noticing little things. Was that not how he had broken the story on "Fast Eddie" Thurston, the new All-Britain darts champion after two of his fellow staffers on the *Herald* had had a go at it and come up with little more than a tired recycling of the biographical details and some well-worn anecdotes about the man who had most of Britain's television viewers aquiver with excitement?

The scoop was all the more remarkable because Ossie did not look at all like the ace tabloid reporter he was. He was a spectacularly obese man who, even on a humid summer day, never appeared to be anything but bandbox fresh: his linen crisp, a tiny rosebud on the lapel of his superbly tailored suit and the shoes on his tiny feet reflecting a gloss that would satisfy a sergeant major.

"Fast Eddie," for all the fact that he could consistently put three darts on a space the size of a tupenny piece, was essentially a dull fellow, and when the interview in his unexceptional row-house on a prosaic Clapham street had elicited little of interest, Ossie had called upon his special gift. Left alone in the living-room when Thurston was called to the telephone, he had cast about for some little thing, a hook on which to hang his story.

There was a writing desk at his elbow with, he had noted, an ornamental brass key in the lock. What harm could there be in turning the key and edging the drawer outward with a finger just to see what might be seen?

What he had seen, projecting from beneath a stack of papers, was a portion of a polifilm envelope. And within it, when he edged it from beneath the papers, a white, powdery substance. He could hear Thurston on the telephone, so he had slipped the envelope from the drawer, tapped some of the powder onto a piece of copy paper, folded it into an improvised packet, and dropped it into his shirt pocket. When Thurston returned to resume the conversation, Ossie, cool as a cat, was in the process of lighting up a cigarette.

The headline, with a close-cropped photograph of "Fast Eddie's" face, covered the *Herald*'s front page: DARTS ACE HOOKED ON COKE. Inside, the blaring headline trumpeted: DARTS TITLE CASH USED TO FEED ADDICTION, "FAST EDDIE" REVEALS. . . . Ossie had followed up his beat three days running with "exposés" on questionable training practices among professional darts players and with a survey of liquor and drug use in sports. Most of it was a gussied-up rehash of materials in the files but it sold papers and earned Ossie a bonus.

Ossie Docherty lived in a quite presentable second-floor flat in Pimlico, the occasionally seedy business and residential area to the southwest of Buckingham Palace. Driving home from a late date with an occasional male friend, he was coming up the Mall and had entered the Victoria Memorial roundabout when the car in front of him began to flash its signal. He realized that it was about to turn into the palace at the Queen's Entrance and so, suddenly alert, hung behind. Craning his neck, he could make out that there were two people in the car but could discern no more than that. As he watched, the policeman at the gate saluted, one of the massive gates barring access to the north side of the palace swung open, and the car moved out of sight.

Ossie pulled over to the curb on Constitution Hill, turned on his map light, and made some notes. Type of car: Jaguar Saloon. Color: dark green. License number: V84-YFY. Checking his watch, he jotted down the time: 2:55 a.m. Now, what in hell would a member of the royal family be doing out at five to three on a Sunday morning?

It was a little thing, but Ossie Docherty prided himself on noticing little things.

♕ THREE

"I WONDER, MA'AM, if before we finish I might have a word with you on another matter? I've had a communication from the Prime Minister."

The speaker was Angus McCrimmon, the Queen's Private Secretary. He and the Queen had just completed their usual morning working session in her sitting-room and she was about to embark on her private correspondence. "Crimmie," as Mary called him, was undoubtedly the most important functionary at the palace but looked anything but. Balding and slightly stooped, with a liver-spotted, cadaverous face and little meat on his bones, he would have gone unnoticed in a group of nondescripts. But there was nothing ordinary about his mind or his manner. Listening, he seemed immobilized, the only movement being in the rapidly blinking eyes; but as he began to speak, every part of his slight, wiry body came into action. The eyebrows leaped or lowered, the mouth flashed fitful smiles and grimaces, and all the while the hands danced digital pirouettes and entrechats – emphasizing, minimizing, advocating, dismissing. At the end of her daily meeting with him, the Queen sometimes had to catch her breath.

But McCrimmon was invaluable to her. He was not only her secretary and confidant but her principal adviser on political, domestic, and constitutional problems. He wrote her speeches. He was the liaison between her and her ministers at home and throughout the Commonwealth. Much of his value lay in the fact that, uniquely among those with whom she dealt, he spoke to her with candor and without artifice.

The son of a Canadian High Commissioner, McCrimmon had come to his post by a not uncommon route. He had graduated from Cheltenham College and, on a scholarship, gone on to Eton from which he graduated with honors, winning a double-blue in field hockey and cricket. Completing his education, he had been enlisted by the War Office at Whitehall and later became Chief Liaison Officer with the Prime Minister's Office. Subsequently, he was transferred to the palace, made Deputy Private Secretary and, on the death of his predecessor, appointed by the Queen to his present post.

Having mentioned the communication from the Prime Minister, McCrimmon had subsided and was now sitting motionless, his black briefcase set squarely on his knees. Mary turned to him, resting a forearm on her desk. "A message from the Prime Minister," she said. "Then, by all means, let's hear it." A small wariness was evident in her eyes and McCrimmon took note of it.

"Mr. Forster called first thing this morning," he said, his eyebrows leaping and gyrating. "He is, as you know, just back from Brussels and seems greatly concerned about what he described as the friendship between Princess Victoria and Mr. Jeremy Walsh of the *New York Times*. He mentioned that he had discussed the matter with you a week ago and asked me to emphasize his concern that the problem not be permitted to develop without due attention.

"He recognizes, as I do," McCrimmon continued, his hands lacing and interlacing atop the briefcase, "that it is a subject more than a bit awkward to raise and begs your forgiveness for so persisting, but he asked me to emphasize that rumors about the relationship – if that's the proper term – are spreading and that immediate consideration must be given as to what steps might be taken in the event that certain contingencies arise."

"And what is your judgement?" Mary asked.

"Granted that the facts are as he reports them, precisely the same as his."

"I presume you've made some inquiries."

"No, Ma'am. For two reasons: the call this morning was the first I'd heard of it and I would not, of course, involve myself in a matter such as this without first discussing it with you."

"Yes, of course."

McCrimmon's eyes were wide and unblinking but the face was without guile. "When from time to time you ask my counsel on . . . family matters, let us say, you usually pay me the compliment of candor and I try to respond by being as direct as I can. I wonder then if I may ask you to fill me in on what precisely the situation is?"

Mary ran her fingers along the edge of her desk to where there was the slightest dent in the polished surface. It was a moment before she responded. "It's a quite straightforward thing. Victoria has fallen in love – very much in love, it would seem – with Mr. Walsh. She intends to marry him. She's aware of the problems. Edward and I have discussed them with her, but I'm afraid she's adamant."

"What do you know about Walsh?" McCrimmon asked. "Is he an adventurer? An opportunist? Putting it bluntly: does he see his friendship with Victoria as a way to advance his own interests?"

"I don't know. I've only met him once, and that

briefly." She looked up at him. "In the final analysis, how would one know something like that for certain?"

"Precisely," McCrimmon said. "So we must keep the possibility before us." He offered an askew smile. "I don't suppose there are any more rogues in the Fourth Estate than in other vocations. It just seems so at times."

He was massaging his bald pate, running his hand over it almost lovingly. It was a habit that, prolonged, irritated the Queen, although she had learned to expect it when he was concentrating with intensity. Content to wait, she went back to observing her forefinger as it examined the dent on the desktop.

"Might I be permitted a moment of reminiscence, Ma'am," he said. "I've been thinking back to October 1936. I was a lad at school, in my first year as a matter of fact, and we had just learned that the King, Edward VIII, was about to abdicate in order to marry that Simpson woman. I remember it well; not least because it was the subject of long and heated debates among my school chums. I remember especially going to the palace with one of my friends to see the crowds at the gates. No one spoke. There wasn't a sound. But the thing that most impressed itself on me was the way they all kept their eyes fixed on the windows, as though they expected the King to come out on the balcony, give them a wave and say, 'All's well, chaps. Off you go.'

"But my most vivid memory," he continued, "is of something said by one of my teachers, a Dr. Lionel Leighton – 'La-dee-dah Leighton,' we called him. Taught history. The morning after the abdication he began class by saying – and it was unlike him to reveal his personal feelings – 'England's back from the grave, men. Back from the grave.'"

Mary had been watching him closely, frowning, wondering if she was hearing amiss. His voice seemed choked. No, she thought, not *Crimmie*.

"I didn't think much of it at the time," he said, clearing his throat, "but later I came to the conclusion that he was undoubtedly right. If Baldwin and Parliament had yielded, if Edward had remained on the throne and been joined there by Mrs. Simpson, it would have been the end of Britain as we know her. Of that I'm certain."

"Victoria is of the opinion that this is a different day," Mary said. "She's certain the people would support her."

"As well they might, Ma'am. As well they might. But the decision won't be made by the people, it will be made by Parliament."

"Even there she believes she would have support. Sizable support."

"Possibly," he said. "Very possibly. And that is, of course, one of the reasons Mr. Forster is so concerned. It could bring him down."

"But what do *you* think?" Mary said, a trace of impatience entering her voice. "Times *have* changed. It *is* a different day. There are moments when I don't know where things are heading. There are days when I don't want to even read the newspapers."

McCrimmon was nodding his head, a dolorous expression on his face.

"Perhaps we should just bide our time," Mary said. "I simply haven't the heart to tell her she must break off with the young man."

"But she *must*, Ma'am," McCrimmon said flatly. He fluttered his hands back and forth almost as though to rebuke his words. "You will forgive me, I didn't intend that the way it sounded. I meant simply that we daren't risk it. We must stop it now. Now, without delay. I said that a confrontation on the matter could bring down the government; believe me, Ma'am, it could bring down the Crown. I have no doubt on that score."

He was more exercised than she could remember him being in all the years of their association, but Mary's impatience was growing. "I can't say I can recall you ever being so unequivocal," she said tartly. "I was looking at one of those public opinion polls yesterday, you must have seen it." He nodded. "The monarchy hardly seems to be hanging by a thread."

His nodding accelerated. "As I recall, approval of the royal family was at an all-time high and Victoria was 'The Most Admired Young Woman' – all of which, if you will permit me, means nothing. There's seldom any serious criticism of the monarchy when things are going smoothly, but let there be some crisis here at the palace and the questions begin to be asked: is the institution worth the millions of pounds it costs? Couldn't the money be better spent on the poor? Isn't the whole apparatus archaic and undemocratic? That's when the mischief can start. This is where Victoria's point is well taken: the times have changed, but not in the way she thinks. The significant change in Britain in the last while has been that the middle-class is disappearing, and the middle-class has been the strength of the monarchy. I for one certainly wouldn't want to see a national debate at this time on the wisdom of the next heir to the throne marrying an American, a man almost ten years older, and divorced at that."

Mary was suddenly weary of the discussion and wanted an end to it. "Well then, what do you suggest? Would it be a good thing for you to have Mr. Walsh in?"

McCrimmon was shaking his head. "I think that would be putting too much of a point on it. If I may suggest: might it not be a good thing to invite Walsh and a few other young people to Windsor for a weekend? Soon. It would give you a chance to get to know him, perhaps to draw some conclusions, and to observe the two of them together."

Mary's relief showed. "Splendid. Edward and I had thought of doing that but we've been postponing it. We'll do it. This weekend."

Victoria and Jeremy were idling on the Long Walk, a three-mile avenue running south from Windsor Castle past the city of New Windsor and on into the Great Park. For three centuries the path had been bordered by magnificent, soaring elm trees but they had been attacked by disease and had all been taken down. In the gathering dusk, with a full moon rising and the evening air laden with the musky scents of spring, they had slipped away from the dozen weekend guests at the castle, meeting at a rendezvous point beneath an enormous oak.

Windsor is Europe's largest surviving castle and the most imposing royal dwelling in existence. William the Conqueror chose the location in the eleventh century and erected thereon a massive timber and earthern structure, choosing the site because the lofty chalk heights overlooked the Thames, England's principal commercial artery, and commanded the area for miles around. Over the intervening centuries the castle went through many changes until today it comprises a hodgepodge of architectural styles in what, from the air, seems to be a random, rambling, and ill-conceived structure. Viewed from the ground, however, it is an imposing and integrated castle of massive grace set at the heart of some twenty-five hundred acres of parkland and playing fields.

The state apartments in the West Wing simply beggar description. Not only are the individual rooms overwhelmingly magnificent, they house some of the world's art treasures and, much of the year, are open to the public.

The Queen's personal suite and the private apartments at the southeast corner and along the South Wing are not.

Their pace leisurely, not daring even in the fading light to hold hands, Victoria and Jeremy strolled on in the soft evening air. That afternoon they had driven the twenty-five miles from London, arriving at different times, and through the afternoon and early evening had mingled with the others, exhibiting no more than a casual interest in each other. Now as they walked on, a dog began to bark in the distance and another answered. Far off there was the muted sound of an automobile horn. Then, suddenly, in a mounting tumult, a great jet swept in, thundered overhead and, running lights flashing, sloped down for a landing at Heathrow not far beyond.

"Nice crowd," Jeremy said when he could be heard again.

"Who?"

"Your friends. The ones I talked to anyway. Looking at them it's hard to believe they've got bags of money, or will have one day."

"The one with the rimless glasses – Bobby. Did you meet him?" He nodded. "His family owns most of Belgravia and part of Mayfair, just for starters."

"I liked him. Most of them, to my surprise."

"Snob."

They went on for a moment in silence. Jeremy, his voice guarded, leaned toward her and whispered, "We're being followed."

Victoria glanced over her shoulder and laughed gaily, "Oh, that's just MacIntyre."

"MacIntyre?"

"My policeman. Anywhere I go he goes."

"Even when you go walking?"

"It's his job. I remember when I got my first car and was about to take a spin. I got in the driver's seat and, next thing I knew, there he was beside me. I said, 'That's all right. I can cope, thank you,' but he said, 'Sorry, I'm afraid I'm going to be part of your life from now on.'"

"The other night at *The Angel*, he was there?"

"The only man at the bar without a drink." She laughed. "He gets to nibble a lot though." She reached over and took his hand as they walked on. "You were saying you liked my friends."

"They were ragging me – isn't that what you call it? – about cosying up to the Queen."

"Well, it was a bit much," she said, smiling. "The two of you on the settee, chatting away like old friends!"

He shrugged offhandedly. "I was just passing by and she happened to be alone for a moment. She patted the cushion beside her and said, 'Do sit down,' so I did. Simple as that. I was a little fuddled and forgot how I was supposed to address her. I almost said 'Your Majesty' and then remembered reading that nobody calls her that except on formal occasions, so I settled for 'Ma'am.'"

"Perfect. And don't worry about it, she's been called everything from 'Your Queenness' to 'Mrs. Majesty.' I've seen men so flustered they curtsied. There was one old gallant who bowed too low and couldn't get straightened up." She laughed and they walked on in silence for a moment. "Well," she exploded, "tell me, for goodness sake! What did Mother say to you?"

"Not much," he said airily. "We chatted about the high cost of tiaras and the problem these days of getting dependable help."

"Seriously."

"Not much, really. She asked me about my work, how I liked London, that kind of thing." There was the suggestion of a smile on his lips. "There *was* one thing she said, about us, that I found interesting."

When he didn't go on, she said, "Well, what, for goodness sake?"

"Nothing much, really."

"Jeremy!"

He shrugged, the smile broadening. "Perhaps I shouldn't have mentioned it. It was just that it surprised me she would make a direct reference to us."

"So help me, I may just have you beheaded and pitched off the top of Round Tower."

"Okay. Okay. She said, 'Victoria tells me you've been seeing each other from time to time.'"

"Good," she exclaimed. "Believe me, that in itself is extraordinary. And what did you say?"

"Well, I thought I might as well be shot for a sheep as a lamb, so I said, 'I'm very fond of her.'"

She laughed aloud and spun around, her skirt flaring. "Oh, I love you, Jeremy Walsh!"

"I haven't told you what she said in response."

"Well, tell me. Tell me."

"She gave me a little smile and said, 'So are we.'"

"Reproachfully?"

"No, sweetly, I thought. And there's more. I'm seeing her tomorrow. She asked me when I was returning to London and I said tomorrow evening. And she said, 'Perhaps we could have a chat before you go. Would you like to come by tomorrow at tea time?'"

She hugged his arm. "Oh, my darling," she said. "That's simply marvelous. You have no idea."

A jet whined overhead, and as it passed, another began the approach. They turned and headed back toward the castle.

The most sumptuous castle on the face of the earth, Jeremy

was thinking, and it's smack-dab on the flight-path of one of the busiest airports in the world.

It was breaking dawn and Jeremy was on his way back to London. The IRA had detonated a bomb outside Selfridges, killing three passers-by and injuring a dozen others. In the aftermath, looters had taken advantage of the shattered display windows, and when the police had used an excess of zeal in making arrests, a small riot had developed. Jeremy, pulled from his bed at four in the morning by a telephone call from his secretary, had thrown his holiday clothes in a bag and left a note for Victoria, explaining his hurried departure and asking her to tender his apologies to the Queen – he wouldn't be able to make it for tea.

He eased onto the M-4 and, once settled into the flow of traffic, smiled at the memory of Victoria's bantering question the night before as they had parted to enter the castle by different doors: "Now that you've become such good friends, how does the prospect of Mummy as your mother-in-law appeal to you?" He'd evaded the question but now had to admit that it was an intimidating prospect. It wasn't that the Queen wasn't a pleasant and, so far as he was able to judge, an intelligent and informed lady, but, as he asked himself, would it ever be possible for anyone not of the palace crowd to be wholly at ease in her presence? Hadn't he read somewhere that even the President of the United States had gotten his tongue tangled when he'd first been presented to the Queen? Perhaps some could adapt to it; the point was, could he?

Jeremy Walsh had been christened Jeremias Wladyslaw Walasciewicz in Gary, Indiana. His great-grandfather, a Polish émigré, had sweated in the Vesuvian inferno of one of Gary's blast furnaces and had died of an undifferentiated respiratory ailment at the age of forty-six. His only son had fled the steel mills and gone into business, finally acquiring an Auburn dealership in Calumet Park, a Chicago suburb, but had ended in the hands of a receiver. Jeremy's father, the youngest of six sons, had himself six sons. From childhood he had shown no interest in the world of commerce and had become a high school history teacher, resettling, oddly, almost in the shadow of the smokestacks in Gary. Supplementing his income by teaching retarded children week nights and on Saturday mornings, he was able to send all six of his sons to university. The eldest, following his father, had become a teacher and had gone to Hong Kong. Two had entered the priesthood. One sold mobile homes. The second youngest died at nineteen when the car he was driving smashed head-on into a trailer-truck.

When Jeremy first went to work for the *Chicago Tribune*, Papa Walasciewicz had not been pleased. Later, he seldom missed an opportunity to drop into a conversation a reference to "my son on the *New York Times*."

They were a closely knit family, and each Christmas the sons and wives and grandchildren gathered from wherever they happened to be living at their parents' home. Jeremy smiled as the thought occurred: what would it be like if, this Christmas, just for the hell of it, he were to introduce Vicky to his father, saying, "Papa, I want you to meet my fiancée, Her Royal Highness, Princess Victoria"? Funny? – not really. The scenario only underlined his and Victoria's essential problem: the depth and breadth of the chasm that stood between them.

As most lovers do, they had been dreaming impossible dreams, each postponing a hard-eyed look at their problems. The whole thing is impossible, he gloomed, turning out to pass a thundering lorry, even our ways of life are alien.

Yesterday had made it even more obvious. Windsor Castle! Although he'd made light of it, the incredible opulence of the place Vicky called home had intimidated him. "It's not much, but at least it's a roof over your head," he had joked. But as the group of young people had gathered with Mary and Edward in the Queen's dining-room, he had found himself ill at ease and perspiring. Yes, the group had been friendly and unpretentious and anything but stuffy. Yes, he and the other men had kicked a soccer ball about on the lawn of the Upper Ward and there had been nothing effete about the way they'd handled themselves. Yet, for all their evident goodwill, he'd been aware that he was odd man out. And for all the kidding he'd engaged in while reporting to Victoria his conversation with the Queen, the few minutes he'd spent with her had left him with a vague feeling of inadequacy. It wasn't that as a journalist he was unaccustomed to being in the presence of the famous – as the saying had it, it came with the territory – it was the overwhelming knowledge that here was a woman who could trace her ancestry back eleven and half centuries to Egbert, King of Wessex, who, it was argued, had begun this whole British royal thing. This was no mere head of state who might be ousted in the next election, no recent Nobel laureate, no Jane-come-lately film star. The Queen embodied in her person the very essence of the British people; as someone had put it, "She's the glue that keeps Britain and the Commonwealth from coming unstuck." Even more intimidating was the fact that all she was and all that she symbolized, his Vicky also would one day be and symbolize.

That is, if he, Jeremy Walsh of Gary, Indiana, didn't muck it up.

Victoria was standing at an open window in Jane Cavendish's Mayfair flat looking off over the rooftops of downtown London. It was a dazzlingly bright early April day. Overnight the sky had been swept clean of the damp, gray dullness that had mantled the city for much of the previous week, leaving a seamless vault of deepest indigo. Before her, retreating to the horizon, was an endless succession of

rooftops, a monotony of mostly red brick buildings sur-
mounting them, like so many duckpins, ten thousand
blackened chimney pots. Interrupting the pattern, and
seeming almost to offend against it, the occasional rectangular office tower, shiny and bare of ornamentation
segmented the skyline.

But as Victoria lowered her gaze, the sameness of the
cityscape ended. On nearby buildings she saw unexpected
outcroppings of marble on cornices and elevations. Tiny,
tended gardens crowded into the most unlikely places.
There, and there, and there were minuscule emerald lawns,
flagstone terraces, blossoming trees, glittering fountains,
and fish ponds, tiny balconies aflame with flowers. Even
the ubiquitous wrought-iron fire escapes were touched with
individuality.

Victoria was surprised to find her eyes blurred with
tears. I love this old city, she thought, it's a rabbit warren
of twisting streets – like a child's maze as it approaches
the river – much of it layered with grime and dirt and
communicating a stultifying meanness. And yet, for all that,
offering evidence of pleasantness and grace and of a
deliberate commitment to excellence, almost as though in
tribute to a vital and engaging old lady.

Her reverie was broken by the rude rat-tat-tat of a
jackhammer from the street below. She smiled and said
half aloud, "And there's life in the old girl yet."

"Talking about me?" Jane asked lightly, entering the
living-room with a tray on which were the makings for
tea.

Victoria laughed. "I was talking to myself."

"Part of the fallout of being in love," said Jane with
mock gravity.

"That cliché, about love being blind. . ." Victoria said
pensively. "Seems to me that when you're in love you see

things you never saw before. Or at least see them differently."

"Or *refuse* to see them," Jane added, setting out the cups and saucers on a small octagonal table.

Victoria joined her. "You're not trying to tell me something?"

"No, my darling Vicky, I'm not," Jane said. "But I do worry about you."

From their early teens, Jane and Victoria had been each other's closest and most trusted friends. They had attended the same girls' school, moved in the same circles, studied dance and drama together. Jane, who was a few years older, had taken Victoria in hand. They had discovered early on that they had much in common, not least being lonely: Victoria, an only child, was raised mostly by her nanny and saw little of her busy parents; Jane's father and mother were so preoccupied with their hatred for each other, spending so much of the time quarreling in divorce courts and in headlines over the disposition of their estate, that Jane and her brother, James, became afterthoughts. James had cleared out, moving to Australia. Jane, on graduation, had done what she had long wanted to do – open a shop specializing in antique porcelain and jewelry. She now had shops in half a dozen cities and was about to expand to the continent.

"You're not too happy about Jeremy and me, are you?" Victoria said.

Jane's tone was emphatic. "I most certainly and emphatically am. I think he's wonderful. I think he's perfect for you, and when I think of the two of you together I want to ring bells and set off rockets."

"But."

"No buts, no ifs, no ands. Romeo and Juliet, Heloise and Abelard, Beatrice and Dante, John Browning and Elizabeth Barrett. . . ."

"My goodness!"

"No, no. It's important that you know I feel this way." Victoria reached across and touched her hand. "Because," Jane persevered, "now we come to the grit in the gruel. Your mother had a word with me yesterday afternoon. At the Academy; the opening of the Renoir retrospective. Incidentally, it's simply smashing."

Victoria sipped her tea. "Tell me – about Mother, I mean."

Jane fiddled with her pearl necklace, swinging it around her forefinger. "Very well, straight from the shoulder. I don't think I'll be betraying a confidence – I'm sure she intended that I speak to you. I took it that she's unhappy about you and Jeremy."

"I'm afraid so." She sighed heavily. "Don't misread me; she's been simply marvelous – so has Daddy – but she's being ... pressured is the best word for it, I suppose. Although even Forster doesn't dare go too far with her; she can be pretty frosty. Crimmie is bending her ear, of course. *He's* the hard nut to crack. He's a Canadian but he makes some of the monarchists sound like abolitionists."

They were both silent for a moment, sipping their tea. Jane offered a flowered china dish on which there were some delicate sugar biscuits. Victoria took one but set it aside.

"The timing couldn't be worse," she said, frowning. "The government is about to introduce a bill making it official. From what I hear, there won't be any trouble on first reading but that the Opposition may – "

"What in the world are we talking about?" Jane was shaking her head, bewildered. "What bill?"

"I'm sorry. I assume that everyone's following my little drama as they do the World Cup on the telly. Forster has decided that it would be good for the country – namely his government – if everyone was to be diverted by a national celebration of my becoming twenty-one. You know the conventional wisdom: nothing so occupies the British people and helps them forget their troubles as a coronation or a royal wedding. So, he's planning an enormous bash for June 30 of next year – I won't even try to give you the gory details. It will cost a packet and go on for three days. He's hoping to ride the wave to a majority in the next general election."

"Aha!" Jane said. "Now I get it. And any controversy about you and Jeremy would rain on his parade. Oh, my god!"

Victoria was surprised to find herself again on the verge of tears. To divert them she went back to the open window. When she was sure her emotions were under control, she turned once more to her friend. "Want to know how I spent my morning? Pretty much as I spend most mornings. Breakfast with the board of the Barnardo Homes. At ten, the opening of the Cheltenham Trade Show. Guest of honor at a luncheon for winners of the Queen's Award for Export and Technology. Jane, I can't tell you how everlastingly boring it all was. Worthy? – yes, but no less mind-numbing for that. Driving here I was thinking about it. Not so much about myself as about my mother. She's been doing this kind of thing for a quarter of a century! I know it matters. I know how important the whole ritualized charade is, or at least how important it's *said* to be, but I'm not convinced. I really am not. And the truth is, Janie – and I haven't whispered this to a soul, not even Jeremy – I've come to where I've decided that, come hell or high water, I am *not* going to give up my life for it."

Jane said nothing for a moment. She had turned her cup upside down and was now rotating it on the saucer. "Can we talk about it? Candidly, I mean."

Victoria's voice was unsure again. "Oh Jane, yes! I've *got* to talk to somebody. There's no one else in the world I can go to, open myself up to."

Jane drew a deep breath and slowly exhaled it. "I'm not sure I know where to start.... Very well, let me ask you this: do you have any idea what it's going to be like if you insist on marrying Jeremy? Any *idea*?"

"Heaven knows, I've thought about it enough."

"Have you thought of what it will be like when the newspapers get hold of it?"

Victoria looked at her bleakly. "Of course. But there's nothing we can do about that."

"They'll dig into every nook and cranny of your life. And into his. They'll investigate his divorce. They'll interview his former wife. They'll snoop around his flat. They'll talk to his neighbors. You'll have to hide. Believe me, you will. He'll have to hide. He certainly won't be able to do his job."

Victoria made no response. She remained at the window, face woebegone.

"And that's just the sound and the fury," Jane continued. "Far worse are the pressures the government and the Church and the editorialists will bring to bear on you and everyone around you." Her concern had borne her forward pell-mell but now, seeing the gloom on Victoria's face, she softened. "I'm sorry. Who am I to tell you these things? Maybe I should mind my own business."

Victoria shook her head. "No. That's why I came here today. I had to talk to you. I've got to face things squarely. Better now than when I'm in it up to my ears."

Jane went to her and put her arms about her and the two friends stood together for a long while embracing. Suddenly brisk, Jane returned to the table. "Another cup of tea; that's what we need. The universal anodyne!" She busied herself with the teapot as Victoria followed her and sat down.

"Sorry to inflict this on you," she said.

"The Jane Cavendish Counseling Clinic," Jane said spiritedly. "Free and sometimes unsolicited advice twenty-four hours a day. Weekends too, if required." She laughed wryly. "Now if I could only manage my own affairs."

Victoria smiled at her. "Your problem is that you just haven't met anybody good enough to deserve you."

"No," Jane said wistfully. "No one who's prepared to let me be me. No one who wants an equal and not just a wife. But enough of that. I'll cry on your shoulder some other time." She took a moment to focus her thoughts. "Vicky, darling, a question: how much have you thought about what it'll be like if the country won't accept Jeremy and you have to ... well, leave the palace? Even leave England?"

"But it'll never come to that. Not these days."

"I'm not so sure. Think of how sticky it got for Princess Margaret. Her marrying Townsend didn't pose a threat to the throne. There was no likelihood that she would ever be queen. But the people who run things – Parliament, the Church, the newspapers that count – simply dug in their heels and agreed that they weren't going to permit it. And I can see their argument. The whole institution of the monarchy ... it looks so solid, so substantial, but it's built on public acceptance, and if that were to go, the entire structure could come tumbling down. It survives by being an all or nothing proposition. So they leaned on poor Margaret until she knuckled under. They said, 'Okay, Maggie, if Townsend's what you want, go ahead, but understand that you'll have to renounce not only your own right to the throne but the rights of any children you may have. And while you're thinking about it, bear in mind

71

that we'll also cut off your income!' Oh they rubbed her nose in it."

"It sounds so . . . heartless."

"Vicky, darling, you had better realize now how unbending people can be when they sense a threat to the things they've built their lives on, the things in which they have a stake. To be honest, I'm not all that sympathetic to Margaret, but, believe me, there was no mercy shown. They even forced her to make her renunciation in public. And guess who was the first person she had to say *mea culpa* to? – the bloody Archbishop of Canterbury. In *his* study!"

Victoria looked at her closely. "How do you happen to remember all the details? It's years ago."

Jane gave her Cheshire-cat smile and then broke into laughter. "I looked it up, for goodness sake! When I saw the way you had your jaw set, I decided I'd better swot up. Just in case."

"I'll wager you've even checked back on Edward and Mrs. Simpson."

"Nothing if not thorough," Jane said airily. "With the Windsors it was even worse, although in their case I agreed with the powers-that-be. A model of consistency, I."

"Why?"

"Can I skip my reasons for the moment? I'd rather talk about what happened to the Duke and his Duchess when they made it clear, regardless of what anyone said, that they were going to get married. Now, maybe what happened to them would have happened under any circumstances – they were a creepy pair – but what needs to be remembered is that when he was your age he was idolized. Not just in Britain, everywhere. Didn't help. They chucked him out of England; in effect, banished him for life. And something happened to the two of them. Something went out of them. Edward had said he couldn't do his work without the woman he loved by his side, but having her by his side didn't seem to help much. They drifted around the world, aimlessly, fecklessly, jet-setting their dreary way from one bit of glitter to another and ended up renting out their celebrity, turning up at American socialite parties for a fee. My god! – the former King of England! And in the end they both looked like nothing so much as two wizened old prunes."

"But Jane, we're not like them. Jeremy couldn't be more unlike the Duke."

"Of course, my darling. But you have to think of what *can* happen. Have you thought about how it would be if you had to live abroad? Has Jeremy faced what it will be like? And don't think the press will go away. They never did with the Windsors."

"But he's not a . . . royal. He works for a living." She put a hand to her mouth. "What I mean is, he's a journalist."

"But will they let him be? Won't he always be the man responsible for the abdication of the future Queen of England? The question is, Vicky, will he be able to be who *he* is? Will you?"

It was Jimmy Shanahan on the telephone to inform Jeremy that the department's pool car would pick him up at 2 a.m. for the drive to Heathrow. Shanahan was a self-consciously gregarious Irishman who had, if anything, deepened his peat-thick brogue since leaving the *Daily Telegraph* to become chief of press liaison with the Department of Trade and Industry. Jeremy noticed that his consonants were slurred and could hear the sounds of partying in the background. As he replaced the receiver, he smiled at the picture of Shanahan and his cronies getting an early start on what undoubtedly would be a hard-drinking junket.

The trip to New York had been laid-on by Trade and Industry to launch a massive export sales program. Stage-managed by an American advertising agency under the theme COOL BRITANNIA! it would introduce a line of summer products ranging from beachwear to a computerized barbecue grill to a personalized hovercraft. A British Airways *Concorde* had been leased to transport, along with Prince Edward and his personal aides, some businessmen, a clutch of civil servants, and an even dozen journalists. It would be a busy three days. There would be a civic welcome, lunch with the mayor at Gracie Mansion, the official opening of the trade show, and a speech at the Waldorf by Prince Edward to a group of buyers and entrepreneurs. Jeremy had been pleased to be included, not only because it might offer the opportunity for an informal word with Edward but also because there would be the opportunity to see his daughter, Merilee.

Suddenly hungry, he went to the refrigerator where he found a leftover piece of smoked ham. Adding a slice of cheddar, a leaf of lettuce, and a smear of mustard, he made an untidy sandwich. Flipping the top off a bottle of beer, he returned to his favorite chair in the living-room. The moon was rising over the docks in Wapping, laying an undulating path on the water and glinting on the squat silhouette of a freighter as it moved massively across the picture window and disappeared. The only sound was the clanging of a ship's bell, distant and faint and somehow sad.

He was conscious of an inner excitement at the prospect of the journey to New York City, but also of a slight chill of apprehension. It would be good to be back in the States, to spend time with old buddies in the editorial offices of the *Times* and to see Merilee again. But all of this was cast in shadow by the realization that Diane would almost certainly prove difficult and that he'd be lucky if the reunion didn't end in ugliness and recrimination.

He had met Diane the day he had gone to work for the *Wall Street Journal*. She had worked as a general factotum in the personnel department and had taken him through the building on an orientation tour, delivering him finally to editorial. She was an attractive woman – there would be no argument on that from any quarter: diminutive, skin the color of alabaster, the eyes round, revealing the entire iris and giving an impression of ingenuousness. Soft black hair framing the face, lying on the shoulders and drawing the eye down to a slender body, voluptuous even in the tweed suit she had been wearing. He was then twenty-two and normally shy with women but managed, albeit awkwardly, to make a case for the fact that he was a stranger in town and she was morally obligated to let him take her to dinner. There had been an immediate affinity struck and soon they were caught up in each other. But for all the fact that he had found her irresistible and saw her on every free evening, he knew he was not in love with her and avoided any talk of marriage, broaching it only after she told him she was pregnant.

Miss Diane Lombard and Mrs. Diane Walsh proved to be the opposite sides of the same coin. Diane Lombard was pert and pretty, engaging in conversation, quick to laugh, and adventuresome in bed. Diane Walsh, although her pregnancy was uncomplicated, soon found it necessary to quit her job, spending her days either on the telephone with friends or absorbed in an unending sequence of television soap operas. The name on the marriage certificate turned out to be not Diane Lombard but Dina Lombardi. The soft black hair began to show brown roots and the voluptuousness gave way to plumpness.

Their daughter Merilee was born in Presbyterian hospital and was adored by both parents, soon becoming, however, a bone of contention much tussled over. Rather than salvage the marriage, Merilee's birth only further estranged Jeremy and Diane, the fragile truce they sought to maintain often breaking out in guerilla forays, sometimes in all-out war. Nor had Jeremy's commitment to his job helped. Merilee was not yet three when he moved out and into a shabby tenement apartment. Jeremy was celebrating her third birthday when, arms loaded with presents, he arrived unexpectedly to find Merilee in her playpen and Diane in bed with the personnel manager at the *Journal*.

Now munching on his sandwich in the dark, Jeremy was questing about in his mind for the ideal venue for his time with Merilee, finally deciding on Central Park, where he could spread a blanket for a picnic lunch and rent a rowboat, then set off to see the toys at F.A.O. Schwartz and finally to the Bronx Zoo.

The telephone rang and he snatched it up. It was Jedd Brownlee. Had Jeremy determined when he would be returning? Thursday morning? Fine. Wednesday was going to be rough, however, and would it be okay if he hired a free-lancer to help out? And would Jeremy mind, as a special favor, calling Jedd's parents in Yonkers? Just a quick phone call to let them know he was okay and would write soon.

When he put down the telephone, he went to the window and stood, legs spread, looking out at the river and the lights of the city beyond.

"Vicky..." he whispered, pressing his brow against the glass. "Why don't you call?"

On those evenings when they were unable to meet, she invariably phoned from her bedroom regardless of the hour. It had been agreed that, for the moment, it would be unwise for him to call the palace, but it galled him nonetheless. He knew he should try to get a few hours' sleep before going to the airport, but knew also that, until he had heard from Victoria, he wouldn't be able to. Perhaps he should save time by getting into his pajamas now and by carrying his bags to the front hall. That done, still there was no call. He lifted the receiver to check that there was no problem with the line, replacing it quickly.

It was eleven o'clock now and there had been no call. Reluctantly, he made his way up the spiral staircase to the bedroom and climbed beneath the covers. Something must have gone awry. A problem with the palace switchboard perhaps. A complication she hadn't been able to avoid. Perhaps. . . . Could she have been taken ill? Of course not. But *something* was wrong; she had never before failed to call.

He had fallen asleep and didn't hear the key turn in the front door, only awakening to the soft pressure of open lips on his and the scent of her perfume.

"Darling! Darling Vicky! . . ."

She undressed quickly and slipped her cool body next to his warmth – jamming against him, her mouth devouring, her tongue questing, her arms like a vise about his neck. He was seized by a sudden, rutting lust and pinned her roughly, holding her wrists, his legs wedging her thighs apart. Afterward, they lay side by side, hands clasped, each conscious of the warm pressure of the other's shoulder and hip and thigh.

"What time do you leave for your plane?" she whispered.

"They're picking me up at two."

"Can you get out of it?" she asked. "I'll drive you to the airport."

"Wonderful," he murmured drowsily.

"And now, my darling love, sleep."

♚ FOUR

"Now," said the queen, touching a button on her desk and rising from her chair, "if there's nothing further, Victoria would like a word with you."

Mary and Hugh Forster had just concluded their regular Tuesday Meeting, an abbreviated one as Mary had had McCrimmon inform the Prime Minister's office in advance that Victoria wished to discuss with Forster the arrangements for the celebration of her twenty-first birthday.

The Tuesday Meeting is a long-established tradition in Britain. The meetings are normally no-nonsense sessions and short on protocol, although, depending on the disposition of the sovereign, they may range from serious discussion to casual chit-chat, or occasionally to little more than the trading of gossip.

It was not always so. In Queen Victoria's time they were starchy sessions, so much so that it was much remarked on in court circles when it was learned that – unlike her meetings with her *bête noire*, Gladstone – Victoria had actually permitted Disraeli to *sit*. When George V first met with Ramsay MacDonald, Britain's first Labor Prime Minister, the King – who had probably not met a live socialist except on a visit to a factory or a mineshaft – had donned a red tie for the occasion and expressed surprise afterwards that MacDonald seemed "quite a decent chap." Elizabeth II found Winston Churchill to be always gallant and courtly in a grandfatherly way. There was a much whispered-about belief that Elizabeth's meetings with Margaret Thatcher, Britain's first woman Prime Minister, were so arranged (either telepathically or telephonically) as to ensure that Mrs. Thatcher's clothes would not clash with what the Queen was wearing that day.

Now, as Mary rose to her feet, Forster followed, expressing surprise when she extended her hand. "You're not staying?"

"No," she said, "Victoria is quite set on speaking to you alone." She smiled. "I have some idea of what she wants to say, of course, and I think it would be best if I were to leave the two of you to yourselves. We can chat about it next Tuesday, perhaps."

There was a tap at the door. She opened it and, as Victoria entered, she put her cheek to her daughter's. Then, with a small nod to Forster, she gently pulled the door closed behind her.

Victoria was nervous but did not betray it. She had prepared for the meeting by reviewing the matter a dozen times, and by putting to herself all possible responses that Forster might make. But now, as she extended her hand to the Prime Minister, she felt a momentary weakness in her knees and for one panicky moment wished she hadn't insisted on the appointment.

As they seated themselves by the fireplace, Forster said pleasantly, "Well now, here we are. I'm given to understand that you wish to speak to me about the arrangements for your twenty-first birthday. Capital."

Victoria had hoped to begin the conversation more obliquely but, concentrating on ensuring that her voice did not falter, she said, "I thought that before your plans are finalized I should mention some of my concerns."

"By all means, my lady," Forster said zestfully. "By all means." He had noted her tension and was conscious of a touch of apprehension in himself. "I wonder," he said, "if we might ask Mr. McCrimmon to join us. He could make some notes as an *aide-mémoire*," he explained.

"Thank you," Victoria said equably, "but I don't think that will be necessary. What I want to talk about are not the details of the celebration but rather a change in emphasis." She took a deep breath, saying to herself, Here we go. "Rather than merely celebrate my birthday, I would like to make it the occasion of my marriage."

Hugh Forster was notoriously difficult to catch out. The Opposition tried to do so almost daily in the House but with little success. On the hustings, when challenged by a heckler, he almost always managed to score off the interruption. But Victoria's directness caught him off guard and brought a rush of blood to his face. He was able to muster only a faint, "Indeed."

Victoria pursued the advantage. "I'm planning to marry Jeremy Walsh. I believe you've met."

"Yes," said Forster, his long experience in the cut and thrust of political debate enabling him to recover quickly. "Jeremy Walsh. The *New York Times*. Of course, he was in for a chat not long ago. An American."

"Yes," Victoria said, "an American."

Forster had now fully recovered his aplomb. "May I offer you my best wishes," he said cordially. "Somehow, your mother failed to mention it. You *do* have her permission?"

"We've discussed it."

"But my question was, if you'll pardon me: do you have her permission? You'll not take it amiss if I raise a small constitutional point. As I'm sure you're aware, under the Royal Marriages Act no member of the royal family may marry before the age of twenty-five without the sovereign's consent. That being true, and your mother not having acquiesced, it would seem that our conversation is a trifle premature."

He made as though to rise but when Victoria didn't move, he settled down again.

"I'll be candid with you, Prime Minister," Victoria said coolly. "Mummy is opposed." She smiled winningly. "But inasmuch as your government will shortly be introducing a bill concerning me, I thought I should let you know my intentions as early as possible."

Forster, his lips tightly compressed, his brows down, studied the young woman seated opposite. He was entirely himself again. Victoria was conscious of an inner tremulousness and kept her hands on the arms of her chair so that they might not be seen to shake.

"I wonder," Forster said, the frown suddenly dissolving, "if I might be permitted a pipe? Your mother is kind enough to indulge me from time to time. Rotten habit." When Victoria nodded, he proceeded to light up, extracting the pipe from its pouch and using the procedure to buy time. "The young man," he said offhandedly, "is he Church of England? No, of course not, he's an American. Episcopalian perhaps?"

Victoria shook her head. "No."

Forster was now occupied in putting away his lighter. "Am I wrong in this? – I seem to remember hearing somewhere that he's a Roman Catholic."

Little wonder the press calls him "Foxy Forster," Victoria thought. "His family is Catholic," she said.

"Mmm," the Prime Minister mused, sending a small cloud of smoke toward the ceiling. "And where, may I ask, does he attend services?"

"He doesn't," said Victoria. "But then, as you know, neither do I."

"Yes, of course. Of course." He looked at her now from beneath his brows. "The matter *has* been raised in some quarters. I shan't comment on it except to remind you that when you ascend the throne, one of your titles will be Defender of the Faith. It's something to think about."

Victoria nodded.

"Mr. Walsh has agreed to convert?"

"I have no idea, Prime Minister. We've never discussed it."

Another "Hmmm." Another pull on the pipe, another jet of smoke directed upward. "I believe you said he was an American?"

Victoria smiled at him sweetly. "I believe it was you who said so. But yes, he is."

"There could be a problem there," Forster said, shaking his head slowly, lips pursed. Now he looked up at her and his eyes were steely. "He *is* aware that he would have to become a naturalized British subject before the two of you could marry?"

"Yes, he knows that."

"And he's agreed to do so?"

"Again, we haven't discussed it."

He looked at her paternally, his expression kindly, a hint of sadness in his eyes. "I really must beg your forgiveness for inquiring so closely, but as I'm sure you can understand – and I can't tell you how it distresses me to speak so negatively in a matter so close to your heart – I am bound to say that the entire arrangement, on the face of it, would seem to be . . . what is the phrase in the song? – an impossible dream." He leaned forward to tap the pipe empty in an ashtray. "And now, if there's nothing further, I really must be getting back to Downing Street."

Victoria had feared that their conversation might reach such an impasse but had not expected it to come so quickly. Very well, she would abandon it for the moment and lock horns with him later when she was better prepared. In the meantime, however, it was essential that he be made to realize that she was not going to be dissuaded.

"Mr. Forster," her voice was soft, "you should understand that I am fully aware of the problems you raise and that I don't underestimate their seriousness. I'll grant you that in the past my marrying Jeremy would have been impossible, but this is a different day and I'm confident that the time is right." She rose and extended her hand. "Please do understand, Mr. Forster – and I mean no disrespect – that I intend to go ahead with or without your approval. I hold the hope that you will find it possible to approve."

"I'm getting that feeling in my left kidney," said Ossie Docherty.

"Fart on your left kidney," said Alfie Hedges, bending down to check on the progress of the rump roast in the oven.

Wearing only underpants, Ossie was lying on a pullout couch in the kitchen of the flat in which he lived with his long-time friend, Alfie. On a chair at his side was a glass of stout and a mixing bowl filled with potato crisps. As he talked, he reached out a massive arm to seize another fistful of crisps. From time to time he would heave his enormous bulk onto one elbow, a great white stomach falling off to one side, drain the glass of stout and flop back spreadeagled on the groaning couch.

Alfie, a short, string-sinewed man of about forty, obviously compensating for the loss of hair on his head with a coarse, ill-trimmed beard, was busy setting a table in a corner of the kitchen even as he checked the roast, kept a pot of potatoes at the boil, and saw to it that Ossie's glass was refilled as necessary.

Ossie Docherty's left kidney had achieved a degree of celebrity in the city room at the *Herald*. From time to time Ossie would announce to anyone within earshot that he was getting signals from his left kidney, a guaranteed augury, he would aver, that the story he was working on was about to fall into place. It had nothing to do with his left kidney, of course, and might have been more accurately described as a hunch, but because the "unmistakable twinges" usually coincided with renewed efforts on Ossie's part – rewarded as often as not by a break in his story – his kidney had come to be regarded by some of his fellow reporters as possessing certain prognostic qualities. No one believed this with more fervency than did the owner of the occasionally omniscient organ. Rationalizing those occasions when the urological forecast hadn't proved correct, he continued unapologetically to proclaim its infallibility.

"Go ahead and laugh," he said to Alfie, wiping his lips with fingers like croissants. "I'm telling you there's something funny going on at the palace."

"Like the time your bleedin' kidney told us we was gonna clean up in the pools," Alfie said. "*That's* five quid I'll never see again."

"That had nothing to do with my left kidney," Ossie protested. "It doesn't perform for a measly fiver. But when I'm on a story and feel her twinge, I know – "

"You know you're overdue to take a leak," Alfie supplied.

Ossie munched a mouthful of potato crisps, musing, "Remember back there when I told you about that green Jaguar with one of the royals in it turning into Buckingham Palace at three in the morning?"

"I remember," said Alfie, fingering some salt onto the potatoes. "That was one of the few good excuses you've come up with for comin' home late."

"Well, last week, on my way to New York, I see that same Jag at Heathrow. There are three of us in the pool car, and just as we turn in at the Departures Terminal, there's that same Jag dropping off a passenger and pulling away. We're not close enough so's I can see who the passenger is, except I can see it's a man, but I do get a good look at the car and it's the same one."

"So?" said Alfie, poking a fork into the roast to check it. "Probably just another of them freeloaders at the bleedin' palace off to the bleedin' Riviera at my expense."

"A royal Jag is ferrying people to Heathrow at 2:45 a.m.?" Ossie asked witheringly. "Any more crisps in the bag there?"

Alfie made a gesture of martyrdom. "'Ow in god's name do I get dinner on the table if I spend most of me day fetchin' the bleedin' crisps?" Nonetheless, he emptied the bag into the mixing bowl and returned to the stove. "That's the last of the stout. I'll open the wine, if you like."

Ossie nodded absently. He was chewing on the crisps, regarding the ceiling with squinted eyes. "I told you about checking out the license plates? The Jag is a hire-car from McIllhenny's Carriage Works. Older'n god, the place is. All spit and polish. I'm doing a story on the cars driven by celebrities, I say, and maybe he can help me out. He's one of those close-mouthed types. It's like pulling teeth to get a yes or a no or a maybe. How about the palace? I say. What kind of car does Princess Victoria, for instance, prefer? He gives me a look like I'm dirt under the world's fingernails, and as much as shows me off the premises. Prick!" He glanced at his glass. "Any more stout?"

"I already told you."

"Maybe I will have some of that," Ossie said, nodding toward the table where Alfie was unscrewing the top on a three-liter bottle of red wine.

"Jeezus!" said Alfie. "You'd think you was one of them Ayrab potentates." He poured a tumblerful of wine and placed it on the chair by the couch, noting that the mixing bowl was empty. "There's some cashews."

"I rang up the press secretary at the palace to ask what kind of motor cars the royal family prefers – you know, I'm doing an article for *Motoring* magazine; who's to know better? They call him a press secretary – won't give you the time of day." He reared up and put away most of the tumblerful of wine, remaining on his elbow. "When's dinner?"

"When it's on the table," Alfie said.

"I don't give a damn what anybody says," Ossie said, beginning to massage the appropriate area on his back and sending seismic waves through the adjacent flesh, "these twinges in my left kidney never lie. Guaranteed."

On most weekends, and as often as could be managed at other times, Hugh Forster escaped London to his country home, a sprawling restored abbey in the heart of leafy Buckinghamshire, an easy one hour's drive from the city. Grendon Abbey was a passion with him. Built some eight hundred years earlier for the Augustinian canons, it had been endowed by Henry V and had on occasion housed such figures as Henry VIII and Cardinal Wolsey. When Forster first saw the forty-six-acre estate, it was rundown and weed-choked and, although it required restoration of the gray granite stone, the redecoration of twenty-two rooms, and the installation of new bathroom and kitchen facilities, he bought it. His expenditures had been well rewarded.

One approaches Grendon Abbey through a massive stone and wrought-iron gate leading onto a broad, winding driveway, lined its full length by soldierly poplars. Past the gently sloping hills that seem almost to enfold the house, glimpses may be caught of the placid meanderings of the river Thame and of a crystal clear artesian pond with enormous willows weeping at its edge. The house, at first sight, intimidates, but the interior is spacious and warm and welcoming, and the broad, gently curving staircase in the entrance hall has made many a woman guest long for a new gown in which she might descend it.

Forster had invited Angus McCrimmon to join him at the abbey for a weekend and McCrimmon had presumed that there would be a number of other guests. But having settled into his room and changed into the comfort of old tweed trousers and a cashmere sweater, he found his host alone on the terrace and learned that he was the only visitor.

"I thought it would be pleasant for you to escape that massive mound of masonry at the end of the Mall and put your feet up," Forster explained. "You work altogether too hard."

McCrimmon had also presumed that he had been invited to Grendon so that Forster might use the opportunity to pick his brains about whatever might be preoccupying the Queen and about the various cross-currents at the palace. But there was no evidence that such was his intention. The two men spent much of Saturday on a protracted walk about the estate, accompanied by half a dozen dogs, with no mention of the palace. Forster proudly showed him through the partially restored bailiff's bungalow down by the river, expanded enthusiastically about his herd of Herefords and about the modern cattle barn with its spanking-clean stalls. ("Got to make the damn place pay for itself," he mock-grumbled.) Then, after a late afternoon swim in the heated swimming pool, a hearty dinner, and a nightcap in the library, Forster, without even the most casual attempt to pry, had suggested that they both be off to their beds.

There was more of the same on Sunday except that after lunch a driver appeared with a bulging briefcase and Forster disappeared into his study for three hours while McCrimmon occupied himself with a book. It was not until the two men had had tea and in the late afternoon gone for a stroll that Forster got around to the reason for the visit.

"Victoria and that young chap, Walsh," he said, swinging his walking stick at a tuft of weeds. "It worries the hell out of me."

McCrimmon said nothing, content to wait for the Prime Minister to develop his theme. "What do you make of him?" Forster asked.

"Damned if I'm sure," McCrimmon said. He puffed out his cheeks and slowly vented a stream of air through pursed lips. "If you want my immediate reaction, I can give it to you in one word: dangerous."

Forster gave him a quick glance. "Dangerous? How?"

"In a number of ways." McCrimmon cupped a palm on his bald head, massaging it. "Victoria is greatly taken with him and won't be dissuaded. He's a journalist, of course, a cut above most of the breed but a journalist nonetheless, and it's been my experience that it's unwise to let such people in close. I'm given to understand that he earned his posting to London simply by working harder and longer than his confreres. As well, he's an Anglophile, and bright. A Rhodes scholar."

"I didn't know that."

"And, according to my information, has said quite openly that he intends to be managing editor of the *Times* by the time he's forty."

"Ambitious."

"And while ambition is an admirable thing, it has been my observation that it may sometimes lead its subjects into . . . how shall I put it? . . .

"Using any means to get to the top."

"Precisely."

At the crest of a small rise, they stopped to admire the view. It was McCrimmon who resumed the conversation. He had picked up a dead branch as they went along and was now snapping off the twigs to make himself a walking-stick. "The Queen asked me if I would see Walsh," he said.

"And?"

"I soon put an end to that notion," McCrimmon said crisply. "I advised her also that it might be wise not to have him up to Windsor again."

"He's been to Windsor? I didn't know."

"She didn't seem particularly pleased with my counsel. She finds it hard to say no to Victoria. As does the Duke," he added.

"You know he's divorced?" Forster said, keeping the pump primed.

"Yes, I've heard so. I must confess I know almost nothing about that. I don't hear much gossip, probably because I don't offer a good ear in such matters." He stabbed at the ground with the stick and it snapped in his hand. "I don't suppose your people have heard anything."

"Nothing except that apparently he was the so-called innocent party." He paused. "I wonder who might be privy to such information? Just as a matter of curiosity."

"Perhaps Sir John."

"No, I think not. The embassy being in Washington I don't suppose he gets into New York that often. The divorce was granted in New York, I believe."

"There's Rowntree."

"Rowntree?"

"The new under-secretary at the U.N."

"Yes, yes. Of course."

"Discreet chap."

The Prime Minister pulled a small notebook from a pocket and wrote in it. They had reached the pond now and paused on its edge to watch a female ruddy duck flee them, a half dozen balls of down paddling frantically in her wake. Forster paused to light his pipe before they went on.

"Let me speak in candor about this business with Walsh," he said. "I had a talk about it with Victoria and it left me troubled. As you say, this is no whim with her. She's got the bit in her teeth and she's a strong-willed young woman. She's quite prepared to carry on with her job but she's not prepared to give him up. Moreover, she's convinced that she won't have to. I'm not overly concerned about the divorce; that could be handled. The problem she hasn't faced up to is the fact that Walsh is an American. I took pains to make it perfectly clear that before she and Walsh could marry he would have to become a British subject. Her response was that they haven't even discussed it. My guess would be that they've both avoided the subject: he because he knows full well that it's something he won't do and he doesn't want to face up to it at the moment; she because she knows what he feels and would rather postpone dealing with it, hoping it will go away."

"I see."

"I would think the chances of his giving up his American citizenship would be small. Wouldn't you agree?"

"I would."

"Nor is it something that would go down well in America. The other side of that coin is, I think it unlikely that our people would accept a consort to the Queen who is an American citizen." He paused, his brows knit. "She and I are going to have another chat about it next week. I'll have to prepare myself carefully; she certainly has her head screwed on right."

As they headed back to the abbey, McCrimmon inquired, "You have no idea how long his term is – as correspondent for the *Times*?"

"Haven't the foggiest."

"It's not impossible that he's nearing the end of it and is due to be shifted."

"Now that," said Forster, "is an interesting thought."

"It occurred to me that, even if he weren't scheduled to move on for a while yet, the *Times* might find it has a need for him elsewhere. Moscow, for instance. Washington." They went on for a few strides. "Did you by any chance meet Chet Sonnenberg when he was in London last February?"

"Chet Sonnenberg?"

"Chester Sonnenberg – he likes to be called Chet. He's the Executive Editor at the *Times*."

"Ah, yes. No, I didn't meet him."

"I was able to do him a few small kindnesses. Managed, among other things, to have him included on the guest list for one of the Queen's private dinners."

"I don't suppose. . . ."

"Very approachable. Perhaps one of these days we may be in touch. I'll pass on your best wishes."

"Yes, please do. By all means."

It had been a long day for both of them, ending at almost midnight following the opening of a new Tom Stoppard play at the Lyceum. Edward had left word with his valet that he would take his breakfast tray in the Queen's bedroom and they had retired to her great canopied bed. Their loving had been long and pleasurable and without restraint, filled with a sure knowledge of the other's needs and climaxing in an overwhelming sense of oneness. Within minutes Mary was asleep.

"Darling? . . ."

"Mmm." Mary stirred.

"Did I wake you?"

"Well. . . ."

"I didn't realize you were asleep."

"That's all right. I'm awake now."

"Sorry about that."

"Oh dear! – I wasn't snoring?"

"No, no, no. It was just that I've been lying here thinking, and. . . ."

"And I've been lying here dreaming. You were making the most sensational love to me."

"But we just did."

"And it was beautiful. You really are quite remarkable, you know."

"Remarkably lucky."

"Isn't it marvelous that, after twenty-two years, it's as good as ever? But you wanted to tell me something."

"Tell you something?"

"When you woke me you said you'd been lying there thinking about something."

"Yes, of course. Vicky – I was thinking about Vicky. I'm terribly worried about her. The last few days she seems . . . I don't know the best way to put it. Depressed."

"Yes, I know."

"I don't know what to do."

"There's not much we *can* do. It's something only she can decide. As her mother I want, most of all, her happiness, of course, but then there's her duty to be done. . . . The whole thing is becoming a nightmare."

"This morning when you were away . . . launching that new destroyer or whatever it was – I talked her into going out riding. She's not all that keen about horses, as you know, and it took a bit of convincing. I brought up the subject of her and Jeremy. She didn't want to talk about it at first but after a while she opened up. I must say, she seemed quite put out about Crimmie. She says he flatly refused to see Jeremy. Did you know that?"

"Yes."

"I got the impression he was pretty adamant about it."

"Well, that's his prerogative. It's his job to advise me, not necessarily to agree with me. I have to remind myself of that from time to time. But he's absolutely devoted to Vicky and I'm sure he wouldn't do anything that wasn't for her good. No, he wouldn't do anything that wasn't for *my* good."

"It must be damned awkward for her; everybody putting in their penny's worth."

"You still haven't told me what you were thinking."

"Mostly whether she'll go through with it."

"Marry Jeremy, you mean? Regardless of the consequences?"

"Yes."

"To tell the truth, I simply don't know."

"But what do you think?"

"I'll tell you what I think. . . ." Her voice broke. "I think, whatever happens, she's going to be a very unhappy young – "

She was suddenly close to tears and reached out a hand to her night table. "Do you have any tissues? I don't seem to have any."

"Here we are," he said cheerily, reaching into the drawer on his side of the bed.

In the dark she daubed at her eyes, finally blowing her nose. "Sorry. It's just that my heart aches for her." She tucked the tissues under her pillow. "You asked me what I think she'll do. I think when it comes down to it she'll marry him." She laughed mirthlessly. "And won't *that* be a pretty kettle of fish!"

"I've been thinking about what happens after that. George is next in line, isn't he?"

"Yes. Oh my god! – George! I haven't been thinking that far ahead. Poor, pathetic George."

Prince George, Duke of Gloucester, Mary's second cousin, was a notorious drunk whose alcoholism had led him into any number of scrapes. The grandson of Mary's uncle, he had survived his older brothers and thus moved to second in the line of succession. When this transpired, the tabloid press had made much of his drinking and even the *Times* and *Telegraph* had clucked editorial tongues. But the public soon tired of his pathetic escapades and dropped him. With Mary a mere forty-two and Victoria not yet twenty-one, he became a person of little consequence.

"It's unthinkable," Mary said. "Absolutely unthinkable. Can you imagine George on the *throne*!"

"I heard he was down at that drying-out spa in Brighton again."

"He should have a permanent suite there. The man hasn't been sober since he was weaned. I'm sorry, I shouldn't joke about it. But you saw him at the investiture last week. I swear, he was actually *talking* to one of the busts. I thought I would die! I kept thinking about that story they tell about Queen Victoria. . . . You know, that she was never amused – which was nonsense, of course. Once, when she was presiding over some function or other, something absolutely hilarious happened. Everybody was splitting their sides, and there was the Queen with an absolutely straight face . . . but with tears running down her cheeks! It was like that when I saw poor George – I thought I would die! Lady Caughtry says he brushes his teeth with Cointreau and rinses with gin. I'm sorry. I shouldn't be laughing."

"They can always go around him. When the Duke of Windsor abdicated, the cabinet considered bypassing

Bertie because of his stammer, and settling on the Duke of Kent."

"But after George comes his daughter, Jessica. And she's what? – twelve. No, it would never do; not a twelve-year-old child, and quite unattractive, poor darling. The dreadful truth is the public simply won't accept it." She shook her head irresolutely. "It's something one tries not to think about."

"Then let me say it right out," Edward said firmly. "It would be the end of the monarchy."

Mary punched her pillow, positioning it against the headboard and sitting up, her arms about her knees. Edward propped himself on an elbow. Neither said anything for a moment.

"Mary...."

"Yes?"

"We're back to what I was thinking about earlier. I've been giving it a great deal of thought.... I'm not quite sure how to put it...."

She reached out and turned on the lamp by her side of the bed. "Why not just go ahead and say it?"

"All right. I've been thinking that perhaps...."

"We should have another child."

"Well, yes."

"I agree."

"Just like that?"

"Just like that."

"But now, hold on a minute. It's not that simple. Neither of us is as young as we used to be. I've been reading up on it. You'll have to go off the pill."

"Already done."

"Already done?"

"After we had that first talk with Vicky and it was clear that she wasn't going to change her mind."

"Then there's the matter of your miscarriage. We'll have to talk to Sir Herbert about that."

"Next Tuesday afternoon at three. I checked with your new private secretary and he says you're free all afternoon."

♛ FIVE

JEREMY WALSH was a man not much interested in possessions. Because he didn't own much of value and had changed his place of residence many times, he had tended to leave behind each time everything but the essential or the irreplaceable. One of his possessions that he considered essential and irreplaceable was a 1957 Aston Martin sports car, the same model – gimmicked up with a smoke-maker, a nail-ejector, and other such frivolities – driven by Sean Connery in the James Bond film, *Thunderball*. Jeremy had purchased the car (naming it, Gridley) on the day he was hired by the *Times*, having discovered it, mantled in dust and with a connecting-rod through the crankcase, in a used-car lot in Chicago. It had taken much penny-pinching and self-denial in his lean years to restore it to something of its original condition, and some persistent arguing to get it shipped to London at the *Times*' expense when he was posted there.

On a brilliant, blue-sky day, with no pressing respon-sibilities, he telephoned the palace on a whim, leaving word that a Mr. Charles LeGrand had called from *Le Soulier d'Or* to say that the shoes Her Royal Highness had ordered from Paris had arrived. Victoria had called back within five minutes, worried – the code name was to be used only in an emergency. Jeremy had told her that this *was* an emergency: she was to put aside whatever she was planning and join him for a picnic in the country. He informed her further that he would be deaf to any arguments. They had both been so busy that they had seen each other but fleetingly and hadn't made love for a fortnight – excluding two long salacious conversations on the telephone late at night. She needed little coaxing.

Jeremy paid his account at the garage, and with an electric exultancy in his veins picked up Victoria in the laneway outside Jane Cavendish's flat. With a brief pause on the outskirts of the city to stow the top in the boot, with the sky unclouded and the sun hot on their shoulders, with Gridley like a blooded horse fighting for his head, and with the outbound traffic light, all seemed right with the world.

The two lovers headed south, and near Tunbridge Wells turned into a meandering country lane, defined by leafy hedges and ending at the heart of a lovely woods. The floor of the forest was dappled with sunlight and springy underfoot with pine needles. They wandered on, pausing to gather wildflowers, following the course of a frolicking creek, arriving finally at a clearing where the grasses were so high that they could spread the blanket Jeremy had brought, lay out the lunch they had stopped to buy, and be alone in the universe.

Sated with food and wine but hungry for each other, they lay naked in the sun, exulting in each other's bodies. Victoria was insatiable. Not content to be the passive partner, her hands and lips were everywhere, and once Jeremy had had to gasp in mock-dismay, "Enough, my darling. Enough!"

Now they lay beside each other, exquisitely undone, their bodies open to the sun. "I've always believed it could be like this," Victoria whispered. "I know now I've never been in love before and that I will never love anyone else."

"My darling, darling, Vicky," Jeremy said, finding her hand and holding it tightly in his.

After a while she leaned on an elbow, and with her fingertips, brushed the hair on his chest. "Tell me about Merilee," she said. "About seeing her when you were in New York."

At first he was awkward in his response, hesitant, but soon warmed to it. "She's such a sweetheart and we have such great fun together. We laugh a lot. She's a real tomboy; loves to be swung around and flung high in the air; that kind of thing." Remembering, he smiled. "She's the world's greatest smoocher. Kisses me so hard I'm surprised she doesn't break her nose." He laughed. "Not that it's much of a nose."

"Is it hard to be away from her?"

"Very hard, and it doesn't get any easier. I suppose it's because I wasn't as close to her as I should have been when she was a baby. Diane and I were having our problems and I was working ungodly hours." He paused, his thoughts far away. "The first six months over here were rough. Now I fly back to see her as often as I can. And to see my family."

"Will you want a large family?" she asked.

"I don't think so." He kissed his fingertips and pressed them to her lips. "Your child. And Merilee, if that's all right with you."

"If we had a girl," she said, "I suppose we'd have to keep on trying. Don't all men want a son?"

"It wouldn't matter."

"I would want a boy," she said. "Because he'd be like you. And because," she said as an afterthought, "he would be king one day, our son."

"Or President of the United States," he said with a slight smile.

She lay down on her back again and neither spoke for a while. It was Jeremy who broke the silence.

"Could you possibly be merely the wife of a newspaperman?"

She was slow to respond. "I'm not sure. If the question is: would I like to be? the answer is yes. If the question is: could I be? I really don't know. I don't know whether it's possible."

"The other half of the equation is, could I be consort to a queen?"

When he left the question hanging, Victoria asked, "Well, could you be?"

"At this moment," he said, "I could be anything so long as it would let me be with you."

She kissed him, long and tenderly and then lay down again, taking his hand.

"But I'm not a fool," he went on, "I know that moments like these, even though they're more important than the so-called important moments, are ephemeral. There is, out there, what is known as the real world and willy-nilly we're part of it. And I'm not at all sure that the real world will let you be married to a guy who chases the news. Or let me be married to a woman who is, to millions of people, something very much like an icon." He thrashed his head back and forth. "I'm not sure I want to talk about it right now."

He sat up, wrapping his arms about his legs, looking vacantly at the ground. After a while he lay down beside her again. He laughed mirthlessly. "You won't believe what's been running through my head," he said. "A line from a sentimental old song: love will find a way." His voice had a tone of incredulity. "Can you believe it?"

She put her lips lightly on his, whispering even as she kissed him. "Yes, I can believe it. I don't dare *not* believe it."

There was a sudden chill breeze. Jeremy glanced at his watch and without a word they both got dressed, packed up, and made their way back to the car. As Jeremy nosed Gridley onto the highway, they saw a car parked on the shoulder of the road off to their right.

"MacIntyre," Victoria said. "Whither thou goest, I will go." Jeremy muttered something but she didn't catch it and didn't ask.

The sky had become overcast and there was a smell of rain. Jeremy stopped and put up the top. The return to London was slowed by blackened skies and a thunderous storm.

Herbert Blackstock, Member of Parliament for Manchester, Wythenshawe and the leader of Her Majesty's Loyal Opposition, was seated in his office at Westminster, his elbows on his desk, his hands clasped, and his chin resting on them. His face was without expression but behind the mask-like visage his mind was racing.

The cause of his preoccupation was a rumor; a few words whispered in his ear as he had turned in at the Bar of the House for the afternoon's Question Time. The whisperer had been a man about whose integrity he had doubts but who was nonetheless not given to casual gossip. David Rhys, the member for Meirionnydd Nant Conwy, had put the flea in his ear, and even though he had prefaced it by saying, "I can't swear to it, mind you . . ." the news had been intriguing. What Conway wasn't prepared to swear to was information to the effect that Princess Victoria had been seen taking dinner in a private room in a pub in Bermondsey. Nor was it the first time, apparently. And more: there was hand-holding going on under the table and a kissy-kissy atmosphere about the whole business. Of even greater interest: the man with whom she was so consorting was an American.

Blackstock had heard the rumor before but had dismissed it. The Princess was a young, zestful, unmarried woman and free, as far as he was concerned, to go about with whomever she pleased. There had been a number of brief romances – or so the tittle-tattle in the press had reported – none of them of the slightest interest to Blackstock. But it so chanced that, not a week ago, he had himself seen the Princess at a palace garden party, talking with a tall, dark-haired young man whom he recognized as the chief correspondent for the *New York Times*. Nothing remarkable in that except that he had seen her pick a bit of fluff from his lapel and brush the lapel with her hand, and had thought in passing that it was an oddly familiar thing for the Princess to do.

The Houses of Parliament, as the old Palace of Westminister is known, are fertile ground for rumor. More than any other place in Britain, they are the locus of power and are therefore rife with what might be categorized as gossip: a conjecturing about motives, a speculation about intentions, an examination of ambiguities, a dissection of auguries. Leaks – some of them unintentional, some deliberate – help to test the winds, establish the climate. Hints are let drop, kites get flown, innuendos are used, and from these fragmentary clues, plans are often firmed up or questioned, strategies are formulated or abandoned.

It was just such an ambiguous set of facts that was occupying Herbert Blackstock's mind this April afternoon. It had been commonly known for some weeks now that the government planned to table a particular bill in the House, a proclamation celebrating the twenty-first birthday of the heir presumptive to the throne, and to seek Parliament's approval of the requisite sums of money to effect the plans. Blackstock was aware that the government would attempt to use the celebration as a means to enhance its standing in the country and had no doubt that the occasion would prove enormously popular; consequently, he too planned to exploit it. He would, nevertheless, even while asserting his unequivocal fealty to the monarchy, mount an attack in the House on the proposed expenditures, arguing waste and redundancy and lamenting the lot of the unemployed poor, on whom, he would argue, some of the monies might better be spent. But he would take care to walk a fine line, seeking not to alienate the anti-royalists and those indifferent to the monarchy while standing foursquare for the perpetuation of the institution.

He had been preparing his strategy for some time and had been puzzled by the failure of the government to table the bill. It was weeks overdue. Had some part of the Prime Minister's plan gone awry? On its face, the celebrations seemed the perfect vehicle for Forster. The Tories were the monarchists. The Prime Minister was skilled at using great occasions. The event would stimulate waves of patriotism. The newspapers and the electronic media, who love occasions, would undoubtedly go overboard. All this being known to Forster, why then had he not tabled the bill?

Was it possible, Blackstock mused, even remotely possible that the gossip he had heard earlier that afternoon and the inconsequential incident of the removal of a bit of fluff from the American reporter's lapel were the keys? Could it be that the Princess had balked at the plans? Did she have her own plans and were they unsatisfactory to Forster? It certainly was possible. She was the model of royal personification but she had a mind of her own. And incredible as the thought might be, did her plans include the American? He shook his head. Impossible. And yet. . . .

He would have a word with his deputy, Ian Barnett, have him sniff about a bit. It would probably be fruitless, but now that the thought had come to birth and was growing he did not want to abandon it without at least checking it out. There was much to be gained; he dare not let it rest unresolved.

27-A Foundry Road

Gary, Indiana

Dear Jeremias:

How good it was to hear from you by telephone from New York and how sorry your mother and I were that time did not permit your coming home for at least a few hours. Having you here would be best, regular letters from you would be next best, but failing both, the telephone call was wonderful. It made our day.

Before getting to the reason for this letter let me bring you up to date on general news from this end. I am well. Your mother is not. I hasten to add that her illness is not serious. It is of the nature of what is commonly described as "women's complaints" – in a word, a problem with the plumbing. Her doctor (a *woman*, I need hardly say: knowing your mother, would she so much as *discuss* such problems with a male doctor?) says that her symptoms result from the onset of the menopause. She tells her not to fret, whereupon, of course, she frets.

As for the latest on your brothers, they are all doing fine. Stanislaus (he now objects to the diminutive Stan) has just been named Senior Rector at St. Stephen's, and when he gets all gussied up for a high mass he does look impressive. With his added responsibilities he grows daily more conservative . . . I almost wrote more conservative than the Pope.

Stephan also is doing well. However, not only is he not mounting the ecclesiastical ladder, he's not interested in doing so. He's more interested in the daily goings-on in his parish: hearing confessions, visiting the sick, running the weekly Bingo, and by and large helping out the Deity in a variety of unspectacular ways.

Hans is the one who has surprised us. You will remember that when you saw him last he was running to keep out of the hands of the bailiffs. That has changed. He now has the Hyundai dealership in this area. He and Maria now each have a car. One nice thing about Maria having a car: she comes by more often with the children, which pleases your mother. And me. Although I'm thinking of charging baby-sitting rates. Hah!

Let me come now to the reason for this missive . . . *your* news. And what news it is! To say that it left me gasping is to understate my reaction. Every so often since, I find myself saying to myself, "Good Lord – *my* son! Her Royal Highness!" I still have difficulty believing it. You will agree that it's not a problem most parents are called upon to face.

But in all seriousness: let me urge you to proceed with the greatest judiciousness. For her sake and for your own, make haste slowly. Let tortoises appear by comparison as hares. You said on the telephone that the biggest hurdle you face is your being divorced. Permit me to differ. Your biggest problem is that you will be perceived as a threat not only to august traditions but to the *guardians* of those traditions. You are, in effect, preparing to go mano-a-mano with (a) the government, (b) the Church of England, (c) the British Establishment, (d) most of the media, and (e) everybody and anybody who has a stake in the British monarchical system. I have not included the general public because they will be divided and will speak with many voices and will, of course, be manipulated by the politicians and the press.

I wonder also if you have looked at the other side of the coin. If the two of you persist, and if as a result Victoria gives up her right to the throne, what then? Will not the remainder of your life be colored by that fact?

My son, you have lived twenty-eight years and you have done well. Your gifts, your ambition, and your commitment to your work have brought you achievements beyond your years. But if you and Victoria marry, all this will be as naught. Turning a page, you will enter into an entirely new life. It will be almost as though you have never done what you have done. Think about it.

But all that aside, you are very much loved here and we wait impatiently to see you. Whatever else, do not fail to join us all for Christmas. And, of course, bring anyone you wish to.

all our love
Papa

"It may interest you to know," Hugh Forster was saying, "that No. 10 Downing Street exists because of an infamous, treacherous turncoat, a disreputable divinity student by the name of John Downing who made a rather handsome living spying for Oliver Cromwell and afterward turned toady for Charles II."

"My gracious," said Victoria.

"It was he who first built Number 10," Forster explained. "Incidentally, it might be of interest to your American friend, Mr. Walsh, to know that, although he was English, Downing was the second student graduated by Harvard University."

Forster was in his best ebullient form. He had invited Victoria to lunch after she had sent him a note indicating that she wished to conclude their earlier conversation. He had been showing her through the Prime Minister's official residence, sketching its checkered history, and now as he walked her up the three-story open staircase, he paused before some of the portraits and spoke anecdotally of his predecessors: mentioning Walpole, the Pitts, the Duke of Wellington, Disraeli, Gladstone, Lloyd George, Chamberlain, Churchill, Wilson, and Thatcher.

The tour had ended in Forster's private flat where Mrs. Forster joined them for lunch and afterward excused herself. Victoria had prepared herself carefully for the meeting and, as became evident when she began to press her arguments, so had Forster.

"My point is," Victoria was saying, "that for all our traditions and for all our reverence for the past, we are a resilient people and have adapted to major changes any number of times in our history."

Forster didn't respond immediately. Head down and frowning, he seemed to be looking critically at the carpet. Without glancing up, he asked, "What, specifically, would you like to see changed?"

Victoria didn't flinch. "To begin with, the law forbidding marriage to a person who has been divorced."

Now he looked her full in the eyes. "Impossible."

"Why?" she shot back.

He betrayed a moment of impatience. "Because the Commons would not pass such a law. And if it did, the Lords would veto it. I'm sure I needn't remind you, my lady, that the nation has addressed the question a number of times, notably twice, and the response each time has been a resounding negative."

"That was years ago," she said firmly. "The times have changed."

"Indeed they have," he said, "and not always for the better. But surely the strength of the monarchy lies in the fact that it *doesn't* change." His eyes narrowed. "Let me go a step further: I could not myself in good conscience recommend such a change."

Her cheeks flushed. "But surely there's an enormous inconsistency here."

"Granted," he said immediately.

"I was about to say, hypocrisy."

"Granted."

She took the bit in her teeth. "Some of the members of your cabinet are divorced. Two dozen or more members of the House. The leader of the Opposition. If it's good enough for the real rulers of Britain, why not the titular ruler? Thousands of couples are divorced every year. There's no disgrace in it anymore."

He had been waiting patiently for her to finish. "But the sovereign is not one in a thousand; she is singular and an exemplar. Members of the House, the members of my cabinet, even I represent only a small number, the people in our individual ridings. The Queen represents us all. She represents our history, our standards, our attitudes. In a very real sense, the Queen *is* Britain. And, as Defender of the Faith, she can hardly contradict in her person the doctrines of the church of which she is head, one of those doctrines being, 'What God hath joined together let no man put asunder.'"

"But," said Victoria, "as everyone knows, the Church itself temporizes on the question. The Church will marry men and women who have been divorced."

"You're forgetting – "

"Permit me to go on. Surely the goal of the Church in all this is to stand for the sanctity of marriage, and isn't the best argument for the sanctity of marriage a good marriage? Many decent people marry and then divorce – the marriage often ending in rancor and hate, with everyone the worse for it. And then, as you know, there are divorced people who, having learned something of the pitfalls, marry again and go on to build a happy home. If the sanctity of marriage is the goal of the Church then it's a mockery to refuse the blessing of the Church to those who want it."

"So, if someone comes to a priest, having been divorced, and wants the seal of the Church on a second marriage, it should be granted?"

"Yes."

"And what should that priest say to someone who has been divorced three or four times? We can both think of some who have pledged their eternal vows a half dozen times, or more. What of them?"

Victoria looked at him, eyebrows arched. "Would it be rude if I were to call that sophistry? Those people are the exceptions. I hardly think they look to the Church. You're more likely to find them at the registry office."

Forster gave the slightest toss of his head as though to dismiss her response, but before he could pick up the argument, Victoria continued. "Let *me* play sophist for a moment," she said, smiling at him ingenuously. "The established church is the Church of England. How did it come to be established? Mostly because the Roman Church wouldn't give Henry VIII a divorce when he wanted to marry somebody else. Some rock on which to build an inflexible doctrine!"

Forster made no acknowledgment of the point, being busy removing a piece of paper from an inside pocket of his jacket. "I suppose," he said, "while we're discussing the question, I should mention other impediments. At your coronation you will be required to repeat under oath the following statement. . . ." He glanced at the paper. "'I, Victoria II, do solemnly and sincerely, in the presence of God, testify and declare that I am a faithful Protestant, and that I will, according to the true intent of the enactments which secure the Protestant succession to the throne of my realm, uphold and maintain the said enactments to the best of my powers according to law.' I put it to you, Victoria; wouldn't that vow have a hollow ring if the man seated beside you is a Roman Catholic? Suppose he were to decide that such children as you may have should be raised in the tradition of *his* family, in the Catholic tradition? Would you then keep the vow you have taken under the law and thus oppose your husband and divide your household?"

"I would hope," she said coolly, "that long before then the oath will have been changed. Parliament can do that. Parliament *should* do that."

Forster turned his palms outward in a gesture of futility. "So much for tradition then. Are we to cast out *all* tradition?" Before she could respond, he pressed on. "Your Highness, how do we come to have traditions? They're not merely the accretions of the past. They are concepts, ways of life, practices that men and women have found useful, so useful that they perpetuated them. Let me speak about one of our traditions, that of the monarch marrying a British subject. Let me posit that you marry an American. You have a son. He marries an American – and why not? What is the result? In one generation the throne of Britain has passed to two Americans. I intend no criticism of Americans, but as I think you will agree, a radical change in the monarchy would come about. Which – and I think you will agree also in this – the British people would not accept."

Victoria was aware of an anger rising within her. Whichever way she turned, this man before her turned with her and cut her off. And his arguments had force. But they were the arguments of a man mired in the past and bound by political expediency. For all the respectfulness of his manner, all his civility, all his apparent reasonableness, there was an iron fist in the velvet glove. He was interested

110

only in countering her, not in helping her to solve the problem. The anger began to seethe. She wanted to shout at him, to rail at him, but realized that that was a kind of surrender and so put a cap on her rage.

"The problem with your arguments, Prime Minister," she said, permitting a tone of weary impatience to enter her voice, "is that at every point you present a worst-case scenario that has little to do with the realities. You said a moment ago that the monarch is unique and that therefore she must not change. I grant you she is unique, but so are the conditions under which she must live. Years ago the monarch *used* the monarchy to serve his own purposes, but that has changed. Today *we* serve the monarchy. As a nation we pride ourselves on our freedom, but of all the people in Britain the Queen may be the least free. She's not free to choose her vocation. She's not free to say what she will. She's not free to marry whom she chooses. She's not free even to go about in public. Parliament may do nothing without her approval but she dare not withhold it. And she dare not object, certainly not publicly. She doesn't rule, she reigns, and even that she does by the sufferance of the powers-that-be. Let me ask you, Prime Minister: when I'm Queen, what may I do that matters?"

He said to her sternly, "You may do your duty."

"Ah, yes," she said, "duty – that hallowed word." She rose from her chair and began slowly to pace as she talked. "England expects every man to do his duty." She shook her head and her hair flew free. "That's fine in wartime but what about in time of peace? What is one's duty? It seems to me that, more often than not, duty is a word used to require some people to do what other people want them to do. You said to me, 'Do your duty.' What is my duty? You see it as foregoing all my deepest desires and doing what others have decided I should do. Let me remind

111

you, Prime Minister, I didn't seek the job, I was born to it. I had no say in it. But, being born to it, I'm expected to do my duty."

She seemed to have exhausted the energy that had driven her to her feet and now returned to her chair, permitting him to sit again. As he adjusted to the chair and crossed his legs, he said casually, "The life isn't *all* bad. There *are* a few perks."

"Yes, but are they perks if you don't want them?"

"If I may say so," Forster said, "your mother is a perfect example of someone doing her duty and doing it with grace and effectiveness. And the people love her for it."

"Yes, the people love her, but let me put it bluntly: you can't go to bed at night and put your arms about the people. It's tolerable for her because she also has the love of my father. But, in my case, the man I love is unsuitable because he can't trace his family back to some royal, no matter how obscure. He may not have blue blood, but if he is cut, do *I* not bleed?" Her eyes suddenly brimmed with tears but she set her jaw and, as quickly, the tears were gone.

Forster took a handkerchief from his sleeve and began to clean his spectacles. "If I may say so," he said, offering the tribute of a smile, "I'm happy you don't sit in the House on the benches opposite." He slipped the glasses into the breast pocket of his jacket, "If you'll permit me, I shan't respond to the point you just made. You didn't ask to see me simply to continue our debate. You must have had something specific in mind."

Victoria was conscious of her heart beating rapidly. "Yes," she said, her voice low. "As I've already told you, I intend to marry Jeremy Walsh. I know this will pose problems, not only for me but for you, and I want you to be aware of my plans well in advance so that things can be worked out as smoothly as possible. The monarchy has gone through many changes, it's time for it to change again." She looked full in his face, her eyes unblinking. "You should have no doubts, Prime Minister – and please do not misread me – I will step down if I am not free to realize a measure of personal happiness and fulfillment."

"I understand," said Forster. "Is there anything else?"

Victoria shook her head. "No."

"Well then, let me give you my immediate reaction. What you are asking is impossible of achievement. Truthfully, I wouldn't know where to begin." He raised his eyes to hers. "Moreover, as the Queen's first minister, I cannot accede to what you ask. However," he added quickly, "I will give the matter serious thought."

They rose and went in silence to the front door where Forster took her hand in his.

"You call someone to mind," he said, smiling at her thinly.

She returned the smile. "Who?"

"The woman you were named for."

Sir Herbert Garvey, MD, Ph D, FRCG CBE, Chairman of the Department of Obstetrics and Gynecology at the University of London Royal Free Hospital, reminded one of a bloodhound. The flesh of his gaunt face fell in folds, festooning beneath his eyes, about his jowls and onto his long, sinewy neck; the woebegone expression being accentuated by a domed forehead that extended in baldness to a close-cropped rim of white hair low on the back of his head. Standing well over six feet, he compensated by stooping, his long arms dangling. As he took the Queen's hand and then shook hands with the Duke, Edward had the feeling of grasping a bundle of warm bones.

But the man belied his exterior. Sir Herbert was world renowned in his field and, at sixty-two, laden with honors. It had been the Queen's pleasure only a few weeks earlier to bestow on him the title of Knight Commander of the Order of the British Empire. Now, seated across from her in her sitting-room, skeletal thighs extended before him, he deposited his empty teacup on the tiny table beside his chair and ransacked his brain for the appropriate response to the information he had just been given.

He had been taken entirely by surprise. Angus McCrimmon's request that he drop by the palace to have a word with the Queen had given him to think that perhaps she was troubled about some minor problem and wanted to discuss it before leaving for Windsor and the Easter holiday. But he had been quickly disabused of that notion. The Queen had put it bluntly, a pleased-as-punch smile on her face: "Edward and I have decided to have another child. Is there any reason why we may not?"

"No, Ma'am," he said slowly, touching his napkin to the corners of his lips to cover his discomfiture. "No reason in the world why not." There followed a clearing of his throat and a slight demurrer. "One would have to bear in mind, of course, the fact of your miscarriage. But that's a dozen or more years past. I wouldn't think your RH sensitivity would pose any problem of consequence." He paused, dropping his eyes as he adjusted the crease of his trousers to dead-center. "I should mention, of course, that conception might not be as simple as one might hope. . . . Your age. . . ."

"Forty-two."

"Yes, of course. No problem there. It's not the ideal time to achieve a pregnancy, one must say, but neither does it necessarily pose a problem." He paused. "We will, of course, want to do a thorough examination and run some

114

tests." He turned to Edward. "And while we're at it, we'll do a checkup on you, if that's all right?"

"No flat-headed sperm, that sort of thing," Edward said in his heartiest manner.

Sir Herbert nodded absently, his mind racing. Why in god's name did they want a child at this stage in life? Didn't they already have an heir in Victoria, and a fine one at that? Hadn't he seen a public opinion poll only recently that showed her to be the most popular woman in Britain, even ahead of the Queen? And with Victoria's twenty-first birthday celebration coming up next summer, wouldn't the Queen be busier than ever? He would not have been overly surprised had he been asked about the terminating of a pregnancy; but to be consulted about the achieving of one shook him.

"You do realize that having a child will require a considerable curtailing of your normal activities?" he asked.

"I wonder if you'd be a bit more specific about that," Mary said.

"Well," said Sir Herbert crisply, something of the pedant creeping into his tone, "if conception is achieved, we'll want to be judicious about physical activity until we're satisfied that the ovum is securely attached. Nothing vigorous for the first few weeks; especially during the week when the menstrual cycle would normally occur. No horseback riding," he added with a thin smile. "Once we feel secure, however, there's no reason why we can't fulfill most of our duties. An event or two in the morning, let's say, and something in the afternoon. Lots of rest. No prolonged periods of standing. We'll want to go off the pill, of course."

"I've already done that," Mary said. "It's more than a month now."

"I see," Sir Herbert said drily. "Then we've had all this in mind for some time." Mary smiled cryptically but said nothing, glancing at her husband. Sir Herbert frowned in concentration. "I'll want to look in on the medical facility here. I'm sure things will be adequate."

"Well now," Mary said, rising. "I suppose that will do for the moment. Mr. McCrimmon will arrange other times as necessary and will keep in touch with Mr. Gracie, the Master of the Household." At the door Mary said, "Incidentally, we've said nothing of our plans to anyone. You might bear that in mind."

"Of course. Of course. May I ask whether you have informed Sir David? As head of the Medical Household and Royal Physician he should. . . ."

"I'll speak to him when the time comes," Mary said, extending her hand. "We do have a few bridges to cross before then, don't we?"

"I have a question," Edward interjected. "We'd like a boy. As I understand it, the sex of the child is determined by the father. There's a preponderance of males in my family, so it's reasonable to presume, I suppose, that we're likely to have a son."

Sir Herbert's smile was more a grimace. "I'm afraid, sir, there are no guarantees. I can only tell you what I tell others when the question is raised – it will be either a boy or a girl."

Jeremy was in the shower when the telephone rang. His first thought was to let whoever it was call back, but when the ringing continued and seemed to grow more urgent he became convinced that it was Victoria calling. He hadn't spoken to her for three days. She was aboard the *Britannia* on a show-the-flag cruise to Gibraltar – an oblique act of response to the increasing rumbling by the Spanish government about the return of The Rock. Unfortunately, the scrambler on the ship-to-shore telephone wasn't working and Victoria had felt it wise that they forgo talking until her return.

"Jeremy? It's Ossie."

"Who?"

"Ossie Docherty of the *Herald*. We met on that Trade and Industry junket to New York. Remember?"

Yes, he remembered. Ossie Docherty, that obnoxious blimp who had overflowed two seats on the Concorde and polished off two trays of food before you could say gluttony. He'd taken an immediate dislike to the man, not merely because of his gross obesity but because of his pushy arrogance and the rudeness he'd displayed at the press briefings. Jeremy had read some of his stuff in the *Herald*, including a whole-cloth snippet of gossip about Victoria, accompanied by a telephoto grab-shot of her in a bikini that had made him grind his teeth in anger. When Jeremy had first arrived in London, Docherty had presumed to nominate him for membership in the Press Association, a dubious honor to which he hadn't bothered to respond in the early weeks of settling in and had later deliberately neglected.

"Hullo," he said. "What's up."

"Nothing special. We didn't get much of a chance to talk on the plane and I thought I'd just ring you up and – "

"Look, Ossie. . . . You caught me in the shower."

"Also, I didn't follow up on that invitation to join the Press Association and I thought that, now that you're an old hand, I'd be happy to put in a good word."

Jeremy had managed to get his feet on a corner of the towel, and with his free hand was mopping as far as the towel would reach. "Very kind of you," he said, "but I really don't have much time for that kind of thing. Hardly find time these days to brush my teeth."

Ossie continued unfazed. "Well, perhaps another time. There *was* something else. . . ."

"Ossie, look! – I'm standing here in my bare ass. Make it quick, will you?"

"Actually, I was wondering if you would do me a small favor."

"Like?"

"Well, I hear by the grapevine that you were up at Windsor Castle for a weekend, and – "

"Where'd you hear that?"

"I hear all kinds of things. It's true, isn't it?"

"So?"

"I mean, why not? – You're with the *New York Times*. Can you imagine those toffs at the palace inviting somebody from the *Herald*?"

"For god's sake, Ossie, will you get to the point?"

"Okay. I'm working on a story about ... let's just say it's an important story, and I was wondering if you'd give me a hand-up."

"Like how?"

"It's a story about one of the royals' cars. A Jag. Bottle green. Marker plate, V84-YFY. I'm trying to tie the car to its owner. I don't mean the actual owner – it's a lease-hire car – but the person who drives it."

Jeremy felt the short hairs rise on the back of his neck. Victoria's car! "For christ sake Ossie, what is this? I'm standing here with an advanced case of the chilblains and you're asking me to do your leg-work." He was about to slam down the receiver but restrained himself. He'd better find out what was up. "What in hell does the car some royal drives have to do with anything? Look, I've got to go."

"Okay, I'll tell you this much. I've seen this Jag twice, late at night – I mean, at ungodly hours. Once coming home late at the palace and once at Heathrow, the night we left for New York. That's all I want to say at the moment. I made inquiries at the palace but you know the bloody press office there. Then I got to thinking; maybe Walsh could ask around. I'd be glad to repay the – "

Jeremy slammed down the phone.

"Bastard!" Ossie said.

Victoria was in an irritable mood. The first day's formal engagements at Gibraltar had not gone well. An out-of-doors stand-up breakfast and reception at the British embassy had fallen behind schedule from the beginning and each subsequent event had taken on a frenetic quality. Even the drive through the town had gone awry. The engine of the aging open-topped Triumph *Stag* in which she was riding had gone stubborn, had coughed and spasmed every few blocks and, finally, with a backfire that sounded frighteningly like a gunshot, had quit altogether. Which led to various levels of official panic, many black looks and muttered imprecations, and to a considerable amount of perspiring in the mind-numbing heat of a sultry, windless day.

Back on the *Britannia*, Victoria had stripped down, showered, and slipped into a bikini and was sunning on the private deck outside the royal sitting-room. She knew that the irritability she was feeling was not simply a result of the foul-up of the day's events – such things happen. It had more to do with the fact that she hadn't talked to Jeremy for four days and with something Jane Cavendish had said the previous night as, in the cool of the evening, they had sat up late.

Victoria had invited Jane to join her on the trip to Gibraltar at the last minute. Her Dresser and her two Ladies-in-Waiting were friends of many years, and while they were good company and amusing, they were not confidantes. Victoria had known that her longing for Jeremy during the eight days absence would be such that she would have a need to talk about him.

Victoria had herself taken on the journey to Gibraltar at almost the last minute when the Queen notified the Foreign Office that she was indisposed and had accepted her physician's advice to take a week of rest at Windsor. She had of course discussed it with Victoria, but only briefly, leaving her bemused by the fact that, rather than ailing, her mother had seemed extraordinarily chipper.

Her Majesty's Yacht, *Britannia*, is the largest private yacht in the world. It is, in fact, a small ocean liner and a Royal Navy ship of the fleet, but functions primarily as a home away from home for the Queen and members of her family when they make official visits to overseas countries. With its crew of twenty-one officers and two hundred and fifty-six men (called "Snotty Yachties" by other naval seamen) it is a favorite target for anti-royalists who frequently decry "the unconscionable extravagance and indulgent lavishness of this floating palace."

And a floating palace it is, a commodious locale for the entertainment of heads of state and a place where the Queen may rest during the rigorous schedule of a foreign tour. The Queen's private quarters are on two upper decks, with her sitting-room and two separate bedrooms below connected by a lift. There is a drawing-room that can accommodate two hundred guests for cocktails, a dining-room that can seat forty, a private movie theater, and a host of other amenities. So that occupants of the royal quarters may not be disturbed, orders on the upper deck are given by hand signals and the crew is required to wear tennis shoes.

Four times the royal yacht had been used as a honeymoon retreat: for Princess Margaret and Anthony Armstrong-Jones in 1960, Princess Anne and Captain Mark Phillips in 1973, Prince Charles and Diana in 1980, and

Prince Andrew and "Fergie" in 1986. With this in mind, Victoria had taken Jane on a tour of the ship, their poking about being accompanied by many conspiratorial giggles.

It had been a splendid idea to take Jane along. For the first three days the two of them had read, gossiped, joined in aerobic workouts, or simply retired to their respective quarters. The malfunction of the scrambler on the ship-to-shore telephone had meant that Victoria had been unable to talk to Jeremy. Instead, she had contented herself by writing him long impassioned letters, sealing the envelopes, and passing them to Jane so that she could address them and include them with her mail.

On their arrival at Gibraltar they had sat up beyond midnight, and through the long evening had too often filled up each other's glass. As the hour grew late, Jane had begun to press her with questions. Reviewing what had been said, Victoria could not recall exactly how Jane had raised the subject nor how she had phrased her questions, but their essence had been: are you absolutely certain that you're not using Jeremy as a way to avoid becoming Queen? I'm not suggesting that you don't adore him, but we all delude ourselves at times, and have you considered the possibility, just the possibility, that you're attracted to him in part because he *is* so unsuitable as a husband? You've told me how you view your mother's and your father's lives, and how the prospect of such a lifelong servitude terrifies you. Could it be that, married to Jeremy, you can have what you want, marriage to him, and at the same time satisfy your conscience and provide yourself with a reasonable way out?

Victoria had made her rebuttals but had been aware that she was feeling unaccountably prickly and oddly resentful. Jane had sensed it and changed the subject and they had gone off to their beds soon afterward. But Victoria had lain awake in the darkness for a long time, half sick with a sense of dislocation and a chill of foreboding, and when finally she did, as she did every night before turning to sleep, whisper "Good night, my dearest, dearest Jeremy," her eyes were stinging and her pillow was wet.

But now Jane, who had skipped the morning's pomp and circumstance to go shopping in town, was back and any sense of estrangement from the night before was gone. She was laden with packages, the contents of which she displayed with flourishes, finally offering Victoria – with breath-held excitement as she watched for her reaction – a tiny velvet-covered box in which reposed a most extraordinary bracelet of filigreed ivory.

And she had news! She had talked to Jeremy on the telephone. He was well but lonely and sent his love. But he had, Jane added, a warning to pass on. A reporter on one of the tabloids was chasing some obscure story about Victoria's Jaguar. The reporter had no suspicion about Victoria and Jeremy, but for some reason had grown curious about seeing the car very late at night: once returning to the palace and once at Heathrow – the night she had driven Jeremy to the airport. His name's Ossie Docherty and he's a creep, Jeremy had said, but he's dangerous, and Victoria should be careful in using the Jaguar when she returned to London.

♕ SIX

MARY AND EDWARD had elected to spend the week at the Royal Lodge at Windsor rather than at the palace. They had banished the servants and rattled about in the big house, relishing even the inconvenience. She had brought him breakfast in bed and prepared the lunches. Edward, who nourished a conceit about being a gourmet cook (and not infrequently put together late suppers when they spent idle evenings at Buckingham Palace watching the telly), had insisted on making dinner each night, managing some minor triumphs and one disaster: a Beef Wellington in which the pastry was like leather and the meat ran red.

Now, tidying up, each aware that it was their final night of reprieve, Edward finished stacking the dishes in the washer, rinsed his hands, and said, "Pregnancy becomes you. I was thinking back earlier to when you were pregnant with Victoria. I can't remember you ever being more beautiful."

"I looked like a horse and buggy."

"You looked like an overweight angel," he conceded, "but the sexiest damn angel in the firmament."

She went along the line of cupboards, closing the doors. "We sound like a couple of proper teenagers."

"We've been acting like a couple of proper teenagers."

She leaned indolently against the countertop. "What's been so marvelous here has been the sense of isolation. Not another soul about. No one to come in with tea or to draw the curtains or to remind me that it's time to dress for this or that. I haven't had the same sense of being by ourselves, even at Balmoral."

They went together to the corner bedroom at the back of the house. It was one of the smaller bedrooms – although only by royal standards – but they had chosen it because it seemed less grand and overlooked the woods. Mary was occupied packing odds and ends in a small leather case, Edward was at a window, hands in pockets, looking out. He, too, had packing to do but was reluctant to get at it.

"Did you get a chance to look at that new book on the coffee-table in the study?" Mary asked.

"*Place and Privilege*? I leafed through it."

"Much of it is rubbish, of course, but there was one section that set me to thinking." She snapped the fastener on the case and set it on the bed. "The author drew this rather fanciful image of a sort of solar system, with Vicky and you and me at the center and a host of planets and satellites orbiting around us. The point he was trying to make was that we royals – not the Commons, not the Lords, none of the various institutions – hold the entire British system together. Nothing terribly new in that, of course, but it started me thinking about us. And the odd part of it was that, for the first time in years, I had the feeling of being . . . a prisoner." When Edward said nothing but continued to look out of the window, she asked, "Do you ever get that feeling?"

"No," he said, not turning around.

"Never?"

"Never."

"But when you get down to it," she said, pressing on, "isn't the reason we're here trying to have a baby because we feel almost duty bound to – "

He turned to face her. "Duty bound?"

"Don't misunderstand me, darling," she said. "I'm not suggesting that that's the only reason. I'm terribly excited about the whole thing. I get the shivers when I think about the baby. All I'm saying is that, being here alone with you and being as close as we've been. . . ." She paused, considering whether to go on. "What I'm trying to say is: isn't what we're doing simply an attempt to see that our whole . . . universe, if you like, doesn't fall apart? Isn't that really why we decided to have the baby?"

"You'll forgive me, darling," Edward said, "but you've lost me. What in the world are you trying to get at?"

She expelled a deep breath and let her arms fall in a gesture of resignation. "It's just that I've been wondering whether we have the right to interfere."

Edward went to her, took her hands in his, and sat her down, seating himself opposite. There was a puzzled look about his eyes, "I just want to be sure I follow you. Are you saying that you'd rather not go through with it?"

"No, no, nothing like that. It's simply that I've had time to think these last few days. It's a mood I've been in, I suppose, but I've been thinking a lot about tomorrows. About Vicky's tomorrows, about the baby's tomorrows. What kind of world will he be coming into? What kind of life will he have? If Vicky's restless, isn't it possible that he will be too? Then what?"

"You *are* in a mood."

"I suppose," she said. "I suppose it's because, in deciding to have this baby, it's as though we're taking it on ourselves to shape the future. And somehow that seems a presumptuous thing to do."

"Doesn't everybody who has a baby do exactly that?"

"Yes, of course. Anybody's baby is a vote for the future and a contribution to it. But it's different with us. Our baby will be King." She smiled wanly. "That's quite a responsibility to saddle a little baby with – the way the world's going."

"But, Mary," he said, "aren't you making exactly the opposite case to the one you intend? If things are bad, isn't that all the more reason for trying to perpetuate what's good? And the monarchy's one of the few good things around. One of the substantial things."

She took her hands back and settled in the chair. "You really believe that, don't you?"

"Of course."

"You say of course, but don't you ever doubt it?"

"Not really."

"I mean at those times when you're doing something . . . something absolutely inane. . . ." She cast about, seeking the appropriate example. "Unveiling a silly little plaque dedicated to . . . the Godmothers of Godalming or whatever! Doesn't what we do much of the time ever seem like a silly, senseless charade?"

Sometimes. But I don't dwell on it. May, darling, listen to me. For some reason you're in some kind of funk. But you're missing the whole point. No, it doesn't much matter when *I* do those things but it does when *you* do. You're the Queen. At a public function you're the one official on hand who doesn't have an axe to grind. You're not looking for votes. You're not trying to get your name in the paper or your picture on the BBC. You're like nobody else. You are the very people who are there to see you. You're the one unchanging thing in their world. You symbolize – what is it, exactly? – you symbolize roots. And doesn't everybody need to be reminded of their roots? Do you know who you *are* if you don't know where you've come from? And all that stems from this business about the line of succession.

126

You're Queen because of your genes, genes that were in your great-grandfather and his great-grandfather before him. Your genes say something. They say the past matters. They say that yesterday is important, perhaps more important than tomorrow. . . ." His thought faltered and he grew silent.

She looked at him closely, the suggestion of a smile on her lips. "My, my!" she said. "Isn't this a day for surprises?"

He glanced up at her. "What's so surprising? Have I ever talked differently?"

She gave her head a contemplative tilt. "Well, no, truth to tell. I suppose that it's that we've never gotten around to talking about it."

"There was no reason why we should; it's one of those things one takes for granted."

She could see that somehow she had vexed him. She was about to offer a palliative but changed her mind. Now that they were talking openly, perhaps she should go all the way and fully divulge her feelings. It's incredible, she thought, we've been married twenty-two years and we've never talked with absolute candor about how we feel; not about *who* we are but *what* we are.

She made her voice light. "Since this is a day for surprises, let's see if I can surprise you. Would it surprise you to know that for not one day of my life have I wanted to be who I am?"

He was puzzled. "Queen, you mean?"

"Queen."

He was flustered and revealed it in the difficulty he had in forming his response. "Are you saying . . . that, all these years you've resented being . . . who you are?"

"It's not that I resent it. Nothing like that. But would I have liked it to be otherwise? Yes."

127

She had begun to feel self-conscious, sitting opposite him talking about fundamental things almost as though they were merely making comment on the morning newspaper. She got up and began to fuss with the bedspread, tugging at it here and there, smoothing it with a palm.

"You have to remember," she said, "that I had just turned fourteen when Daddy was crowned. It hadn't entered my mind that one day I would be Queen. I knew it was remotely possible, of course, but it wasn't something that was going to happen. And then one morning, without five second's warning, I was out riding with some friends. Somebody had a portable radio and there was this voice saying, 'The King is dead. Long live the King!' And the new king was *Daddy*!"

She puffed out the pillows and adjusted the coverlet. "Fourteen years old! I was trying to cope with puberty, never mind with becoming the heir to the throne!" She smiled at him, a small, wistful smile. "It was all quite unreal, believe me. Unc's funeral. Moving out of Kensington into the palace. Daddy's coronation, with everything so solemn and with me worrying about doing the wrong thing – any one of a *thousand* wrong things! All of a sudden everybody curtsying. People advising me, tutoring me, guarding me. Not being able even to go shopping without cameras flashing and people peering and whispering. Not seeing Mummy and Daddy nearly as much. It took a bit of getting used to, believe me."

The bedspread had had enough attention and she now took to running a finger along the surfaces of the elaborately carved headboard, checking it in a reflexive way for dust. "For a while, I rebelled against it. They were stealing everything important from me! But I didn't say anything to anybody; the rebellion was all inside. Then one day I said to myself, 'Look, Miss Gloom and Doom, if you're for it you're for it. Stop the nonsense.' And that made things somewhat better."

She was silent, apparently intent on tracing the pattern of the inlay on the headboard. "That's why I feel so deeply for Vicky," she said, reaching quickly into a pocket for a handkerchief. She got past the moment with a dab at the corners of her eyes, finally breaking into a sudden, fragile smile. "Then, just when I'd earned my honors degree in princessing, Daddy was gone."

She sat for a moment at the edge of the bed and then eased forward onto it, her body shaken by a series of silent sobs. Edward went to her; putting his arms about her, holding her tightly, pressing his lips into her hair, whispering, comforting. After a while she was herself again and went into the dressing-room. When she rejoined him, there was no hint of the lapse save a slight redness of her eyes.

Nothing further was said in the sudden realization that they were due to leave for London in half an hour with all kinds of preparation yet to be made. It was not until the Rolls was on Bayswater Road approaching the turn onto Park Lane that Edward returned to the subject.

"That, uh, business we were talking about back at the Lodge . . ." he began.

"The baby?"

"No, your feelings about being Queen."

"Well, it's all past now. Truth to tell, I haven't thought about it for years. I suppose it was all brought to the surface by my thinking about the baby and about what the world will be like when he's crowned. . . ." She turned to him. "Isn't it odd how we both talk about *him*, as though it were certain it's going to be a boy? We don't even know there's going to be a baby." She patted her stomach. "Although I'd be willing to wager a fiver on it."

129

But Edward's mind was on what he'd already broached and he pressed on. "You were quite candid back at the Lodge, May, and it's been on my mind since that I should be more frank with you on something that's been bothering me."

She smiled at him. "You're not going to tell me that *you're* having second thoughts about going through with it?"

"Of course not," he said a trifle peevishly. He hesitated. "I'm not quite sure how to put this. . . ."

She turned to him. "It's not like you to be so tentative."

"Very well, then," he said. "I've been troubled about Victoria's attitude in this whole business about young Walsh. I'd never say it to her, of course, but I expected better from her. I can understand a young woman, especially one as full of ginger as she is not being all that happy about her duties – heaven knows, the old daily grind can get frightfully tiresome – but as you yourself came to see, it's one's duty and one does it."

Suddenly, a battered and rusting Austin, a torn rear fender flapping erratically in the wind, drew up alongside their Rolls, its horn blaring. Jammed together in the front seat were two young men and a woman, all of them with spikey, multicolored hair, and all mouthing obscenities. The passenger on the near side put a bare arm out of the window, fist clenched, middle finger upraised. The driver quickly accelerated and veered toward the Rolls, forcing it to give way and swerve into the oncoming lane. Then, as suddenly as it had appeared, the car sped off, leaving behind a stink of exhaust. Mary saw her policeman in the front seat shouting into a microphone. In a moment, a black, unmarked police car sped past them, followed immediately by another.

"Filthy rotter!" Edward shouted, shaking a fist after them. He turned to his wife in concern. "Are you all right?"

130

"Fine," she said, fishing in her purse. "Probably had a pint too many." She flipped open the lid of a compact and checked her face and hair. "You were saying?"

"Saying. . . ."

"That you were disappointed in Vicky."

"Ah, yes. Yes, I don't actually mean disappointed. She's a simply super girl and I'm sure she's very much in love with him and all that, but one can't help feeling that she's letting down the side, as it were. I'm sure Walsh is an interesting fellow, but marriage! Surely there's someone in her own crowd . . . Billy Carnarvon, or that Leigh-Robertson chap."

"But she's in love with Jeremy."

"Yes, yes, we've been over that. But surely all that can be managed somehow. My god, it's not the first time such a thing has happened. I'm not sure she realizes the unholy row there's going to be."

"You'd like her to marry Billy, say, and have Jeremy visit her by the back stairs?"

"Of course not. But if you want to put it that way, why not? It's been done for centuries. My god, May, we won't name names but we both know some of our friends who have managed very well. One does what one must do. It's important to keep up appearances, very important where families and heirs and so on are involved."

"And you'd want that for your daughter?"

He made a gesture of exasperation. "No, dammit, I wouldn't want that for my daughter. I'm looking for a way out of a bloody mess, that's all." His exasperation grew. "You know, sometimes you women can be so damned – what's the word I want? Sentimental, that's it – so damned sentimental. You act as though love is everything. Well it is, but it's not." She had turned away and was looking at the cluster of hotels at the end of Park Lane. "There now, I've said too much."

131

She turned to face him, unperturbed. "Not really. The thought had crossed my mind." She leaned across to put a kiss on his cheek. "I think you and I have found the best way to work things out."

He didn't understand for a moment, looking at her blankly. As he caught her meaning he began to smile. "Right! Right on!" The smile broadened. "Yes, by George, looks like it's up to you and me to take up the slack."

She looked at him fondly, shaking her head. "You are such a goose!" She began to laugh. "Yes, my darling, it does look as though it's up to you and me to...." She could hardly finish for giggling. "To, one might say, take up the slack."

Maidy Lightstone, a night housemaid at the palace, was on her break. Sunday night was the beginning of her week, and, as always, there was more work than usual. With the royal family away weekends, there was only a skeleton staff on duty Friday and Saturday nights and quite a bit of catching up to do. She'd had an eye on the clock, however. At fifteen minutes past four, she'd told her friend, Hetty Gorman, that she was going to catch a breath of air and was now standing in the shadow of the massive stone doorway leading to the Belgian Suite at the northwestern-most corner of the palace. The hazy crescent of a waning April moon seemed to be resting on the grove of trees ranging along Constitution Hill, casting just enough light to permit her to see forms and shapes and silhouettes. Immediately to her left was the looming bulk of the swimming pool with its Corinthian columns and its gleaming expanses of mullioned glass. Above and to her right were the windows of the royal apartments. The usual surf of sound from the nearby traffic was muted. The night was still but for a rustling in the trees and the insistent creaking of crickets.

Kevin had instructed her on how to open the door and set the lock so that she wouldn't trigger the alarm in the security room and had impressed upon her where she could walk without breaking one of the photoelectric beams that crisscrossed the gardens. She'd been surprised to find the lock already set, but in her preoccupation gave it no second thought, peering instead into the darkness, straining to see the darker form that would be Kevin.

He'd explained that he might not be able to meet her. His new post was at the Queen's Entrance gate, not far away, but as he'd reminded her, security procedures changed twice a month and he wasn't certain exactly when he'd be expected to check in on his transceiver. "We've got to be super careful," he'd warned. "If anybody was to catch us, I'd be put on report. I could even get shipped out."

And now, after ten minutes, for all the craning of her neck and squinting of her eyes, there was no sign of him. She was about to turn back into the palace when she heard a sound off to her right. Her heart leaped – Kevin! After all!

But no. . . . There, on the small balustraded balcony that ran along the Principal Floor at the window level, was the dark form of a man. So swiftly that she wasn't quite sure what she was seeing, he stepped over the balcony, swung down until he was hanging by his hands, and dropped to the ground. Now he was coming toward her, crouched low, moving swiftly, clinging close to the building, obscured at times by the shrubbery. She stepped behind the great concrete urn standing by the doorway, wanting to scream, her heart pounding until she was certain he would hear it. He passed within a foot of her and, without a sound, went quickly through the door into the palace. So close was he that she saw his face. . . .

"Holy Mother of God!" she breathed, a hand to her lips. "In the Queen's bedroom!"

Part 2

♛ ONE

A VAST ABYSSAL HORROR. She lay motionless at the center of it, not feeling, not thinking, every muscle, every sinew drawn taut; eyes wide open, dry and unfocused, lips drawn back, teeth bared in the grimace of the dead. Her chest rose and fell in quick, panting breaths; the sounds like the whining cries, the muted yelping of a puppy in a nightmare.

She began to be conscious of her body. The refusal to think that had frozen her brain was beginning to lift and the horror was beginning to descend. Suddenly, the calves in her legs knotted in cramps and she uttered a strangled groan, doubling up in the bed, fighting the reflex that had drawn her feet into arches of pain. But she daren't cry out. The voice had hissed in her ear, "One sound when I'm gone and you're dead!"

How long ago had that been? A minute? An hour?

She began to tremble and suddenly realized that she was cold. She fumbled at her nightgown, tugging it down to cover her nakedness. Now the shivering swept over her in waves, jerking at her arms and legs and chest and belly, causing her eyelids to flutter and her eyes to go out of focus.

In a few moments the trembling passed and she lay still in the bed, suddenly, acutely, totally aware. Her body was inflamed with pain, every part of it reacting now to the long moments when she had lain rigid as a stone, afraid almost to breathe lest the dark horror return. Her palms felt wet and she realized that they were bleeding where she had dug her fingernails into them.

Before she could react, she vomited, the gouts gushing over her chin and neck and chest. She struggled to get out of bed but was seized with another paroxysm and fell to her knees on the carpet, heaving, retching, gasping.

"Oh, God," she cried. "Help me!"

In the darkness of the bathroom she fumbled for the taps. The bath filled so slowly. When finally she was able to climb in, she realized that she had forgotten to take off her nightgown but was unable to muster the will to move. She lay there as the water mounted to her chin and wondered if she should simply slide beneath the surface, breathe the warm, welcome water and let it wash away her life.

She heard the words repeating beguilingly in her brain: "To die. To sleep. To sleep. . . . No more."

She stirred and then awakened with a cry and a jerk of an arm that curled a wave of water over the rim of the bathtub onto the floor. She was immediately alert and lay still, as a bird freezes until the predator has passed. Slowly, laboriously, she climbed out of the tub, stripped away her soiled nightgown and let it slump in a sodden heap on the tile floor. Through the bathroom window the sky had that leaden lightness of the onset of dawn. She noticed that her body was wrinkled and white in places from its immersion in the water. How long had she lain there since exhaustion had overcome her fear and given her sleep?

She turned, and on a sudden notion went to the bidet. She ran the water, letting it jet with powerful force; staying there, head thrown back, face twisted in a grimace for a long time. It was painful to walk to the towel rack.

But now she was back in the bedroom, dry and warm and wrapped in a bathrobe. She was very tired and wanted to lie down, but the sheets on the bed were twisted and soiled with vomit. She jerked at them, tugging them loose, and dropping them on the carpet to cover the stains there. For a moment she didn't move, standing at the center of the bedroom, commanding her clouded brain to concentrate. Then she went to the bedside table, pressed the button that would summon the chambermaid, and waited by the door. There were footsteps and a soft tap-tap. She opened the door a crack but stood where she couldn't be seen.

"I seem to have had an accident and soiled the bedsheets," she said. Her voice sounded surprisingly normal. "Will you please get clean sheets and blankets and remake the bed. I'll be in the bathroom. Let me know when you're finished. Right away now; I'm not feeling at all well. It's Jenny, isn't it?"

"Yes, Ma'am."

In the bathroom she emptied the tub, wiped it clean with a towel and filled it with warm, clean water. She was drying her body when there was a soft tapping at the bathroom door. "Ma'am."

"Yes?"

"The bed's ready, Ma'am. I've tidied up the carpet for now but I'll have it taken care of properly later on. Is there anything else, Ma'am?"

"Yes, Jenny. Will you tell the kitchen that I won't be wanting any breakfast, nor anything else until I call for it. Do you understand?"

"Yes, Ma'am."

"And would you see to it that the footman speaks to Mr. Gracie and tells him to be in touch right away with Lady Hammil and Billie – you know who Billie is?"

"Oh, yes, Ma'am. Your Dresser."

"To tell them that I'll be staying in bed and won't need them today. I'll see no one, do you understand?"

"Yes, Ma'am."

"There's a good girl. Off you go now."

"Yes, Ma'am. I'm sorry you're not feeling well, Ma'am."

"And tell Mr. Gracie to tell Mr. McCrimmon that I won't be able to keep my appointments today, that I'm indisposed."

"Yes, Ma'am."

"You have all that?"

"Yes, Ma'am."

"That will be all then."

When she heard the door close, she returned to the bedroom and turned the keys in the doors leading to the corridor and to both her dressing and sitting-rooms. The bed had been turned down and looked inviting. She slipped between the cool, fresh sheets and lay there, staring at the canopy with unfocused eyes.

Jenny hadn't seemed to sense anything wrong. She'd been a trifle more timid than usual but that was understandable, her mistress being ill. Obviously the intruder had raised no alarm or the policeman who stood guard nights outside her apartment would have been at the door inquiring. The officer on duty Sunday nights was Sergeant Trumper and, while talking to Jenny, she'd heard his voice in the background conversing with the footman who was replacing him. Clearly there was no problem there.

The intruder had entered her bedroom through the door to her sitting-room and presumably had left the same way, although she wasn't sure about that. But how had he gotten into the apartment without raising an alarm? And gotten out? He couldn't have come through a window; her apartment was on the Principal Floor, at least twelve feet above the ground, and there were alarm devices everywhere in the driveway and gardens below. Even if he could have avoided them as well as the guards posted about the grounds, there were no chinks in the smooth facing of the building, no crevices to offer footholds. An air-conditioning duct ran down the wall near the windows of the dressing-room, but surely no one could climb that. He must have come from within the palace. But how was that possible? – Trumper was in the corridor outside her rooms. Could Trumper himself be the man? Impossible. He'd been with the palace police force for forty years – she'd made a little presentation to him only a few weeks ago; he was to retire soon. And Trumper affected a bushy moustache drawn to two waxed tips; the face that had been pressed to hers was clean-shaven, although there was a stubble on his cheek.

The memory of the horror began to sweep in on her again and she started to tremble. The muscle in her right thigh began an involuntary twitching and persisted for a few minutes. A grayness began to close in and she knew she was about to faint. She set her jaw and forbade it, and after a moment it cleared.

She was surprised by tears. They streamed from her eyes and ran down her cheeks into her hair and ears. The weeping became a soft sobbing, a kind of mourning. She felt again that sense of desolation that had depressed her from time to time after Unc died. She didn't struggle against it but let the tears flow and ebb, and then overflow again. Now the sobs were coming from deeper down, shaking her entire body, constricting her throat, and she clutched at the bedsheets, holding on. Then that too passed and she was quiet again.

She must have fallen asleep. A thin bar of dazzling sunlight shafted through the narrow opening in the drawn window drapes, streaking across the carpet and halfway up the wall. What time was it? She glanced at the clock on the night table. Almost ten! How grateful she was that Edward had had to be up early for his flight to Wales and that Vicky was aboard the *Britannia* on her way home from Gibraltar. She could at least go through the day without having to see anyone.

She got out of bed. In the bathroom she was surprised that her image in the mirror reflected almost nothing of what she was feeling. She looked a little pale. There were shadows under her eyes and her hair looked frightful, but that was all. She gave her hair a vigorous brushing. There was a small cut on her cheek where the intruder had put the tip of his knife to ensure that she wouldn't cry out, but it was little more than a nick and had already begun to heal. She washed her face – cupping and holding handfuls of cold water against her eyes as she did so. She looked tired but not unwell; her skin shone with a healthy pinkness.

The telephone jangled. She leaped at the sound. It was a moment before she could pick it up.

"Good morning, Ma'am." It was Crimmie, his voice solicitous. "I do hope I'm not troubling you, but in simple truth I couldn't go any longer without at least knowing firsthand how you are. Better, I trust."

"That's all right, Angus," she said. "It's kind of you to inquire. Just a bit under the weather, I'm afraid."

"A little stomach upset, I'm told."

"I'm afraid so."

"Mr. Gracie filled me in. I've headed off everyone so you won't be disturbed. There was some disappointment with the people in charge of the flower show when I told them you were indisposed but they took it in good grace. The Duchess of Kent was kind enough to fill in. Ah. . . . I was just wondering about tomorrow. . . ."

"Tomorrow?"

"You're to lay a cornerstone at the new Salvation Army headquarters. If you don't think you'll be up to it, I could arrange for someone, I'm sure."

"Just give me a minute to think," she said. "What we'd best do is plan on my being there, but have a word with the people in charge so that they can prepare for the possibility that I might not make it. Perhaps someone could stand by."

"Of course. Of course." He paused a moment. "Tomorrow being Tuesday, there is of course your meeting with Mr. Forster. . . ."

Forster! She couldn't possibly do her boxes and be prepared to see him. She was about to say so but decided not to. "I'm sure I'll be fine by then. I'd prefer, incidentally, that my . . . indisposition not get blown up into anything of consequence. You'll see to that?"

"Indeed I shall. I've been describing it as just that, a slight indisposition. It will be a bit awkward with the press, I'm told, following on the heels of the cancellation of your trip to Gibraltar, but that can be managed. You don't think you would like to see Dr. Knight?"

"No, no, no. It's nothing really. If I do, I'll ring you up and you can ask him to come round. I'm going to spend the day quietly. I should be fit as a fiddle tomorrow."

"You'll forgive my pressing the matter, Ma'am, but you're not running a temperature? You're quite sure you don't want Dr. Knight to pop in for a minute?"

"Thank you, no." She was about to end the conversation but a cloud passed across the sun and, with the drapes drawn, the room was suddenly quite dark. What would she do when night came? How could she remain alone? There was a sudden constriction in her throat and she felt her heart pounding.

"Angus. . . ."

"Yes, Ma'am."

"You haven't heard anything about a problem in the palace last night?"

"A problem?"

"A fracas of some kind."

"In the palace?"

"I was up much of the night, and around four, four-thirty perhaps, I heard what seemed to me odd noises."

"Odd noises? What kind of noises?"

"That's the trouble. I was quite ill at the time and not exactly concentrating. It sounded as though there was . . . a scuffle. I couldn't tell whether it was in the palace or out in the gardens. It frightened me, I must say, and I've been wondering since what it might have been. I'm always a bit nervous when Edward's away. It's possible I dreamed it – I was asleep off and on. You might look into it. Do let me know."

McCrimmon was back on the line within ten minutes. "I've talked to the security people. They have no report of any kind of dust-up last night. The only thing out of line was a problem with a lock on one of the doors to the Belgian Suite. A malfunction of some kind. Nothing of consequence."

"Nothing that went bump in the night," she said, making her tone light.

"Nothing, apparently. But inasmuch as you mentioned feeling a bit tense – Edward being away – it occurred to me that it might be useful if we were to put a younger

144

man on the night shift. It's a lot of standing for Trumper's old legs. I gave instructions that it be handled in such a way as to seem like a reward for his years on the job."

"I wouldn't want to hurt his feelings."

"Actually, Gracie tells me he's been hinting pretty broadly about being assigned to a post where there's more sitting, so all's well. Trumper's replacement, for your information, is Terrence Austin. Twelve years on the palace force. Splendid record. You'll feel a shade more assured with him in the corridor."

She lay down on the bed, not troubling to get under the covers. Perhaps that was part of the answer. Perhaps Trumper had grown weary and had gone off to sit on that chair in the pantry and dozed off. She'd noticed not long ago that there was a cushion on it where there had been none before. Or perhaps he'd slipped away for a chat with one of his mates, or to the loo, and the intruder had seized the moment. But how had he gotten into the palace in the first place? The malfunction of the lock on the door to the Belgian Suite might explain that. But surely not. The intruder, whoever he was, would have had to by-pass all the other security devices to get that far. But wasn't that exactly what had happened to Lilibet back there when that madman wandered about the palace for ages and then broke into her bedroom?

She was certain the man couldn't be a member of the staff. There had been a stubble of beard on his face and she knew that Gracie was a martinet about neatness; even the gardeners were required to be clean-shaven. The thought nagged at her: was it possible that the intruder had managed somehow to get inside the palace grounds and had then, perhaps, clambered up the drainpipe? Wasn't that what Lilibet's crazy had done?

She had to know. She went to the sitting-room. There! – the window was open. She disliked the stale smell of the

145

air-conditioning system and usually left a window or two ajar even in winter, but it was open more widely than she'd left it. She checked that there was no one in sight below and put her head out of the window. There was no drainpipe. Of course not; all those on the north wing had been removed in Lilibet's time. Then how had the man come and gone? She craned her neck, looking upward. Yes, he could have come from the roof, could have lowered himself down a rope to the tiny balcony outside her apartment and escaped the same way. She made a tour of all the windows in the apartment, securing them.

While she was about it, she thought, she'd better check Edward's apartment. As she opened the connecting door, she heard a sound from within. In a sudden panic she closed the door and turned the lock, standing with her hand to her throat, her entire body atremble. After a moment she ran to the door leading to the corridor, flung it open, and then took a step backward, loosing a small, involuntary cry. Joseph, the senior footman, was standing in the doorframe, his back to her.

"Joseph! . . . Joseph, there's someone in my husband's apartment."

"Yes, Ma'am."

"But he's away."

"Yes, Ma'am. Until tomorrow, Ma'am. Jenny's in changing the linen and doing a tidy up." He was looking at her, his brows furrowed.

"Jenny? Yes, of course." She was aware that she must look distracted. "I heard a sound and. . . . Thank you Joseph."

She returned to the bedroom and, feeling unnerved, took off her bathrobe and got into bed. She must try to get some rest. Perhaps she should call the kitchen and have them send up something to eat. The thought nauseated her.

But she would have to eat something later on or she would leave herself weak, and with Edward arriving back tomorrow –

Edward! . . . Oh, my God – *the baby*!

♛ TWO

"Maidy?..."

"Kevin! I've been waiting for your call. Where are you calling from?"

"The phone box down the street. I had the devil of a time getting out of the flat. Annie's beginning to think something's going on the way she asks questions when I'm going out. Something else before I forget: don't send me any more notes by the post. I'm taking a ragging from my mates about who's the fancy lady who uses purple ink."

"But what if it's important? Like now?"

"I'll think of something, but we've got to be careful. I've applied for a transfer out of the palace. Captain Groat thinks I've a good chance at gettin' into Traffic Division and I've got my fingers crossed. It would mean a rise in my pay packet and, Maidy, love, more chances for us to see each other."

"Oh, I do hope so. I'm going out of my mind lately, hardly ever seeing you and then for only a few minutes."

"It's just that it's too risky at the palace. Some tourist chap came in through the tradesmen's entrance last week and was wandering round near the post office. He might still be there if he hadn't asked if he could get a letter postmarked so he could send it home to Canada to let them know he'd visited the palace. Believe me, there were some tempers frazzled about that."

"I love you, Kev. Do you still love me?"

"Of course I do."

"Well then, say it."

"Haven't I told you dozens of times?"

"Yes, when we're alone, but I like to hear it."

"Okay . . . I love you."

"Sounds like you're ordering fish and chips. Say it like you mean it."

"You know I mean it. Don't I prove it when we're. . . ."

"You still haven't said it. I love you – like you really mean it. Want me to count to three?"

"I don't need anybody to count to three. Okay. . . . I love you."

"Like drawing teeth! But anyway, you said it."

"What is it that's so important?"

"Important? Oh yes, in my letter. Kev, remember Sunday night when you were supposed to meet me – "

"Of course I remember."

"Well, I was there at four-fifteen right on the dot, hoping against hope, and no sign of you. And just as I was going to give up, I heard this noise. It wasn't actually a noise – more like a squeak of some kind. I thought maybe he's been able to get away after all. If you only knew how much I look forward to seeing you. Last night I even dreamed – "

"What was the noise?"

"Kev, you're not going to believe this. I've been asking myself over and over again should I mention it. I mean, I still can't believe that I actually *saw* it."

"Maidy, will you get to the point!"

"You don't have to take my head off."

"Sorry."

"All right then. So I hear this noise, this squeak – I know how you policemen are about getting all the details and like that."

"Maidy...."

"I'm telling you. I'm telling you. So I look around, hoping it's you, and you won't believe this – there's a man coming out of the Queen's window – "

"There's a *what*?"

"I knew you wouldn't believe me. There's a man climbing out of the Queen's window. I mean, I had to look twice to be sure I wasn't seeing things. Coming out of her window. And so fast I couldn't believe my eyes, down to the ground."

"You're absolutely certain?"

"I knew you wouldn't believe me."

"I do believe you; I just want to get things straight. It was pretty dark Sunday night – "

"Kevin, I *saw* him! I not only saw him, I know who it was."

"Now, wait a minute. You say he came out of the window and down to the ground so fast you couldn't believe your eyes; how could you recognize him?"

"Because he came right toward me. Well, not right toward me, but ducking behind the bushes, sort of. And, oh, I forgot to tell you: when I went to set the lock on the door the way you told me, it was already set. Anyways, he went right past me and into the palace. I could have reached out and touched him. Kev? ... Kevin, are you still there?"

"I'm still here. I've been trying to digest what you just told me. This isn't some kind of joke?"

"Would I joke about something like that?"

"I certainly hope not. Now, let me be sure I've got this straight. Sunday night – Monday morning, actually – at approximately half past four, you observed a man exit the palace through a window on the Principal Floor, a window that you know opens into the Queen's apartment. Correct?"

"Correct."

"Wait a minute, how did he get down from the balcony?"

"He swung down. You know, hung by his hands and dropped."

"Upon reaching the ground, the suspect proceeded west, following the palace wall, and apparently trying to conceal himself behind the shrubbery?"

"Correct."

"Upon reaching your vantage point. . . . Just a minute. If he passed so close to you, how come he didn't see you?"

"Because there's that big concrete urn there. You know the one in the corner by the swimming pool. Because I ducked behind it when I saw him coming."

"I see. Whereupon, the suspect turned left and entered the palace through the door to the Belgian Suite, which door was standing open at the time."

"Well, not exactly standing open; not quite closed. You know, so I could go back in."

"And despite the fact that it was quite dark, you were able to recognize him."

"Correct. I'm not sure you know him but it was – "

"Hold it! Hold on a minute. I don't want you to tell me who it was. It's not information I wish to have at the moment."

"But, Kev. . . ."

"Maidy, listen to me very carefully. *Do not* tell me who the man was. I don't want to know. Understand?"

"No, I don't understand. I can't see why you wouldn't want to know who he was. Why not, for goodness sake?"

"Maidy, love, I wonder if you have any notion how serious this whole thing is? Imagine if it got in the press? Or even if it got out at the palace? I don't want to know who it is because what I don't know I can't perjure myself on. Somebody was asking questions about the door lock on the Belgian Suite. It looks like it's all blown over, but you never know. If it should come out in some way – this business about the man on the balcony – and there was to be an investigation, I won't even guess where that might lead! If I'm questioned, I saw and heard nothing. In something like this, the less you know the better. The same with you. Don't tell a soul. Follow me now: to see the man you must have been outside the palace. Right? How did you get out without triggering the alarm? How did you know how to set it? Who told you? There'd be no end of questions and you'd end up crying and telling them everything. You haven't mentioned it to anyone?"

"Of course not."

"You're sure? None of the girls on your shift?"

"I was dying to tell Hetty, Hetty Gorman, but I didn't."

"Maidy, listen to me; you mustn't tell a soul! Nobody! You could get the sack, I could get the sack. Worse!"

"But aren't you curious to know who it was?"

"Well, you can tell me this much – was he Household or Staff? Not the name, mind you."

"Staff."

"My god! – not Household. And with the *Queen!*"

"I couldn't believe it either. If it was one of those high muckety-mucks in Household it wouldn't be . . . well, you know, so bad. But a footman!"

"Maidy! Not another word! I think we'd better ring off."

"Wait a minute. When am I going to see you?"

"Friday. I'll pick you up at the usual spot. And

remember, you don't tell a soul no matter how you're tempted. Mum's the word."

"Morning sickness!"

Such was Edward's diagnosis of her indisposition when, on his return, Mary offered her reasons for not being up to scratch. In fact, she seemed entirely herself except for a slight tremor in her hands and a tendency for her mind to wander. She'd made it through the night by taking a sedative she'd found in the medicine cabinet. But when even the medication hadn't eased her tension or her startled reaction to the slightest sound, she had gone to Edward's bed and finally fallen into an unbroken sleep.

She was roused by the sound of Joseph's voice and a loud banging in the corridor. What had happened, she learned, was that when the maid arrived with the breakfast tray, Joseph had knocked on the Queen's dining-room door and, growing alarmed when there was no response, had begun to call out and hammer on it with a fist. Mary went to the door and took the tray, offering no explanation, finding that after the first few mouthfuls she was ravenous. Afterward, having steeled herself for the ordeal, she kept her engagement to lay the cornerstone and, although at times her voice was a trifle unsure and her knees shaky, managed her public persona so skillfully that there was a consensus among the larger than usual contingent of reporters that she seemed entirely fit.

Mary was in her sitting-room when Edward returned from Wales. He was zestful and full of news, noticing only that she seemed tired. She offered as a reason that she hadn't been able to keep anything in her stomach the previous day. It was at that point that he had come up with his instant diagnosis – forefinger raised aloft and a broad grin on his face – "Morning sickness!" and gone off to an appointment.

There was one unexpected stroke of luck. When McCrimmon arrived to review her correspondence and other pressing matters, he brought news that the Prime Minister's plane had been grounded by fog in Bonn and that, regretfully, he would have to cancel their Tuesday Meeting.

Later, a nurse came by from the Royal Free Hospital to take three vials of blood and a urine sample. As she was leaving, Mary asked her to have Sir Herbert ring her up on the telephone at his convenience. He called within the hour.

"I read in the press you're a little under the weather."

"I must have eaten something that disagreed with me. It's nothing, really. They make it sound as though I was terminal."

"I'm not surprised. Following on your change in plans for Gibraltar, you cancel some engagements. . . . What more do the newsmongers need? It's the glass house you live in."

"Edward diagnosed my problem as morning sickness."

Sir Herbert gave his braying hee-haw laugh. "A bit premature, I would venture."

"When will you have some word for me?"

"Within the week. I want to double-check the work-up on the blood. Another nurse will come by for some more blood and another specimen on Friday and yet another on Monday next. Different hospitals. We don't need any more rumors flying."

"Agreed."

He began to chuckle. "The three ladies whose names are on the blood samples are: Mrs. Angela Throckmorton, a Ms. Eloise Wilberforce, and a Miss Cynthia Revelstoke – all fictitious inventions of mine. Agatha Christie had better have a care."

154

She went listlessly through the apartment, straightening a picture, rearranging a bouquet of cut flowers, puffing up the down pillows on a sofa. There was no point in returning to her desk; she was unable to concentrate. If only there was someone she could talk to about the horror and about the questions arising from it. But to whom? She had decided to keep it from Edward unless she found she was pregnant. The fact that she had been violated by another man might, for all his best resolutions, come between them. Nor could she tell Sir Herbert. If the tests showed that she hadn't conceived, there would be no need to; if she had, there would be no option. She knew what her first question would be: is there any way of determining whether I was impregnated before or after Sunday night? And then there was the question: what would she do if the baby forming within her was not Edward's?

She felt utterly alone. She went into the sitting-room, drew the drapes, and sat in a chair in the darkness of a corner.

"Hey, what would that bunch of meddlers at Westminster do if I got you pregnant?"

Jeremy and Victoria were in the shower together following a languorous, loving Sunday afternoon in his flat. She had come straight from Portsmouth after a press conference and photo session on the *Britannia*. Jane Cavendish, who had left her apple-red Ferrari parked in the naval enclosure during their absence, had served as chauffeur and, in part to shake off some paparazzi who were following, had demonstrated her driving skills if not her restraint in a mad dash for London.

Almost simultaneously, Jeremy had cleared his desk at the *Times'* office, fretted at the slow descent of the lift and – rare good luck! – collared the first taxi in sight. They had arrived within fifteen minutes of each other, and before the door closed, Victoria was in his arms, her purse and parcels falling about their feet.

Now they were toweling each other dry, ravenous and eager to set out on the table – already laid with linen and silver and candlesticks – the goodies Jeremy had stacked on the kitchen counter or jammed into the refrigerator. ("There's gazpacho cooling; the most incredible lobster thermidor in history; broccoli, asparagus, and the makings for a monumental salad; grapes the size of plums and two pears that would have put Eve off apples for life!")

"You didn't answer me," he said as they went, arm in arm, wrapped in terry towelling bathrobes to the kitchen. "What *would* Foxy Forster say if suddenly he learned you were pregnant?"

"Never mind Forster, what would you say?" she asked as she began to open containers and he got the stove functioning. "You'd have to make an honest woman out of me," she said, popping an olive into her mouth, "or I'd lay charges in magistrate's court."

They'd moved on to other subjects, both chattering about what they'd done in the ten days they'd been apart. But now, sated and sipping cognac, the candles burning low on the table, Victoria returned to Jeremy's question.

"We were kidding about my getting pregnant," she said, "but it's something I've thought about. Don't panic, it's not going to happen, but there is that one in a million chance. Never mind Forster, what would we do?"

"Go shopping for some smashing maternity clothes?"

She was not to be so easily dissuaded. "If you want to know what I would do, I'd have the baby."

"Damn the torpedoes."

"The torpedoes? . . ."

"Farragut, an American admiral said it: 'Damn the torpedoes! Full speed ahead.'"

"Right. Damn the torpedoes!"

Jeremy was silent for a moment, musing. "You say you've thought about it," he said. "I'm afraid I haven't. But I wonder. . . . What *would* we do? What *would* Forster do?" Elbows on the table, chin in his hands, he looked at her. "You'd have the baby. Tell me why."

"First, of course, because it would be your baby." He reached across and put his hand on hers. "But mostly because I couldn't bear to contemplate anything else."

"You wouldn't worry about contributing to the world's overpopulation?"

A frown shadowed her brow. "I thought you were being serious."

"I am, I am," he said quickly. "Sorry."

"Would you want the baby?" she asked.

He was slow to answer. "I'm not sure." He hastened to go on. "I know that's the second most unromantic answer possible, but we've always talked honestly and the truth is I haven't actually thought it through. I'm a funny guy, I have to go over the ramifications before I make an important decision." He gave a humorless laugh. "And like, Wow! – would there be ramifications!"

"I'll tell you who my mind flashed to," she said. "To Martin."

"And who, pray, is Martin?"

"The Most Reverend Martin Staples Sutherland, Archbishop of Canterbury," she said, making her voice clerically lofty.

"And how does he ramify?"

"By leaping off the top of Westminster Abbey. It's one thing for a royal to marry a Catholic, but throw in a wee papist out of wedlock! . . ."

"He wouldn't buy it?"

"As they say in the best circles, not bloody likely."

"So we lose one?"

157

"Actually, he's not a bad fellow, but yes."

"Leave us move on then to the Right Honorable Hugh Anthony Forster. My turn. He joins the archbishop on the roof of the Abbey. Right? No, wait a minute, with Forster you've got to ask what the political consequences are. Let me think about this for a minute." He was wiggling his toes, watching them, eyes squinted. "You see, I've always thought that my being a Catholic is not the major roadblock. A generation ago, yes, but today. . . . I'd be willing to bet money that if that were the only objection Forster would stand tough. More than that, I'm a Catholic only in name and he probably knows that. It matters to my family, but not to me. It's not that I scorn it, I'm indifferent to it. Would I convert? I suppose, if that's what it came down to. So, my converting could become a kind of bargaining chip, Forster could argue that he'd insisted on it and could present it as a small victory for Anglicanism, and would thus be able to pressure the Archbishop to bend the rules in some way to overlook the divorce. As a matter of fact, if I converted, and my being divorced was the only issue, we might find Forster ready to champion our cause. I'd go so far as to say that he could make political hay with it. He'd have the public behind him – I'm convinced he would. And the Opposition, especially Blackstock, who is himself divorced and wouldn't let himself be put in the position of opposing it. Not least because Labor's constituency would be more for it than would the Tories'."

He paused, deep in his thoughts, and sipped his drink. When the silence extended with no sign that it was about to end, Victoria asked, "Are you going to say it or am I?"

"No, I'll say it: the real clinker is that I'm an American."

"Yes," she said. "I've known that all along."

"You understand what I'm saying?" He turned toward her so that they were face to face. "I'm not talking about anti-Americanism – although that could be a problem. It's that the GBP – the Great British Public – would never go for an American sitting on the throne with their Queen. I'd have to become a naturalized British subject."

"Yes," she said. "You would."

"Therefore, the problem isn't the Church or Parliament or the GBP, but Jeremy Walsh."

"Or," she said, "me."

He was puzzled. "I don't follow. . . ."

"Let me come back to that in a minute. Right now, help me out with something. There's one subject we've never discussed – I suppose it would be more accurate to say one subject we've avoided – and that is your feeling about *being* an American. You don't say much about it, which," she said with a sly smile, "makes you almost un-American."

He grinned at her. "No heart on my sleeve, huh?" He rose from the sofa and went to the small bar in the far corner of the living-room. "Pour you one?" he asked, holding up the cognac bottle. She shook her head and he splashed some of the liquid in his own glass. "Are you sure you want to hear this?" he asked, glancing at her.

"As much as you want to tell me."

"Okay," he said, pulling a camel saddle stool around until he was facing her. "Let's start at the beginning. I'm a third-generation Polish-American. Which means, I guess, that I'm an American citizen whose forebears came from Poland but who has no memory or emotional connections with it other than through my parents. I'm an American. Period. And from the day I was born it was drummed into me to be proud of that. There's a lot of that in my country, but I've been around enough to realize that Americans are no more patriotic than other people, they just make more noise about it. But you mustn't misread that. For all the unabashed chauvinism, it's no less real. I don't know why Americans are so insistently, so unapologetically, so overheatedly proud of being Americans, although I have a theory about it: it's because, unlike most of the rest of the world, we don't have a long history. We started with nothing not much more than a couple of hundred years ago, and that's yesterday compared to England, say, or the rest of Europe. Or Asia. And we started with people who were pretty much the world's leftovers: immigrants who were mostly poor and mostly uneducated, or so stubborn they were ready to leave their homes and families in order to worship or believe the way they wanted to. And now I'm going to sound like your prototypically American braggart; but what this sorry lot did was to tame a wilderness and turn it into the richest and most powerful nation in history.

"Don't get me wrong," he said, "there are a thousand things I don't like about the States. I don't like the racial discrimination, the violence and crime, the rampant materialism, the coarseness and the crudity, a lot of the politicians. . . . It's a long list. But there are ten thousand things I *do* like, and hokey as it may sound, all things considered I don't know any place on earth where I'd rather live. England, for instance. It's a great place, perhaps the most civilized spot on earth, but its best days are behind it. The same is true of the rest of Europe. There are any number of places in the world I might like to visit, but would I like to live there? The answer is no. Could I be happy here in London? Of course, dammit! – I am. But the question is: would I rather be an Englishman than what I am and, again, the answer is no. Which doesn't make me better or worse, it simply makes me . . . who I am."

He went to the window to stare out at the night. Victoria rose and went to stand beside him, putting her hand in his. Neither of them spoke for a long time. Victoria could see their faces dimly reflected in the glass and, behind them, the guttering candles. Then the reflections blurred as tears formed in her eyes. But when she spoke, her voice was unwavering.

"A few minutes ago we were talking about our problems and they seemed to come down to one thing: would you be prepared to renounce your American citizenship? The answer seems to be no. That leads to a second question: would I be prepared to renounce the throne?" She paused until she was certain her voice wouldn't betray her. "And the answer to that is: unless Parliament will agree to our getting married, I would."

He was squeezing her hand so tightly that she had to bite her lip to keep from crying out. "I'm afraid . . ." he began, pausing to clear his throat. "I'm afraid that only leads us to another problem. I don't know whether I could let you do it. I think we might be haunted by it for the rest of our lives. There would always be that unspoken thing between us: you loved me enough to give up the throne but I didn't love you enough to give up my country." He turned to her and they stood facing each other, arms loosely about each other's waist. "Darling, if that was the real problem, I'd be willing to do what's required, but it's not. There's another question, a larger question and I'm not quite sure how to put it. . . . Okay, let me put it flatly: what would worry me would not simply be saying good-bye to being an American, but saying good-bye to being me."

"But – "

"Let me explain. If I were to become the Queen's husband, what would I do with the rest of my life? Yes, we'd have each other, but what would I *do*? I'm a journalist. These days that's not saying a hell of a lot but it means a great deal to me. It's what I've wanted to do since I was a kid. And I try to do it well. But, ask yourself: could I do it after we were married? Can you imagine the byline: 'Story by Prince Jeremy, Duke of Whatever!' Impossible. On the face of it, impossible. So what could I do? I could write other things: books, novels maybe. But would they be accepted on the basis of their merit? The answer is no. And if the answer were yes, could I ever fully believe it? So, in effect, there wouldn't be a Jeremy Walsh, journalist, anymore, there'd be this . . . this gelded celebrity, this former person."

She put her arms around his neck, her face against his shoulder. He put his arms about her and held her close. There was the sound of the door knocker. Loud. They started, and drew apart.

Jeremy put a finger to his lips. "Shh."

Again, a knocking at the door, this time more insistent. Now a voice, shouting, "Jeremy? Jeremy?"

"I'd better answer," he said. "It may be important."

The sound of the knocker seemed magnified by their silence. "Jeremy! . . ."

"Stay out of sight," he whispered. "I'll get rid of whoever it is."

He went down the hall and opened the door. Bulking hugely on the porch step was Ossie Docherty, hand upraised to knock again. "Jeremy!" he said heartily. "Hello! I *knew* you were in there – the lights in the kitchen."

"What the hell do you want?" Jeremy asked.

"I was in the neighborhood. Tim Finnegan of the *Mirror* – you've met him – lives over on Maltby Street. We were having a pint and he said, 'Know who lives around the corner on Rotherhithe? Jeremy Walsh.'" Ossie was craning his neck, peering down the hall. "Uh oh! – candles." He glanced at Jeremy's bathrobe. "Looks like I'm interrupting something." He offered a leering smile.

Jeremy stepped back and slammed the door shut. A mirror in the entrance hallway jumped off its hanger and smashed on the floor.

The Most Reverend Martin Staples Sutherland, Archbishop of Canterbury, Primate of the Church of England, was aware that his thoughts might accurately be described as uncharitable. He was and knew he was being maneuvered and resented it. He was being maneuvered so skillfully, however, that to offer a remonstrance would surely lead to a plausible denial and to the suggestion that he was misreading the Prime Minister's intention. Best to hear Forster out, he thought, to say no more than was necessary, and to listen carefully for the overtones.

Forster had suggested that they meet following the Easter Sunday morning services at Westminster Abbey. The Prime Minister's Bentley was idling near the door to the vestry when Sutherland, having doffed his robes, emerged in his street clothes, an oxford-gray suit, a roman collar, and a red vest on which a gold cross dangled. The Archbishop was not a physically impressive man – middling height, lean, graying, balding – but he communicated an unfeigned serenity that was sometimes misread as asceticism. He had had the Christian ministry as a goal from childhood and in his youth had been something of a zealot. But somewhere across the intervening years he had lost his sense of mission and was now, in his early sixties, a skilled ecclesiastical politician dedicated to the perpetuation of the Anglican communion and to the fostering of an intellectually respectable Christian idealism.

On this cloudy Easter morning, as the Prime Minister's limousine made its meandering way through the relatively deserted streets, Hugh Forster was recounting his conversation with Princess Victoria. A student of history, Forster was fully aware that during the crises surrounding Edward VIII's attempt to make Wallis Simpson his Queen and Princess Margaret's move to marry Peter Townsend, the Church had been inflexible in its opposition and, as a consequence, much criticized. It was his hope that should a storm break over Victoria's plan to marry, the Archbishop might serve as a lightning rod.

"Now," he said briskly, "you have the picture before you. The problem may resolve itself but I think not. Victoria is an absolutely first-rate young woman but, and I say this with affection, she is stubborn. So it seemed wise that the two of us take the time to get the situation and its dangerous potential clearly in our sights. I presume you agree."

Sutherland nodded slightly. He had learned long ago that when the Prime Minister came seeking his counsel, the first and best response was a noncommittal attentiveness.

"There are three potential trouble spots," Forster was saying. "Walsh is an American, he's divorced, and he's a Roman Catholic. I would imagine that the Church would have something to say on the latter two."

Sutherland nodded, but only just.

"Let's look first then at the matter of his faith. I presume that as a member of the Roman Church he would be unacceptable to you as the husband of the heir presumptive. Am I right in that?"

This time Sutherland's nod was more pronounced.

"You would feel it incumbent upon you to protest?"

"We wouldn't rush to battle," Sutherland said, "but, yes, we would find it necessary to demur."

"Not least because of the Act of Succession?"

"Precisely. As the Act states, its purpose is to secure the Protestant succession, and although the faith of the monarch's spouse isn't specified, it is clearly implied."

"I would agree," Forster said. "Let me raise a question

here: if I were able to convince the young man to convert, would he then be acceptable?"

Sutherland was swinging his cross back and forth like a pendulum. "Perhaps I should clarify our position. If a young woman in our communion wished to marry a Roman Catholic and wanted to be married by one of our priests, there would be no objection. He would not have to convert. The problem posed in your scenario is that the young lady involved is the heir presumptive. Rather a different matter."

"You would not consent?"

"Shall we say; the Church could not consent."

"I take that to be a flat no."

"Mmmm."

"Let me move on. Let me posit that Victoria were to come to you. She tells you that she wants to marry Walsh and that Walsh is prepared to convert. She tells you that he is divorced but he's the so-called innocent party and she asks you to marry them. What would be your response?"

"I would want to ask a few questions about the young man's divorce. Did he divorce his wife or she him? What were the grounds? Has she since remarried? Were there children of the marriage? Are they being taken care of?"

"I can speak to that: he sought the decree, charging adultery. There was no counter-suit. The woman remains unmarried. There's one child, a girl of five. She lives with her mother."

"How long were they married?"

"I'm not certain. Less than three years, I believe."

When Sutherland made no response, Forster asked, "Would the Church find it possible to consent?"

"I'm afraid not."

"Why not? As I'm sure you're aware, Ben Wickshire, my Home Secretary, was married by one of your people a month or so ago.

"But not in the sanctuary. In the recreation hall, if I remember rightly."

"Not in the sanctuary?"

"No. Church law forbids it. Neither the Convocation of York nor the Convocation of Canterbury permit the use of the marriage service in the case of anyone who has a former partner still living. Some of our clergy will hold a service of prayer and dedication, and of course they're free to do so under the provisions of civil law, but not in a church building. I hardly think such arrangements would be suitable for a royal wedding."

"No special exception could be made?"

The Archbishop shook his head.

"Let me posit one last scenario," Forster said. "It becomes known that Victoria and Walsh are set on being married. The press is having a field day. The public is entirely caught up in it and divided. Parliament is in an uproar, and divided. I'm beleaguered and under attack, and so are you. Does your no remain unequivocal?"

Sutherland turned to Forster, his expression guileless. "What is the government's position? Has it said no? Is its no unequivocal?"

Forster smiled thinly. "The government is not saying anything at the moment."

"Ah, well . . ." Sutherland said with a small shrug.

"You're not being very forthcoming," Forster said, his voice testy. "The government doesn't yet have the question before it. It would first want to know the position of the Church. If the Church forbids the marriage, that becomes an important consideration. If Parliament were then to consent, it would be, in effect, repudiating the established Church. No small thing, as you will agree."

Sutherland turned from the window where he had been watching the horseback riders on Rotten Row. "Do I catch a hint that such a possibility exists?"

There was some impatience in Forster's voice. "I'm sure, old friend," he said, "that you are cognizant of the fact that Parliament is a reflection of the people. I think it fair to say – and I say this with the greatest respect – that the Church no longer is. I'll be candid with you: I don't think the British people would accept a flat refusal by the Church in the matter. I have to be aware of that. And if I may say so, so do you."

♕ THREE

SIR HERBERT GARVEY was not a man easily unsettled. In the delivery-room at the University of London Free Hospital, he was known to his colleagues as "Old Unflappable." Nothing, it seemed, could rattle him. Once, so the story was told, engrossed in the delivery of the last of a set of quadruplets, he had murmured – not as a jest designed to relieve the tension but in dead earnestness – "What are we up to now? Has anyone done a head count?" In a difficult delivery he was always slow to resort to a Caesarian section but swift to do an episiotomy. "Easier for the mother now; better for the father later," he would say without a wink or so much as a twinkle in his eye.

Sir Herbert had come to the Queen's sitting-room, the bearer of what he thought would be good news, and had been jocular during the small talk that accompanied their settling down in chairs. He noticed that the Queen looked drawn and a bit pale and made a mental note to inquire about it later. Having asked if Edward was going to join them and being told that he was out of the city, he had said, "Then I'll leave it to you to break the good news to him. Yes," he said, rubbing his hands together, "I've reviewed the tests and gone over the reports and it looks like success. Jolly good show."

168

Mary's voice was flat and expressionless. "I take it that I'm pregnant."

He masked his surprise at her response. "We mustn't be unequivocal, of course. There's always the possibility of a false reading, but I would think not. I'll go so far as to say, yes Your Majesty, you are pregnant."

She sat for a moment, head lowered, twisting the wedding ring on her finger. Then, without preamble, she told him in a dozen sentences about the intruder who had broken into her bedroom. "So, Sir Herbert," she concluded, "my question is – and I'm afraid I know the answer – is there any way to know for certain whether the father of my child is my husband or?...." The voice was dead, the timbre toneless.

For the first time in his life, Sir Herbert was dumbstruck. Eyes wide, jaw down, mouth agape, he stared at her. "Your Majesty," he gasped. "Your Majesty.... Surely what you're telling me.... Surely it can't be true."

"I'm afraid it is."

He sought to gather himself. Then, as he looked at her, her head still down, her fingers turning the ring almost mechanically, his professionalism returned. "I don't quite know what to say," he murmured. "I can't tell you how sorry I am. Is there anything I can do?"

"Yes," she said. "Can you answer my question: is it possible to know for sure if it is Edward's child?"

"I take it you want me to speak to you straightforwardly?"

She raised her eyes. "In absolute candor."

"Very well, then." He drew a deep breath that was more a sigh and held it for a moment. "What we're faced with here is a question of probabilities, and there are many factors in our favor." He tailed off, looking at her compassionately. "You wouldn't like to take a day or so to accustom yourself to the news?" His voice was kindly, his manner like a father's. "Perhaps wait until you've had a word with your husband?"

"Sir Herbert," she said, "I couldn't face the next hour, much less the next day, without knowing everything you can tell me. Please, do go on."

"Let's begin then," he said with a briskness he didn't feel, "with the fact that we have a normal menstrual cycle. You seldom deviate, you tell me. Which means that on the week in question, the week you and your husband were at Royal Lodge, our peak period of fertility would have begun on the Thursday. Let's just review for a minute. Our cycle is a healthy, normal twenty-eight days. Ovulation is going to take place on days thirteen through fifteen, somewhere centering on that. Now, you will remember that, as we expected, we felt a transient pain, on the right side as I recall, and registered a slight rise in temperature, all of which suggests that everything was bang-on.

"Now," he said with growing animation, "we had intercourse on days thirteen and fourteen, namely Friday and Saturday, and it's probable that conception took place. All the more likely because my tests demonstrate that your husband suffers no lack of healthy sperm. And even though the unhappy circumstances of which you spoke took place late Sunday night, we must remember that some of our husband's spermatozoa would continue to be on the job for forty-eight hours or more. Therefore, bringing what might properly be described as logic to the data, it would seem highly probable that the ovum would have been fertilized prior to Sunday night."

Her face had lost some of its pallor. "Highly probable, you say." There was a tremor in her voice. "What do you mean by highly probable? Ninety percent? Seventy-five? Fifty?"

"Well, now," he said, fussing a bit, setting the seam of his trousers dead center on his knobby knees, "we must not think of ourselves as a computer. Without in any way diminishing what I've been saying, we're dealing here with probabilities, not certainties. And although there are no guarantees, we do have a high degree of probability. Enough, I think, to put our minds at rest."

"There's no way of knowing for sure?"

His voice was all reasonableness. "How many things in life do we know for sure? Who of us can be sure even of tomorrow? But we go on, confident that it will come."

She was fighting her emotions now. An enormous pressure was building in her chest and constricting her throat. She had thought in the past few days that she had no more tears, but now they were welling behind her eyes. "If I hear you rightly, Sir Herbert, you're telling me to have the baby."

"It's not for me to tell you that," he said. "That's something you and your husband will decide. If you're asking me what I would counsel, I would say that you should proceed as planned."

"As planned," she said bitterly. Suddenly, all her defenses were swept away and she bent forward, great, wrenching sobs convulsing her. As the pent-up agony poured out, Sir Herbert went to her and stood by her chair, patting her shoulder and saying again and again, "There, there. . . ."

Now she was in control again and slightly embarrassed, but with her spirits beginning to rise. "I must look ghastly," she said, attempting a smile. Sir Herbert was back in his chair blowing with great honkings into a handkerchief. "I do have another question."

"Of course," he said huskily. "Of course."

"Let's say we go ahead as you suggest. Since we can't be certain the baby will be Edward's, one must be concerned about what might be described as . . . undesirable traits in the child. I've been worrying about that."

171

Sir Herbert was shaking his head rapidly. "We're now into an area in which I have no competence. I'll be happy to discuss the matter – discreetly, of course – with a colleague of mine, Dr. Wilson Smythe-Cooper. He's a geneticist. As far as I'm concerned, without peers, at least here in England. I'll get right on it, if that's your wish."

She nodded and rose from her chair. At the door, it became obvious that there was something he wanted to add.

"Yes, Sir Herbert," she said, offering her hand.

"Have you spoken to your husband about ... the incident a week ago Sunday?"

"No," she said. "I'll probably have to, won't I?"

"I would think so," he said. "I would think so."

Ossie Docherty had, as he put it, "invested" in a waterbed, thereby justifying the throwing out of a standard mattress not a year old. He'd bought the water-bed for a number of reasons, not least because none of his friends had one and because there was a certain trendiness, even a connotation of sexiness, in owning one. Mostly he'd bought it because his enormous bulk often made him uncomfortable, even in bed, and he hoped the water-bed would add to his ease. As well, the manufacturer had offered him a discount if he would work the company name into a news story.

But the bed had not been an unqualified success. Ossie liked it, but Alfie did not, mostly because of the disparity in their weights. When Ossie turned over, a minor tidal wave would sweep across the bed and loft Alfie upward. Whenever Ossie moved, there would be seismic repercussions. Even an arm raised and dropped during sleep would set off wavelets and rills and ripples that might take an entire minute to subside. Alfie had protested and for two nights had slept on the pull-out couch in the kitchen, afterward returning to the bed pleading a bad back. It was not in him to say, simply, that he had been lonely.

This night had been particularly tempestuous. Ossie had come home in a flushed rage and, after an assault on the refrigerator, had stomped into the bedroom without a word. Stripping to his underpants he had collapsed on the bed. After ten minutes of being tempest tossed, Alfie had said plaintively, "Will you stop floppin' about. I'm gettin' seasick. Whatever's eatin' you?"

"I've got it all figured out," said Ossie, punching a fist into a palm. "I'll do a series for the *Herald* on the rotten way we're being portrayed in America by a crummy reporter we've treated like a king. Six parts. It'll run a whole week." He raised a massive arm, pantomiming a banner headline in the air. BETRAYAL ON FLEET STREET: *Yank Journalist, Feted by Royalty, Stabs Britain in Back!* Vocalizing his anger seemed to ease it and, after a few minutes, he reared up on one elbow to punch up his pillow and fall back again.

Alfie clutched the side of the bed and hung on. "What *are* you goin' on about?" he asked. "Oo stabbed us in the bleedin' back?"

"A creep named Walsh," Ossie replied. "Works for the *New York Times*. Fat pay packet. Aston Martin classic. Hangs out with the palace crowd. Lives in this fancy flat on the river and he's just written a series in the *Times* that stinks."

Jeremy had indeed filed a series of reports under the heading: BRITAIN: *The Lion Doesn't Roar Anymore*. In it he had done analyses of the UK's economic woes, the decline in her balance of payments, her differences with other European Common Market countries, the glaring inequities of the National Health Service, and the general political malaise. For all its emphasis on Britain's problems, the series

173

was upbeat, depicting a nation in decline struggling valiantly against great odds.

Hearing about the series, Ossie had dug into back copies of the *Times* and filed the stories, not realizing how soon they might become useful.

"*Pampered Yank Wipes Boots on Britain!*" he muttered, still thinking in headlines.

"I know what's eatin' you," Alfie said. "You 'aven't 'ad a invite to the palace. They're afraid you'd clean out the larder."

"I can pull enough quotes out of the series to crucify him," Ossie exulted.

"I'm in the dark," Alfie said. "Wot's got you off on this tear?"

"I put him up for membership in the Press Association and does he say, 'Thank you, mate'? Not him. I hold out the hand of friendship and he slams the door in my face! Had some upper-class bird in his bed, I'll wager." He brought a massive fist down on the bed with a thump, straightening Alfie's spine. "I'll fix his clock, I will."

"Where's this fancy flat of 'is?" Alfie asked.

"In Bermondsey."

"There's nothin' fancy in Bermondsey," said Alfie. "Except your fancy friend, Tim Finnegan," he added sourly.

"Just this one building smack-dab in the middle of a public park, and he has the first two floors. Pulled some strings to get that or I miss my guess. Right on the bloody river. I drove round to the other side, to Wapping, and used my binoculars. Nothin' to see; he'd turned out the lights. But we'll see, Mr. High and Mighty, we'll see! . . ."

The Queen, having completed the Investiture, slipped through her "secret door" and went on leaden feet toward her apartment. The semi-annual ceremony was always a tiring affair, but today's had seemed especially so. The recipients of the various honors had been named in her Birthday Honors list and, as instructed, had arrived early in all their finery and with their allotted number of guests to await the Queen in the Throne Room. There, they had been lined up according to the honor to be conferred, and at the appropriate moment had approached the Queen who was standing on the dais beneath a crimson velvet canopy. Sword in hand, she had dubbed the more favored ones Knights or Dames, touching each with the sword on the right and then the left shoulder, afterward pinning the appropriate medals on the others.

In her dressing-room her change of clothes was laid out but, oddly, neither Lady Hammil nor Billie, her Dresser, was anywhere about. She closed the door, leaning against it for a moment, full of fatigue. There was a sound from Edward's apartment. Was he back early? The door opened and there he was, smiling broadly, his eyes shining with excitement. "Come," he said mysteriously, beckoning with a long finger and leading the way. With a grand flourish he threw open the door to her bedroom. "Ta-da!" he said, flinging his arms apart theatrically and stepping back so she could precede him into the room. Banked about the head of her bed were enormous, overflowing baskets of fresh flowers, filling the room with their fragrance. At the foot of the bed was an elaborately ornamented baby's cradle and, lying at the center of the white pillow, a single white rose.

"Surprise!" Edward cried.

The Prince would not be moved; she had never seen him so adamant. None of her entreaties swayed him. "The answer is no," he shouted. "We will *not* have the baby. You'll have to talk to Sir Herbert and have it taken care of."

"Abort your *son*?"

"My son! How would we ever know it *was* my son? My god, Mary, the man might be insane and pass it on through his genes! He could be a moron, a congenital criminal. You must be mad even to consider going on with it."

"But it won't be his son, it will be ours. I've been trying to explain what Sir Herbert said. He'll be your son, *our* son!"

She watched him deliberately rein himself in. His voice softened, and as he took her hands, his were trembling. "Mary, darling, listen to me, listen to me: you mustn't have the baby. I know myself; I could never think of him as mine. Nor could you ever be sure. We'd find ourselves wondering. We'd read things in his face, in his walk, in a thousand ways. . . . And if he looked utterly unlike me – as he may! – could you expect me to love him? Could you?"

"But Edward, if we were to adopt a child would we not come to love him? And if he were adopted, neither of us would be his parent. But we *are* his parents. He's my son. Your son. I'm certain of it. Darling, you must remember why we made the decision to have a child in the first place, and you must remember what Sir Herbert told us. At my age it's often difficult to conceive. And if the pregnancy is terminated it may be even more difficult in the future. We were lucky. He said as much. Edward. . . ." Her voice was filled with pleading. "This could be our one chance. . . ."

"I'm sorry, May," he said flatly. "I won't consider it. And that's final." He turned and left the room.

Maidy Lightstone had fully intended to keep her promise to Kevin not to tell anyone what she had seen that Sunday night in the palace garden. And for ten days she kept her word despite almost irresistable temptation. Even then she told no one but her mother, and what harm could there possibly be in that? – her mother was confined to her flat in a wheelchair and the flat was in Hounslow East, miles from the palace. Maidy had told her mother, in part, out of feelings of guilt. She had failed to visit her for almost three weeks and the poor soul had nothing to brighten her life other than the telly and a weekly flutter on the pools. Perhaps a juicy piece of gossip would give her something to dwell on other than her arthritis and "those six screaming brats" who lived on the other side of her living-room wall.

So, with a preamble of the most solemn warnings "not to tell a living soul," and with her voice lowered and an eye on the door as though someone was about to come through it, she told her.

Mrs. Lightstone told no one but the Victorian Order nurse who came on Thursdays. The nurse, disbelieving and certain she would not be believed, hesitated for a week before telling her husband. He told two of his mates at the shop, swearing them to secrecy. They each told their wives who told their families and a few friends. And the neighbors. In one month four hundred and thirty-seven people, one of them deaf and one living as far away as the Isle of Skye, had heard the story.

♛ FOUR

"IF I MAY SAY SO, YOUR MAJESTY, this is probably as unpleasant a task as I have ever undertaken," Sir Herbert said. "But if I am going to be responsive to your concern, I will have to ask you a few questions of some delicacy. You do understand?"

"Yes," Mary said, her voice almost inaudible. "Please go ahead."

It had been a week since she had seen the doctor and in the meantime Edward had remained inflexible: there would be no baby, and the sooner the matter was taken care of the better. The fact of her pregnancy lurked between them like a dark presence, alienating, hindering communication, barring intimacy. It chanced to be a particularly busy time for both of them. They shared breakfast but otherwise saw little of each other through the day. And evenings, when Edward was home, he stayed in his apartment, pleading work or fatigue. He hadn't come to her bed for a week. She had had the cradle removed to the nursery, but had left his flowers about the head of the bed until, on the third day, beginning to look bedraggled, they had to be removed. When they were together there was no lack of conversation: both rattled on about friends, about items in the news, and about incidents in the palace. But there was a brittle quality to the conversation and, on a number of occasions, they found themselves changing subjects when a casual remark took on uncomfortable overtones.

Through it all Mary's determination to have the baby deepened. She was sympathetic to Edward's concern that the child might not be his and would therefore be unpredictable in appearance and character, but the conviction that she had been pregnant before the return to London had become certainty and the thought of destroying the foetus had become intolerable.

"His Royal Highness expressed concern as to whether character traits could be transmitted through the genes," Sir Herbert was saying. "He seemed particularly troubled about the possibility of passing on criminal tendencies. I've had a talk with my geneticist friend, Smythe-Cooper, and have been doing some reading on the subject, so before I put my questions, let me offer you a note of reassurance."

His voice took on a slightly professorial tone. "There is a considerable body of research on the subject and, as one might expect, some disagreement in certain areas. Nevertheless, I think it fair to say that there is consensus on this: the children of parents with distinct criminal tendencies do themselves seem more disposed to become criminals. But most of this can be accounted for on the ground of environmental factors: parental neglect or abuse, neighborhood influences, peer pressures, and so on. However, even allowing for these influences, we do encounter criminal tendencies apparently derivative of the parent, Nonetheless, and this is the good news, except where a parent is demonstrably a criminal psychopath, there is strong evidence to indicate that, granted parental affection, satisfactory role models, and a reasonably decent environment, such genetic tendencies can be overcome." He paused. "Are we clear on that now?"

179

"Yes," she said, her voice flat.

Sir Herbert was occupied for a moment rubbing his jaw with long, bony fingers. "Now we come to the transmission of physical characteristics. As is obvious to even a casual observer, there can be great variations in the appearance of children of the same parents. Some bear a resemblance to the mother, some to the father, some to both. Others may bear little resemblance to either. So, we begin with the fact that the so-called 'spitting image' is rare.

"There are, however, certain transmitted characteristics that are obvious. They have to do with physical size, skin color, the configuration of the face – slanted eyes, high cheekbones, and so on. Which brings me to my question about our ... shall we say, unfortunate experience of a week or so ago." He peered at her from beneath his eyebrows, noting that she was pale and had her hands clasped tightly on her lap. "Shall I proceed?"

"Yes," she said softly. "Please get on with it."

He removed a piece of paper from his jacket pocket and unfolded it. "A few notes," he said by way of explanation. "Now, first, did you get a good look at the man?"

She shook her head. "The room was dark and the curtains were drawn." She corrected herself. "Not entirely. I always leave them open a bit for the night air."

"You weren't able to see then whether he was Asian, say, or black?"

"I was asleep when he entered the room. Even now I'm not sure how he got in. He must have made a sound of some kind because I was suddenly awake. There was enough light that I could see him at the side of the bed...." Her voice faltered. "Before I could cry out he put his hand over my mouth. I saw his face for just a moment...."

She was breathing quickly, her chest heaving. Sir Herbert saw that her hands were shaking. "Would you like a glass of water?" he asked solicitously.

She shook her head quickly. After a moment she said, "He was a white man."

"I don't suppose you could tell anything about hair color?" She shook her head. "His build? Was he tall? Short?"

"Average. About Edward's height, I think."

"Did he say anything?"

"I'd rather not say."

"Of course. What I'm getting at is, did he have an accent of any kind?"

"I really can't say. English, I suppose."

"Only one more question. He was a young man presumably?"

"I think so. It's difficult to say."

Sir Herbert replaced the paper in his pocket. As he spoke, there was a forced quality to his enthusiasm. "Well, now, that's all very encouraging, although I must say, probably irrelevant. There's little doubt in my mind but that conception took place before your return to London and, while it's not my decision, I would recommend that you have the baby." He leaned forward and put a hand on hers. "And I'd try not to worry about it too much. I know it's difficult but. . . ."

She looked up at him, her eyes glittering with tears. "I *want* to have the baby."

When Mary told Edward about the intruder that day in her bedroom, his first reaction had been disbelief. As it broke upon him that it was a fact, he had felt the blood roaring in his head and had had to steady himself with a hand on a chair. Later, alone in his apartment, his impulse was to shout, to rant, to drive a fist through a door.

The initial shock having passed, he found himself filled with a contained fury. Evenings, alone, he paced the floor, fists clenched and jammed deep in his pockets, his face a brick red, his jaws jammed shut. His wife's trauma was almost forgotten in the waves of revulsion that swept over him when, for all his forbidding it, imagination played before him the scene in the darkened bedroom. And when the images would not be dislodged, he sometimes bared his teeth and flung his head about, spitting out curses, groaning in a furious, frustrated rage. He felt himself wronged, affronted, violated. At times he found pleasure in dwelling on precisely how he would exact vengeance were the intruder in his hands.

But in time the fury subsided. The measure of his wife's agony began to penetrate and soon he was upbraiding himself for his preoccupation with his own hurt. He resolved when next he saw her to tell her how much he loved her; but when the moment came he found himself unable to do it. It was not until she came to his study, having just talked to Sir Herbert, that his hesitancy was swept away by the measure of her need.

"Darling," she was saying, "please try. Try, just for a moment to put aside your feelings about what happened and look only at the facts. Think, darling! Remember! Think back to how carefully we planned. Remember how certain we both were that we were going to have a child. We were sure of it. And Sir Herbert is convinced we were right. He's telling us to go ahead, to have the baby. Darling, you mustn't allow your anger, your sense of outrage, to destroy the beautiful thing that has happened to us."

Standing behind his chair, she put her hands on his shoulders, placing her cheek against the top of his head. "Edward, my darling, I love you. I love you so. We love each other, and we mustn't let ourselves add to the pain we've already suffered."

182

She slipped her arms about his neck and then down to his chest, crossing them, holding him tightly, putting her cheek alongside his. "Darling," she whispered, "I have never in my life been so sure of anything. We *must* have the baby. We must have it for its own sake, for our sake, and for Victoria's. We must trust in the power of our love. If, as I know it is, the baby is ours, that love must be given entirely, with all our heart. If – and it must be said – if in the unlikely possibility that it isn't ours – yours and mine – it becomes even more important. We will love him and *make* him ours. He'll be ours *because* we love him."

She could feel the emotion surging through him and held him tightly, her arms strong. He tried to speak but was unable to get the words out. After a moment, he raised a hand to the side of her head and pressed her cheek against his. His voice choked, he whispered, "I love you, May. I love you."

Afterward, Edward said, "We must tell Victoria."

Mary's face was troubled. "I'm afraid we can't. Not yet. Sir Herbert warned me, we're not out of the woods yet. I could still miscarry. The greatest risk is at the end of the first month. I've told Crimmie to ease my schedule that week. You mustn't worry, but I did have that miscarriage after Vicky and we won't be able to feel entirely easy until after the first trimester."

"Trimester?"

"Three months. It would be terrible to raise Vicky's hopes and then dash them. We'll have to keep it to ourselves for a while yet."

♕ FIVE

OSSIE DOCHERTY HAD LOST HIS APPETITE. Such was the excitement churning within him that for days he had not been able to eat between meals. Alfie, who lived in constant fear of losing him, presumed that he had found a new friend, and even though his almost reflexive grousing had continued unabated, the cutting edge of his malice was dulled.

Ossie's exultancy stemmed from the fact that one of his nurtured hopes had been realized: he had "that bastard Jeremy Walsh" exactly where he wanted him. Not only was he now in a position to strike devastatingly at the man who had rebuffed him, but he would, in the doing, be able to break what would undoubtedly be the news story of the year.

It had all begun the night Jeremy had slammed the door in his face. Sulphurous with rage, he had crossed the Tower Bridge to Wapping and driven slowly along the High Street, from time to time glancing across the river. There! – there it was. Easily identifiable beyond the broad sweep of the Thames, the only building in the tiny park on the edge of the river. He'd nosed his car down to the river's edge, parked, and, running down the window, stared across the distance. But there was nothing to be seen; the

184

picture window spanning the entire width of the flat was dark, the only glintings of light being the reflections of the running-lights on the barges moored in the middle of the river. He got out of the car, opened the boot, took out his binoculars, and focused on the window. Yes! Those wavering pinpricks of light were undoubtedly the candles he had glimpsed earlier. Other than that there was nothing visible in the living-room, but as he drove home his heart was beating wildly. Jeremy Walsh didn't know it but Ossie Docherty, by god, would soon know what went on in his fancy goddam flat!

Ossie made an arrangement at a shop on Regent Street to lease-hire a Baush and Lomb 15X-60X zoom telescope and a lightweight tripod, ideal for viewing at short distances and small enough to be inconspicuous. He had no opportunity to use it during the early part of the week, being occupied with assignments, but on the Thursday shortly after dark he had driven to the location he had selected and, in the lee of a shipping shed at the foot of Sampson Street, set up the telescope. His hands were shaking and it had taken a few minutes to register a focus on the window of the flat. It was incredible! He was able to see that the paint on the window frames was peeling! He felt a rush of elation, dampened a few minutes later by disappointment: Walsh was not home. But when he had packed up after a wait of an hour and headed back to his flat, his excitement had returned. It was only a matter of time.

Unable to contain himself any longer, he told Alfie what he'd been up to. "I'll be able to tell whether the bastard needs a shave," he crowed.

Alfie had listened, silent, not sure at first whether this wasn't another of the stories Ossie trumped up to explain his absences. "I don't get it," he said. "What's the point of your peepin'-Tom rig? So you see 'im wiv 'is bird; what's the good of that?"

"The little things," Ossie said definitively. "Remember? It's the little things that juice up a story. What do you know anyway?"

"So I'm not Rupert Murdoch. What little things?"

"If I knew I wouldn't have to look, would I?" Ossie said witheringly. "For all I know, he has orgies. Maybe I'll recognize his bird. Don't tell me it wouldn't spice up my series if I could say he was carrying on with somebody's wife or having an affair with the Duchess of Fiddle-dee-dee."

On his second vigil, a police constable attached to the Thames Division, London's water police, spotted him and wanted to know what he was up to. Despite Ossie's noisy dudgeon and the brandishing of his press card, the constable insisted on taking him to Wapping headquarters. By the time they arrived, Ossie's nimble mind had worked out an excuse. He was, as he explained to the sergeant, preparing a series for the *Herald* on London at night and was scouting sites for the photographer who would follow on. After all, he did have credentials, didn't he? A call to his city editor confirmed his story (the city editor, playing it by ear; not unaccustomed to handling such inquiries) and Ossie was released.

He now realized he'd have to be more careful. He wrapped the telescope in a blanket and kept it in the boot of the car and, rather than risk another run-in with the police, moved further along the river, coming upon an ideal site for his reconnaissance: *The Prospect of Whitby*, a pub bearing a sign boasting that it was London's Oldest Riverside Inn. A three-story structure, built during the reign of Henry VIII, with massive brass lamps on the face and with bowed, bottle-glass windows, it looked the part. But what interested Ossie more than the pub itself was an alley beside it with a sign: *The Pelican Stairs*. He went down the dark, narrow passageway to the end where a set of concrete steps ran down to the water. A locked metal gate barred passage but, as he noted with satisfaction, the upright bars were widely spaced; he could easily position the lens between them.

He began to drop into the pub just as darkness was falling, ducking out every half hour or so to check whether there were lights in the window across the Thames.

On the third night, at about 10:15, the window was aglow. He went quickly to the car and, hands clumsy in his excitement, set up his equipment. Just then it began to rain, a driving rain that splattered drops on the lens, distorting the image. Cursing, he fetched an umbrella from the car but found that when he bent over the eyepiece the umbrella tilted and the rain slanted in. Frantic lest the moment escape, he took off his jacket and draped it over the lens hood, arranging it so that it offered a further shield against the rain.

The rain was cold and the wind blustery. By the time he was set up, he was chilled to the bone and shivering. He had difficulty operating the two focusing mechanisms but after a while got it dead on.

Now he could see the interior of the room with startling clarity. A pair of table lamps by a sofa and an overhead light gave spotty but sufficient illumination. But there was no one in the room and no sign of anyone down the long hallway. His back began to ache and he had to straighten up and press his hands against it. "The bastard," he muttered.

When he bent over the eyepiece again, he saw Jeremy in shirt-sleeves coming down the hall. As Ossie watched, Jeremy went to one side of the great window and drew half of the curtains closed. As he moved to the other side, he paused, apparently responding to someone calling from the kitchen, and returned to the hallway. Ossie waited, tense, shivering uncontrollably. The pain in his back was such that he knew he would soon have to straighten up.

I'll count to ten and take a break, he said to himself. On the count of six a woman entered the hallway from the kitchen and came toward him. She was carrying a tray on which there were dishes and cutlery. Her face was in shadow and Ossie couldn't make out her features. Jeremy came down the hall and went to draw the other curtain. As he did, the woman bent over to transfer the dishes to a low coffee table and her face was clearly illuminated by the table lamp.

"My god!" Ossie gasped aloud. "Princess Victoria!"

"I've got a really mad idea," Jeremy said. "Want to hear it?"

"Mmm hmm," Victoria muttered, busy munching some salad.

She had stopped by after attending the premiere of a new film and they were seated at the small table in the kitchen of Jeremy's flat eating a late supper consisting mostly of leftovers put together from the refrigerator.

"I warn you in advance that it's unorthodox," he said, "but I've been thinking about it for days. Suppose you and I were to get married but I was to remain, officially and in every other way, Mr. Jeremy Walsh. Not Prince Consort, not the Duke of Whatsis, not seated on a throne to your left on ceremonial occasions – none of those things. Simply Jeremy Walsh, commoner, who happens to be married to the Queen."

She looked across at him. "This isn't one of your jokes?"

"Dead serious. I was in the Press Gallery last week for Question Time, and with not much happening, I began to look about. There, on the topmost row in the gallery, was Mrs. Forster. Nobody around her seemed to have twigged to who she was. Nobody spoke to her or bothered her. Once I saw Forster look up and give her the slightest smile, but you'd have had to be watching for it to see it. Anyway, it got me thinking. He's the Prime Minister, the head of state, but his wife is merely that, his wife. As Prime Minister, he has all kinds of powers and prerogatives. She has none. Which is precisely the way it is with the Queen and her husband."

She looked at him, bemused. "I'm listening."

"Follow me now," he said, taking a moment to wolf down the better part of a croissant. "Take Queen Victoria's husband, Albert. He was quite a guy, I gather. But his vested right to do anything on his own was zilch. Another example: the Duke of Edinburgh. In 1952 it was announced that – and this is the exact wording – 'henceforth, upon all occasions and in all meetings, except where otherwise provided by Act of Parliament (the Duke of Edinburgh) shall have, hold and enjoy place, pre-eminence, and precedence next to Her Majesty.' Now, what had been done? Nothing. Nothing of consequence. They had merely codified what was already true in practice. It left the Duke with position, but no power, certainly no real power. And now I come to my point. Why couldn't the next Queen's husband – I now refer to yours truly – why couldn't he be no more than that – your husband? As Queen you'll have all sorts of titles and a flock of prerogatives, but they'll be yours and yours alone and not shared with your husband. Quite properly. So why, apart from his vanity, is it necessary to give him titles and a throne and a stipend and all the rest? Let him be the Queen's husband just as Mrs. Forster is the Prime Minister's wife, and leave it at that. Why not?"

Victoria was slow to answer, chewing meditatively. "The argument against it that first comes to mind is tradition. And seemliness, I suppose. No, there's something much more important: you would be the father of the heir to the throne."

"So?"

189

"So your analogy won't work. The Forsters have a son, an heir if you like, but when Forster dies, his son doesn't inherit his office."

"But isn't that irrelevant? The important thing about an heir to the throne is that he or she be in the direct line of succession. It doesn't matter a damn who the sovereign's mate is."

"But it does. The heir must marry a member of the nobility, another royal."

"That's the tradition, but it doesn't always get observed. Take George VI, for instance. He was married to a commoner, Elizabeth Bowes Lyon, the Queen Mum as they called her."

"Yes, but George wasn't the heir apparent. He became King only because his elder brother, Edward VIII, abdicated. If I had a brother, even an older sister, there'd be no problem in my marrying a commoner."

"But my point is that it's not unheard of or forbidden for the sovereign to marry a commoner."

"So what are you saying?"

"I know it's unorthodox as hell, but as you've said dozens of times, this is a different age, a different time, and. . . . Okay, I'll state it flatly: I'm proposing that we get married, with whatever pomp and ceremony is requisite, but not as in a royal wedding. You alone ascend to the throne, exactly as you would if you weren't married or if you'd been married and your husband had died. I'd be your husband but I'd have no part in the functioning of the monarchy. No say, no powers, no rights."

"But," she said, "what happens to any child we might have?"

"The child, being in direct line of succession, would be heir to the throne. Nothing's changed. And I'm prepared to covenant that I forgo my right to determine where he – and forgive me for presuming that it's a boy – would be

190

educated, to which church he would belong and so on. You'd decide such questions and I'd abide by your decision. I'd get on with my life, and just like many other married couples, we'd each follow our own careers while sharing our children and our private lives." He glanced at her. "Well, what do you think?"

She turned to him and they looked full into each other's eyes. Victoria found herself quivering with excitement. "Oh, Jeremy," she said, her voice trembling, "is it possible? Could it be?"

♔ SIX

HERBERT BLACKSTOCK, the leader of Her Majesty's Loyal Opposition, was late arriving at his offices in the Parliament buildings, as was pointed out to him by his new secretary as he went by her on the half run wearing his usual distracted air. I must remember to sack her, he thought. I have enough critics without paying one a salary.

Ian Barnett, Blackstock's deputy, and David Rhys, the member for Merrionnydd Nant Conwy, half rose as he entered. There was no reason for him to apologize; they knew him to be habitually late but knew also that, having arrived, he would move immediately to the business at hand.

"Ian?" he asked inquiringly, unlocking a desk drawer and removing a manila folder.

"Nothing new to report, Herb," Barnett said. "David may have something."

Rhys opened the briefcase on his lap, extracted a piece of paper, lowered the lid of the briefcase, placed the paper at the exact center of it, and smoothed it out with a hand. Self-important bastard, Blackstock thought. You'd think he was about to release a ruling by the Queen's Bench. The people you get in bed with in politics, he gloomed.

The meeting had been convened to discuss, of all unlikely things, gossip. There were fragmentary reports that Princess Victoria was having an affair with an American journalist, which in itself was a matter of no great interest to Blackstock, and yet important enough because it might relate to something else: the fact that, although the Commons was due to prorogue soon until early autumn, the government had yet to introduce its much touted bill authorizing a national celebration on the occasion of the Princess reaching her twenty-first birthday. The Prime Minister had told a press conference some weeks earlier that such was his intention – managing in the telling to emphasize his close relationship to the royal family – but the bill had not been tabled, and it was the political illogicality of this that puzzled the Leader of the Opposition. He knew what he would have done were he in Forster's shoes: he would have presented the bill with a flourish and forced the Opposition either to concur or to take on the politically unwelcome task of criticizing it without seeming to attack the palace. The question nagged at him: why had the bill not been tabled and why did the Prime Minister appear to be fudging on it?

Padding his part, David Rhys was well into a review of the background.

"Get *on* with it, David," Blackstock snapped. "*Is* the lady in love, and has it anything to do with Forster's dillydallying?"

Rhys trimmed his sails to the wind. "Of course, Herb," he said ingratiatingly. "I presumed that you wanted a full – "

"The lady. The bill," Blackstock snapped.

"Yes, of course," Rhys said. He shuffled his papers. "Ian asked me to check into the matter, I being the one who had drawn it to your attention, and I have been able to establish that, yes, Princess Victoria is enamored of one Jeremy Walsh of the *New York Times*, and, yes, they have been observed having dinner together privately, and, yes,

Walsh has been a guest at Windsor on two weekends in the past month. . . ."

"All that we know," Blackstock broke in. "My question is: Is the lady in love?"

Rhys stumbled. "The problem with that – "

Blackstock turned to his deputy. "Ian?"

"Nasty business, this," Barnett said, a look of distaste on his ruddy countenance. "There's ample reason to believe that she is, I wouldn't want to be unequivocal, but the case can be made."

"But?"

"It seems to me the relevant question is: why *else* would Forster delay the bill?"

"Could he be worried about criticism of the cost? These are hard times."

"Agreed. And we'll have something to say on that when the time comes. But in the end, except for the lunatic fringe, we'll all close ranks. And everybody knows that, including Forster. There are no votes to be won these days carping at the palace."

Blackstock frowned in concentration, pulling at the fold of skin below his jaw. When he spoke, it was as though he was still musing. "I wonder if perhaps we should turn our guns on him tomorrow in Question Time and see if we can blow him out of the water?"

The British House of Commons acquired its first permanent home in 1547 when St. Stephen's Chapel was made available by King Henry VIII. The general seating arrangements today are merely an enlargement of those in use then, when members sat in the choirstalls and the Speaker's chair stood on the altar steps. The chapel was destroyed in 1834 when fire ravaged almost the entire Palace of Westminster. The elegant new chamber, designed by Sir Charles Barry, was first used in 1852, but it too was destroyed, by German bombs in 1942. The present chamber, almost a replica of Barry's but simpler in decor, was opened in 1950.

There are 635 members of Parliament, with seating accommodation for only 437. The restriction is deliberate. Most debates are of a routine nature or are specialized in subject matter, and as a consequence few members are present. Thus a small and intimate chamber is convenient. But on great occasions or when large issues are being debated and the House is full, members crowd the side galleries, sit in the gangways, or cluster about the Speaker's chair, and the drama is heightened. At such times there is, as Winston Churchill once put it, "a sense of crowd and urgency." So it was that, on this day, on the eve of the House rising for the summer recess and with word having gone out that the Opposition had "a bee in its bonnet," the benches and galleries overflowed and there was an air of heightened expectancy. At exactly 3:15, the Speaker recognized "The Right Honorable Member from Manchester Wythenshawe, the Leader of the Opposition."

Blackstock rose and moved to the Table of the House, placing his notes on the dispatch boxes. There was a murmur of conversation and he waited for it to subside. "Mr. Speaker," he said, addressing himself to the Chair, "as is well known and much anticipated by her many admirers, Her Royal Highness, The Princess Victoria, will on June 30 of next year celebrate her twenty-first birthday."

There was a murmuring of "Hear, hear!" from all parts of the chamber.

"There are, I am sure Mr. Speaker, few, if any, in this company who would not agree that the admiration and affection all Britons feel for Her Royal Highness demands that, on this significant anniversary, appropriate and wholehearted tribute be paid."

"Hear, hear!"

He paused until the sounds of approval died. In the silence there came a shout from someone on a government back-bench. "Question!" It was the cue Blackstock had been looking for.

"The Honorable Member calls for the question," he said, his voice rising. "He may wish, Mr. Speaker, he may shortly wish that he had asked rather that it be deferred!" There were good-natured hoots and catcalls from the government side. Blackstock pressed on. "Five long weeks ago, Mr. Speaker, the Prime Minister announced – not in this House, as he should have done, but to the press – that he would shortly introduce a bill proclaiming June 30 next as Princess Victoria Day and seek the approval of this body for the expenditures required properly to observe the occasion. In making his announcement, the Prime Minister reached new heights of political opportunism. Was syco-phancy ever so self-serving! Listening, one might have thought that this nation's commitment to the royal family needed shoring up. He pleaded his fealty. He pleaded his devotion. He pleaded his admiration. . . . One could hardly see the Forster for the pleas."

There was laughter and groaning; Blackstock was renowned for his contrived jibes. It was a minute or so before the entreaties of the Speaker for "Order! Order!" could be heard. Blackstock waited it out, head up, jaw outthrust, managing to mask his glee at the response to his outrageous pun. But now a silence settled in as both sides of the House awaited the main thrust.

"What the devil is the man up to?" Chips Chippendale whispered behind a hand to Forster.

"But, Mr. Speaker, *but*, I say, for all the cackling, where is the egg? For all the posturing, where is the bill? Most practitioners of hocus-pocus wave their arms about and then produce *something*. Not so with our master of deception. He waved his arms about and then, to nobody's

196

surprise, produced nothing. Nothing but empty air. One might say, *hot* air."

There were wild shouts from the Opposition benches, yelps and whoops and howls. The government side, except for some token heckling, sat silent.

On his feet, the Speaker waited until the din diminished. "I wonder," he said, his tone measured, "if the Right Honorable gentleman may now be ready to ask his question? I think he will agree, the Chair has been more than indulgent."

"Question! Question!" came the echo from everyone on the government side – everyone save Hugh Forster. Forster sat at his ease, legs crossed, right foot bobbing, face composed in a benign smile.

Blackstock offered the Speaker a courtly bow. "I stand rebuked, Mr. Speaker. But in the circumstances, one may hope to be forgiven." His voice rose in indignation, "Such a flagrant disregard of the House, such a subverting of the parliamentary process stirs outrage." Before the uproar could begin, he hurried on. "The question, Mr. Speaker ... ah, yes, the question. The question, very simply put, is this: the Conservative party has often posed as the staunch champion of the monarchy. Why then has it not tabled in this House a bill, a proposal that we may, with near or full unanimity, make into law? When precisely do we get the bill? Give us, sir, not generalities but a specific date."

Forster uncrossed his legs and, feigning an attitude of weary patience, stepped forward to stand with his hands on the dispatch boxes. "Mr. Speaker," he said, shaking his head slowly, "I must confess to some bafflement. One grows accustomed to watching the Leader of the Opposition, as is his wont, tearing a passion to tatters. Observing him, one eventually arrives at an axiom: the louder the sound, the less the substance. It would seem that what he lacks in lightning he seeks to make up for with thunder."

Now it was the government's turn to howl, and they did, setting up an incredible din. Through it, Forster maintained the pose of a patient adult forced to deal with a recalcitrant child.

"The Right Honorable gentleman asks, 'Where's the bill?' I would ask him in turn, 'What's the date?' Today's date? For his information, today is July 4. The twenty-first birthday of our esteemed heir presumptive falls on June 30 of next year. Almost a year from now! Has this House *ever* heard more ado about nothing? The Right Honorable gentleman will get his bill. . . . But *will* he? We come now to the heart of the matter. Between now and next June there will be a general election. May we not therefore reasonably conclude that the Right Honorable gentleman's frantic pleas that the bill be introduced now, *immediately*, stem from the fact that he has been sniffing the electoral wind. . . ." His voice suddenly changed from weary patience to a shout. "And he knows that, come next June 30, *he will no longer sit in this place!*"

He returned to his seat as both sides of the House roared their reactions. Blackstock was on his feet immediately.

"Mr. Speaker, I will not labor the point – "

"The Labor party labors *every* point," a voice cried.

Blackstock pressed on. "We are not going to get a date, that is now clear, although a judicious government would know that a mere twelve months is barely enough time to prepare for an event of the magnitude we are discussing here. So I will not further waste the time of this House beating with bare fists against the monolithic ineptitude of this government. But there is a related question, and although I realize that I move now onto a slippery slope, I feel I must nonetheless venture to ask it."

Blackstock had decided to gamble. He had become convinced, with not much more evidence than a gut conviction, that, despite Forster's insistence that there was sufficient time to prepare for the celebration, it was uncharacteristic of him not to move strongly and immediately on an issue so obviously to his advantage. Blackstock stabbed in the dark.

"My question, Mr. Speaker, is this: does not the Prime Minister's delinquency in this matter stem from the fact that there is a major difference of opinion, an actual impasse, between the government and the palace?" The silence in the chamber deepened. Blackstock was indeed venturing on perilous ground. "The Prime Minister has undoubtedly discussed the matter with the palace – he would hardly have the effrontery to announce publicly, as he has done, that there would be a celebration had he not first consulted with Her Majesty and Her Royal Highness. And having done so, is it not reasonable to expect that he would proceed apace? Instead, he delays. And when asked why, obfuscates. The question demands asking: why? *Why?* Would the Prime Minister be considerate enough to rid us of our concern in this matter? Will he reassure us all that, having presented his plan, it has not been rejected, that there is not indeed a impasse between himself and the palace?"

There were no shouts from anywhere in the chamber. All realized that the Leader of the Opposition had acted with daring, perhaps recklessly. Controversy that touches on the royal family is normally eschewed. One might criticize the amounts allocated in the Civil List and deplore the expense, but except for members known for their eccentricity and consequently disregarded, one did not draw the person of the Queen or other members of the royal family into the cut and thrust of parliamentary debate. Blackstock was not a foolhardy man and was acknowledged to be a skilled and sagacious parliamentarian. He would not have put his question were he not sure of his ground. On the benches on both sides of the House and in the galleries, members, newsmen, and visitors tensed and leaned forward as the Prime Minister rose in his place.

There was no hint in Forster's demeanor of the tension roiling within him. Dammit! he was thinking, somehow, somewhere Blackstock had learned not only of Victoria's intention to marry Walsh but of the demands she was making. *Surely* he would not dare to put his question were he not sure of his facts. But how, in god's name, had he found out? It was no time for speculation. He must act to defuse the explosive situation, a situation that had the potential to bring down his government.

The decision had been made in his seat – despite the possiblity of being caught out, he must draw the sting from the issue. He was aware that if his hastily conceived plan could not be realized, he might well be charged with misleading the House, but he knew also that he must chance it.

"Mr. Speaker," he said, his voice low, almost inaudible in the upper reaches of the chamber, "in the face of a notable lack of restraint, I will be restrained. The Leader of the Opposition has – and I say this to him directly – permitted his zeal to overpower his judgement. Because I do not wish to see and will not permit, at least for my part, the royal family to be the subject of partisan debate, I have decided on a change in the government's plans. I had hoped that our intentions in this matter might be revealed in ideal circumstances and at the proper time and therefore had decided to withhold the details for the time being. However, because it has today become clear that preparations for the celebration are going to be made a bone of partisan contention, I here and now inform the House that it will learn of the government's intentions at the most appropriate time possible and from the most appropriate source possible: from the lips of Her Majesty the Queen herself when, come autumn, she delivers in this chamber The Speech from the Throne."

Angus McCrimmon caught up with the Queen in the Picture Gallery as she was returning from a reception for the newly appointed Commander of British Forces Cyprus. "May I have a word with you, Ma'am?" he asked. When she nodded, he fell in stride with her.

"Have you had an opportunity," he asked, "to read *Hansard* or the news reports on what happened yesterday in Question Time?"

"I'm afraid not," she said, a small reproof in her voice. "You've had me too busy, Crimmie."

"Sorry about that," he said. "The rest of the week should be easier, I think."

"You mentioned Question Time."

"Yes. I'm reluctant to trouble you about it but there was a most remarkable performance by Mr. Blackstock. He managed to suggest quite plainly that there is a difference of opinion between the government and the palace – a major difference, he managed to convey – about the arrangements being made for what is being called Princess Victoria Day."

"Really?" she said, pausing at the door to her sitting-room.

"It would seem that he is privy to the reasons for that difference of opinion. It's difficult to know how he might have come by that information. So far as I'm aware, no one knows of Princess Victoria's views other than you and His Royal Highness, the Prime Minister, and me. And, of course, Her Royal Highness and Mr. Walsh. It occurs to me that Mr. Walsh may have confided in a friend, or that during the voyage to Gibraltar, Victoria might have said a word to Miss Cavendish. It is, of course, entirely possible that Mr. Blackstock may simply have leaped to a conclusion. Whatever his reasons, it is of the greatest importance that all of us guard against any hint that there is truth in the rumor. I cannot, as you will understand, speak to Victoria or Mr. Walsh, but if I may, I would ask you to impress on Victoria how important discretion is in this matter. You may also wish to suggest that she convey your concern to Mr. Walsh."

♛ SEVEN

O SSIE FOUND HIMSELF INTIMIDATED by the enormity of the story he had chanced upon. He had been planning a series of articles in which he would portray Jeremy Walsh as *The Ingrate American*, but that was peanuts compared to the story he was now about to break. He could win The Scoop of the Year award! Scoop of the Year, hell – scoop of the *decade*! The old left kidney had been right again.

He hadn't slept that first night, threshing about in bed, sending Alfie bobbing like a floater on a fish line. He wrote the lead in his head a dozen times, visualized the headlines. The *Herald* would copyright the story, of course; make a bundle syndicating it. And he'd get a bonus. But right away, there's a raw deal. It was *his* story, *his* persistence that had paid off. Maybe he should quit the *Herald* – it was a penny-ante rag compared to some of the rest of them. Maybe he should go over to the *Mirror* or *The News of the World*. But how could he approach them without revealing the story and without the bastards stealing it right out of his hands? No, he'd be loyal to the *Herald* but they'd damned well better come up with a whopping bonus.

He decided finally to talk to Monty Haslett, his city editor, and get his advice on the approach to take. But wait a minute; you could wager Monty would find some way to take the credit. Probably claim the idea was his, claim he'd originally assigned it to Ossie, and then leave him out in the cold. No way he was going to let that happen! He'd go see Ed Replogle, the managing editor. No, not even Replogle; he'd go right to the top, to Tim Osterwald, the editor-in-chief. Why not? How often did the *Herald* get a story like this dropped in its lap?

But Osterwald wouldn't see him and sent word through his secretary that Ossie should discuss whatever was on his mind with Replogle. Ossie knew he might also get fobbed-off by Replogle and kicked back to his city editor, so, waiting until Replogle had left for the day, he hung about Tim Osterwald's door until he caught him on the way out.

"Mr. Osterwald. . . ."

"You're?"

"Docherty. Ossie Docherty."

"Yes, I know. Ossie Docherty. Nice to see you."

"Mr. Osterwald, I wonder if I could have a minute of your time?"

"Ossie, I'm sorry." He glanced at his watch. "I'm already late for an engagement. Have you spoken to Mr. Replogle?"

"He's gone for the day, and it won't wait. Believe me."

"I'm afraid it will have to. As I said, Docherty, I'm already late."

Ossie seized his arm, dropping his voice. "Princess Victoria is having an affair – "

"For crissake, Docherty – "

"She's screwin' around with Jeremy Walsh of the *New York Times*. I have absolute proof. I've been working on the story for – "

"What kind of proof?"

"I've personally seen her in his flat. Twice. And there's more. Plenty more."

"Facts?"

"Absolutely, Mr. Osterwald. Guaranteed."

Osterwald frowned. "Will you be home later tonight?"

"Yes, sir."

"I'll get back to you."

But he didn't; Monty Haslett did. "Hey, Ossie, goin' over my head, huh? Bloody marvelous. Makes me love you more."

"I'm sorry, Monty, but you were gone for the day and-"

"Now, Ossie, I want you to listen to me carefully. I want you to fill me in on what you told Mr. Osterwald but I don't want any names. Not on the phone, understand? No names." Ossie provided a quick rundown of what had happened and was told to meet Haslett at the *Herald* the following day. In his office, Haslett was brisk but, Ossie thought, oddly formal. Ossie had no knowledge that Ed Replogle and Tim Osterwald were in Osterwald's office listening on the open intercom.

"Now, Ossie," Monty said, "fill me in." Before Ossie could respond, he held up a hand. "No bullshit, Ossie. Understood?"

"You still think I went over your head. Look, I – "

"Forget all that," Monty said. "Fill me in. I'll get you started. I assigned you a series on Walsh and the negative stuff he's been sending back to America. Now go on from there."

"Well," said Ossie, "it doesn't actually start there. It starts when I see one of the royal cars, a green Jag, turning in at the palace at 2:55 a.m. I make a note of the markers so's I can check on whose car it is. I'm pretty sure it's Princess Victoria's and I'm curious, naturally, why she's getting home so late. So I start to check around. . . ."

"Ossie, look, I've got a meeting in ten minutes. What

I need now are the bare facts. Okay, so it's Victoria's car and she's out late. Let's get to the meat."

"I next see her car around 2 a.m. on the night of April 17, the night I left for New York on that Trade and Industry junket. The Princess pulls up at the departures terminal at Heathrow, lets Walsh out, and drives off."

"Hold on a minute. Did you actually see the Princess? Did she get out of the car? Are you sure it was Walsh? Was there anybody with you who can corroborate it?"

Ossie was getting hot. "Jeezus, Monty, he was on the plane with me afterward. If you mean, did she do a walkabout, no, but it was her car and her driving."

"Go on."

"Anyway, I talk to Walsh on the phone a few days later. I ask him to find out for me – he hobnobs with the palace crowd – who at the palace drives a green Jag, marker plates V84 YFY."

"Wait a minute. I thought you'd already found out that the car belonged to the Princess?"

"Jeezus, Monty, you're being sticky today! I was sniffing him out. Fishing. Anyway, he hangs up on me, *bang!* soon's I mention the Jag, and this gives me a twinge in the old left kidney, you know what I mean. Anyway, last week I drop by his flat in Bermondsey, checking things out. He doesn't answer the door but I can tell he's home so I keep banging away. He finally opens the door and he's wearing a bathrobe with nothing underneath. No pajamas, I mean. And in the living-room, which I can see down the hall, everything's real cosy. There's this coffee table set up for supper. Candles, the whole bit. Having dinner with the Princess."

"You saw her?"

"Jeezus, Monty, she's not exactly going to be parading

around in a bathrobe, having a little supper with her boyfriend on the QT. But it was her all right."

"The point is: you didn't actually see her."

"The proof it was her is coming. His flat is right on the river and it has this big picture window. So I say to myself, Ossie, get yourself a scope – "

"A telescope."

"So I leased one at Picto-Camera and set up on the Wapping side of the river. Perfect. I'm there, night before last, in the bloody rain. Anyway, there's this cosy little scene again: the two of them setting out a private supper in the living-room. Candles, lights low, the whole thing."

"Now, Ossie," Monty said a trifle portentously. "I want a straight answer absolutely devoid of bullshit. Did you actually *see* the Princess? Not a woman who might have been or maybe looked like the Princess? Her, herself?"

"For chrissake, Monty, what am I – a cub or something? I see her clear as I see you. The Princess and Walsh, all cosy and snug."

After a few more questions, Monty excused himself, saying he would be right back. He was gone ten minutes.

"Ossie, it's a hell of a story but we don't have enough to go on. Here's what we do. First, we keep the lid on. Not a word, not even to anyone in the newsroom. I'm going to put Jill Martin on a stakeout outside Walsh's flat. For the next week from dark to 3 a.m. she'll check all comings and goings, get license plates, etcetera. If any woman goes in, she'll call me on the radio and I'll sent out a cameraman. He can stand by with Jill and try to get a grab-shot of the woman leaving. Also a shot of the car. Would there be any chance of a telephoto shot from across the river?"

"Hard to say. The river's maybe two hundred meters across at that point. And sometimes they pull the curtains."

"What are the possibilities of running a boat in close?"

"Well, I – "

"Don't worry about that. Leave it with me. In the meantime, play it by ear and see what you can come up with. And not a word. Even Jill won't know what story she's on."

Ossie's face had gone red and was running with perspiration. "You mean you're not going to run the story?"

"Ossie, ease off. What have we got? You want us to run a story saying one of our reporters was playing peeping-Tom with a telescope and claims he saw, on the other bank of the Thames at night, a fellow journalist getting his with a member of the royal family? It's a hell of a story but we're going to have to nail it down. Otherwise, dear boy, there *is* no story."

The stakeout at Jeremy's apartment didn't work. Days passed with no sign of him. Jill Martin groused to Monty Haslett about the near-terminal boredom of sitting most of the night in a mini-van parked on Fulford Street, the while living on soggy, take-out meals and a fat thermos of tea. The second night, there had been complaints by neighbors about the van and an inquiry by the police, none of which amounted to anything. Jill found the temptation to lie down on the makeshift bed in the rear of the van almost irresistible and, having succumbed once, arranged to be called on the radio every half hour as a safeguard. She complained of "feeling like a cooped-up zoo animal." There was no way she could take a break; she was on duty from darkness to three in the morning and, despite having a canister of mace and a police whistle in her handbag, didn't feel free to go for a stroll. Twice, late-night drunks had thumped on the side of the van, shouting obscenities, and one had urinated on a tire. What Jill didn't know, nor had she the wit to check out, was that Jeremy had been recalled to New York for consultation with his editors.

Victoria was miserable. She had grown so accustomed to seeing Jeremy at the end of the day, or at least to talking to him on the telephone before going to sleep, that her days seemed to have an almost palpable void at their heart. So intense was the sense of apartness that occasionally it dizzied her, sometimes edging her toward tears. She berated herself for her callowness – he'd be back by the end of the week, for goodness sake!

They had covenanted that, on his first full day away, he would call at 10 p.m. sharp, London time, but he'd missed the first call. ("Darling, I was in a meeting that continued through supper. You have to remember the six-hour time difference. It would have been three in the morning your time.") And now she hadn't talked to him for two days. Not that it was his fault. She knew his schedule and knew that, after three days in New York, he'd gone on to visit his family. The previous day, having returned to the palace after a wearying afternoon, she had found, among her telephone messages, two slips bearing the name I.M. Hankering, Gary, Indiana. Depressed, she rang up Jane Cavendish the following day and, disguised, they had gone on a shopping trip to Harrod's, which ended suddenly when Victoria was recognized and followed by a squealing gaggle of girls.

In Jane's flat, Victoria put down the telephone, having checked vainly with the palace switchboard for messages.

"Men," Jane said, crunching on a crisp cheese stick. "I sometimes wonder if the game's worth the candle. I love them, the wretches, but on balance I'm not sure they're worth the price you pay." She munched the remainder of

209

the cheese stick and followed it with a sip of wine. "Men are God's way of getting even with Eve."

Victoria was lying on the carpet, propped on her elbows. She smiled into her glass. "I'm on God's side, he made Jeremy."

"So far as I know," Jane said, "he may have made a lot of Jeremys. But why doesn't he lead some o   em into these green pastures? You have no idea how good I could be for the right man." She took a sip of wine. "If such exists."

"What about Colin?" Victoria asked. "By my count you've been seeing him at least twice a week since we got back from Gibraltar."

"Shipboard romance. Moonlight. Stars. A uniform. A pretty face. An itch in my unscratchable."

"He seems nice enough to me."

"He *is* nice enough. He's sweet. Always arrives with a little something that says, 'I've been thinking about you,' but nothing so expensive that you feel compromised. Knows nice places to go to. Opens doors. But from that point on, until, mind you, things get interesting late in the evening, it's *sports!*" She combed her fingers through her hair, pushing it from her face. "Why are so many grown men obsessed with sports? Not so much in playing them as in cheering while others play. The mad part of it all is that the people they cheer are total strangers who don't even live in the city they play for. Millionaires, most of them, with as much muscle between the ears as they have in the rest of their bodies. Why do men *care* about whose mercenaries beat whoever's mercenaries? Maybe it has its good side," she conceded. "Maybe if they didn't holler at their heroes they'd take it out on their wives or sweethearts." She paused in her mock tirade. "Ron was the same."

Victoria shifted until she was sitting, her feet tucked under in the lotus position. "I don't want to rally to an unpopular cause," she said, "but really, Jane, Ron *wasn't* like that."

"All right," she allowed, "he wasn't. A bit maybe, but within reason."

A silence descended. Victoria looked up at her friend. "Can we talk about Ron for a minute?"

"Whatever for?" Jane said, feigning indifference. "He's filed under missing-in-action. Maybe deserter would be a better description."

"If you'd rather not," Victoria said, not pressing. "It's just that you were once as absolutely bonkers about him as I am about Jeremy. And the fact that it could go flat as fizzwater sometimes worries me. But . . . not if it's a no-no."

Jane spent a long moment looking off, her eyes unblinking. Suddenly she grew animated, leaped to her feet, went to the bottle of wine on the sideboard, and curled some of the golden liquid into her goblet. She glanced at Victoria who raised her glass to show that it didn't need replenishing.

"It might be a good thing to talk about him," Jane said, returning to her chair. "Like dusting the attic, getting rid of the cobwebs, exorcising a ghost."

When she didn't go on, Victoria prompted, "You met him at one of our garden parties."

"There I was: a nineteen-year-old blossom, fragrant with Arpege and ready to be plucked. Nobody who knew me then had any idea how naive, how chockablock over-flowing I was with pubescent naiveté. Yes I'd been in the back seat of a car and, yes, there had been moments, but silly child that I was – violins, please! – I was saving myself for *the* man." She smiled wryly. "So, everybody dreams, but not many pinch themselves and find the dream isn't a dream. There he was! In the flesh! And such exquisitely arranged flesh. Ron, that darling, adorable, considerate, intelligent, wish-fulfilling, fascinating, sexy . . . rotter!"

She took a deep swallow of wine and once again her gaze went far away. "I was talking earlier about how God plays tricks. First he shows you the apple of your eye, all polished and shiny, and then when you've come to realize that there isn't a single thing in all the world you want as much as you want this man, when you realize through the haze that was once your mind that you simply cannot go on living without him, he lets you have him. For a while. And you nibble away, and it's heaven's ambrosia – and *isn't* it! And then you bite deeply . . . and it's rotten at the core."

Victoria saw that her friend was poised on the edge of either tears or fury and then saw it all resolve into hurt. She was tempted to remain silent, to let Jane finish the painful journey into her past, but she seemed mired for the moment, so she said, "Did you never sense that? Never suspect it?"

Jane was shaking her head in slow, solemn, sideways movements. "Never. He talked about marriage and I said yes, of course. Yes, yes, yes! We even made plans. I went shopping for a wedding dress – you remember that, you went with me."

"I know, and you looked like – "

"A princess."

Victoria smiled and gave her head a quick tilt. "If you like. . . ."

"And felt like one, too."

Victoria heard herself asking, "When did it go wrong?"

Jane gave a short, suppressed, bitter laugh. "In the space of one hour on one afternoon. I got back from the doctor's office, having been informed that I was pregnant and wanting to shout it from the housetops, and the phone was ringing. On the other end of the line was a woman's voice telling me that she was his wife, and warning me that he would never leave her. Their parents were lifelong family friends, their fathers were in business together. . . ." She paused and then said in a choked voice, "And she was right."

Jane was silent for a moment, swallowing hard. "You think I'm about to cry, don't you?" she said in a strangled voice. "Well, you're right."

She put her head down, her hands to her face and, making barely a sound, was shaken with sobs. Victoria put her arms about her, trying to will an end to the pain. In a few minutes Jane went off to the bathroom to dash cold water on her face. When she emerged she was herself again.

"I was wondering in there," she said, gesturing with her head toward the bathroom, "how I've kept from telling you all that. All the years we've been friends."

"I'm glad you shared it with me now."

"I think what brought it on was something you said earlier about the two of us being bonkers about a man, and that not knowing what happened between Ron and me worried you."

"It has. Not often, but sometimes."

"Like right now?"

"Not really. Well . . . perhaps. But for no good reason. It's because Jeremy's so far away. I always feel a bit insecure when he's away or when I haven't heard from him for a few days. Silly."

Jane rose, went to the sideboard and left her empty glass there. "You asked me if I needed to talk about Ron. Do you need to talk about Jeremy? You're worried."

Victoria gave her head a vigorous shaking, as though to scatter her thoughts. "Yes, I am. Even though I have no reason to be. I'm *so* lucky."

"But worried."

Victoria drew a deep breath and expelled it. "Yes."

213

"And not sure why."

"Exactly."

"Do you doubt him? Is there a little corner of your mind in which? . . ."

"No, no. Nothing like that. It's the future that worries me. I'm absolutely certain that he loves me, he shows it in so many ways. And if he was looking for a way out, heaven knows he's had lots of excuses. He's been marvelous, simply marvelous. The trouble is – and I suppose I'm borrowing trouble – he's being asked for too much." She was suddenly distraught. "Oh, Jane, there are so many people, so many . . . *forces* against us. So many reasons not to go ahead, and only the one to continue on: that we love each other. I'm afraid they're going to push us both into losing sight of what's important. I'm afraid that something will happen that will cause us to run away from the whole complicated mess, because that would be the easiest way out, or that we'll bend to the pressure and wake up one day to find that we've thrown away the one thing we wanted more than anything else."

Jane was looking at her intently. "Now that we have that out of the way," she said, "what's *really* worrying you?"

Victoria yielded a wan smile. "He's in New York. The paper called him back all of a sudden for no apparent reason. We've talked twice since and he hasn't mentioned what it was. That's not like him. And today he's with his family in Gary. A while ago he showed me a letter from his father. He has great respect for his father and his father is dead set against our getting married."

"My, my, my!" Jane said. "Now I understand. What you need is The Jane Cavendish Marriage Counseling Service. Remember? I have just the ticket."

She got to her feet and went to a closet. "First, you must close your eyes." Victoria heard her open and close a door, and then something was placed in her hand. "You may look now," Jane said.

It was an envelope. "Arrived this morning by messenger with a note telling me I was to find the right moment to giv it to you," Jane said. "Right now seems as good a time as any."

Within the envelope was a note under the *New York Times* letterhead. It read: *"What do you give someone who has everything? Flowers? – she has her own conservatory. Something to wear? – she has the couturiers of the world begging her to accept their clothes. A bauble to reflect the sparkle of her eyes? – she has all the jewels of Araby. So, because it* needs *to be shouted from the housetops, I send this instead. (Cue Jane)"*

Jane brought her hand from behind her back and passed over a long cylindrical paper tube tied with a ribbon. Within it was the front page of the day's *Times*, the headline replaced with the words in bold type: JEREMY LOVES VICTORIA.

Jeremy sat back in the sagging sofa, put his feet on the coffee table and belched, a great rumbling resonant belch, a most satisfactory, reverberating belch.

"Thank you," his mother said from the dining-room. She was scraping and piling dishes on a tray preparatory to removing them to the kitchen.

"Can I give you a hand?" he asked, making no move to do so.

"You can sit there and talk to your father. How often does he get to see you these days? Hans and Maria can help with the dishes. Just because they have two cars and a condominium they mustn't forget how the rest of the world lives. Stephan can sit with you after he gets the lawn mowed. Come on Stephan, take off your collar if you're afraid you'll look undignified. Leave the lawn to

215

Papa and some of Mrs. Kowalski's half dozen will get lost in the weeds out there."

Dinner had been an enormous feast with plates heaped high and the variety unending. The reunited family crowded the small dining-room. Jeremy, knowing what was in store, had skipped lunch, and, after drawing his chair up to the table, had loosened his belt. Papa sat at the head of the table, presiding, offering thanks in a rambling informal way that suggested that the Deity was a familiar and as nearby as the attic. Mama hovered at the foot of the table, standing more often than not, pressing each serving bowl on everyone, eating little herself. Hans and Maria managed to take something of everything that passed by, the while pressing food from their own plates on the twins. Stephan, lean as his father, protested as his plate was laden but sampled everything. Stanislaus, corpulent as his mother, displayed a considerable talent as a trencherman before dashing off to a meeting of the Diocesan committee on African relief.

Now, with the velour curtains drawn between the dining-room and the living-room, with the table cleared, the clatter of china and conversation muted in the kitchen, and with the drone of the mower in the background, Jeremy and Papa Walasciewicz took their ease. The living-room was small and made more so by an oversize sofa and two matching overstuffed chairs, each with handmade antimacassars on the arms and backs. The table lamps wore rose silk shades, their fringes undulating in the breeze from an open window. A fireplace that had never worked provided an alcove for a brass jardiniere filled with paper flowers. On the wall were three paintings in elaborate gilt frames and an untidy cluster of family pictures. Over the mantelpiece was a large lurid portrayal of an expressionless Jesus, drawing aside his immaculate robe to reveal a bleeding heart.

"Moscow," Papa said, drawing deeply on a skinny cigar and venting the smoke toward the ceiling. "Imagine, a son of mine in Moscow. I wonder what your grandfather would say." He smiled tightly at the thought.

"I may not go," Jeremy said.

"Not go?" Papa said. "You tell me it's the most important bureau other than Washington and then you say you may not go? Not go, when the President agreed only a few weeks ago to a summit there?"

"I've been in London less than three years. I'm only finding the handle."

"London is a backwater."

"Papa – "

"The glory has departed. The locus of power, outside of Washington, is Moscow." He peered closely at his son. "You said something about the posting being an intermediate step. What did you mean by that?"

Jeremy shifted in his seat. "The idea is that, if all goes well, they'll bring me back to New York in a few years and give me the foreign desk. There was even talk, nothing definite, of a shot at a regular column. They were pretty high on the series I did on the U.K." He drew a deep breath, frowning. "It's tempting."

"Tempting! It's that well-known offer you can't refuse." When Jeremy didn't respond, he said, "Well, isn't it?"

"Yes, yes, of course," Jeremy said, a touch of irritability in his voice. "It's just that it screws up my plans."

"What plans – if a father may ask?"

"I'm thinking of getting married. You *know* that, Papa."

Papa was rotating the cigar between his lips. Thin ribbons of smoke ascended past his eyes, causing him to squint. "I was hoping that that was over and done. You haven't mentioned it since your phone call and I. . . . Well, enough of that. You know my feelings on the subject."

"Papa," Jeremy said sharply, "please *don't* say any more about it." He softened his tone. "I don't think there's anything you can say I haven't said to myself in a hundred ways. It'll work out. Some way."

"There is one thing," Papa said. As Jeremy grimaced, he added quickly, "Not by way of advice, but something you should do. You should tell your mother. I promised you I wouldn't and I haven't, but I feel guilty keeping it from her. She talks all the time about when you'll meet the right girl. She misses seeing Merilee. There's the possibility of Hans and Maria buying a bigger dealership in St. Louis and that will mean not seeing as much of them and the twins. You're twenty-eight, with no family started, and she keeps talking about who and when. If you're serious about Princess Victoria – I'll *never* feel comfortable saying it! – you should at least let her know."

Jeremy sat motionless, frowning in concentration. There was a sound of childish laughter from the kitchen. "Why don't I do it right now?" Jeremy said.

"Right now? You don't think you should wait until? . . ."

"Will you ask her to come here for a minute?"

Mama stood just within the parted curtains to the dining-room, wiping her hands on her apron. She sensed something amiss and there was a troubled look about her eyes. "Papa said you wanted to talk to me. Alone, he said. Is something wrong?"

"No, no," Jeremy said, patting the cushion beside him. "Come sit here."

There was a small wariness as she sat beside him, which increased as he took her hands.

"There's bad news," she said. "I know it."

He shook his head, laughing. "No, no, no. Will you stop that. It's good news. I'm thinking of getting married."

"Oh, my," she said, relief flooding into her voice. "That *is* good news!" She was suddenly excited, animated. "Tell me, who is she?"

"First," he said, "you have to make me a promise: that you won't tell anyone. Anyone."

"I won't. I won't. Who is she? Where did you meet her? An English girl? Of course, an English girl."

He smiled, having trouble restraining the smile. "Yes, you could say that. An English girl. I'm glad you're sitting down. Mama, the girl I'm going to marry is Princess Victoria."

"Of England?"

"Of England."

Her face mirrored a sequence of swift reactions. She looked at him closely, he was joking; appraisingly, why was he telling her such a thing; eyes twinkling, they like to play tricks on their mother; smiling, she wasn't that easily fooled; frowning, he was smiling but he seemed serious. "This is another of your jokes," she said.

"No, Mama, I'm dead serious. Ask Papa. We met at a garden party at Buckingham Palace. We've been seeing each other for months. I haven't said anything because it has to be kept secret for a while. You mustn't tell a soul."

"Why is it such a secret? Her parents don't approve?"

"Let's say they don't disapprove. It's a very complicated matter."

She mused. "Princess Victoria. . . . Jeremy, she'll be Queen some day. *You're* going to be King of England?" She looked at him with pleased suspicion. "It *is* one of your jokes."

He burst into affectionate laughter. "No, Mama, it's not. No, I won't be King of England. I'll explain it all to you another time. In the meantime I wanted you to know."

"No joke?" she said.

He shook his head. "No joke. Okay?"

Again she mused for a moment. "When do I meet her? It's only right I should meet her. Papa and I'll never get to England. Perhaps you should bring her here. Maybe at Christmas or on St. Stephen's Day with the whole family here." She was suddenly distracted. "There won't be room at the table. . . . Perhaps the twins should eat early. . . . Perhaps we should. . . ."

"Relax, Mama. It'll all work out. In the meantime, remember. . . ." He put a finger to his lips.

♕ EIGHT

"MAIDY?. . ."

"Oh, Kevin. Yes, it's me. I've been waiting – "

"Hold on a minute. Where are you calling from?"

"From the phone box down at the corner. Like you said to."

"Good. Now, Maidy, I want – "

"Oh, Kev, I've missed you so. You haven't answered my letters, even though I was careful not to use the fancy envelopes or my purple ink. I know you don't want me to write you at work but how else am I going to get in touch? I'm not supposed to ring you up at your flat, but you don't call."

"Maidy – "

"Do you realize how long it's been? Kevin, I love you, don't you know that? Did I say something, do something? If I did, I'm sorry. The last thing in the world I'd do – "

"Maidy, hold on a minute. I've got something to tell you. Something interesting. Day before yesterday I was on duty at the turn onto Constitution Hill – you know the spot. Anyway, this American tourist came up to me. American, mind you! Have you got that? He'd been taking pictures, you know the way they do, and he began to talk

221

to me. We don't encourage conversation with tourists – start with one and it never stops – but this one's very persistent. From Pawtucket, Rhode Island, he says – wherever that is. Anyway, just as I'm about to tell him to move along, he says to me – pointing, mind you, at the royal apartments – 'Is that the window over there?' I don't say yes or no, of course, and then he gives me a sort of wink and says, 'Is that the window – the curved one – is that the one the Queen's lover sneaks in?' Now, Maidy, I have a question for you: what am I to make from that?"

"Kevin, that's terrible. That's just terrible."

"Yes, it is. But my question was: what am I to make from that?"

"What do you mean, what am I to make from that?"

"I think you know what I mean."

"I certainly don't know what you mean."

"I mean, how would anyone – much less an American, for god's sake – know anything about the Queen's window?"

"How should *I* know, for goodness sake! I don't know any Americans."

"But that's not the point. The point is: how would anyone know about someone being at the window in question? How would they know unless somebody has a big mouth?"

"Oh, sure, I rang up a stranger in whatever that place is in Rhode Island and told him. Oh sure!"

"No one is suggesting you told somebody in Rhode Island, but you certainly must've told somebody."

"Oh, and who did I tell?"

"Maidy, you're being ridiculous. You must've told somebody or how would the story get out?"

"Oh, so it's me. It couldn't be somebody else? Somebody we both know. It couldn't be him. Oh, no."

"Maidy, be careful now. Only one person says she saw what she saw. So, if – "

"Wait a minute. What are you trying to get away with? You said, 'Only one person says she saw what she saw.' Well, don't put it all on me. You know what happened."

"I know nothing except that you came to me with a cock-and-bull story about seeing something and I told you not to be going around telling such nonsense."

"Kevin, what's got into you? I can't believe what I'm hearing! And what do you mean I came to you with a cock-and-bull story. I told you all about it and you asked me all kinds of questions. You didn't call it a cock-and-bull story then."

"I repeat, you told me this story and I warned you not to say a word about it or you'd get yourself in trouble and you chose to ignore my advice."

"*I* could get in trouble! We *both* could get in trouble. That's what you said. All of a sudden it's all me. Isn't that just lovely!"

"There isn't any trouble . . . yet. But if you keep spreading this made-up story around – "

"*Made up!*"

"It has to be made up; it couldn't have happened, and I said that when you told me. And if I'm asked about it, that's what I'll tell them. I just thought you should know."

"Kevin – "

The line had gone dead.

Victoria had had a vague sense of foreboding through most of the day. The feeling had surfaced during Jeremy's telephone call on his arrival at Heathrow. "I've only got a minute," he'd said, explaining that his plane was an hour late and that he was overdue at the office. She'd been able to tell him no more than that she was happy he was back and that she would see him at his flat around eight. There was a feeling of let-down even as she hung up the receiver – there hadn't even been the opportunity to say "I love you."

Her day had been full, and meeting Jane for tea had been a welcome diversion. She'd said nothing about her concern, but her mood had led Jane to say, "*This* is the woman whose love has just flown in from overseas!" But when Jane dropped her off at Jeremy's flat and she had let herself in, the doubts dissolved. She walked from room to room, seeing the evidence of him, smelling the scent of him, running a hand along a jacket hung on the back of a chair. . . .

She'd been there an hour and a half before he arrived. There'd been "a problem at the office," he explained. But, for all her anticipation, there had been something lacking in their reunion. She wasn't sure whether it was in Jeremy or herself, but from their first embrace in the hallway there had been an overtone of restraint, the slightest sense of holding back. And it was only later, as they set out the supper Jane had packed for them, that Jeremy, having talked animatedly about the flight and about his family, had said, "Oh, yes, and about New York. . . ."

"How wonderful for you!" she enthused when he told her about the posting to Moscow. "What a tribute to what you've accomplished here." He made no response, being occupied licking his fingers after buttering some toasted rolls. "When do they want you to go?" she asked.

"They want me to spend at least a month in New York – briefings, getting all the clearances, that kind of thing." He put his arms about her waist. "Vicky, darling, it's not *settled*. I haven't accepted. I told them only that I'd give it serious thought."

She was tempted to press him for more details but didn't. Nor did they discuss it further until after they'd eaten and made love and were lying indolently in his bed.

"About Moscow," she ventured. "It would be very difficult to say no."

He gave a short laugh. "That was my father's first reaction." He was silent for a moment. "Yes, it would be hard to say no. With the summit there and signs of softening on both sides, it would be a reporter's dream."

In the distance a boat was hooting with angry persistence. In the darkness of the room it was impossible to see the tears in Victoria's eyes. She blotted them surreptitiously with a corner of the bedsheet. "You'll have to accept," she said. "If you don't, you may never forgive yourself." Or me, she almost added.

Jeremy got up, pulled on some pajama bottoms and began to stride about the room. "It's a real son of a bitch!" he said angrily. "You'd almost think the fates were against us."

"Or the Prime Minister," Victoria said softly.

He stopped in mid-stride. "What do you mean?"

"Simply that I wouldn't put it past him."

"To do what?"

"Politicians can be pretty ruthless. We're a threat to Forster."

Jeremy's voice had a note of disbelief in it. "Vicky, what in god's name are you talking about? I thought we were talking about Moscow."

"I am. I said I wouldn't put it past Mr. Forster to do anything in his power to separate us. Even getting you shipped off to Moscow."

Jeremy sat on the edge of the bed. A thin vertical line of light from the bathroom traced the contours of his body. "Thank you," he said, his tone dispirited. "Thanks a bunch."

She sat up quickly. "What's the matter? What did I say?"

"Nothing. Nothing at all. But thanks for the vote of confidence."

"Jeremy, will you stop that. What do you mean, the vote of confidence?"

"Well, it's pretty obvious," he said. "You believe the reason I was offered the job was because Forster pulled strings. Isn't that what you're saying?"

"Of course it's not what I'm saying, you silly goose. I was merely pointing out that we, you and I, are a political threat to Mr. Forster and that he is perfectly capable of various kinds of skulduggery in order to preserve his government. You think that because our politicians are more polished than your own that they're less given to duplicity than yours. Don't be fooled."

His voice was punctiliously polite. "Victoria, aren't you forgetting something? Politicians are my business. I'm not exactly a babe in the woods."

Now her blood was heating. "Oh, Jeremy," she said, "will you stop deliberately misunderstanding me? I was merely – "

He got to his feet and began again to pace the room. "It's very interesting," he said, "the little things that slip out, the revealing things. First you suggest that I don't rate the promotion and then you say I'm naive – "

Victoria was pulling at the sheet, covering herself. "I can't believe what I'm hearing. You're twisting everything I say. And what do you mean, the little things that slip out?"

"The things you were saying."

"But what did they reveal? Did they reveal that I love you? – although that's hardly a secret. Did they reveal that I believe in you? – as I do. What were these revelations that have you so upset?"

He came to the foot of the bed and stood there. "Let's go back to square one. In the past few days I've flown thousands of miles, through god knows how many time zones, managing an average of about four hours sleep a night. I've got a lot on my mind. I've got serious problems at the office. I've got a major life decision to make. I arrive here an hour and a half late and there's something in the air. I have no idea what, but I can feel it. I tell you about Moscow, and you know the feeling I get? – that you want me to go. Then, if that's not enough, you suggest that I don't rate the posting but that Forster pulled some strings at the *Times*! And then, to cap it off, you as much as tell me that I don't understand politics. Now maybe you can understand why I am, to use your words, so upset."

Victoria flung the sheet aside, got out of bed, and began to gather her clothes, bumping against the bed table and letting out an "Oooh!" that was partly pain, partly exasperation.

"What are you doing?" Jeremy asked.

"I'm going to get dressed," she said, hopping on one foot, "and then I'm going home."

"Wait a minute," he said. "Wait a minute. Tell me one thing I said that isn't true. One thing."

"Not a word. Nothing," she said. "When the oracle speaks he utters only truth."

"Oh, come off it, Vicky!"

She was hugging her clothes to her, covering her nakedness. "Really, Jeremy! I'm beginning to wonder if this storm isn't a kind of smoke screen to hide what's really on your mind. I can understand your wanting to go to Moscow. It's a reward you've earned. I said as much. I think you have to go or you'll regret it. But you're feeling uncomfortable about us and you have to find some sort of justification for that, so you misread what I say. Jeremy, you should know by now that there isn't anything good for you that I wouldn't want. And just so you won't feel

227

guilty, let me say now that I won't stand in your way. . . ."
Her voice broke and she made a dash for the bathroom.

Outside the bathroom door, he shouted, "Sorry. I hadn't realized the entire misunderstanding was all my fault."

When Victoria came down the spiral staircase, heading for the hallway, Jeremy was standing, hands behind his back, looking out over the river. She picked up her coat. "Good night," she said. "I'm sorry."

"I'm sorry, too," he said almost inaudibly.

At the front door, her hand on the knob, she slumped in dejection, her forehead against the doorframe. "Jane dropped me off. I don't have a car."

"I'll go get Gridley," he said. "Won't take me a minute to get dressed."

"Why don't I just call a taxi," she said.

"Impossible," he called from halfway up the stairs. "Imagine *you* arriving at the palace in a taxi."

She wandered unhappily down the hall and sat on the sofa in the living-room, her trench coat folded on her lap, her handbag atop it; misery's model. Jeremy came clanging down the staircase, pulling on a New York *Mets* wind-breaker. "Back in five," he said, striding down the hallway.

Jeremy opened the front door: a sheet-lightning storm of flashbulbs. She saw him standing legs apart on the threshold, silhouetted against the popping lights. He stepped back, slamming the door closed. "That sonofabitch!" he said.

"What is it?" Victoria whispered.

"A creep by the name of Ossie Docherty. He's a reporter on the *Herald*. He's been snooping around for weeks." He slammed a fist into the kitchen door, sending it crashing against the wall. "He must know you're here."

"Oh, Jeremy!" she said, dismay in her voice.

Seeing the expression on her face he went to her, putting his arms about her. "I'm terribly sorry," he said.

228

"I've certainly mucked it up." He broke away, running up the hallway. "Quick! Turn off all the lights. I'll get the kitchen."

It was a minute or so before he returned. "There are five of them: Docherty, three photographers, and a woman. They've got a radio-phone in a news van parked outside. Docherty's on the phone talking to somebody. Probably his city desk." He checked the curtains, tugging them securely closed. "I wouldn't put it past the bastards to be out on the river."

Victoria essayed a smile. "Maybe I should call out the Horse Guards. Or the navy."

He smiled grimly. "I'm afraid, my darling, we are well and truly trapped."

"Oh my!" she said. "Oh *my!*"

"What is it?"

"I was just picturing tomorrow's headlines." She was silent a moment, pondering. "Maybe I should call Crimmie. He's the world's best fixer. Maybe he can do something."

Jeremy shook his head. "The one thing we must do is keep the palace out of it. If we can." He snapped his fingers. "Maybe we can wait them out. You could spend the night here, and tomorrow I'll go to the office, pretend everything's normal."

"Tomorrow's Saturday."

"Yes, of course," he said. "Damn! And it's just a matter of time until the other papers hear about it. We'll have a mob out there."

"Do you know the people upstairs?" she asked. "Are there any other women in the building?"

"There's a man and his wife above. The top floor's a bachelor."

"Maybe we could get the lady upstairs to join us here and then do a kind of diversionary thing. You drive off with her and I duck out later."

He made no response.

"It was just an idea," she added.

He slapped his hands against his thighs. "*Got* it!"

"What is it?" she cried. "What is it?"

He picked up the telephone. "Operator," he said, "would you give me the number for *The Famous Angel*. It's a pub on Bermondsey Wall East. . . ." He gave Victoria an extended wink. "Thank you, operator."

"Jeremy. . . . What in the world?"

He had finished dialing and held up a hand to silence her. "Mr. Cottingham, please." Another broad wink. "Cottie? Jeremy Walsh. . . . I'm fine, thanks. And you?. . . Cottie, as you may have noticed, we've got something of a problem over here and I was wondering if you might do something to help out. . . . They're newspaper reporters. The *Herald*. . . . Exactly. Cottie, how's the turnout tonight? Full house, I suppose?. . . Good. Now, Cottie, here's my problem: I have a lady with me here and those creeps outside are after her picture. You understand?. . . I knew you would. Now, I wonder if this would be possible? Could you tell your usuals that a friend of yours is in something of a jam. He's got an American movie star with him and they've been trapped by a bunch of paparazzi from – tell them from *Paris Match*, just for the hell of it – and that you'd like to help him out. Tell them anything that appeals to your fancy. What I have in mind is that a dozen or so of them might come along and act as a sort of diversionary force – you know, generally get in the way, and let me and my friend make a getaway in my car. . . . Lovely! Lovely!. . . Yes, say it's Joan Collins, if you like. Probably make me a local hero. . . . Right. I'll go fetch the car and drive by *The Angel* in about five minutes. I'll blink my lights as I go by. Cottie, you're a gem. Just for that I won't report you to the health department for selling moldy pretzels. See you in about five."

He put down the telephone and grinned at her. Even in the near darkness she could see the gleeful smile.

"You look like a cat with canary feathers sticking out of its mouth," she said.

He had a sudden inspiration and dashed to a closet. "Here we are!" he said triumphantly, placing a pair of glasses on her nose. She raised a hand and felt a celluloid nose with a brush of moustache beneath it. He guffawed, pleased with himself. "It's a pair of Groucho Marx spectacles left over from the Christmas office party. Got a kerchief?" She nodded. "Put it on your head, turn up the collar of your coat, and I'll be right back with the car."

In the darkened kitchen she peered through a gap in the drawn curtains. She saw Jeremy go off on a half-run in a storm of flashing lights, turning only once to shout something at a grotesquely obese man standing in the middle of the street. A woman in a trousers-suit and one of the photographers went off in pursuit. The fat man and the others moved in on the front door. Victoria shrank back to the far side of the kitchen. There was the sound of shouting and a loud banging on the door.

Now Jeremy was back with the car. He pulled to the curb, left the lights and engine running, and sauntered to the door. The staccato flashing reminded her of a stroboscopic film.

She was standing in the darkness of the hall. "Ready?" he asked.

"Aye, ready," she said, suddenly aware that she was trembling from head to foot and that her knees were weak.

"You're sure you're okay?" he asked, concerned.

She nodded.

"I love you," he said, and put a kiss on her lips.

From the front doors of *The Angel*, shouting and laughing as they came, a raucous, rag-tag crowd of perhaps forty revelers spilled into the street. As they marched raggedly down the street, some raised glasses of beer, others pumped arms up and down. A few had brought along metal serving trays and they banged them with spoons or with the heel of a hand. In the vanguard, prancing like an ungainly hackney, knees high, head back, a skinny little man pumped and pulled at a concertina.

Waltzing Matilda. Waltzing Matilda,
You'll come a-waltzing Matilda with me. . . .

The trays banged and the spoons clanged and the ale slopped onto the cobblestones. Boisterous, dissonant song jangled the night air.

And he sang as he watched
And waited till his billy boiled;
You'll come a-waltzing Matilda with me.

Now they had reached the flat and, as Jeremy and Victoria watched through the window, they flowed about Gridley like a hive of bees swarming, oozing in an uncoordinated fashion toward the front door of the flat. One of the marchers, a burly, bearded giant in a leather vest, seized Ossie Docherty about the waist and swung him around and around.

Waltzing Matilda. Waltzing Matilda,
You'll come a-waltzing Matilda with me. . . .

"Now!" Jeremy shouted, and flung open the front door. Crouching low, they scuttled along a path through the crowd that opened before them. Into the car they piled in a mad scramble, Victoria clambering over the console, glasses askew on her nose, and Jeremy plumping into the driver's seat. The photographers sighted with their cameras but upraised trays blocked lenses and bodies bumped and jostled. Jeremy revved the engine and leaned on the horn. The crowd parted like the sea and, tires smoking, the car sped off.

Ossie broke free of his involuntary dancing partner and ran toward the news van. But the crowd flowed about it, massing in front of it, blocking access to the doors.

Suddenly the man with the concertina changed the tune and dozens of voices roused the night:

Rule Britannia.
Britannia rules the waves. . . .

Crash-bang went the trays. Ring-a-ding-ding went the spoons. Raised aloft were the glasses.

Brit-tons never-ever-ever
Shall . . . be . . . slaves!

Despite the headlines, the story in the *Herald* was a damp squib, making only veiled references to "a royal," "a prominent American journalist," and "a love nest fit for a princess" on the bank of the Thames. Jeremy gutted the promised "sensational revelations" of the follow-up story with a telephone call to Ed Replogle.

"Replogle," he said, his voice crisply accented, "I think you should be clear on my intentions in this matter. We both know the laws of libel. We both know you can write virtually anything about a public figure, even a journalist, so long as two things obtain: first, your story must be true, and second – "

"Look here, Walsh, I don't need anybody to lecture me on – "

"And second, it must not demonstrate malice. Now, for reasons that aren't clear to me, your man Docherty has a personal grudge against me. His series on my pieces on Britain is demonstrably full of distortion. Then, last Friday – "

"Now hold on a minute – "

". . . he and four of your people harassed me in my home. I had a guest at the time, a young lady from the area – "

"From the area, hell!"

"And for reasons any juryman would understand, she did not want her picture in your newspaper and we had to call on some of her friends to help. Their rallying around should make it clear to you that references in your story to an anonymous royal were so much bilge water."

"Now, see here, Walsh – "

"Don't take my word for it, Replogle. Ask around. Docherty's a liar with an ax to grind. The two of you are going to end up in court."

"Look, Walsh – "

"That's all I have to say. One more word about me in that rag of yours and you'll be served with a writ."

♛ NINE

On July 18, 1944, during the Normandy invasion of France, the United States First Army, after fierce fighting in the easily defended "hedgerow country" south of Cherbourg, finally took the vital communications center of Saint-Lô. The city was virtually destroyed. During its reconstruction, a memorial bearing a bronze plaque had been erected. Before this plaque, decades later, on a humid July day, Princess Victoria stood with the Prime Minister of France and the Vice President of the United States as bands played and wreaths were placed and the Vice President made an emotion-laden speech. On the fringe of the crowd, wearing a driving cap and dark glasses, Jeremy Walsh watched but did not take notes.

Happily, July 18 had fallen on a Saturday and Victoria and Jeremy had laid plans to seize the opportunity to escape to the continent for a holiday. On the Friday afternoon, Jeremy had taken the ferry from Dover to Calais and driven Gridley to Deauville where he registered at L'Hôtel Auberge. Sunday morning he continued on to Saint-Lô where Victoria, all official obligations fulfilled, had slipped away from her entourage and her policemen. The two had made a rendezvous near the villa where the royal party was quartered.

"There's not going to be an all-points alert out for you?" Jeremy asked, putting the car in gear and nosing along the country lane. "You left a note for someone?"

Victoria nodded, smiling happily and removing the kerchief that covered her blonde wig. "I left a note for Billie, my Dresser, telling her I had a date with a dashing if somewhat disreputable fellow by the name of Henri Gridley and would be back tomorrow in time for the return to London." Looking in the visor mirror, she tugged and fussed with the wig, turning her head from side to side. "You certainly do keep company with some tarty-looking women," she said.

Jeremy threw his head back and burst out with a robust if occasionally off-key baritone:

> She had a dark and a roving eye-ay-ay
> And her hair hung down in ring-a-lets.
> She was a nice girl,
> A proper girl,
> But one of the roving kind.

They were both in high spirits, feeling loosened, free. But the weather proved contrary. As they passed through Bayeux and came in sight of the Bay of the Seine, long, dark rows of rolling clouds were moving in from the Channel and, as they skirted the coast, heading for Deauville, it began to rain: fat, heavy drops at first, smacking into the windshield, and then a deluge that slowed Gridley's progress and had Jeremy leaning forward, peering past the whacking windshield wipers through the downpour.

"It'll clear," he said. "I checked the forecast."

But it didn't.

Deauville, whose waterfront can dazzle in the sunlight, sat somber and sullen in the rain. The white casino, the pastel-toned bathhouses, the white and brown Normandy houses with their carved bargeboard eaves seemed lifeless and abandoned, as did the gray waves and the sweeping strand of dun-colored sand. Even the streets were deserted, and those venturing on them scurried heads down, hunched beneath umbrellas.

Their suite was lovely, but deathly cold: the groom who settled Jeremy in had opened a window to air the room but, hurrying off to meet Victoria, Jeremy had left it open. The polished floor was puddled and running and much of the carpet was wet. They busied themselves, mopping with bathtowels and hanging them to drip in the bathtub.

"It's just a a shower," Jeremy said, peering out of the window. "It'll clear."

When it didn't after an hour, he borrowed an umbrella from the concierge and dashed into the storm to buy two oversize oilskins and matching sou'westers, not thinking to get anything for their feet. It didn't matter; there was no going out. The rain became a lashing, tempestuous storm, rattling on the windows and penetrating with frigid fingers into their rooms. They bundled into bed, shivering, and made a nest of fragrant warmth.

"Hey!" Jeremy said, feigning delight. "Blondes *do* have more fun," and Victoria, simulating outrage, flung the wig across the room.

They decided that the dining-room, jammed with marooned tourists, would be too risky and ordered dinner in their suite. The kitchen, busier than usual, didn't do well and when, after more than an hour's delay, the food arrived, the soup was cold and the entrée and vegetables overcooked. But the baguette was fragrant and crisp, the cheeses were nippy, and the wine, a Moillard Mersault, was superb. So they called for another.

As it grew dark, the rain suddenly fell off and they decided they needed some fresh sea air. Enveloped in their capacious oilskins, the brim of Victoria's sou'wester pulled low over the blonde curls, they went quickly through the lobby and down a hill to the boardwalk, only to be driven back as the storm, having regrouped, suddenly launched another assault.

"It won't last," Victoria said. "I checked the forecast." He made as though to strike her, then put his arms about her and together they dripped ragged circles on the floor.

There was no place to get warm except in bed, and after soaking their feet in a hot tub and showering together, they raced in a wild melee and leaped beneath the covers where their loving was long and leisurely and sometimes sheer fun; with teasings and experiments and explorations, and with a culmination that was almost unbearable in its intensity. After which, even as Jeremy was doing a fair imitation of the Vice President's valiant but hilarious attempt at speaking French, Victoria fell asleep. He covered her bare shoulders, put the lightest of kisses on her lips, and, with the sounds of the driven rain against the windows, lay for an hour before sleep, his heart swollen with happiness.

Fog! A vaporous, motionless, enveloping, impenetrable grayness isolated them when, the following morning, they peered out of the window. From their third-floor room they couldn't even glimpse the street. Nor, as Jeremy went to fetch the car, could he see a hundred feet ahead.

"It'll lift as we head inland," he said.

They'd had the kitchen prepare a picnic lunch so that, driving at an easy pace, they might stop to eat en route and have Victoria back in Saint-Lô on time for the departure of the regal party for London. Because of the fog, Jeremy's mind was concentrated on the road and Victoria's attempts at conversation received only brief preoccupied responses.

But his weather prediction proved accurate; they slowly emerged from the fog ... into more rain, a soft misty rain that seemed to hang in the air and that wriggled snakelike across the windshield. At noon, for want of a better option, he pulled off to the side of the road and parked beneath an ancient, enormous oak. The chef had prepared a feast of tiny sandwiches, cold smoked meats, cheeses, and fruit, with strawberry tarts to surfeit them. And, of course, a bottle of wine. As Jeremy poured the claret into plastic glasses, he said, "I've been waiting for a chance to talk to you about a problem. Perhaps now's as good a time as any."

"Sounds important," she said lightly, glancing at him out of the corners of her eyes, sensing his change of mood.

"I had a phone call from New York yesterday as I was leaving the office. They're not happy about the delay in responding to the Moscow offer." He tilted his head, throwing back the wine. "They want a decision by next weekend."

Victoria was nibbling meditatively on a sliver of cheese. "Have you made up your mind?" Her voice betrayed nothing of her anxiety.

"Yes," he said, suddenly urgent, turning toward her and propping a knee on the console. "Darling, we're going to have to bring things to a head. If we don't move, Forster won't. I've studied him. He's either swiftly decisive or he'll postpone as long as possible, hoping some solution will present itself. With us, he'll wait things out, figuring we'll change our minds or simply give up. We've got to seize the moment or lose it."

"But how do we force his hand?"

"We put before him the proposal I worked out – you know, we get married but I remain plain old me. I've been taking some soundings among the political gurus and there's a pretty firm consensus – Forster's in trouble. He's got to go to the country soon and his polls are bad. He has all kinds of problems – the economy, unemployment – the last thing he needs is a constitutional brouhaha."

Victoria's face reflected her puzzlement. "But how does that work to our advantage?"

"You've already made it clear to him that you intend to get married. He's flat-out opposed. But if it's done my way, the legal and traditional problems will be more easily resolved and Forster – you can bet on it – will find a way to turn it to his advantage. I know it's a long shot, darling, but can you think of a better way?"

"Let's suppose he does say yes. What then?"

"Then I accept the Moscow posting. I come back to London for our wedding and you and I go off to the Soviet Union for a few years where we can keep each other warm while we make an heir to the throne."

The half-jocular tone disappeared as he leaned across to take her hand. "Darling, think: your mother's just past forty. English monarchs don't retire. We'll have grown children by the time the crown passes to you. In the meantime. . . ." There was pleading in his voice, "Let's buy some time, some happiness."

She was full of doubts. They discussed them on the remainder of the journey to Saint-Lô, and when he dropped her off beneath the *porte cochère* at the villa, she had agreed to speak to the Prime Minister.

She was able to arrange to see Forster the following Tuesday after his regular meeting with the Queen. His first reaction had been to avoid the session, but after a discussion with Chips Chippendale he'd decided to meet her in order to be able better to appraise her mood and her intentions. "You never know in a love affair," Chips had said. "One or the other may be cooling off."

Forster perceived immediately that Victoria was even more tense than she'd been at their previous meetings and read this as a good augury. Consequently, he was momentarily put off balance when, with few preliminaries, she presented Jeremy's proposal.

"I must say," Forster responded, "it *does* have the virtue of novelty." Begging time, he raised his empty cup. "May I?"

While Victoria attended to the tea, Forster, taking care to avoid any note of challenge in his voice, said, "I suppose my first question must again be: have you Her Majesty's permission?"

"No, Prime Minister," she said, "I haven't mentioned it to her." She passed him his tea, filled her own cup and sat down. "But you know and I know that if the government is opposed she'll have no option but to say no."

Forster nodded. "Then let me give you my immediate reaction: it would have no chance of acceptance in Parliament. Don't misunderstand me, there would be those who would welcome it. Mr. Blackstock and most of his front bench would like the sound of it. The Alliance? – hard to predict. I wouldn't be surprised if, after the initial shock passed, you found considerable backing from the general public. The press? . . . A split down the middle, I would think, with the more conservative journals opposed. It would be a rum go."

"And where would the Conservative party come down?"

Forster looked off, squinting his eyes, appraising. "Divided," he said. "Yes, divided."

"Then why would the idea have no chance in Parliament?"

"Because, Victoria – and I say this with all the good will in the world – I would feel required to fight it with such influence as I may have. And because, if Mr. Blackstock were, opportunistically, to champion your cause, he would make himself vulnerable. Even more important: suppose the proposal were to squeak through the House, it would be turned down by the Lords."

Victoria looked across at him, her eyes wide and unblinking. "I can't argue the political ramifications with you but it does seem to be a logical solution. The Protestant Succession remains secure. Jeremy will become Church of England. Our children will be raised in that discipline. As to his divorce: there have been so many divorces among royals in recent years that I can't see Jeremy's being regarded as scandalous. And wouldn't the fact that he's an American be a good thing? Wouldn't it strengthen what we like to call our special relationship with the United States?"

"I'm not entirely sanguine about that," Forster said with a wry smile. "Uncle Sam's not every Briton's favorite uncle."

"I wonder though, Prime Minister, if you haven't left out the most important part of the equation: namely, the alternative. Bluntly, and I don't mean to be unkind here, do you believe that anyone – Parliament, the press, the people, the Church – would accept poor sad Prince George as the heir? Or failing that, his daughter? What option do you have?"

Forster smiled at her; a tight, thin smile. "My dear Victoria, you wouldn't be trying to blackmail me?"

"Of course not," she said sharply. "I'm trying to deal with the realities. I've always believed that much of life consists of making choices and, in making those choices, choosing the lesser of evils. George or Alice would mean the end of the monarchy, and I don't think – to paraphrase one of your predecessors – you became Her Majesty's first minister to preside over the liquidation of the monarchy."

Forster seemed not to have heard her. He was preoccupied, looking down, rubbing his hands on the elaborately carved arms of his chair. "I've been wondering," he said, "what it would be like to have a Queen who reigned alone?"

"The woman I was named for did. For more than forty years."

Forster nodded. "Ah, yes, but her husband had died. You would *have* a husband, but he would be out there in the workaday world making a living." He glanced up at her. "Have you thought of the security problems that would lead to? Our enemies look for chinks of vulnerability. Why did the IRA murder Mountbatten? Wasn't it because he was close to the royal family and was vulnerable? You'll forgive my plain speaking, but Mr. Walsh would make a tempting target. For kidnappers! And I feel it my unpleasant duty to warn you, Ma'am, that were you to step down and become with your husband plain Mr. and Mrs. Jeremy Walsh, you and such children as you may have will be in constant jeopardy." He smiled wanly. "I'm sorry to raise such unhappy matters."

Now it was Victoria's turn to be silent, her thoughts skittering off in many directions. Forster was studying his hands which rested on his lap, the fingertips lightly touching. "Believe me, Victoria, I am truly caught between a rock and a hard place. It would please me to see you and the man you love married. I want your happiness. But I want also to see the monarchy, the institution, and all that it means and has meant, perpetuated. You must remember this: that for all its longevity, it's a very fragile thing. It has endured while other thrones have disappeared but, believe me, it too could be gone tomorrow. And if it were, would this nation ever be the same? And how will you feel if you are the cause of it?"

He paused, gathering his thoughts. "I would like you to understand my position. I've been chosen at this particularly precarious time in our history to serve as leader of our country. As such, I see quite clearly what the result will be if you renounce your right to the throne. My hope is that this very real danger will be at the forefront of your mind when finally you do make your decision."

He reached into his sleeve for a handkerchief and engaged in a vigorous blowing of his nose. "I am bound to tell you, my dear princess – and I say this with the deepest regret – that if you persist in your intention, I will have no option but to actively oppose you."

"Jeremy, I can't do it. I simply cannot do it."

They were in Jane Cavendish's flat. Jane had gone to the continent on a buying trip and had offered them the use of the flat. "For a love nest," she'd said. "Wasn't that the term they used in that ghastly piece in the paper? Sounds wonderful."

Victoria had been in despair since her meeting with Forster. He had shaken her by his appeal and by his manner. She had repeated his arguments to Jeremy but he had turned away in scorn before she was finished.

"Vicky, remember who you were talking to – one of the wiliest politicians this country has had in generations. He played you like a violin. Ah, yes, you will be personally responsible not only for the end of the monarchy but for the disintegration of England. And Jeremy will be in mortal danger, poor fellow. Not to speak of your children. And then, with tears in his eyes: I am bound to tell you, my dear princess – nice touch that! – that I will have to actively oppose you. Good god! The man should be writing for the films."

Nor was he content to drop the matter with Forster's refusal. As he paced the floor, fists clenched, brows beetled in concentration, Victoria retreated to the kitchen to put together some sandwiches and coffee. Not five minutes later he burst in on her, almost manic with excitement.

"I've got it!" he exulted.

He sat her on a kitchen stool and arranged another so that he was facing her. "Correct me if I'm wrong," he began. "Forster as much as admitted that we would have the support of most of the GBP – right? He said that Blackstock's people would probably be on our side, and some of the Alliance. And the popular press – right? And as I understood you, he even admitted that his own party would be divided."

"Well . . . yes. He also said, however, that even if it passed the House it would be vetoed by the Lords."

"The Lords are a fusty, archaic collection of upper-class nonentities," he snorted. "With a few exceptions they represent raw privilege, and their opposition might be the best thing that could happen."

He couldn't remain in the chair for his excitement. "Here's what we do," he said. "I'll have an off-the-record chat with Blackstock and sound him out. If Forster's right and the Opposition would be with us, and if we can pick up a few votes from the Alliance plus a few Tories, that could make for a majority in the House. It was obvious in his speech in the House that Blackstock knows something about us, so if he were to get up and say that he'd learned of our intention to get married and of my solution to the problem, he could move that the House express its approval. Then, if Forster opposes it but the motion carries, it could be taken as a vote of non-confidence. Forster would have to resign and ask the Queen to call an election."

"But Jeremy, you couldn't have a general election on whether or not we get married. It's unthinkable."

"Hear me out," he said, his eyes gleaming with excitement. "There wouldn't *be* an election. The House dissolved, Blackstock would be able to go to the Queen and ask her permission to try to form a government. It's one of the few real powers the palace has." Elated, he smacked a fist into a palm.

"Jeremy...."

"Yes?"

Her voice was small. "I couldn't do it."

"Why not?"

"First, because the royal family doesn't get involved in politics, and second – "

"But the royal family wouldn't be getting involved in politics. *I'm* certainly not a royal. What's your second reason?"

"Simply that I couldn't put my mother in a spot like that."

"How would you be putting her in a spot? It's her constitutional duty to ask whichever party can put together a workable majority to form the government. The situation wouldn't be any different than if, after an election, there was a tie and one party could make a reasonable argument that it was able to govern. That's what happened back in 1974, and the Queen called on Harold Wilson to form a government. In such cases, it's the sovereign's *duty* to decide."

"But this would be an entirely different situation. She'd have a conflict of interests. Her daughter's intentions would be the reason for the vote of confidence."

"It sounds to me like the normal operation of a constitutional monarchy," he said grumpily.

She shook her head. "I'm sorry. I couldn't do it. It would mean that the election would be fought in part over our marriage. It would divide the country."

"For goodness sake, Vicky, *whenever* we announce our intention it's going to lead to a division of opinion. We've always known that. There's got to be an election soon, and if you're not prepared to have it discussed, we'll have to hold off our announcement until after the election. And bear in mind what will happen if Forster is reelected. He'll refuse to go along with *anything* we suggest, and that will leave you no option but to forfeit the throne. Under pressure."

She shook her head. "I can't do it."

She returned to the sandwiches she had been making. He went back to the window, looking into the night. "What you really mean," he said, "is that you *won't* do it."

"No, Jeremy, that's not what I mean."

"Well, what am I to think?" He turned back into the room, his face inflamed with disappointment and anger. "I'll tell you what I do think; Forster's got you spooked. We've got him by the short hair so the wily old fox starts manipulating you. First he talks flag and country and sentiment. Then, about face, he's all piss and vinegar – he'll fight you on the beaches and all that guff. Vicky, if we're going to win this battle, we've got to fight him in the only way open to us: in *his* arena. But you say you can't do that, that you won't put your mother on the spot – which, as I've pointed out, you wouldn't be doing. All she'd be asked is to do her constitutional duty. She wouldn't be taking sides."

"But she'd appear to be."

"Nonsense. If Blackstock could demonstrate that he has the numbers to govern, it's her responsibililty to give him the chance."

"But Jeremy," she said, her voice pleading, "don't you see that the issue that has brought the question before her is her daughter's right to marry as she pleases?" She shook her head. "I'm sorry."

"You can't put your mother on the spot but you're willing to put us on the spot." There was bitterness in his voice. "I thought we were in agreement."

He went into the living-room. In a moment he was back, shrugging into his topcoat.

"Where are you going?" she asked.

"I don't know," he said dispiritedly. "I'm going for a walk. I've got to think."

He turned and was gone.

"Chips," said the Prime Minister, "let me try an idea on you for size."

The two men were in Forster's study at No. 10 Downing Street, feet up, jackets off, ties loosened, shirtcuffs rolled back, and drinks in hand. In a corner, an exquisite Whichcote long-case clock began to strike midnight and both Forster and Chippendale waited out the near minute of its solemn chiming.

"Damned if I know why I haven't pitched that ponderous thing out or put a mute on it," Forster said. "It's been here since Walpole. God knows what tales it could tell – except it would take all day to tell them. Never mind, it gave me a minute to shape my question. Subject: my conversation yesterday with Princess Victoria, about which I've already filled you in. Problem: she and Walsh are about to put pressure on us to approve their marriage on the basis of that ridiculous solution he's come up with. Proposal: that we go to the country before the whole thing blows up in our faces."

Chips took his time before responding, slowly revolving the glass in his hands. In the half-shadow his normally lugubrious face resembled a gargoyle's. "We're going to have to go soon at any rate," he said. "And by dissolving the House now we'd at least have good weather for the campaign."

"What in blazes kind of response is that?" Forster grunted. "My question is: facing the very real possibility of a constitutional crisis – which I need as much as I need

248

three thumbs – are we better to be in summer recess or on the hustings?"

Chippendale wasn't about to be hurried. "Let's begin by reminding ourselves that we have an outstanding promise to the House – namely, to bring forward the details on Princess Victoria Day come early autumn. If we go to the country and lose, we'd certainly be getting Blackstock off to a good start, handing him that prize."

Forster grinned. "You've given me an idea. We don't wait till October. We announce the plans immediately – say, on Friday. That will make points for us with the monarchists and certainly bring Walsh up short. I say Walsh because I'm certain he's the *éminence grise* behind Victoria. With the press full of plans for the celebration, it will hardly be the appropriate time for him to throw a spanner in the works."

Chips continued to peer into his glass. "I think everything is in hand. I'll ring up Cecil first thing tomorrow and double-check. Last time we talked everything was gung ho." He pursed his lips. "We might want to cut back on the estimates a bit – the cost is pretty steep. There's no need to give ammunition to the Opposition."

"Especially with the latest figures on unemployment." He shuddered. "You've seen them?"

"Pretty grim."

"They're to be released when?"

"Friday."

"Then perhaps we should make the announcement about PV Day on Thursday and move to dissolve on the heels of it."

"I would think we might."

Forster grinned mirthlessly. "In that way, neither Blackstock nor Walsh will have the House for a forum." The grin widened.

"You'll want to be ready. Blackstock will come out all guns blazing. You made quite a thing about delaying the announcement till the Throne Speech."

Forster's eyes glinted with the fire of battle. "Let him try. I'll cut him off at the knees."

"Mr. Speaker. . . ."

There was a rustle of sound in the House as Question Time began. The clock above the Speaker's Chair showed exactly 3:15. A few delinquent members bobbed the knee at the Bar of the House, made perfunctory bows toward the Speaker and slipped into their places. Others made their way to the galleries. The few final whispered conversations died.

"Mr. Speaker. . . ." Herbert Blackstock's resonant voice rang out in the chamber as the silence settled in. "Over a period of time one comes to expect the unexpected from this government. Not, I hasten to add, because of inspiration of thought or novelty of idea but rather because of a general fuzziness about goals and a certain muddle-headedness of intention."

There were murmurs of approval from the members behind him.

"But enough of that. I do not ask your concurrence, Mr. Speaker, but I would presume that you are as astonished as we are on this side of the House by the actions of the Prime Minister. You will recall how, not many days ago, he announced that the celebration of Princess Victoria Day would be observed next June 30. When questioned here about the date and the details, he began to obfuscate. One could not, try as one might, elicit from him anything of substance. Then, suddenly reversing himself, flying in the face of the reasons he had just given, we were informed that his earlier reluctance stemmed from a desire to have the announcement made, and I quote, 'in ideal circumstances and at the proper time.' And more, 'from the most appropriate source,' namely her Majesty the Queen."

"Hear! Hear!" from the government benches.

"Well and good. It seemed at that moment a not unreasonable if belated response. But we come now to the present moment and we find that that which only days ago was 'ideal' and 'proper' and 'appropriate' no longer is. Today, without warning, a bill is tabled detailing plans for the celebration. The question is, of course: why this sudden reversal? Are we to take it that, once again, the Prime Minister has changed his mind, and that he no longer regards Her Majesty as 'ideal' or 'appropriate' for the task?"

There were cries of "Shame," but even they were swept away in the thundering roar of disapproval. When finally order was restored, the Speaker, standing in his place, said, "I shall take it that in his zeal the Right Honorable gentleman did not intend what he seemed to imply and would ask him if he is now ready to state his question?"

Blackstock placed his hands on his hips as though sweeping back a gown, thus betraying his origins as a barrister. "My question, Mr. Speaker, is this: what is the government's reason for moving forward from this autumn to today the introduction of the necessary legislation? One cannot but wonder if it is that he wishes to divert the attention of the public on the eve of the release of the new unemployment figures? If that be so, what a cynical and cruel smoke-screen!" His voice rose to thunder. "What an unconscionable act of self-serving flimflammery."

In the ensuing uproar, Forster moved to the dispatch boxes. He had no notes in hand and seemed in a high good humor. The tumult subsided and then fell away.

"Mr. Speaker. . . ." His voice was warm, his manner avuncular. "When we last touched on the subject of Princess Victoria Day, the leader of the Opposition made an enormous fuss about, 'Where's the bill?' Well, the answer to his question is. . . ." He pointed with an outthrust forefinger at the clerk's table, "*There!* There, where all bills rest when they are tabled in this House. There! – on the clerk's table.

"But," Forster continued, his voice mocking, "now that he has his answer, is he satisfied? Of course not. First, he is all for a celebration. Then he takes umbrage when preliminary intimations are given to the press. Then he demands that a date be given here. Right here! *Right this minute!* And such was his foot-stamping petulance that, to pacify him, I reluctantly specified the time and the place. But now, now that the date has been moved forward, is he satisfied? As they say within earshot of Bow Bells, 'Not bloody likely!' One wonders, will anything please this man?"

"Hear! Hear!"

"But to be responsive to his question. The bill has been introduced today for one reason: because of the government's growing concern that participation in the celebration be open to all the people of Britain, and not only to them but to all the people of the Commonwealth as well. We are anxious on this side that anyone, anywhere, who wishes to participate in any way be given ample opportunity to plan to do so. Thus, today's date.

"Now," he continued, a look of patient resignation on his face, "I await only the Right Honorable gentleman's predictable supplementary question, in which he will seek to play off one segment of the population against the rest by raising niggling quibbles about the cost."

He turned toward his seat, but before Blackstock could rise, stepped again to the table.

"Mr. Speaker, if I am not out of order . . . I should like, before I sit down, to present a motion in this House. I move, seconded by the Honorable Member from Taunton, that this House herewith be dissolved."

Pandemonium.

*   *   *

"Mr. Forster," the Queen said sternly, "cliché though it may be, I cannot resist saying it: I am not amused."

Immediately following Question Time, Forster had rung up Angus McCrimmon to ask if he might drop by the palace to have a word with the Queen. "A word of explanation," he'd said, "for what may have seemed a precipitate action." Crimmie had conveyed the message to a woman coldly angry. "He seems quite contrite, Ma'am. It was obvious in the few words we had that he realizes his action was presumptuous." There being no response, he added, "I would suggest that you see him."

Forster's head was down as Mary continued. "Awaiting your arrival," she was saying, "I took a moment to turn up a few pages in Walter Bagehot's *English Constitution*. He is, I've been given to understand, your favorite historian." Forster nodded. "Among the rights of a sovereign in a constitutional monarchy, Bagehot states – and I quote – 'are the right to be consulted, the right to encourage, the right to warn.' You would not disagree with that?"

"No, Ma'am, I would not."

"I must ask you then for an explanation. You have dissolved Parliament and have announced the details of a celebration of my daughter's birthday without either consulting me or giving me the opportunity to advise you. I consider what you have done to be an act of the most extreme discourtesy."

Forster's demeanor was close to sycophancy. "I wonder, Ma'am, if I might offer an explanation as to why I took the actions I did?"

"No, Prime Minister, you may not," she said icily. "I can imagine a circumstance of such urgency that you might feel required to move the dissolution of the House without being able to communicate with me in advance, but I am aware of no such emergency. Beyond that, what possible reason could there be for tabling a bill that has been weeks and months in the planning without giving either me or my daughter prior notice?"

"Your Majesty, if you will allow me – "

"Good afternoon, Prime Minister," Mary said, rising from her chair.

Forster rose, bowed, and took three backward steps. In the corridor on his way to the lift, he gave a small shrug of his shoulders.

They had quarreled like this too often lately, so often that Victoria had come to wonder if they wanted the quarrels, needed them, were each using them as a way out. It could happen, she knew that. You could want something very much and at the same time, contrary to everything you felt, almost have a need to thrust it away.

That consciously she wanted Jeremy close she had no doubt. When his assignments took him away from her or her duties took her away from him, she longed for him with the obsessive single-mindedness of an addict for a drug. Even as she nodded and smiled and shook hands and said all the vapid mandatory things expected of her during her public appearances, his memory intruded. At the heart of a solemn ceremony, even as she read the words prepared for her, a large part of her mind dwelt on him; on his face, on his touch, on his hard body against hers. . . .

And yet so often in recent days when they were together in Jane's flat, with the door locked and bolted, the telephone off the cradle, and the heavy velvet curtains tightly drawn, there would be, as the evening went on, something said or left unsaid or misunderstood or bridled at, and a somber, awkward alienation would suddenly mock their nearness and, worst of all, conspire to keep them from easing the tension between them with the balm of their lovemaking.

She was in the kitchen making all the familiar noises, doing all the familiar things. Jeremy was in the living-room, reading and underlining with a highlighter a thick, austere-lookng book. How many times had they put together meals from take-outs or odds and ends from the refrigerator or delicacies carefully packed by the palace kitchen? She was thinking: what is there in this? For him? For me? For all our playing house, for all the passion that flashes fitfully through us as in a distant storm, for all the times when we have each seemed to the other to be the beginning and the end and all of life, is there any hope? Is it all ending as the fond dream of fools?

She had decided that when next the distancing between them came she would risk getting the whole thing out in the open. So now, with the supper growing cold on their plates and unaccountable lulls in their conversation, she looked across the table at him. "Jeremy," she said, her voice sounding foreign to her, "what's happening to us?"

His eyes were on his plate, but he flicked a glance at her. "What do you mean, what's happening to us?"

She should have begun better than that, but the problem was to say what needed to be said in a way that wouldn't be challenging or be misinterpreted. "Sorry," she said. "Let me try again." Inwardly she cursed the iciness she heard in her voice. "For the past few days – it's going on weeks, actually – we seem to be at odds much of the time. And I don't know why. I was wondering if perhaps you did."

Again he gave her that quick look from the corners of his eyes, as though assessing her mood. "I've been thinking about it, too," he said, his voice dispirited and almost inaudible, his eyes on his fork as he filled it again and again without bringing it to his mouth. "And I've been wondering if we're not both trying to tell each other something, not knowing quite how."

"Trying to tell each other what?" she said, knowing the answer but knowing that it was better to face it than to have it lie between them like some foul beast that might rear up without warning. When he didn't respond and continued to push the food around on his plate, she said, "Jeremy, darling, let's both try to get said whatever it is that needs saying. We can't go on the way we've been for the past few days. It's too painful."

He pushed his chair back suddenly and, hands plunged deep in his pockets, began to stride back and forth. "I don't know what to say," he said. "I've been thinking about it, worrying about it so much that I can't sleep and my work's gone all to hell." He strode on. "It was that son-of-a-bitch Forster who drove the last nail in the coffin."

"Can we really blame Mr. Forster?"

"Who else? At least there was some hope before he moved to dissolve Parliament. What can we do now?"

"Are you saying there is no hope?"

He pivoted to face her. "I'm beginning to wonder if what's between us isn't foredoomed. I think perhaps that . . . the sense of alienation we've been feeling is the rational part of us saying, 'Face it. For all your dreaming, in the *real* world, the future Queen of England doesn't marry a divorced, Polish-American, Catholic, commoner news-paperman.' Tell the truth, could there be anything worse?"

Her face and voice were expressionless. "You could be the head of the IRA."

"Not funny," he said, returning to his pacing.

An acute sense of desolation descended. Her heart seemed to swell until it filled her chest. A flutter of panic ran through her and she suddenly felt cold. She gathered herself; she must think. They must talk it out. They must deal with what they were feeling, but equally important with the realities that were crushing the life out of the love they felt for each other. It was dangerous, but she must ask him some of the hard questions. She began to gather the knives and forks, preparing to remove them to the kitchen.

"Darling," she said, "can you talk to me with absolute openness about your work? It's not possible, is it, for you to turn down the posting to Moscow? I can understand how it wouldn't be."

She had been afraid that he might react adversely to the question, but instead he returned to the table and sat opposite her, reaching across to take one of her hands. "Let me try to explain to you how it is," he said earnestly. "You set your sights on something and you work your butt off trying to achieve it, not expecting anything for years. And then, out of the blue the door opens. The fact is, the job shouldn't come to someone like me, at least not yet. There are half a dozen men, older men, more experienced men than I am, but they've offered it to me. And I think I can handle it. To turn it down would finish me at the *Times*. It would say something about my commitment. I'd dared to hope that somehow you and I could work things out, that I could keep on being me and you could keep on being you and that we could get married and you could join me in Moscow. I had this picture in my mind of the two of us together during all the years before you would have to take the throne. Times change, I told myself, attitudes change, governments change. People can get used to anything and perhaps they could accommodate even to us. I've been trying to believe that, but I'm afraid I no longer can."

She felt her heart pounding. "So what do we do?"

He shook his head, almost as a swimmer might, surfacing after a dive. "I don't know."

She looked at him across the table. It was there to be read; he had given up hope. It was there even in the way he was sitting, turned half away, an elbow on the table, his head down. She had been about to tell him that she was ready to marry him and, when the moment was right, follow him to Moscow. It hadn't been a precipitate decision; it was where she'd been weeks ago when they had faced up to their final options. But with all the complications, she'd lost sight of it for a while and had, only this morning as the sun was rising, decided that her earlier instincts had been right. She'd reviewed all the judgements that would be made about her: that she had shirked her duty, that she had let down the side, that she had, for selfish reasons, put the monarchy in jeopardy, even that she had betrayed her country. They would say all that and more. But if a nation's institutions could be toppled by the decision of a girl of twenty, what was their worth? She was asking no more than any normal woman would: the right to love, the right to open her life entirely to someone else, and as the result of that commitment to create another life. Yes, she could do as she was told and there would be many to tell her what a good and obedient and dutiful child she was and then go off to their own concerns, leaving her with her hedged-about, circumscribed, empty world. "No!" she had cried out. They had made do once before when someone in circumstances not unlike hers had said he would not go on without the woman he loved by his side. They could manage again.

But now as she looked across the table at Jeremy, a line from a poem sounded in her mind: "The center will not hold. Mere anarchy is loosed upon the world." There he was, the heart of her hopes, the strength she had counted on, with his head down and his tongue stilled.

"So what do we do?" she repeated insistently. "What do we do now?"

He looked up, surprised at her tone. "What is there to be done?" he said, turning his palms outward in a shrug of impotence. "Forster's made it impossible to put forward my plan. You aren't prepared to put your mother on the spot. I'm being bugged to make a decision. . . ." Again he left his thought hanging.

"Then I don't suppose there's anything to do but say good-bye." Her voice sounded matter of fact.

He looked at her fixedly. "Maybe I'm misreading you, but I get the feeling that you think it's my fault."

She was gathering the dishes, piling plate on plate recklessly. A knife fell to the floor but she didn't retrieve it. "It's not anybody's *fault*. It's just the way things are. The way *we* are. You have to do what you think is best, and apparently you've worked it out in your mind that. . . ." She stopped, not certain that she could trust her voice. She picked up the dishes and went to the kitchen. He followed, remaining in the doorway.

His voice betrayed some irritability. "You said I'd worked it out in my mind to do something, but you didn't say what."

"I'm not sure what," she said, scraping the food into a garbage bin. "Except that, I take it, it's time to call it quits."

"You make it sound as though that's what I want, and that's hardly fair. No one knows better than you how I've tried to find solutions. It's just that now, belatedly, I've come to the conclusion that we're beating our heads against a wall."

She wasn't going to give him anything. "Well, then, there's little further to be said." She was conscious that he was staring at her. "You could at least have waited another few weeks."

"What difference would a few weeks make?"

"The election would be over. Labor might win. Some of the polls say so. You said yourself that you might have a talk with Mr. Blackstock."

"That was before Forster called the election. It wouldn't work now. He's not going to put his neck in the wringer."

"You thought he might."

"Not now. He's a politician. He won't want anything to muddy the waters."

She picked up a tray and went past him into the dining-room to pick up more dishes. Passing in the doorway she took care not to touch him. When she realized what she'd done she was suddenly close to tears. Damn tears! They change the character of a conversation. Men read tears as weakness and are embarrassed by them, or they see them as an attempt to play on their own weakness and resent it. She set her jaw: there would be no weeping.

Back in the kichen, she asked. "When do you leave?"

He hesitated. "Friday."

She turned toward him, putting the tray on the countertop. "But that's the day after tomorrow."

"I know, I know, I know," he said dejectedly, leaning against the door frame, moving the toe of a shoe from one square to another on the linoleum.

She was filled with a rush of despair rimmed with anger. "When was that decided?"

"This afternoon. On the phone with Jack Patterson in New York. He simply insisted on an answer – yes or no. Vicky, I've been stalling them for *weeks*." He saw the stricken look in her eyes and a note of pleading entered his voice. "Darling, I had no option. The publisher is having a small supper for the new ambassador to the Soviet Union and he feels that it's imperative that I meet him." He went back to tracing the pattern of the linoleum. "There'll be a month to six weeks in New York and Washington, and then a week to ten days here to pass over the reins."

There was that frightening pounding of her heart again. She put her hands behind her and leaned on the countertop for support. "Jeremy," she said, "I love you. Is this all the chance I get to say good-bye?" She shook her head in disbelief. "The day after tomorrow. . . . And you don't tell me till now?"

"I didn't know myself until this afternoon."

"But, I'm in Birmingham and Worcester tomorrow. I won't be back until midnight. When do you leave Friday?"

"Early, I'm afraid."

She was shaking her head slowly, a dazed look on her face. "They couldn't wait a week. You couldn't tell them there are some loose ends to tidy up. . . . Like saying good-bye to an old friend," she added with a touch of bitterness.

"Darling, I've stalled as long as I can."

She turned to the sink and aimlessly began to run water over one of the dishes. She closed her eyes, and with her back to him, the tears came. She let them fall, scrubbing mechanically with a brush at the dish in her hands. Her emotions were in tumult. She wanted to turn, to run into his arms, to crush herself against him, to pull herself within him, but there was an anger and a resentment that forbade it. He had no right to do this to her. Were all their days and weeks and months together to be cast aside because of a silly little supper for a bureaucrat? It was a courtesy thing. A ceremonial thing. She'd been a part of dozens of them. Nothing ever happened; they were matters of form. They stroked the egos of people of importance. And for *that* he would have stolen from her the chance for a decent farewell.

It was Jeremy's fault; he could have said no. She could understand that it would be difficult to delay his decision much longer, but he could have told them yes and then requested more time before leaving. If they wanted him all that much they would agree. She had to concede that at this point things did look hopeless, but who could predict what might happen given more time? Why then had he agreed without argument or laying down conditions of his own? The anger began to rise again.

Jeremy went to her, put his arms about her and pressed his lips to the top of her head. "Don't you think you might have that dish clean by now?"

But she would not be so easily humored. "I want to go back to what I asked you earlier. Is this good-bye?"

"Of course it's not," he said, tightening his arms about her. "We can stay the night here and you can go with me to the plane on Friday."

"No, we can't," she said. "I'm having breakfast with the Lord Mayor at eight about my damned birthday."

"Couldn't you postpone it?"

She turned on him. "Couldn't *I* postpone it! Couldn't *you* postpone your meeting with your silly ambassador? And while we're at it, why didn't you let me know you'd made your decision on Moscow? Why am I the last to know?"

"Vicky, darling, hold on a minute. It wasn't planned that way, it just happened. I'm not the enemy. I'm the guy who loves you and was hoping to marry you."

"Was hoping," she said hotly. "Past tense! Now the picture's coming clear – it's already over in your mind. Hoping to marry me, yes, until it became inconvenient. Until – "

"Vicky, stop it!"

"Until it came to a choice between me and your work. Until – "

"Will you stop it!" he shouted. "Stop it right now!"

"Yes, I'll stop it," she cried. "Right now. Officially. Forever!"

She flung out of the kitchen, running to the bedroom, slamming the door behind her, throwing herself on the bed, and cupping a hand over her mouth so that the sound of her sobbing wouldn't be audible. But even as she did, she listened for any sound that would tell her what he was doing. All was silence. Then, after a few minutes, she heard the front door open and close and, faintly, the sound of footsteps in the hallway. The lift whined. The whine grew louder and ended with a thump. There was the distant clash of metal as the door opened and closed. The whine began again and faded. And then there was no sound save the occasional spasmodic intake of her breath.

After Jeremy's phone call, Ed Replogle had taken Ossie Docherty off the story and Ossie had reacted by going on an eating binge. Within a week he had put on fifteen pounds. He devoured cakes and pastries, wolfed down chocolates and sweets, scoffed double orders of fish and chips. A long-time preference for cream buns became an addiction. On the way home for dinner he took to dropping in at a Wendy's take-out, ordering two Whoppers and a double coke. Before dinner he polished off a bowlful of potato crisps, washing them down with a pint of ale. When he couldn't sleep he made midnight raids on the refrigerator. As well, the tumult in Ossie's mind made him more restless in bed and Alfie's dreams came to be filled with trampolines and storms at sea.

Finally, he objected. "Instead of bouncin' about like a bleedin' grampus, and makin' me ready to flip me biscuit, why don't you *do* somethin' about it?" he demanded.

"Don't think I'm not working on it," Ossie said.

And he was. To hell with Replogle, he would run down the story on his own. His first thought had been to keep track of Victoria and thus catch the two of them together when they met. In contemplating it, the task didn't seem too formidable. It wouldn't be necessary to monitor her through the day; her official engagements were published daily in the *Court Circular*. All he'd have to do would be to shadow her after her public responsibilities had been fulfilled. But as he soon realized, her appointments often took her out of the city and it was impossible to anticipate either the time or the means of her return. She might arrive at the palace by limousine, driving her own car, or even by helicopter – she, an accomplished pilot, more often than not at the controls. Even tracking her in the city was difficult. She was invariably accompanied by her personal policeman who spent much of his time keeping a sharp watch on the traffic following. On official journeys she was preceded and followed by unmarked police cars.

Instead, he would keep track of Jeremy. It soon became evident that Jeremy was not spending his evenings at the flat. On the night that had subsequently become renowned in some parts of Bermondsey as "The night we formed *The Famous Angel Marching Band*," one of Ossie's fellow reporters had located the garage in which Jeremy parked his car. Ossie made an arrangement with his friend Tim Finnegan to check it each night on his way home from work, but it had proved to be of no help; the car was never removed. It suddenly dawned: "They've got a new rendezvous. I'll have to follow Jeremy from his office."

He badgered Alfie into taking a drink each late afternoon at a bar named *Dizzy's*, not fifty yards from the entrance to the *Times'* offices at 76 Shoe Lane. Alfie, who was happiest when life was routine and unhappy when not at home in his kitchen, argued against the assignment.

"You want me to sit there like a bleedin' boozer, nursin' a drink and lettin' on I've been stood up by me bird! Is that it?"

"What do you care?" Ossie said. "Just sit where you've got a view of the entrance and keep an eye peeled. Mind you don't run up a big bar tab, and pay for your drink when you get it so you can skedaddle out of there fast when the time comes. And have a taxi standing by."

"An' what do I do for me supper? It's nothin' to you – you'd eat your bleedin' shirt cuffs – but I like a good home-cooked meal, not sittin' in some fancy bar listenin' to me bowels growl."

As it happened, Alfie's indenture wasn't for long. On the second night, Jeremy emerged from the Press Center and paused on the corner until his driver came by with the car. By the stop light at Fleet Street, Alfie's cab was tucked in behind.

"It was a doddle," Alfie reported. "I follow 'im to Park Street, couple of blocks from Grosvenor Square – you know, where all the bleedin' embassies is. Dolphin 'ouse is the name of the apartment. Very posh. 'A Mayfair address wiv a Park view' it says on the sign out front. An' right beside it, a gold fountain wiv a bleedin' dolphin spittin' at the sky. A lobby you could 'old the bleedin' Olympics in. Your Mr. Walsh is a sly one. 'is driver drops 'im at the side door where the deliveries go in. There's a service lift there with nobody to see 'oo comes or goes. After which, 'is driver 'angs about until a parkin' space opens up and leaves the car. I 'ang about myself, and 'oo else arrives? – 'er Royal bleedin' 'ighness, that's 'oo. I nip inside for a look-see and notice the lift stops at the top floor. There's a list of everybody what lives in the place and 'ere's the names on the top floor. And you owe me one pound, fifteen."

Ossie handed Alfie his wallet and Alfie extracted the money as Ossie scanned the paper. "Jane Cavendish!" he shouted. "Alfie, you're a doll." Alfie passed it off as nothing, but his face was pink with pleasure.

Then began a nightly vigil at the Dolphin House, with Ossie down the street in his parked car. The lovers had arrived four of the next five nights, separately and at various times. Ossie had hired a freelance photographer, a nondescript man whose equipment included an attaché case fitted out with a concealed camera that could take photographs through an opening at one end, the shutter triggered by pressure applied to the handle of the case.

On the fifth day, Ossie, all avuncular affability, entered the lobby in the afternoon and inquired after Miss Cavendish. "My niece," he explained, emanating heartiness. "She's been away, I know, but I was around the corner at the United States embassy and thought I'd pop in on the off chance she was back."

It wasn't difficult to elicit the information that Miss Cavendish was away on the continent.

"I wonder then if I might leave a note for her?" Ossie said.

The concierge produced a piece of stationery and an envelope. Out of view, Ossie scribbled a meaningless scrawl and sealed it in the envelope, addressing it only to "Dear Jane."

"Would you be good enough to give this to Miss Cavendish on her return," he asked. "And would you tell her that her Uncle Trevor dropped by and that I'll ring her up first of the week. It's Sunday she's back, isn't it?"

"Sunday night," he was told, and went off jaunty and pleased with himself.

Jeremy gone, Victoria had rolled onto her back and lain motionless on the bed, the tears gathering in the wells of her eyes and running unnoticed down her cheeks and into her hair. It was over. All over. Her brain seemed drugged and she had the feeling of being enveloped in a sea of enormous sadness.

She may have slept for a moment, or more – there was no way of knowing – but suddenly she came alert. There! Yes, the whine of the lift ascending. Jeremy was coming back! Of course he was; how foolish of her to have thought even for a moment that he wouldn't. She heard the clash of metal as the door to the lift opened and the sound of footsteps coming down the hall. "Jeremy!"

She leaped from the bed. The tears wet on her face and her hair askew, she flew from the bedroom. Her heart leaped as she saw the door handle turn and heard the gentle knock. Quickly she opened the lock and threw open the door, her arms outstretched.

"Jeremy!"

Three blinding flashes in swift succession dazed her and sent her reeling back. Dimly, beyond the overlapping circles of pale blue light, she saw two men: one an enormous hulking figure and another with a camera before his face, the light flashing. . . .

♛ TEN

THE STORY BROKE ON THE WEEKEND. The front page of the Sunday *Herald* bore the headline in bold black type:

WORLD EXCLUSIVE
PRINCESS VICKY'S
STEAMY ROMANCE
WITH YANK NEWSMAN

Most of the front page was devoted to a blown-up photograph of Victoria's face, her eyes wide and staring, her hair disheveled, her mouth open. It carried the caption: *HRH Princess Victoria registers surprise at the doorway to her hideaway love nest at Dolphin House where she and American reporter, Jeremy Walsh, have met secretly in lovers' trysts.*

Pages two and three were given over entirely to a world copyrighted double-truck spread under the headline:

MARRIAGE IN THE WIND?
OUR VICKY'S LOVE AFFAIR WITH DIVORCED
AMERICAN POSES THREAT TO THE MONARCHY

The facing pages were highlighted by a photograph of Victoria, clearly identifiable despite the dark glasses and the scarf covering her head, slipping through the Service Entrance at Dolphin House, and bearing the caption: *Britain's future Queen on way to secret rendezvous.* There were two smaller

268

pictures of Jeremy; one of which showed him with fist upraised and fury on his face outside the front door to 44 Rotherhithe Street.

The story carried a by-line in 14-point bold type: BY OSWALD STEARMAN DOCHERTY.

Her Royal Highness, Princess Victoria, Britain's heiress-presumptive, has been involved for the past eight months or more in a torrid love affair with the *New York Times'* London Correspondent, Jeremy Walsh, a passionate and clandestine relationship that Buckingham Palace and 10 Downing Street fear may pose a threat to the throne.

Walsh, 28, a Polish-American Roman Catholic, is divorced and the father of a five-year-old girl who lives with her mother in New York City.

Princess Victoria, whose 21st birthday will be celebrated next June with an elaborate and costly day of Commonwealth-wide festivities, has been a regular late-night visitor at Walsh's bohemian-style flat at 44 Rotherhithe Street in Bermondsey, a romantic ultra-modern hideaway on the south bank of the Thames.

Their hush-hush retreat, having been discovered by the *Herald*, the runaway lovers have for the past two weeks changed their place of romantic rendezvous to a penthouse flat at posh Dolphin House on Park Street in fashionable Mayfair.

The flat is owned by Miss Jane Cavendish, a former classmate and longtime friend of Princess Victoria and the owner of a chain of exclusive high-priced antique shops in London and abroad.

Cavendish made the flat available to the royal lovers during a two-week absence on the continent.

Last week, the Princess and her American lover spent four of five evenings alone in the flat, on three of those evenings not leaving until after midnight.

Wednesday evening they spent the night together and were observed leaving separately at 6:43 and 7:18 a.m. respectively.

Their sizzling love affair has been one of Buckingham Palace's best-kept secrets but has not gone unnoticed.

On the evening of July 12 last, a group of approximately 40 people from the neighborhood gathered outside Walsh's Rotherhithe Street flat in hope of catching a glimpse of the royal lovers.

The Princess, wearing a disguise, made her escape in Walsh's car.

Her Royal Highness, who has heretofore appeared to be the model of propriety, has sometimes seemed indifferent to the risk of having her open affection for her divorced American boyfriend publicly observed.

Walsh has been a frequent weekend guest at Windsor Castle and at Buckingham Palace garden parties.

Even more flagrant has been her and Walsh's behavior in the confines of his flat.

Boat traffic on the Thames has from time to time had an unobstructed view through Walsh's picture window of the living-room where the young couple have frequently shared intimate suppers and more, attired in nothing but matching bathrobes.

It is reliably reported that the lovers have seriously discussed marriage.

The possibility has shaken both the palace and the Prime Minister's office. Neither Grady Hamilton, press secretary at the palace, nor Mr. Forster's press liaison officer would comment.

Under the Act of Succession, Princess Victoria may not marry without the Queen's permission until she reaches the age of 25.

It is highly unlikely that the Queen's permission would be granted, Walsh being a Roman Catholic and divorced and the Queen being titular head of the Church of England.

Even if she were to approve, experts on Britain's constitutional law concur in the opinion that Parliament would withhold consent.

When the question was put to a highly placed spokesman in the office of the Archbishop of Canterbury, the response was, "Impossible. Unthinkable."

But divorce is not Walsh's only problem. He is an American citizen and would be required to become a naturalized British subject before Victoria would be permitted to marry him.

Those who know him (one of whom described him as "terribly ambitious") believe such a renunciation is unlikely.

Usually reliable sources say that there has been an extraordinary difference of opinion between the palace and the Prime Minister's office about Princess Victoria's attachment to Walsh and her apparent desire to marry him.

Rumors are rife at Westminster that this was the reason for Prime Minister Forster's recent about-face on the introduction of the bill authorizing the celebration of Victoria's 21st birthday.

Insiders report that Forster demanded guarantees from the palace that there would be no marriage.

But, apart from their plans, there can be no doubt that Princess Vicky and her American lover are involved in a sizzling affair. Here is the schedule of their meetings in the past week:

Sunday: 6:23 p.m. HRH arrives at Dolphin House in black chauffeur-driven Daimler, license number RPS-176. Enters apartment through Service Entrance and takes lift to eighth floor. Walsh arrives 6:47 p.m. in lease-hire Mercedes, licence marker UYR-316S. Enters through Service Entrance. Lights out in Number 801 (the Cavendish flat) 9:43. Lights on 12:03 a.m. Walsh departs 12:27, hailing taxi at intersection Mount Street and Park Lane. HRH departs 12:33. Her car waiting outside Service Entrance.

Monday: HRH arrives at Cavendish flat 4:31 p.m., coming directly from opening ceremony at Heatherstone Delinquent Children's Home, of which she is patron. Walsh arrives at 8:48 p.m., having attended the Conservative Party's Greater London Rally at Albert Hall. Both parties leave within ten minutes of each other shortly after 6:45 a.m., Tuesday.

Wednesday: HRH arrives at Cavendish flat 5:17 p.m. Walsh arrives twelve minutes later. HRH and Walsh observed at 9:19 p.m., arms about each other's waist, on landing at top of fire escape leading from Cavendish flat, apparently taking the air. Lights out at 10:01 p.m. Lights on again at 11:44. Walsh leaves at. . . .

Jeremy first learned of the *Herald*'s story on his arrival at New York's Kennedy airport. As he emerged from the Customs and Immigration area, he was surprised to see Tom Hammersmith, the assistant city editor at the *Times*, waiting for him. In a limousine heading for the city, Hammersmith showed him a copy of the story and, pulling from his briefcase carbons of the stories by UPI and *Reuters*, told him that it had been picked up by the various wire services. Jeremy, a bleak look on his face, read them as the limousine, heading for the city, found itself stalled in the morning commuter traffic.

In his room at the Park Lane hotel he placed a telephone call to Buckingham Palace and gave the switchboard operator his name. "I'm sorry, Mr. Walsh," the operator said, "Her Royal Highness is not accepting calls."

"Dammit!" he shouted. "Tell her who's calling. *Do it, woman!*"

He stayed on the line, pacing at the end of the cord for ten minutes. He hadn't realized that Ossie's photographer had arrived at the flat only minutes after he had left that night. When Victoria had stormed into the bedroom he had remained in the kitchen for a few minutes, feeling an admixture of anger and umbrage and guilt. When she didn't reappear, he had decided to go for a walk in the evening air to cool his head and to try to regain his perspective.

The night had been chill and dark, with layered gray clouds at treetop height. He had turned up the collar of his jacket and plunged his hands deep in his pockets. His predominant emotion soon became concern. He saw Victoria in the bedroom, weeping, hating him perhaps. He could understand why; he seemed to be putting his own interests before his love for her. She should know that that wasn't true; they were enmeshed in one of those grotesque dilemmas that sometimes thwart lovers and occasionally destroy them. At every turn, it seemed, there were roadblocks. Well and good to act for the moment, but the moment led to tomorrow, and in the tomorrows, different men and women than those who made the decision of the moment would face each other in the reality of the aftermath.

His decision had not been forced by the ultimatum from New York; he had already decided what they should do. With the House dissolved and an election in progress, they must buy time. Painful as the separation might be, he would go to Moscow and Victoria would continue to fulfill her obligations. Their moment would come, perhaps sooner than they now dared believe.

There was so much at stake. For Victoria, for himself; indeed, for Britain. He could understand Forster's adamancy; their love was a threat to the nation's most cherished institution. But life is change, and institutions accommodate to change or die. The monarchy had already changed; there was no longer a "divine right." Rulers had changed; power no longer rested in the hands of kings or autocrats but with the people. Even the church had changed; its temporal power was gone as was much of its spiritual influence. There was no reason the monarchy could not adapt even further. Britain would still have her monarch and her succession. The pageantry and the symbolic significance of the throne would remain. The royal family might be less royal, but more family, perhaps, and thus closer to the people.

He had turned in at the Dorchester Hotel and used a public telephone to call Jane's flat. He had let it ring for a full two minutes but there had been no answer. Perhaps he'd misdialed. Again there was no response. He glanced at his watch. How long had he been gone? Forty minutes. Why did she not answer? She must know it was him. It was unlike her to harbor resentment.

Back at the flat, he turned the key in the lock, opened the door and called out, "Vicky?...." There was no answering voice. He looked about. She had gone, and hurriedly; there were dishes in the sink and articles of clothing about. In the bedroom he could see the impression of her body on the bedspread and the pillow into which she had wept.

He'd called the palace, disdaining code names and subterfuge. "I'm sorry," the operator had said. "Her Royal Highness is not taking any calls. Do you wish to leave a message?"

Now, in his hotel room two days later, he was waiting on the transatlantic line, his anger mounting as the connection hummed and the minutes passed. Even as he was considering hanging up and placing the call again, the palace operator came on. "Are you there, Mr. Walsh?"

"Yes, I'm here."

"I have Mr. McCrimmon for you."

McCrimmon's voice was brisk. "Good afternoon, Mr. Walsh. Or perhaps I should say, good morning, you being in New York."

"Good morning," Jeremy said. "May I speak to Princess Victoria, please."

"I'm terribly sorry but I'm afraid she's not available," McCrimmon said. "I believe the operator informed you that she is not taking any calls."

"Mr. McCrimmon," Jeremy said, striving to contain his mounting anger. "I have just read a transcript of the story in the Sunday *Herald*. I would like to speak to Victoria. Will you be so kind as to put me through."

"I'm afraid that's not possible," McCrimmon said. "Her Royal Highness is not in the palace."

"Where is she?"

"I'm not at liberty to disclose that."

"Mr. McCrimmon, you're not talking to the press or to a stranger. I will ask you once more: will you be kind enough to put me in touch with Victoria?"

"I'm sorry, Mr. Walsh, I can't do that."

"Then put me through to the Queen."

"*Really*, Mr. Walsh!" McCrimmon said, his voice frosty.

"Look, dammit! I – "

McCrimmon broke in on him. "Now, look here. I don't think we need that kind of talk. I've given you the facts. Her Royal Highness is not available. She's not here. As a matter of fact, she's not in the city, and she has instructed me not to forward any inquiries."

"This is not an inquiry, dammit! I will wait on the line until you get in touch with her, wherever she is, and tell her who's calling. Now will you please take care of that?"

There was a brief pause and then the sound of McCrimmon's voice, flat, controlled. "I'm sorry, Mr. Walsh, I don't mean to be rude but I must go off the line now. It's been a very busy day here, as you might imagine. Good afternoon."

♛ ELEVEN

BALMORAL CASTLE is the royal family's summer home, the place where nerves untangle and hearts beat happiest, the one place in the world where the family may come close to total privacy. All this, of course, on a scale of grandeur and opulence foreign to ordinary mortals.

Unlike Buckingham Palace and Windsor Castle, Balmoral is owned by the Queen and has been the royal family's summer home since the original medieval estate in Aberdeenshire, Scotland (known then as Bouchmorale, Gaelic for "Majestic dwelling"), was purchased by Queen Victoria and Prince Albert in 1852. Albert hankered for a reminder of his native Thuringia in Germany and had the house rebuilt as a mock Gothic castle in the style of his ancestral home. The great house is set at the center of a twenty-four-thousand-acre estate among rolling hills and woodlands and is notable for its many conical turrets – reminding one, incongruously, of a substantial and stately Disneyland. The dominant feature is a square eighty-foot tower surmounted by a twenty-foot turret on which the Royal Standard flies when the Queen is in residence. It's a welcoming and inviting place but no modest country home. The ballroom, for instance, is twenty-five by sixty-eight feet. The impressive, marbled entrance hall contains a statue of Prince Albert –

frequently used nowadays as a hat rack – and the castle can house as many as a hundred people. But it seldom does; it is essentially a retreat and the guests are usually family members or close friends.

It was to Balmoral that Princess Victoria had fled on the Sunday morning after her private secretary, face flushed, rushed to her a copy of the Sunday *Herald*'s first edition. She bade a brief farewell to her parents and flew to Balmoral by helicopter, accompanied only by her co-pilot and MacIntyre, her personal policeman. Much of Sunday and Monday had been spent in her rooms or on long walks about the estate accompanied by the exuberant romping of a dozen dogs. The hunters among them, visibly disappointed when it became evident that she had no gun, nonetheless raced about flushing grouse and tearing off in pursuit of real or imagined game.

On Tuesday Jane Cavendish arrived unannounced, greeting Victoria by saying, "Queen of the tabloids that you are, being here will probably destroy what reputation I have left but, what the hell!" To escape the servants – who had only days before come up to a full contingent in anticipation of the arrival of Mary and Edward the following week – the two friends moved out of the castle into Birkhall, a commodious but relatively small old-fashioned house on the estate.

Jane was full of news about the continent, about mutual friends encountered, and about the latest in fashion in Paris and Rome and Madrid. Typically, she came bearing gifts: a bolt of exquisitely woven black and scarlet silk shot through with gold and silver threads and an exquisite Chinese bud-vase that duplicated exactly the stem and leaves of a rose and permitted the insertion of a single bloom. Finally, making an impish face, she handed Victoria a gaily wrapped box in which reposed a diaphanous and outrageously cut black nightie. "Sorry it's too late to wear it at my digs," she said. "But there'll be other places and other times and, who knows, maybe even other men."

It was only then that Victoria told her about the quarrel with Jeremy.

"Ah!" said Jane, "the light dawns. And here I was about to chide you for overreacting to that rubbish in the *Herald*."

"It was the suddenness of it all," Victoria said, tucking her emotions back into place. "Out of the blue – bang! It's over. That's what I can't accept. Or understand. It's now the better part of a week and I haven't heard from him. He *must* know about the story – it's in all the papers, I'm told – and yet he hasn't called. I would never have believed, never, that he could be so . . . unfeeling. Not Jeremy."

"He's a *man*," Jane muttered.

Victoria, her emotions only precariously in control, told her friend the details. "Fine," she concluded. "We've quarreled before. Everybody does. But it's obvious now that he was looking for an excuse." She shook her head in bewilderment. "I'd made up my mind to go with him to Moscow and damn the torpedoes. . . . It's an American expression," she explained. Now her eyes flashed with anger. "But as we talked it became obvious that he was no longer keen on my going with him. His head had been turned by the job."

Jane was seated cross-legged on the bed, letting the story spill without interruption. When it became clear that Victoria had finished, she played with a piece of ribbon from the parcel, curling and uncurling it about a finger as she spoke.

"In my vast experience," she began, a hint of self-deprecation in her tone, "I've learned one thing about men – and I'm speaking of the better ones, few as they may be. The object with which men fall in love – in a lasting, lifelong commitment to which everything and everyone else is secondary – is their work. *That's* the love they dream about most of the time. *That's* where their minds are most of their waking hours. Not with Mrs. cook-and-bottle-washer out in the kitchen or the nursery. Sure, he'll fall in love with you. Yes, he'll love, honor, and cherish you in sickness and in health, but don't make the mistake of thinking that he loves you more than he does himself. And remember: his work is who he *is*. You can compete for his affection with those wide-eyed and high-busted sweet young things who come along from time to time, but not with that beguiling finger that beckons and whispers, 'Say there, old chap, you can be vice president here, maybe even chairman of the board if you work at it.' Delilah could shave Samson's head once she had him asleep on her lap, but when he woke up, what was he interested in? – in bringing down the columns of the temple on his enemies, that's what!"

Listening to her friend, catching the overtones of bitterness in her voice, glimpsing the cynicism in her eyes, Victoria was shaken by the realization of how much of a misanthrope Jane had become. Jane . . . loving, giving, openhearted Jane, soured on men! And yet, paradoxically, still fascinated by them; never missing an opportunity to talk about them. Never wanting for a date and pursued by some of the most interesting men in Britain. And little wonder; she was good company and strikingly beautiful, more often than not the most attractive woman in a gathering. But, as Victoria had noticed, none of her relationships seemed to jell. She had presumed that it was because Jane's rapier-swift mind and occasionally acerbic tongue could be offputting. She had only begun to understand her friend's brittle quality when Jane had told her of the disastrous ending of her love affair with Ron. There had been other unhappy endings, but Jane never discussed them. Asked about them, she'd dismiss them with a quip and a quick grimace.

280

Victoria had not had a really bad experience with a man. In truth, she'd had few involving relationships and had never been in love until Jeremy. She'd had crushes, of course; brief, exciting, light-headed feelings about some of her male friends, but most of those had passed within a few days. It had been somewhat different with Billy Carnarvon. She'd been infatuated with him and looked forward eagerly to those weekends at Windsor when she knew he'd be there. He was as handsome as one could hope for, titled and heir to an enormous estate in Devon. He had an extraordinary easiness about him for a man of twenty (she had just turned eighteen at the time) and was fun to be with. They'd gone to parties together and once to the theater. He'd held her hand in the darkness and had kissed her good night with a passionate possessiveness. Once, at Windsor, as they stood in the darkness atop the Round Tower looking out at the lights of the city, he had moved his hand upward slowly until it was touching the side of her breast, and she hadn't forbidden him or drawn away. But later that night she'd chanced to see him steal a kiss from Angela Hawthorne and that had been the end of that.

There had been others: flirtations, brief flares of attraction, some wild imaginings, but no one to stir her blood or set her heart to soaring until Jeremy.

Jane's voice brought her back to the present and she felt a sudden need for some fresh air. It was an invigorating Scottish summer day but, with a threat of rain off to the west, they donned raincoats and pulled on Wellingtons, and struck out at a hiking pace toward the river.

Off in the distance there was a soft, fluttering sound that suddenly mounted to a roar. Before they quite knew what was happening, a helicopter skimmed a nearby hill at tree height and swept in above them, its wings thudding in the air, the turbulence flattening the grasses and buffeting them. Victoria looked up. Leaning from the cabin was a man, sighting with a camera. She turned her back and crouched to the ground. Beside her, Jane, her face distorted, was shouting something, but the words were lost in the tumult.

Usually, the legitimate purveyors of news pay little attention to stories broken by the tabloids, but the *Herald*'s story was picked up by all the media. It was obvious, despite the florid prose and overt sensationalism of Ossie Docherty's account, that there were, in the bare bones of the story, authentic factual details that could not be dismissed. Nonetheless, the *Times* carried nothing in its first edition on the Monday and thereafter ran only a brief item low on page two under a one-column heading. The *Daily Telegraph*, industriously checking it out, had no story in its first edition either, but quickly came abreast, running a restrained account on the front page below the fold, emphasizing in the second paragraph that the palace had dismissed the story as unworthy of comment. The other dailies ran the story on their front pages, varying in their emphases from the carefully contained to the wildly speculative. The BBC carried nothing on Sunday. On Monday, BBC radio took note of the *Herald*'s allegations in a brief item well into its newscasts. BBC television, having had time to check the facts and do its own digging, dealt with the affair in its Nine O'Clock News, including, for want of something better, file footage of Princess Victoria and a dated still photograph of Jeremy. Independent television rang the changes.

In the days that followed, as the public's appetite grew, the story burgeoned. No one in any way related to it went unreported. Reporters and cameramen fanned out like military assault teams. 44 Rotherhithe Street was photographed from every vantage point, including the river and the air. The proprietor and the regulars at *The Famous Angel* grew accustomed to the flash of cameras and the presence of microphones in their faces. The tenants who lived in the flats above Jeremy's were interviewed. Soon editorials were asking unanswerable questions and pondering potential constitutional problems. Features pages were dominated by major articles reviewing the contretemps brought on by Edward VIII's romance with Wallis Simpson.

In New York City, Diane Walsh accepted a fee of one thousand dollars from the *Daily News* for an exclusive interview, revealing little of substance other than some details of Jeremy's and her courtship and divorce. Merilee was waylaid by newsmen as she emerged from Mrs. Foster's Day School in Oyster Bay and fled in tears. Jeremy's whereabouts remained the great mystery until a bellhop at the Park Lane recognized him from a photograph on one of the television news shows and sold the information to WPIX, forcing Jeremy to flee for sanctuary to a friend's apartment.

In all this the *Herald*, not to be outdone, managed to score a beat on the opposition by tracking down Victoria, trumpeting on its front page that she was hiding out at Balmoral and proving it by running a fuzzy, blown-up photograph of her and Jane, neither of whom would have been recognizable without the caption: *Our Vicky and best friend Jane Cavendish wave at Herald's Copter-Camera at Balmoral!* – the "wave" by Jane resembling more a brandished fist.

The news of Victoria's whereabouts led to an invasion of the quiet countryside surrounding Balmoral Castle. Reporters and cameramen, telephoto lenses at the ready, swarmed about the gate on the main road leading to the estate, descending on and temporarily blocking the passage of any vehicle approaching the entrance. A resourceful reporter-cameraman from a West German tabloid bribed his way aboard a delivery van, hiding beneath a heap of provisions, but was discovered and charged with trespass by the police.

No one was more harried by the media than Prime Minister Forster. Nor could he hide. Campaigning daily, junketing from appointment to appointment in city after city, he was entirely vulnerable. Early on he had announced that he would be conducting a "close-to-the-people" campaign and had at first kept the promise, moving about in crowds, shaking any hand in sight, patting backs, and encircling shoulders with a comradely arm whenever there was a picture to be taken. But now the strategy backfired. Most of those crowding about him, jostling for position, were reporters. And because they were more zealous – and many of them armored with such hard objects as portable television cameras and battery packs – they outmuscled even his coterie of party workers. Finally, even as a beleaguered animal will, after a show of defense, turn tail and run, Forster abandoned his "press-the-flesh" approach and instead plunged head down through the crowds, offering no more than an upraised, restraining hand and a glowering, "No comment. No comment."

♛ TWELVE

THE QUEEN had taken the unusual step of inviting her husband to join her for her meeting with the Prime Minister. The Prince Consort is seldom if ever privy to the subject matter of the monarch's conversations with the Prime Minister or to the inner workings of the government – but this was not the usual Tuesday Meeting. They had ended when Parliament was dissolved. Forster had requested the audience when "The Vicky Affair," as the press had dubbed it, began to be perceived by the Conservative party's central campaign committee as a serious threat to Forster's bid for reelection.

In the opening days of the campaign, reaction to the announcement of Princess Victoria Day had been almost unanimously favorable and Forster had immediately appointed himself her champion, seeking to transfer to himself something of her popularity. But the revelations of her love affair with Jeremy, with all its concomitant ramifications, had made too close identification with her perilous. Snapshot public opinion polls and discussions in the press and on radio and television began to reveal a pattern: more conservative Britons, the backbone of the Tory party, tended to respond negatively while a preponderance of the "working classes" seemed to be saying, "Why not?" and even "Good luck, Vicky!" Especially worrisome was the evidence that the majority of women, especially younger women, appeared to be sympathetic to Victoria.

In the first few minutes of his meeting with the Queen and Edward, Forster mentioned none of these concerns. He had spoken only in a troubled manner about "our problem" and of the need to deal with it before it could mushroom into a major constitutional crisis.

"I'm sure you'll agree with me, Ma'am," he was saying, his tone all reasonableness, "that time is the enemy here. The debate is heating up. Positions are hardening. The question is beginning to polarize the country. And yet, it seems, little is being done to resolve the dilemma. Victoria, so I'm informed, remains incommunicado and young Walsh has gone into hiding in New York. A very unhappy state of affairs and one that must not be permitted to continue." His voice turned sharp. "Something *must* be done. And quickly."

He had not met with the Queen since the day Parliament had been dissolved and had been concerned that he might find her in the mood in which he had last seen her. Instead, she seemed relaxed and cordial.

"I'm not quite sure what you would like me to do, Prime Minister," she said. "Perhaps you have a suggestion, Edward," she added, turning to him. He shook his head.

"I presume you've been in touch with Victoria," Forster said. "What are her plans?"

"Yes, we talk to her every day. So far as I've been able to gather, she has no specific plans. Her friend Jane Cavendish is with her, and I gather they intend to remain there through the weekend. Edward and I hope to see them on our arrival Saturday."

"There's talk of a press conference," Forster said, fishing for information.

Mary looked at Edward, eyebrows upraised. "Not to our knowledge," she said. "I would think the last person on earth Victoria would want to see at this point is a reporter."

Forster showed his exasperation by drawing a deep breath and expelling it slowly. "You'll forgive me, Ma'am, if I say that she is not being very helpful. We have a problem on our hands, and no small one at that. In my earlier conversations with Victoria about her intentions, I tried to be as understanding as I could be under the circumstances, but to little avail. And now that her unwillingness to accept my counsel and do her duty has precipitated what can only be described as a crisis, I would respectfully suggest that you – and you, sir, if I may be so bold – talk to Victoria without delay about issuing a statement to the press. My office will be happy to prepare it for her." Beads of perspiration glinted on his brow. "I should tell you," he said, "that I am already in receipt of queries from a number of the Commonwealth countries. They're deeply concerned. So am I."

"And so am I," Mary said crisply. "Among other things, I'm concerned about my daughter." Color had flooded to her face and neck. Her eyes were flashing. "I will tell you quite frankly, Prime Minister, that much of this is your doing. If you had shown any flexibility, if you had tried to understand her feelings rather than give her penny lectures on her duty, we might not find ourselves at this pass."

"Your Majesty. . . ."

"If I may finish," she said. "The situation is this: she and Jeremy – Mr. Walsh – have quarreled. It's a serious quarrel and it happened before that story appeared in that despicable tabloid. So far as I'm able to tell, they have broken off their relationship and it is final."

The tension flowed out of Forster's body and his face softened. "In that case, Ma'am," he said, "perhaps what should be done is to – "

"If you will excuse me, Mr. Forster, there is more. I hadn't intended to tell you this for another week or two, but Edward and I are agreed that perhaps now is the time. It's very good news but it is shadowed by the problem we're all facing." She paused and then said in a firm, unemotional voice, "Edward and I are expecting another child. I am pregnant."

Forster's jaw fell agape. "You are *what*?" he gasped.

"Pregnant."

"Pregnant?"

"Pregnant. The baby is expected in mid-January."

Forster's reflexes had been trained to respond quickly, but it was a moment before his normal aplomb asserted itself. Eyes blinking in astonishment, he asked, "And you've known this for some time?"

Mary smiled. "Of course."

"Forgive me," he said, still flustered, "you caught me off balance. Permit me to offer my congratulations and my best wishes. And to you, sir," he added, turning to Edward and rising to shake his hand. He managed a wry smile as he seated himself again. "You will understand me if I say that had I known this earlier it would have made things a great deal less trying." The smile faded. "You've told Victoria?"

"We intend to tell her Saturday."

Forster was stroking his jaw, almost thinking aloud. "But this could alter everything. If it's a boy, Victoria will be able to marry as she wishes, granted your approval, of course. If it's a girl, the repercussions would not be calamitous were Victoria to step down – there would be someone to replace her. My, my," he murmured. "Interesting. *Very* interesting." He noted that the Queen's eyes were near to overflowing. "It's been a difficult time," he said lamely.

"Especially for Victoria," she said.

Forster reached across and patted her hand. "Things will work out," he said reassuringly. "All lovers quarrel."

"I'm afraid this is more than that," Mary said. "I don't think Victoria is prepared to forgive him."

Arriving at Balmoral, Mary and Edward were surprised to find Victoria in good spirits. "I must say," Edward enthused, giving her a great bear hug, "you're looking absolutely smashing!"

And she was. The redness about the eyes was gone, the pallor, the distractedness, the occasional heavy sigh. Jane had been good for her: full of irreverent fun, making outrageous comments and doing hilarious takeoffs of some among the more pompous of the palace circle. And cheating shamelessly at Scrabble.

"Craxwycz," she'd argued. "It's a little-known Australian marsupial. No, don't bother to look it up. They discovered it only a few years ago in the outback. It's almost extinct. Ask any paleontologist."

"But paleontologists deal with fossils."

"I said it was almost extinct."

"But you've misspelled it. You put down CRAXWYZ. You're missing a C."

"I don't have another C. Sometimes they leave off the second C." Whereupon she'd burst into wild laughter and on they'd gone to other things.

After dinner Mary asked Jane if they might be excused, and she, Victoria, and Edward withdrew to a small parlor of which Mary was particularly fond. She wasted no time in coming to the point. "Your father and I have some news for you," she said, a small smile playing at the corners of her lips. "Edward, you tell her."

"Yes, of course," he said, clearing his throat and quite obviously searching for the right words. "Well now. . . . Your mother and I have been planning to – No, no, that's not right. Let me put it this way. . . ."

Mary laughed happily. "Oh, do get on with it, Edward."

"Very well," he said, clearing his throat again. "You'll be pleased to know that we're about to add another member to our little family. Your mother and I have decided that, for a number of reasons, it would be a good thing if. . . ."

Mary broke in, laughing. "What Daddy's trying to tell you, darling, is that your mother is pregnant. We're going to have a baby."

Victoria looked from one to the other of them, incredulous. "You're not serious?"

"Couldn't be more so."

"Oh, Mother!" she cried and ran to her, throwing her arms about her. Then to her father. "Darling Daddy!" After a moment she released him, smiling happily. "Ooooh!" she said. "That is *some* news! I think it's just bloody marvelous!"

They returned to their chairs. "How long have you known?" she asked, and then turned to her father. "Daddy, you gay old dog."

"Not all that old," he said, beaming.

"Three months," Mary said. "I completed the first trimester a week or so ago. We're expecting sometime in mid-January."

Victoria was accustoming herself to the news. "I still can't believe it. You certainly are good at keeping secrets."

"Well," said Mary, "there was some doubt that I could carry the child and it seemed wise to keep it to ourselves until we were sure. I can't tell you how difficult it was not telling you. Especially when you and Jeremy were struggling to work things out."

Edward broke in. "In hindsight we might have been wrong about that. We've talked about it by the hour. We finally came to the conclusion that we didn't have the right to inject something into your – what shall I call them? – discussions, when to do so might have influenced you, and then May might have miscarried and all we'd have done would be to confuse you."

"I hope not telling you had nothing to do with. . ." Mary said.

Victoria had been listening in silence, her eyes lowering and then her head. "It didn't," she said. "As a matter of fact, things have worked out for the best. It's all helped me to . . . to regain my sense of perspective." She smiled at them wanly. "Our getting married was a mad idea from the beginning, I suppose." She shrugged. "I'll get over it." Suddenly, her eyes widened. "Oh, my goodness! If it's a boy, I'm out of a job." She smiled at her mother. "Oh, Mother, *do* let it be a boy!"

Things had not gone well for Jeremy. On his arrival in New York he'd expected to be plunged immediately into briefing sessions and intensive research on the forthcoming Summit. There would be, he'd anticipated, a week or two in Washington, interviews with people in the State Department, get-acquainted meetings with liaison staff who would be accompanying the advance negotiators, and rafts of background material to be absorbed. Instead, there had been an oddly ambiguous character to his too-brief conversations with Jim Handleman, the managing editor, to whom he was finally responsible, and with Jack Patterson, who ran the foreign desk. After two weeks of wondering what was up, he decided to broach his concern, and at the end of the week, with the final edition away, he sent a note to Handleman. Within ten minutes he received a call asking him to come by.

Handleman's was an extraordinary success story. Raised in the wilds of Brooklyn, he had grown up street smart and able to succeed at virtually anything he turned his hand to. He'd observed two older brothers become shiftless and cynical and had decided that he wanted more from life than what they were getting. His size and lightning-fast reflexes had made him something of a neigh-borhood celebrity in basketball and football, and won him a scholarship at Cornell. His athletic ability, his straight A's in the classroom, and his editorship of the campus newspaper led to his being named valedictorian, and after graduation, to a job as a reporter on the *Brooklyn Eagle*. On his fortieth birthday, he had become managing editor of the *New York Times* and the driving, sometimes tyrannical force of the city room. He was the antithesis of an outsider's preconception of a *Times* man; he was earthy and often coarse in speech, boisterous, indecorous, sometimes brash. But he knew what needed to be done and saw that it was, and those who, on first meeting him underrated him, soon revised their opinion.

"I think we've got to face the facts," he was saying. "The situation has become materially different."

Jeremy and Jack Patterson were seated opposite Handleman's heaped-up desk. Patterson had been there when Jeremy arrived. "In what way different?" Jeremy asked.

Handleman had a habit of balling sheets of copy paper and lofting them toward a wastebasket in the far corner of his office and was now making compact the missile in his hands. "Jer," he said, "let's be realistic. There's been a radical change in . . . let's call it the public's perception of you. Two weeks ago you were, as far as the public was concerned, our guy in London, a by-line over a story.

But the reader knew little, if anything, about you. Today. . . ." He looped the ball of paper toward the basket and scored. "Today you're . . . there's no other word for it . . . a fucking celebrity. People are reading about you, seeing your picture on television, being filled in on your background, your religion, your family affairs. . . . Why? Because you're romantically involved with a fairy-tale princess who lives in a great castle across the sea and who will one day be Queen of England. That's the stuff of a certain kind of journalism. Even we carry it."

"Jim, look – " Jeremy began.

Handleman held up a restraining hand. "Let me make the case." He leaned back in his chair, put his feet on the desk, and laced his hands behind his head. "Last night I'm at the Waldorf – the governor's speech. Mixed bag – politicians, business types, high-rollers, the whole schmeer. Half a dozen people ask me about you. Not soap opera buffs, legit people. Where is he hiding out? Is the story true? Coming in today, the guy downstairs, the majordomo in charge of the elevators – what's his name, Jack?"

"Tony."

"Right, Tony. Tony says to me, sidling up to me while I'm waiting for the elevator, 'Hey, Mr. Handleman, what kinda guy is this Jeremy Walsh?' Elbow in the ribs, jab, jab. 'Really sumpin' wit' the women, right?' Right."

Seeing Jeremy draw breath to break in, Handleman pressed on. "What am I saying with all this? Not that these little outcroppings are important in themselves, but that they manifest one thing: the public's perception of Jeremy Walsh. Good god, man, I'll bet you can't walk the street without people bugging you for your autograph. They tell me you come in the back way and up in the freight elevator."

He wadded another ball of paper, arced it across the office, and rimmed the basket. "Now," said Handleman, suddenly all business, "now we come to the heart of the matter." He sat forward, putting his arms on the desk. "You're the living embodiment of Andy Warhol's dictum about everybody being famous for fifteen minutes. The trouble is, being in the spotlight cripples you as a reporter. A reporter should be nobody: a fly on the wall. The personality journalist gets in the way of the story. Fine, if you're a columnist or on television, but too many people in our business have forgotten that the subject is the story and not some knothead's view of him.

"Anyway," he went on, "my point is this: we've been having second thoughts about you going to Moscow, at least for the time being. We think you should lie low until this business in London cools. Couple of months, maybe three, then we can take another look."

"You've lost me somewhere," Jeremy said. "The Soviets couldn't care less about the brouhaha in Britain."

"You don't think it would make a difference in the atmosphere, say, at a press conference? You don't think correspondents from London or Brisbane or here in the States aren't going to be asked to file a story on Princess Victoria's lover out there on the job? They're not going to take your picture? Not going to try to interview you?"

"I can handle it."

"Maybe you can. The point is, handling it is going to get in the way – your way, everybody's way. The Summit's the story of the year and distractions and sideshows we don't need."

Jeremy leaned forward. "Question: is there any point in my arguing this or has the decision been made?"

Handleman glanced at Patterson, who gave the slightest shrug. "In a word, yes. For now."

"Then," said Jeremy, sitting back in his chair, "the question becomes: what do you want me to do? London's out, I presume?"

Handleman nodded. "Look, Jer, I still see you in Moscow. Cool it for a few months. In the meantime I want you to work with Jack here. He's going to be up to his ass. I'm talking about you coordinating our coverage of the Summit. Also, it'll be the ideal way to come abreast of things out there. Right? Right." He turned to Patterson. "Right, – Jack?"

"Right," Jack said.

"I'm afraid I have something of a confession to make," Angus McCrimmon said.

He'd found the Queen with three of her cats in the orchid conservatory, busy with a handful of camel's-hair brushes transferring with deft, painterish strokes the pollen from the stamens of some of the blooms to the pistils of others.

"A confession," Mary said. "I've never thought of you as ever regretting an action."

"I'm afraid my transgression is more in the nature of a presumption," McCrimmon said. There were deep, vertical furrows at the center of his brow.

"Off with your head, then," said the Queen.

McCrimmon winced. "You may not find it amusing."

She turned to him, taking a tiny handkerchief from the pocket of her smock and touching it to her brow and the base of her neck. It was hot and muggy in the conservatory. "Well, then," she said lightly, "I'd best pay attention. What is it, Crimmie?"

"As I say, I acted presumptuously. The day after that story about Victoria and Mr. Walsh appeared, Mr. Walsh rang up from New York City wanting to talk to Victoria. He was quite insistent. The switchboard operator wasn't sure how to handle it and referred the matter to her supervisor who spoke to me. Mr. Walsh was quite upset when I came on the line. I told him, as the operator had, that Victoria wasn't taking calls, which was, of course, true. When he pressed me, I informed him that Victoria was not in the city and that she had given orders that calls were not to be forwarded. He took this with ill grace and insisted on speaking to you. I told him that was not possible and that was the end of it." He looked at her directly. "I'm afraid I said nothing about it to Victoria then or since, and it's been troubling me."

"But why, after a month, are you telling me this now?" Mary asked, her eyes on his.

McCrimmon's gaze didn't waver. "Because yesterday, as you know, the decision was confirmed that Victoria will be taking your place on the tour to Canada and New York City where it's entirely possible Mr. Walsh will try to contact her."

"And Victoria might learn of your duplicity and raise it with me."

"That's part of it."

"But only part," she said ruminatively. She turned and, hands deep in the pockets of her smock, walked slowly down the center aisle of the conservatory. At the far end she turned and came back to where she'd been. "And what's the other part, Mr. McCrimmon? The more important part, I presume."

He began to rub a palm over his bald head, his eyes on the floor. "We were confronted by a crisis," he said slowly, "and it seemed important to gain some time. If you'll forgive me, they'd both been behaving badly and I was having very serious doubts about their judgement. I was concerned that if Mr. Walsh were to come dashing back to London and they were, to indulge for a moment in the theatrical, to throw themselves in each other's arms – the two of us against the world, if you follow me – it might have greatly exacerbated the problem and moved it beyond containment." His eyes were on hers again, unblinking. "It was simply that at the moment it seemed wise. For all concerned."

Mary broke away to walk again to the end of the aisle, pondering. From that distance she said, "Yes, Angus, as you say, you did act presumptuously. But apart from what your motives might have been, have you given any thought to how much pain you may have caused?"

The blood had drained from McCrimmon's face. He reached into an inside pocket of his jacket, brought forth an envelope and placed it on the table beside the brushes Mary had been working with. "If it pleases you, Your Majesty," he said. "My resignation."

"Leave it there," Mary said. "I'll give it thought."

She wouldn't accept his resignation, of course, but she would let him dangle in the wind for a few days. He'd seemed contrite – as contrite as anyone could ever hope for Crimmie to be – but clearly there was a need to put on a check rein. He *had* been presumptuous. In a matter affecting her daughter he had not only acted without informing her but had subsequently said nothing about it. She knew he'd acted as he had because he thought it was in the best interest of all concerned, but that was not excuse enough and he needed to be made to realize it.

But she wouldn't accept his resignation, wouldn't even give it a thought. Heavens, no! – what in the world would she do without Crimmie? Crimmie knew her mind so well that she hardly needed to instruct him in most matters. And she was old-shoe comfortable with him. He never showed pique. There were no silent sulks or outbursts of temperament. He was neither patronizing nor obsequious. Yes, he could be irritating, but his devotion to her and his commitment to the Crown more than compensated for that.

But the problem he had raised remained. Now that she knew Jeremy had not acted as badly as she thought, should she inform Victoria? Yes, she must. But. . . . But. . . . To tell her what had happened might lead to a reconciliation and to a resurrection of all the problems that had been there before the quarrel. Moreover, he was now even more deeply committed to going to Moscow and would surely be unable to renege. Nor was Victoria as free to act as she had been; she would certainly have to continue her duties until the baby was born and for a few months after that, at least until she, Mary, was delivered of the child and able to resume her routine.

And would it be a kindness at this stage to intervene? Might she only twist the knife in the wound? Suppose Victoria's hopes were rekindled only to learn that Jeremy had cooled. Wouldn't that add to the pain?

But what of the problem Crimmie had anticipated? During Victoria's trip to America she would be in New York. There, if Jeremy wanted to get in touch with her, he surely could manage it. The whole story would come out and she and Crimmie both would be in an awkward position. In such a circumstance, Crimmie would probably have to go. Dear me! Dear me!

She'd better talk it over with Edward. She'd do that at lunch; they would soon have to discuss the public announcement of her confinement anyway. The two announcements could be combined: because of her pregnancy, she was canceling the trip to America and Victoria would be taking her place. So, best to bite the bullet and get it done immediately.

"Jane? Jeremy Walsh here. How are you?"

"Jeremy! Well, isn't *this* a surprise."

"I hope I haven't caught you at a bad time. I'm calling from New York."

"Well, I was in the middle of getting dressed to go out to dinner. . . ."

"I tried earlier at your office but you were in a meeting."

"Really? I didn't get the message."

"I didn't leave my name. Tell you the truth, I wasn't sure you'd take the call."

"To tell *you* the truth, I wouldn't have."

"I understand. I do. Do you have five minutes?"

"Look, Jeremy, I don't want to seem rude but. . . ."

"Hold on, Jane. Just for a minute. Please, I want a word with you about Vicky. How is she?"

"As well as might be expected. And, dammit Jeremy, no thanks to you. Otherwise she's fine."

"I miss her terribly."

"Oh, come *off* it!"

"No, I do. Every day. And more all the time."

"Look, Jeremy, I'm going to break a rule I have about staying out of other people's business and be absolutely candid with you. You've acted like a rotter. Vicky had made up her mind to go with you, even if it meant freezing in Moscow, but you were so preoccupied with your own concerns that you didn't give her a chance to tell you."

"Now wait a minute, Jane. That's not fair. Let me ask you: do you think that's what she should have done? With everything that was at stake? Do you really?"

"That's hardly the point. You never gave her the chance to tell you. But I'm not going to get into that. That's your decision and you're stuck with it. Now, I'm afraid I. . . ."

"No. Please. Hold on a minute. I want to get a message to her and I was wondering if you would pass it on."

"I'm sorry, I really don't think I want to do that. She's just beginning to get back on her feet. I don't think you have any idea how much that girl loved you – still loves you, unfortunately – and I'll tell you frankly, I don't want to play any part in the two of you getting back together again. She has her life to live and you have yours. The whole notion of the two of you getting married was harebrained from the beginning. Jeremy, listen to me, let it be. Leave her alone."

"Then you won't give her a message for me?"

"No, I won't. I'm sorry but I won't be a part of it. And what do you need me for? If you're determined to muck things up again, write her a note or ring her up, for goodness sake!"

"I have called. She won't take the calls."

"Well, what would you expect? You walk out on her. You leave her to face the aftermath alone – that filthy story in the *Herald* and all the other rot your carrion-eating friends in the press could dredge up – and you don't have the decency to pick up a telephone and say, 'Sorry about that. Are you all right?' "

"Wait a minute. Wait a minute. I did exactly that. I called your flat that night and she was gone. The minute I landed in New York, the minute I heard the news I called the palace and they wouldn't put me through. She'd left word that she wasn't taking any calls. I raised hell with the switchboard operator and finally she put McCrimmon on. He said she wasn't taking calls and that she wasn't in the city. But he wouldn't tell me where she'd gone. I tried Windsor but they referred me back to Buck House. It was pretty obvious she didn't want to talk to me."

There was a long silence on the line. "Jeremy, you're telling me the truth? . . ."

"Yes. Yes. It was made quite clear that she didn't want

to hear from me. I called you but your office said you were out of town."

"I was with Victoria at Balmoral. Where else?"

"Yes, but I didn't know that. And when you didn't return my call, I figured you weren't talking to me either. Then, yesterday, I thought: dammit, I'll try again. There's been a change in my plans and I want her to know. Jane? . . . "

"I'm still here."

"I think it's something she'd want to know. It changes everything in a way."

"Oh, Jeremy, I don't know. I really don't."

"At least let me fill you in. Then if you don't want to tell her about it . . . well, that's your decision. Okay?"

"I suppose."

"Well, first, I'm not going to Moscow. It was their feeling here at the *Times* that all the publicity would make that unwise. Impossible, as a matter of fact. Their idea was that I should go on the foreign desk. I gave it a try, but on day one I knew it wasn't for me. I'm a reporter. Anyway, I came up with this idea and presented it to them: to do a series of feature articles for the magazine. The overall title will be something like 'The Shape of Democracy,' and each article will deal with how the major democracies actually work, comparing the way each handles the various problems they all have in common. How each system tries to solve them – that kind of approach. Anyway, to skip the details, there's to be one on France, one on West Germany, Italy, Sweden, and so on. I tried to swing it to do the first one on the UK but they want France. The point is, I'll be in Europe for the next six months or more. *And* working out of London."

A note of quiet urgency entered his voice. "Jane, I want very much to see her again. Maybe some of the things we hoped for will never happen but. . . . Even if we could only see each other once in a while. . . . I love her, Jane."

Jane sounded dispirited. "Why do you *do* this to me?"

"At least, tell her I called. Then she can make up her mind what she wants to do. Will you at least do that?"

Again there was an extended silence. "No," she said suddenly. "I won't promise anything. Very well, I will do this: I'll think about it. Damn you, Jeremy!"

"I think this might do very nicely," Edward said, passing to Mary a piece of typewritten paper on which he had penciled out some lines and made some notations in his precise hand. It read:

COURT CIRCULAR
Her Majesty Queen Mary III and His Royal Highness Prince Edward, the Duke of Connaught, are pleased to announce the anticipated birth of a child next January. The Queen hopes to continue to undertake some public engagements during her pregnancy but regrets any disappointments which may be caused by any curtailment of her planned program. Her Royal Highness, The Princess of Wales, has agreed to assume some of Her Majesty's public responsibilities.

Mary returned it to him. "That seems fine," she said. There was the hint of a repressed smile on her face and it caused him to look at her closely. "We might make one small change," she said, the smile growing beyond containment.

"*Now* what mischief are you up to?" he asked, beginning to smile himself. "I know you too well. Something's up."

"Perhaps you could change the first sentence so that instead of reading the anticipated birth of a child it reads the anticipated birth of a son."

He looked at her blankly and Mary laughed outright

at the expression on his face. "Are you trying to tell me something?" he asked. "You're not putting me on?"

She shook her head vigorously. "No, my darling. It's official. Sir Herbert was here this morning with a Dr. Charlton. He specializes in pre-natal ultra-sound examinations. He brought along his equipment and they're agreed. No doubt about it, it's a boy."

She went to him and kissed him on top of the head. "I hadn't realized they could tell the sex of the baby, but there was his little tassel. I couldn't make it out on the screen but they could."

"Well, I'll be blowed," he said. "A boy."

Mary had returned to her chair and to her lunch. "In some ways I'm sorry I know; not knowing till the baby's born adds to the miracle somehow. But because of Victoria's problems it was important to take some of the pressure off her if we could." She was munching on a piece of french toast. "I was joking, of course, about making the announcement that it's a boy. We mustn't breathe a word of it – except, of course, to Victoria."

Victoria's senses were reeling. Suddenly dizzy, she had to put a hand on a table to keep from falling, and then to lower herself into a chair.

Within one hour the entire direction of her life had changed!

First there had been the conversation in which her father – with Mary's arm linked in his and she barely able to repress the excitement that flushed her skin and made her eyes seem almost to dance. "The baby will be a boy," he'd said. "A brother. A son." Even as he spoke, the words she had involuntarily uttered a few days earlier when her mother had told her she was pregnant resounded in her memory: Oh, my goodness! If it's a boy, I'm out of a job. Mother, *do* let it be a boy!

And if that weren't enough news for one day, add the telephone call from Jane Cavendish. Jeremy *hadn't* failed her. He *had* called. He loved her and missed her and wanted to see her! Incredibly, within one hour all the barriers were down. She was free to marry him if she wished and no longer would he be miles away, across the sea, out of reach, out of touch. They could get married and live reasonably normal lives. All the requisite protocol would have to be followed, of course, all the proprieties observed. There'd be some fuss and bother but it would be no more than that. An almost liquid warmth flooded into her chest and then suffused her entire body. "Oh, Jeremy, Jeremy.... I love you. Oh, world, I love you. Oh, gloomy, windy, drizzly day, I love you...."

Part 3

☒ ONE

"WELL NOW, WHAT HAVE WE HERE?" Edward said.

Mary and Edward were in his sitting-room idling away the evening; he watching television. Mary, having tired of the program, was posing in front of a full-length mirror, alternately standing face-on and sideways, sometimes frowning as she drew in her stomach. She had spent much of the afternoon practising reading the Speech from the Throne, occasionally seated – as she would be the following day during the State Opening of Parliament – and sometimes with a replica of the crown on her head. Hugh Forster's Conservative government had been returned to power with the slimmest majority – and only after a recount in three ridings – and the following day Mary would play the leading role in the official ceremony she dreaded most.

Edward rose and went to the door. A white envelope had been slipped beneath the crack. He opened the door and peered into the corridor. There was no one in sight.

"What is it?" Mary said absently, positioning her head before the mirror in various attitudes, finally patting the skin beneath her chin with the backs of her fingers.

"Someone slipped a note under the door," he said. "and Terrance is nowhere is sight. Odd."

He returned to his chair, ripping open the envelope. As he unfolded and read it, his face clouded and his lips drew into a grim line. When a minute passed and he'd said nothing, Mary turned to him, curious. "What is it?" She saw his face and was immediately alarmed. "Edward, what *is* it?"

He held out the note and she saw that his hand was trembling. In a scrawl reminiscent of a schoolboy's it read:

Oct. 7

Your Royal Highness:

I read in the newspapers a few weeks ago that the Queen is going to have a baby in January. It didn't take me long to figger out who the father is. Namely me. I'll prove that to you by even giving you the date. It will be born the second week of January. How I know this is because that will be nine months from the night I was in the Queen's bed. You can be shure this is no crank letter because I will give you the code words 'ask the Prince about Samantha.' Nobody else in the world could know those code words except me and the Queen. And you, naturaly.

I demand a meeting with you and Her Majesty. I will ring up Mr. Gracie in Household tomorrow morning to set a time for our meeting. Let me warn you if you try anything fancy I will go strait to the newspapers and tell the world. If you send round the police it won't do you any good. A freind of mine has a seeled letter from me with *all* the facts. If something happens to me he has orders to open it and give it to all the newspapers. I wish neether of you any harm but I demand to see you tomor- row. I know you have to go to the opening of parlament but there will be sometime in the day you can see me and you better. That's all for now.

yours truly

Eric Mulholland

"Oh my God!" Mary said, sinking into a chair.

Edward's face was gray. "What does he mean, code words?"

It was a moment before Mary could gather herself to respond. She was struggling to catch her breath and had a hand to her throat. The blood had drained from her face and the makeup showed starkly, giving her the appearance of a cadaver. She licked her lips with a dry tongue and said haltingly, "When he. . . . When. . . ." She stared at her husband, stricken. "Oh, Edward . . . I can't bear to think of it. I can't."

He roused himself. "I'll get you a glass of water."

He returned quickly. Her hand trembled and some of the water spilled on her dress. He took the glass from her and put it to her lips but she shook her head. He then fetched a wet flannel and passed it to her. She put it to her brow and then to the base of her neck.

He pulled a chair opposite hers and sat on it, leaning forward, elbows on his knees. "Do you think you should lie down?" he asked. She shook her head. Her chest was rising and falling as she sought to breathe. "You're sure?"

The color was returning to her face. "I'll be all right," she said. "Just give me a minute."

He put out a hand and laid it gently on her knee, and so they sat for a while. Now she had her emotions in hand. "I'm sorry," she said, folding the damp cloth and placing it on the table by her chair.

"There," he said. "That's better."

She looked at him bleakly. "What are we going to do? Whatever are we going to do?"

"You mustn't worry about it," he said. "We'll work it out. We will. You'll see."

Her spirit was reviving. "But we must decide what we're going to do. It's impossible. I can't believe it." She was close to tears but willed them away. "We've got to talk about it."

"Whenever you're up to it."

"Now," she said. "Now. We've got to talk about it now." She put a hand to her hair. "Would you turn that lamp off," she said. "I must look frightful."

"Ready?" he said, returning to his chair. She closed her eyes and nodded. "Do you think it's from . . . him?"

She nodded.

He picked up the note. "I don't understand this business about code words. What does he mean, 'Ask the Prince about Samantha?' Did he say that to you?"

She nodded, head down.

"But what does it mean?"

She looked up at him. "I don't know. I thought you might."

"Why haven't you mentioned it?"

"I was going to, and then I thought I'd better not. It just seemed better to let it go."

His brow furrowed. "Can you talk about it? When did he say it?"

She drew a deep breath, held it, and expelled it. "Just before he left. He had his knife to my cheek and he said, 'Ask the Prince about Samantha.'"

"But I don't know a Samantha. Yes, of course, there's Lady Samantha. . . . What's her name?"

"Rutland."

"Yes. But I don't know her. I was introduced to her once – at the reception for the new Belgian ambassador, as I recall. Samantha. . ." he mused. "I'm at a loss."

"Well, that's nice to know," she said dryly.

"Really, darling!"

"That aside, what are we going to do? Shouldn't we have a word with the police? No, we can't do that. The more people who know, the greater the danger of it getting out. Maybe we should just ignore it. No, we daren't do that. He sounds like he means business, and if the police were to take him in, there's his friend, the one with the letter. Oh, Edward, what are we going to do? We *can't* see him."

Edward had been drumming with his fingers on the arms of his chair. "I'm afraid we're going to have to."

"But if we do, it just gives him credibility. Why would we see such a madman if we weren't afraid of him?"

"But if we don't see him and he speaks to the press, there's no telling what mischief it might cause. We've *got* to see him. At least then we'll know who he is and what he wants."

She was unconvinced. "Maybe I should talk to Crimmie."

"No!" he said sharply. "It's a nest of snakes. Nobody must know of it. Not a soul."

She was shaking her head slowly. "I'm sorry, I can't do it," she said quietly. "I couldn't bear to see him, to be in the same room with him." She looked at Edward. "I don't know what I might do. I might faint. I might scratch his eyes out."

"Well then, I'll see him alone. The letter was addressed to me, there's no need for you to be drawn into it. Yes," he said decisively, "I'll see him alone. Tomorrow afternoon, after we're done with Westminster."

Britain's Great State Coach is surely the ultimate extension of flamboyant transport. Each early autumn it is hitched to four pairs of magnificent matched grays (with eight pages in medieval uniforms astride) and its four tons of rococo elegance is drawn along lined and festive streets from Buckingham Palace to the Palace of Westminster for the State Opening of Parliament.

The coach, known as the Irish State Coach, was acquired in 1762 by George III and cost £7,587 19s 91/2d. In its construction, no square centimeter was left unornamented. Joseph Wilton, a leading sculptor of the day, undertook the carving which, on the body of the coach, details eight gilded palm trees rising and branching out to support the domed roof. At the front, two gold-encrusted male figures may be seen heralding the coming of the sovereign by trumpeting blasts on conch shells. At the rear, two similar figures bear fasces on their shoulders – bundles of rods and tridents, emblems in Roman times of magisterial power. At the peak of the roof, three gilded cherubs, representing England, Scotland, and Ireland, bear aloft the royal crown and hold in their hands the Sceptre, the Sword of State, and the Ensign of Knighthood. Oil painted panels on the doors represent Mars, Mercury, and Minerva sustaining the Imperial Crown of Great Britain. And there is more, much more, the whole of it gleaming with gold or polished to a dazzling gloss.

Seated within the coach on this gray October day, a glittering diadem atop her head, a fixed smile on her face, and a gloved hand upraised from time to time in a slight regal wave was Mary III, the haunted look in her eyes evident only to the closest observer. Beside her, in the gold-braided and bemedaled uniform of a full Admiral of the Fleet, was her husband, and opposite, Princess Victoria, she too dazzling and diamond-bedecked. From time to time, out of sight of the crowds lining the Mall, Edward reached across and squeezed his wife's hand.

Mary had not slept well the night before, awakening every so often to cry out. When she did, Edward had half roused to murmur words of assurance, and Kong, a black Labrador brought from Balmoral some five months earlier to sleep on a mat at the foot of her bed, had reared his massive head to sniff the air and then gone back to sleep.

To the crowds massed along the streets the Queen looked serene, but behind the smile her mind was in tumult.

312

Might that scowling countenance or that sullen face be that of the man who had marred her life and who would turn up at the palace later that afternoon to meet with her husband? Or that man there! – could he be the one? Or was it that unshaven man in the filthy cap who seemed to glower at her as she passed? She shuddered, and again Edward reached out to touch her hand.

Ahead, at Westminster, the ritual search of the basement was concluding – a hold-over from that November day in 1605 when Guy Fawkes and a band of English Catholics had secreted thirty-six barrels of gunpowder beneath the chamber of the House of Lords, planning to kill James I as he attended the opening of Parliament. Ten minutes before the Queen's arrival, the House of Commons had assembled for prayers. The Sergeant-at-Arms, having been informed by the Second Principal Doorkeeper that Black Rod was on his way from the House of Lords, had barred the door. Black Rod, the chief ceremonial Usher of the Lords, knocked on the door three times and, having been identified through a grating, was permitted to enter. Having bowed three times, he delivered his message, commanding the House to attend Her Majesty immediately in the Lords. A procession had then formed up and moved off through the Commons lobby to, as it is known to Parliamentarians, "that other place."

The Chamber of the House of Lords is the masterpiece of Westminster. A visitor's first impression upon entering it is of red: red padded benches rising on each side, red robes on the peers, a red velvet curtain running around the gallery, a red three-tiered dais on which twin thrones sit. Even the Queen's long train, draped diagonally to the left after she has seated herself on the throne, is red. The second impression is of a gleaming medieval cathedral. The elaborate wood and marble walls rear some forty-five feet above the floor to a paneled ceiling. Ranging along each wall and separating the huge stained-glass windows are eighteen bronze statues: the barons who fought for the Magna Carta. At either end of the great chamber are frescoes: allegorical above the Strangers' Gallery and historical – depicting incidents in Britain's history – above the thrones. At the front, rising high above the dais, flanked on each side by towering two-tiered candelabra and looking very much like an altar, a reredos, airy in the delicacy of its detail, forms the setting for the two thrones. Before it, Edward was seated to Mary's left and, one tier below, Victoria was to her right.

Mary had been the focus of attention as she entered. Every eye had assessed her face and, in the knowledge that she was pregnant, especially her figure. So expert, however, had been the ministrations of her dressers and her hairdresser that few noted the underlying pallor of her skin and the slightly drawn look on her face.

Now, reaching the last paragraph of the speech, having previously committed it to memory, she looked up from the manuscript.

"And finally," she said, her voice ringing strong and clear in the chamber, "what of the future for those of us so fortunate as to live on 'this sceptered isle, this earth of majesty. . . this blessed plot, this earth, this realm, this England'? For what tomorrow may we reasonably hope?"

Her eyes fell on a man to the far left of the Strangers' Gallery alongside one of the television cameras. He stood out from those about him because of the studied carelessness of his clothes, the unkempt tangle of his hair, and the cold disdain on his face. Her eyes met his and her memory faltered.

"For what tomorrow may we reasonably hope?" she repeated, her eyes again on the manuscript, her voice a trifle uneven. "For a tomorrow of security and better living conditions, a day of growing prosperity and more meaningful work, an era of diminishing deficits and a strengthening economy, and above all else, a time of peace. My government," she said, looking up again to find the man gone, "pledges to work toward these goals, and with God's help, to see them realized."

Earlier that morning, having completed his correspondence, Edward had instructed Tom Hornpayne, his private secretary, to inform the Master of the Household that a Mr. Eric Mulholland would be telephoning to ascertain a suitable time for an appointment. He was to be told that four-thirty would be suitable and that Edward would receive him in his sitting-room. Within fifteen minutes Hornpayne was back.

"I'm sorry to trouble you, sir," he said in his overly deferential manner, "but Mr. Gracie has a question about the advisability of your seeing Mr. Mulholland."

"He does, does he?" Edward said. "What kind of question?"

"It seems, sir, that Mr. Mulholland was a footman here until he was dismissed some months ago. Mr. Gracie says he's not reliable."

"Well," said Edward, betraying nothing of his surprise, "isn't *that* a bit of news. Did he say why Mulholland was given the sack?"

"A number of things apparently. He was observed trying the door to your apartment and given a severe reprimand – he had no business on this floor. And there was a question about pilferage – some of the silver service went missing. There was no proof, mind you, but good reason for believing that Mulholland might have been the culprit. He was quite cheeky when being questioned about it and there was nothing to do but dismiss him. There were other things. Small things."

Edward was silent, busy making doodles on a sheet of paper. "I hadn't realized he'd been in trouble," he said. "He's a poor relation of an old navy friend who's asked me to give him a leg-up. Sad story. Tell Mr. Gracie that I'll have a word with him anyway."

Following the ceremony at Westminster, Mary and Victoria had gone on to a reception at Clarence House and Edward had returned to the palace. His valet had laid out a pair of gray slacks and a dark-blue, double-breasted blazer. He changed, and as he was adjusting his cravat was surprised to see that his hands were trembling. He went into his sitting-room and poured himself a whiskey. At four-thirty there was a knock on the door. "Come!" he called out.

Bryce, the senior footman, entered. Following him was a man in his mid-twenties, tall, with a shock of dark hair, brown eyes, and a fair complexion against which the shadow of a clean-shaven beard showed. "Begging your pardon, sir," Bryce said, "Mr. Eric Mulholland." He made no attempt to hide his look of disapproval. "I'll wait outside, sir," he suggested.

"Thank you, Bryce, but that won't be necessary," Edward said. "I'm sure Mr. Mulholland knows his way back."

He remained seated at his desk, indicating with a hand a chair nearby. Mulholland moved instead to stand before the world map on the wall opposite. He had a hand in one pocket and was feigning a casual air. "This must be the famous UFO map," he said, the slightest note of amusement in his tone. "What are the different colored pins for?"

Edward felt an irritability stirring in him. "I don't think that's what we're here to talk about," he said. "Do sit down. I haven't much time."

Mulholland, looking about the room as he went, crossed to sit in the chair Edward had indicated. "You won't mind if I smoke?" he asked, reaching into a pocket.

"Now, look here, Mulholland," Edward said, his voice reflecting his mounting anger. "I've had about enough of your acting like an invited guest. Let's have no more nonsense and get to the business at hand. I have some questions to put to you and I'd bloody well like straightforward answers. Now that we understand each other, my first question is: what's your game?"

Mulholland shrugged, still looking about. "No game," he said. "I just want my rights."

"Your rights? What rights?"

"I'll get to that in a minute," Mulholland said coolly.

Watching him closely, Edward was surprised at the younger man's composure. He seemed in no way intimidated by the fact that he was in the royal apartment. Other than the fact that his hands were clasped in his lap with the knuckles dead white, there was little evidence of any underlying tension. Edward decided to put him on the defensive.

"Before we go any further," he said, "I want to know how you managed to get into the Queen's apartment."

"It wasn't all that hard. Not if you've got a job here at the palace and you've set your mind on it."

"And how did you manage to be taken on here?"

"You probably won't believe this, but I looked up the number in the telephone directory, rang up, and asked the personnel office if there was anything going in the way of jobs. They told me to write the Sergeant Footman, which I did. It wasn't a fortnight before there was a letter back – the Royal Crest on the back of the envelope and all that – telling me to turn up for an interview."

Edward was about to tell him to get on with it, but restrained himself. He was learning something about the palace hiring procedures, perhaps some things he should know.

"Bryce asked me a few questions and took me along to see Oldcastle, Mr. Oldcastle, that is. The only thing he seemed interested in was how tall I was. Hardly asked me anything. They sent for Jocko – Jocko McKnight, that is – and had him and me stand back to back. Seemed like all they was worried about was me being tall and matching Jocko. He was to be my 'pair,' they said. Then it was off to see Mr. Gracie who didn't ask me anything but just listened to Bryce reel off what I'd written in my application. Ten days later there was a letter in the post telling me what the pay was, and three days later I had the job."

"I find that hard to credit," Edward said. "But, be that as it may, what has it to do with my question: how did you get into Her Majesty's apartment?"

A certain cockiness had entered Mulholland's manner. It was evident that he was beginning to half enjoy what was happening: sitting with a royal, chatting, answering questions. Wait till he told Alice; she'd never believe it.

"That part was easy," he said. "I wasn't in a hurry. The pay's not much, but it's easy work." His face darkened. "Then, out of the blue, those bastards in Household – if you'll pardon my French – give me the sack. They told me I was to finish on Friday, and that meant if I was going to do what I come here to do, it had to be done right away." He smiled slyly. "Then, there in the *Court Circular* was the news that you were off to Wales early Monday. I knew the two of you'd be back from Windsor Sunday night, so it was easy. I didn't turn in my uniforms Friday like I'd been told, and I still had my identity card, so Sunday night I come back to the palace. The weekend staff's just a few, and us who work weekdays don't know many of them or them us." He shrugged. "I'm friends with Jenny, the chambermaid who does your apartments – I've chatted

318

her up a few times – and she'd mentioned once that when you go out you leave your door unlocked so's the maids can tidy up.

"I'd been hiding in one of the wardrobes on the attic floor, and around four I come down here to the Principal Floor. There's that big closet down the corridor from where old Trumper used to sit – sleep most of the time, if the truth was told – and I hid in there till I hear you leave. Then it was just a matter of slipping across the hall and nipping in here. After that. . . ."

He turned and looked at the door leading to the Queen's apartment, a smile that was half leer on his lips. Edward gripped the arms of his chair to keep from hurling himself at the man opposite and smashing his face with his fists. Drawing on all the years of masking his emotions in public, he made his normal voice speak the words, "But why? Why?"

Mulholland looked at him boldly, and Edward could see the flinty hate in his eyes. "Why? Don't play innocent with me. Why do you think I told your wife, 'Ask the Prince about Samantha'?"

"But who *is* Samantha?"

Mulholland tilted his head back and looked at Edward through lidded eyes. "You don't remember?"

"Remember what, you fool?"

"Samantha Mulholland. My mother."

"Your mother? What in god's name have I to do with your mother?"

Mulholland balled his hands into fists and brought them down on his thighs. He leaned forward, eyes squinted, teeth bared. "You and my mother, you rotten bastard, spent a weekend together when you were in the navy and on shore leave in Belfast. Twenty-five years ago. *Now* do you remember?" He raised his eyes to the ceiling. "My god, he doesn't even *remember*!"

But Edward was remembering. Yes. He'd picked up a girl in a pub, a pretty little thing with green eyes and a saucy way about her. What had they done? A dim memory began to form: something about hiring bicycles and taking the road toward White Abbey. Yes. And about an idyll in a leafy woods. Samantha? . . . Yes, her name had been Samantha. He remembered now teasing her about wanting to be called Sam. Good god! And this was her son sitting across from him, malevolence in his eyes. A sudden thought invaded his mind and his head reeled. "You're not saying that I'm? . . ."

"My father? No. Thank god for that! I was going on three at the time. But you got my mother pregnant, you bastard, and then just sailed off and forgot the whole thing." He was swinging his head back and forth like a caged beast. "To think, you didn't even remember her *name*!" He put his head down, fighting his emotions, breathing thickly.

After a moment he looked directly at Edward, and when he spoke his voice was little more than a hoarse whisper. "My mother went to some quack to get an abortion." He hissed the words. "He was a butcher. She bled for weeks. My father started asking questions and the story came out. And then the rotten bastard beat her up. Broke her jaw. She lost the sight of an eye. . . ." He fought to contain his emotions. "We never saw him again. And good riddance."

He got out of his chair and, to vent his rage, sent the chair spinning across the room to crash into a bookcase, spilling a torrent of books onto the carpet.

"I am sorry," Edward said. "I didn't know."

"Didn't *know* – you didn't give a damn! Then, or since, or now." Mulholland had gone to the window and now stood looking out. "One day my mother showed me in the paper where you were going to marry Princess Mary. And since then, every goddam week of my life it seems like, I see pictures of you: riding round in a Rolls, playing polo with your toff friends, living on the fat of the land. And my mother. . . . What man was going to look at her, her face smashed and all?" He turned from the window. "Do you know how she's lived all these years? By doing other people's stinking laundry and on what I send her! And me? . . . I had to quit school when I was twelve and make out the best I could. I made up my mind that one day I'd pay you back."

He paused, his fists clenched, a hard, tight smile distorting his face. "Want me to tell you something? What happened to your wife wasn't supposed to happen. It was supposed to be Princess Victoria. She's twenty – right? That's what my mother was."

He flamed with a sudden rage. "Want to see what she looks like now?" He went toward Edward, pulling a warped snapshot from a pocket. Here! Look! Take a *good* look!" He thrust it in Edward's face. "Look at it, you bastard! Look at it!"

Edward stood up, thrusting him away. The picture fell to the floor. Mulholland picked it up and returned it to his pocket. The two men stood facing each other. Edward was pale but was himself again.

"All right, Mulholland," he said sternly, "that will be *all*! I'm not going to listen to any more of it. I can understand what you feel, but it in no way justifies what *you've* done. I could kill you for that. I want you out of here. Now!"

Mulholland gave him a contemptuous smile. "Or you'll do what?"

"I'll have the police in. . . ." Edward put a hand on the telephone.

"Go ahead. Call the police. Nobody's stopping you.

And tomorrow it'll be in all the papers who's the father of the Queen's baby."

Edward balled his fists, but then reined in his anger. There was danger here. He must tread warily. "I'm not going to argue with you," he said, turning away. "You've done what you came to do. Now get out."

"I'm not finished yet," Mulholland said. "Like I said, I want my rights."

"What are you talking about? What rights?"

"My rights as the baby's father. It's time for you to play the man and do what you should've done years ago. I want a house for my mother back in Belfast with a hundred quid a week as long as she lives." A grin stole over his face. "And another ten thousand for my trouble."

Edward looked at him, his gaze impassive. Mulholland made a point of not dropping his eyes, the grin widening, if anything. After a moment Edward said, "And as we both know, every so often there'll be another note under my door and more demands."

Mulholland's anger was spent now. He seemed suddenly indifferent. "You'll not have to worry about that. I'm off to America Monday. That'll be it. You'll have seen the end of me. Guaranteed."

It had been Jeremy's intention to slip into town unobtrusively and, having been reunited with Victoria, to tie together some loose ends at the office, pack some clothes and sort out some papers at the flat, and return to New York the following day. The plan would have worked had he not asked one of his staff, Jedd Brownlee, to bring Gridley to Heathrow so that, his driver having been laid off in his absence, he might have the use of the car during his brief stay.

Leaving the airport, he'd dropped Brownlee off at his flat in Knightsbridge and gone directly to Clarence House where there was to be a small reception following the opening of Parliament. "Just family," Victoria had said on the telephone. "All very informal. Nobody to worry about."

As it happened, Jeremy arrived first. Victoria had been delayed by the need to attend a formal reception in the Speaker's Drawing Room, from which she had slipped away as soon as her sense of responsibility permitted. Not bothering to change, other than to entrust to one of the Ladies-in-Waiting the diadem and some of the jewels she'd been wearing, she went directly to Clarence House.

Flushed with excitement – she'd spotted Jeremy the moment she entered the salon – she accepted the various light embraces, shook the requisite hands, and made chit-chat with those who insisted on telling her how lovely she and the Queen had looked. Only then did she make her way to the furthermost corner of the room where Jeremy had positioned himself beside a grand piano, wine glass in hand.

"Hullo," he said a bit shyly, accepting her proffered hand.

"Hello, Mr. Walsh," she said, and added *sotto voce* with no change in her normal mien, "My darling. Oh, I love you so."

He raised a hand as though to stifle a cough and said behind it, "If only you knew how much I've missed you."

"Do be careful," she said, her voice low. "There's not a person in the room looking at us, but there's not one who isn't watching."

"No fear," he said, smiling civilly, giving the slightest deferential nod of his head, "I shall outdo Caesar's wife."

"You've been well?" she asked, and then added in a lowered voice, "As though I haven't talked to you every day this week."

"I've been fine. Other than the fact, Your Royal Highness . . ." his voice fell off, "other than the fact that I've been out of my mind with longing for you. By the way, how long do we have to play this game? I want to put my arms around you and crush the life out of you."

"As indeed you must, sir. At the earliest opportunity," she said gaily. "And when, may I ask, will that earliest opportunity be?"

"I know when it *must* be," he said, his face impassive. "Tonight. Somewhere. Somehow. . . . Have a care; footman approaching off the right bow."

"Ma'am?"

"I believe I will, John," Victoria said. "The white, please." She accepted a glass of wine, took a sip of it, and placed it on the piano.

Jeremy surrendered his empty glass and took a full one. As the footman moved off, he sipped the wine, looking over the rim of the glass with slightly lidded eyes. "I drink to us, my darling. I hope my face isn't betraying what I'm thinking."

"You'd have made a great actor," she said with a slight smile. "You just communicated something absolutely lewd without so much as raising an eyebrow."

"And you'd have made a great critic," he countered. "You read my intention exactly."

"But where, where, where can we meet?" she said, retrieving her wine glass. "We daren't go back to Jane's. I could ask one of my friends to loan me her house – Jenny Gloucester's in Bermuda – but I'd feel a bit awkward. . . ."

"Why don't we. . . ."

"General alert," said Victoria, her eyes flicking to the doorway. "Prepare to repel boarders."

A woman in a flowered dress had just arrived, a middle-aged woman of ample proportions with an enormous, bobbing bosom, and was bearing down on them. "Darling,

darling, Vicky!" she exclaimed, touching her cheek to Victoria's. "You look simply smashing, simply smashing. But then you always do. And wasn't your mother just ravishing? Sorry to be late but it's been that kind of day since sun-up. Dreadful. Dreadful." She turned to Jeremy, the smile affixed, the eyes appraising.

"Beverly," Victoria said, "may I present Mr. Jeremy Walsh. He's with the *New York Times*. Mr. Walsh, my cousin, Lady Beverly Ransome.

"Mr. Walsh. Yes, yes, of course. I've been so looking forward to meeting you. I trust you're well?"

Jeremy nodded. "Yes, thank you. I am.

"I hadn't thought you were in London. What a pleasant surprise." She looked at Victoria archly. "For everyone."

"Just for the day," Jeremy said.

"Lovely to see you, dear," Victoria said, putting a gloved hand on her cousin's arm. "We must find the opportunity later to have a chat."

"Wouldn't that be lovely," said Lady Beverly. "Well now, if you'll excuse me, I haven't so much as greeted our hostess. Ta ta, Mr. Walsh. Do come again soon." She dipped in the slightest curtsy, backed away, and made her undulant way across the room.

"Why don't we meet at my digs?" Jeremy said into his wine glass.

"I'd love that. But do we dare?"

"Nobody knows I'm in the city. I've been gone for weeks." He reached into his pocket for a handkerchief and, as he brought it to his lips, whispered, "I want you in my bed, my lady."

She laughed as though at a witticism. "Naked against your nakedness," she said softly, smiling as though relishing his quip.

His voice was low and throaty. "Vicky darling, will you, without being obvious about it, monitor my face while

I tell you that I am at this moment stripping that gown from you, holding you in my arms, putting my hands to your breasts, pressing deep into that warm, cozy nest of yours."

"And I," she said, apparently occupied in tucking into place an errant tendril of hair, "am opening myself to you, my love. And will you please stop this instant, my cheeks are burning. . . ."

♕ TWO

SCOTLAND YARD is not, as is commonly believed, Britain's federal police force. Nor has it anything to do with Scotland, apart from the fact that it was first established by London's police on a short street in Whitehall at the original site of a palace used in the twelfth century as a residence for visiting Scottish kings. When that accommodation was outgrown, a larger headquarters was built on the nearby Thames embankment, the name being perpetuated by calling it New Scotland Yard. However, when in 1967 a further move was necessitated to larger quarters in the Westminster area, it too was called New Scotland Yard and so, to avoid confusion, it was renamed New Old Scotland Yard; making sense, but only just.

Actually, New Scotland Yard is merely another name for London's Metropolitan Police which, to confuse things even further, is responsible not only for policing Greater London but also parts of the counties of Essex, Hertfordshire, Surrey, and Kent, but *not* the City of London which, being the original London town, has its own force.

What is commonly thought of as Scotland Yard is a relatively small part of the Metropolitan Police known as the CID, the Criminal Investigation Department. The head of the CID, when Edward rang him up on the telephone, was Assistant Commissioner Benjamin Benbough. Benbough was a disarmingly ordinary looking man, just gone sixty, whose bearing was anything but paramilitary and whose voice was soft to the point of sometimes being inaudible. He had begun in police work as a constable on a beat but, in part because of his almost courtly civility, was soon transferred to the Buckingham Palace Police. Because he was not a large man – barely meeting the minimum physical requirements – he had compensated by studying the oriental martial arts long before such activity became fashionable. His proficiency in these skills led to his being named bodyguard for Princess Victoria in her childhood and finally to being assigned to the Queen. In this responsibility, he and Edward had spent many waiting hours together and had established a relationship that grew to be as close to friendship as their stations would permit. So it was to Ben Benbough that Edward turned the morning after Eric Mulholland's visit.

For privacy and "to take the air," they had decided on an idle walk in the gardens back of the palace and had now come to the near edge of the lake. It was a windless, brassy-bright November day and the few final leaves of autumn were falling about them as they paused to watch some water birds foraging.

As they turned away to walk on, Edward resumed the conversation. "Sorry," he said, "I've been skirting about it. Let's call it what it was: a youthful fling. I was in my twenties." He recounted in a dozen sentences his brief encounter with Samantha Mulholland but said nothing of her pregnancy. Benbough listened dispassionately, his expression reflecting nothing.

"The problem is, Ben," Edward continued, "the damn thing's come back to haunt me and I'm afraid I've handled it badly. The lady, it would seem, has exaggerated the episode over the years, and her son has convinced himself that he – *he*, mind you! – has a grievance. He went so far as to get a job as a footman here at the palace and, once on the inside, began to slip hate notes under the door."

"Hate notes?"

"You know the sort of thing – who do you think you are, Mr. Big Shot, riding around in a Rolls-Royce while the rest of us have to grub for our money? That sort of rubbish."

"You reported this to Mr. Gracie?"

"I'm afraid not."

"Do you have the notes?"

"I didn't want them around so I flushed the damn things down the WC."

"I see," Benbough said. "Well, that shouldn't be much of a problem, sir. We'll have a word with him."

They paused at a bird-feeding station and Edward reached into it, flinging handfuls of grain in semi-circles onto the water. "I'm afraid there's more to it than that," he said. "Some months back he was given the sack and he blames it on me."

"How does he get these threats to you now that he's been sacked?"

"One of the footmen, I suppose. A friend."

They stood for a moment on the bridge. Surprised, a flock of ducks burst from almost beneath them, running on the water, settling with raucous complaints some fifty yards away. "Lately," Edward said, "he's begun to turn up where the Queen is making an appearance. He'll stand there in the crowd, glaring at her. As you might imagine, he's got her quite petrified."

They followed the edge of the lake. "I had him in yesterday," Edward said.

Benbough's eyebrows arched. "Really?"

"He'd insisted on seeing me. He's been threatening to go to the press with any number of what he calls his revelations and, foolishly, as I now realize, I decided to see him. I don't know what I was thinking. . . . That I could talk sense into him, I suppose."

"If I may say so, sir, that was most unwise. He might have made an attempt on your life."

"I realize that now in hindsight. I'm afraid I've handled the whole business rather badly."

"As well, it would give some credibility to his claims if he actually were to go to the press. Did he make any demands on you? Any threats?"

"He wants a few thousand pounds to, as he says, keep his trap shut. But that would be just the beginning. He's a . . . a ruddy psychopath."

"You didn't give him anything. Promise him anything?"

"No."

"Well now," Benbough said, "ease your mind, sir. We'll have a word with him. Not to worry."

"I wouldn't want to lay charges or get involved," Edward said.

"No, no, don't worry about that."

"You should know that he has apparently left a sealed letter with a friend with instructions to open it and give it to the press if he's arrested."

Benbough made a small, deprecating motion with his shoulders. "We'll find him, sir. Just leave it with me."

They started back toward the palace. "You understand that it would be embarrassing if . . . if his threats were bandied about. You do understand?"

"Of course, sir. Leave it with me, sir."

"You'll take care of it personally?"

"Indeed I will, sir."

"His name is Mulholland. Eric Mulholland. Household will have his address in their records." They were approaching the palace. "You *will* exercise the greatest discretion? There's been enough bad press lately."

"Ossie? It's Tim Finnegan. How are you?"
    "Fine."
    "It's been a long time."
    "Yeah. Right. I've been wildly busy. What's up?"
    "I was just wondering, that's all. It's been at least six weeks."
    "Look, Tim, I was on my way out the door. Can I get back to you?"
    "Sorry, I don't mean to be pushy, but. . . . Anyway, the reason for my call was to ask if you're still working on that story about Jeremy Walsh?"
    "You're damn right I am."
    "Well then, this may be of interest. You'll remember you asked me to keep tabs on his car. It was no problem. His garage is just three away from mine and I got in the habit of having a look on my way home from work. The past six weeks it's been gathering dust, but last night I noticed it had just been washed, and this morning it was gone. That probably means he's back and I thought I should let you know. Ossie. . . . Ossie, you still there?"
    "Sorry. I was thinking. Maybe he's loaned it to a friend. Maybe he's going to put it up for sale."
    "Could be. I just thought you'd like to know."
    "Yes. Thanks. Thanks, Tim. I appreciate the call."
    "It's nothing. Maybe we can get together over the weekend. I'll be here Saturday, most of Sunday. Why don't you stop by for a drink?"
    "Great idea. I'll get back to you. Right now I'm going to have to beetle out of here. Ta."
    Ossie put down the telephone and for a full minute sat gnawing on a thumbnail. Things had not been going

well for him. The story about Victoria and Jeremy had brought a short-lived firestorm of notoriety but had left him soured and profoundly disquieted. Hundreds of newspapers around the world and most of the electronic media had scalped the story without giving him a credit, and those that did make attribution referred not to him but to the *Herald*. He dismissed the thousand-pound bonus he'd been given as "pisspot cheap," but it had induced in him a sulphurous rage that fumed for weeks.

The story had faded surprisingly quickly. With not the slightest reaction from the palace, with Jeremy in New York – by all accounts, permanently – and Victoria back to her royal rounds, no amount of flogging could keep it alive. And the attitude of Replogle and company seemed to move overnight from "Super!" to "What have you done for us lately?" The answer was, not much. Ossie had chased a number of promising leads only to have them die aborning, and even his not inconsiderable skill at making much out of little hadn't been enough to earn him a by-line, much less a headline, for weeks. Consequently, the news that Jeremy might have slipped into town, possibly for a rendezvous with Victoria, set his heart to thumping and his nerve ends to vibrating.

In a sudden burst of activity, he snatched a telephone directory from a drawer, flopped it open on the desk, and rustled through the pages: Walsh. . . . Walsh. . . . Walsh, Albert; Walsh, J.A.; Walsh, James F; Walsh, Jeremy, 44 Rotherhithe Street, Bermondsey! He scribbled the number on a pad by the telephone and dialed it. On the eighth ring the receiver was picked up. "Hello. Hello. . . . " Ossie hung up the phone, pounding with a massive fist on the top of the desk. "*Hah!*" It had been Jeremy's voice; no question about that. The rotten bastard was back!

On the way home he went by way of Wapping, turned into the dockyard area, and, using his binoculars, stared across the Thames at Jeremy's flat. Yes, he was home; the drapes were open. They hadn't been for the past six weeks when occasionally he'd checked. On the drive home his mind was racing.

"Alfie, I want you to pack me a midnight snack. That bastard Walsh is back and I'm going to do a stake-out at his flat tonight."

Alfie flapped his apron in a flutter of irritation. "You couldn't of told me earlier. Of course not. I don't know what I've got in." He went first to the refrigerator, poked about, and then to the cupboards, banging each door shut. "What am I supposed to be – a bleedin' mindreader?"

Ossie had followed him to the refrigerator and was prying the top off a bottle of ale. "Where's the crisps?"

"I'll tell you where they'll be two minutes from now," Alfie said sullenly, spilling a heap into a serving bowl. "Gone!"

"See what you can come up with," Ossie said in zestful good humor. "I see you've got some pigs' feet in the fridge. Throw in a few of them and whatever else you can come up with. I could be up most of the night. What's for dinner?"

"Breaded pork chops," Alfie sighed. He went about setting the table. "You could of at least let me know," he groused, "I'm gonna get me a bleedin' crystal ball." He gestured with a fork. "There's some brie and crackers in the cupboard next to the fridge to tide you over."

Victoria was finding the temptation to tell Jeremy the secret almost irresistible: the baby would be a boy and they would be free to marry. But there remained a small wariness, a residual doubt, and she wanted it out of the way first. Then there was, of course, the promise to her parents not to tell anyone for a while. But did the "anyone" include Jeremy?

Hands in the sink, rinsing the dishes on which they'd eaten their late supper, she heard him thumping about in the room he used as a study, gathering whatever it was he had to take back to New York with him. She could picture him: pulling papers from drawers, fingering through files, tipping down books from the shelves with that fearsome concentration that sometimes made him oblivious to what was happening around him, sometimes even to her. It had taken a little getting used to.

She was suffused with warmth in the knowledge of his presence just beyond the wall. Only yesterday he'd been three thousand miles away, and would be again tomorrow. But that would soon pass. He'd be back in another ten days to begin his series on the democracies, and although it would mean being away as often as he was in London over the next few months, it would mean also that the apparently unbridgeable chasm that had lain between them for so long would be gone with the birth of the baby and that, with the passage of only a few months, they would be together for the remainder of their lives.

She was wondering what he would say if she were to call to him and, as he entered the kitchen, greet him with: "I say there, old chap, want to get married? I've grown rather fond of you, you know. I have my parents' consent. Come mid-January we'll have the world's consent. I've got a church picked out in Westminster, and a parson – an Archibishop, possibly – who might be free. The date? How does next June first sound? Happens to be my birthday and they're planning a small party. Might as well economize and use the decorations. What do you say, old bean?" She let out a small squeal of delight.

Borne on the thought, she raised a hand to tap on the wall between them to summon him. But as quickly as her fantasy had come to warm her, a chill of apprehension followed. The wall between them. . . . So often there had been a wall between them. Walls of circumstance and of tradition. Walls that others had interposed to keep them apart. Walls they had themselves erected; *these* were the barriers that now gave her pause. For all the fact that they loved each other, they were so different. They'd talked about it. Often. He'd talked about his childhood, about his parents and family, about his home in Gary, about the schools he'd attended, about the tiny clapboard church with the electronic bells in the steeple in which he'd been confirmed, about his working, during summer vacations and on weekends hauling slag from the mill in a dump-truck to make enough money to pay his tuition at Northwestern. Even as she listened she'd been remembering her own childhood and how utterly unlike his it had been. She hadn't been nearly as close to her parents as he had to his; they'd been too busy. In her childhood years she'd been more attached to Katie, her nannie. Most of her schooling had been with tutors, and when she switched to Knightston, a small college near Harrow, she'd been driven to school each day in the big, black Daimler with her chauffeur and her policeman in the front seat. She'd prepared for her confirmation under the instruction of the Right Reverend Hamilton Jamieson Cheam, the palace rector. When not attending services with her parents in cathedrals here there and everywhere, she had gone, when there was no avoiding it, to the family's own Church of England chapel in the palace.

Jeremy had had his brothers; she'd had only cousins or friends. Jeremy had talked about wandering the streets of some of the great cities of the world. She'd traveled more widely than he but had never been free to explore an interesting street or poke about in exotic shops or nip into a gallery or a bar that looked inviting. Certainly not alone, never without her ubiquitous policemen hanging about nearby or without crowds gawking. Jeremy had had to scrimp and save when he wanted something; she'd never earned a pay packet. Indeed, as was true of her parents, she never carried money.

And how different they were in their relationships with the other sex. She'd had few profound or involving experiences with men. There had been flirtations and escapades of a sort, but nothing to speak of, certainly nothing comparable to the variety of experiences some of her friends had had. Jane, for instance. There were good reasons for her lack of emotional involvement. Her circle of acquaintances was wide but intimate friends were few. Especially among young men. Many of them treated her like one of themselves, but she could sense that they were afraid of her – she was, after all, the heir to the throne.

Moreover, Jeremy had been married. He never talked about it and she would not, of course, ask about it. She'd read about his wife and daughter in those dreadful stories in the press, and somehow she hadn't seemed to be the kind of woman Jeremy would be attracted to. But he must have been in love with her or he wouldn't have married her, wouldn't have given her a child. And probably there had been other women. Of course there had. When she wondered, as she occasionally did, how many, she was momentarily made ill by the thought and banished it by an act of will. Things he'd said had made it obvious that he disliked his former wife, disliked her intensely. Why? What had she done? What had gone wrong? Could it happen again? To herself, perhaps?

She thrust the thought away.

Yes, they were *so* different, but wasn't it his being different that had first attracted her to him? He was unlike most of the men she knew. Most of them were nice enough – although, heaven knew, not a few of them were bubble-headed ciphers – but they were the kind of male friends she had grown up with. Some of them were interesting and aware and pleasant to be with, but for all their individuality they seemed, oddly, to be cut from the same cloth. It was the fact that Jeremy was different that had made her want to see him again after their first meeting. He was older than she, eight years older, and wiser in many ways; more experienced, more worldly. All of which was good. She liked his directness, although sometimes it could be offputting. He had strong opinions, but then so did she. Would they wear well together? It would help that they would both be busy. With her mother back in harness and her new brother the heir apparent, she would be able over the months and years ahead to cut back on her official duties and have more time for herself. She'd be able to reserve specific times for her writing. She'd discovered that there was a certain rhythm to writing; you needed to do it nearly every day and she hadn't been able to manage that. Imagine, being able to control your own time! . . .

She suddenly burst into song. *"Wouldn't it be luverly? Luverly, luverly, luverly? Wouldn't it be . . . luv-er-ly?"*

What a godsend, the new baby being a boy! His birth would bring her an entirely new life. She really must call Jeremy in and tell him it was going to be a boy. She was free! *They* were free!

"Oh, God, please protect dear little whatever his multiple name will be from all harm! . . ."

Ossie Docherty switched on the map light in his car and looked at his watch. 12:52. He'd been parked on Fulford Street for just over four hours and was beginning to do a slow burn. "The bastard!" he muttered.

He knew she was in there. He'd made sure of that before choosing the parking place for the stake-out. He'd cruised the area, and on the second tour around had spotted the royal car, parked in the shadows up a tiny lane, lights out, easily within range of a summons on the radio phone.

Ossie was in an ideal spot: behind a parked car not one hundred feet from Jeremy's flat and with sufficient clearance to permit him, when the moment came, to pull into the street and roar up to the front door of the flat with the entire area in the beam of his headlights.

The problem at the moment was that he was exceedingly uncomfortable. His right leg was asleep and his left was tingling. The pain in his lower back had become almost unbearable. Jammed behind the steering wheel he was almost immobilized. He'd had the seat-adjustment mechanism set back when be bought the car, making it possible for him to wedge his great bulk behind the steering wheel without too much difficulty, but even so, it was a tight fit. Yet he dare not get out of the car to stretch his legs. You could bet that that would be the moment when the hall light would go on and Victoria's driver would glide into position at the front door to pick her up. And by the time Ossie squeezed back behind the wheel and got his car in motion, it might be too late. Maybe it would help if he undid his belt and unzipped his fly. Ah yes! There. . . .

He reached across the seat for the brown paper bag Alfie had packed for him. Three sandwiches, a few stalks of celery, a half dozen date squares, a pear, and, wrapped in wax paper, four pickled pigs' feet. He'd almost finished his snack when he saw the light go on in the entrance hall.

Harry Newly was in his living-room watching Greer Garson and Walter Pidgeon in *Mrs. Miniver* when he heard the sound of an automobile horn from the street. When it continued unabated, he went to the window and, shading the glass with cupped hands to eliminate the reflections, peered into the near darkness. The sound was coming from a car parked at the curb immediately behind his. There was a man in the car – he could make that out in the ghostly gleam of the street light – but he seemed to be doing nothing to end the piercing, sustained howl of his horn.

Harry threw up the window. "Hey there, mate!" he shouted. "Will you shut that damn thing off?" He realized immediately that, in the din, his voice couldn't be heard a dozen feet away and, seeing no one else in sight, decided that he would have to deal with the problem himself.

As he approached the car, he realized that something was wrong. The man behind the wheel had fallen forward, his head was on his chest, and the great bulk of his body was pressing against the steering wheel. Harry pulled open the door, seized the man by the arm, and shook him. "Hey! Hey, Mister! You all right?"

He could see the man clearly now. His eyes were open and staring. His mouth was agape and strings of spittle dribbled from it. His face and neck were a blue-gray in color and shining with perspiration. "Heart attack," Harry said and ran toward his flat.

The police were first to arrive and were followed within minutes by a fire-department pumper and an ambulance. A crowd had begun to gather, most of them with coats or windbreakers over their night clothes. Harry identified himself to a policeman as the one who had placed the call to 999, but the policeman paid no attention and ordered him back on the sidewalk with the others.

Harry watched the swiftly efficient procedures of the emergency teams. A paramedic leaned into the car, did a quick examination, and stepped back. Two of the firemen tugged at the man's body, struggling to pull it free of the

339

steering wheel. As they hauled him from the car, his trousers pulled down, pale, hairless legs revealing underpants embroidered with tiny forget-me-nots. With the man on his back on the pavement, a fireman leaned over to give artificial resuscitation, only to pull away after a few seconds, shaking his head. There was an urgent heads-together consultation. Two of the firemen then seized the man's arms and pulled him into a sitting position while one of the others squatted behind him, wrapped powerful arms about the man's chest, knotted his fists, and pulled with hard, spasmodic jerks.

After a moment he, too, stopped. A paramedic kneeled beside the man, who was now spreadeagled on the pavement, placed his palms on the man's chest, and, matching his moves to a count, delivered sharp downward thrusts. One of the medics pulled an instrument from a pocket of his white coat, unfolded it, turning on a light, and inserted it down the man's throat. In a moment he got to his feet, said something to his partner, and went to the radio telephone in the ambulance. Someone covered the body with a blanket, someone else fetched a stretcher. The sense of urgency had passed.

Pulling a small notebook from a pocket, the policeman came over to Harry Newly. "You're the one who called in?" he asked. Harry nodded. "Just a few questions, if you don't mind," the policeman said.

"What was it?" Harry asked. "A heart attack?"

"No," said the policeman, flipping the pages of his book. "Asphyxiation. He choked on some food. Pigs' feet, it looks like."

When Mary returned to her apartment from the formal reception at which she had welcomed the new Italian ambassador, she discovered a sealed envelope on the writing desk in her sitting-room. She recognized the single word *Mary* as being in her husband's handwriting and ripped open the envelope. There was no note, just a one-column clipping from a newspaper.

POLICE ARREST IRA SUSPECT

Officers of the Special Branch of the Metropolitan Police today arrested Eric Sean Mulholland, 28, of no fixed address on charges of illegal possession of a firearm and various explosive devices.

Mulholland, unemployed, and a native of Belfast, Northern Ireland, resisted the arresting officers and had to be restrained before being removed from a vacant flat at 92-A Borough Road in North Southwark where he has apparently been living. He is suspected of being a member of the IRA.

Mulholland was arraigned at Magistrates Court, Newington, and committed for psychiatric examination at Lambeth Hospital.

♛ THREE

"MR. WALSH?"

"Yes."

"Just a minute now, I want to be sure I have this right. You're, like, the reporter with the *New York Times*?"

"Yes."

"I hope you don't mind, Mr. Walsh, sir, if I don't give you my name. Is that all right?"

"Well, no, as a matter of fact. I don't talk on the telephone to people who won't give their name. You'll have to understand that I get – "

"Would it be enough if I was to tell you that I work at the palace? Buckingham Palace."

"And you want to tell me about something dreadful going on at the palace."

"Well, in a way, yes. But – "

"I'm sorry, miss, but I'm busy. I'm going to have to hang up now."

"Wait a minute, sir. Please! If I do give you my name you won't put it in the paper or tell nobody it was me rang you up?"

"Now, look here – "

"Maidy. Maidy Lightstone. I'm a chambermaid, sir, at the palace. Bedroom floor."

342

"Well, that's very interesting but. . . ."

"You said a minute ago, sir, that I wanted to tell you about something dreadful going on at the palace, and in a way that's true. At least it *was* true. And it still could be. I mean, that's why I rang you up. I didn't know who to talk to, and then I heard you were back from America and I thought maybe I could tell you. I mean, like, you're a reporter and, if I may say so, sir, a friend of Her Royal Highness, and I thought, well, he'll know what to do. It's got me so worried I can't sleep. I'm afraid if I tell what I seen I'll be in trouble, and if I don't. . . . I don't even want to think about that! And I've been told not to tell nobody or I'll get the sack. Or worse. But ever since I seen that article in the paper I've been just sick with worry. . . . Sorry, sir. Like my mother says, I run on sometimes."

"Perhaps, Miss Lightstone, you should just out and tell me what it was you saw that has you so frightened."

"I hope you don't think, sir, I rang you up because I want it in the paper, because I don't. I hope you know that."

"I understand. You don't want it in the paper. But you said a minute ago that it was already in the paper."

"No, no. I didn't mean that *it* was in the paper but that *he* was in the paper, and that's what's got me worried. I mean, about him being a member of the IRA, which nobody I'm sure at the palace knew. And if he knows a secret way to. . . . I'm sorry. I'm not sure I should even tell. I mean, I've been warned not to tell. By a policeman. But since I seen in the paper he was IRA, I've been thinking that maybe it's something that's *got* to be told even though I'm not supposed to."

"Maidy. . . . May I call you Maidy?"

"Well, sir. . . . I mean, yes sir, if you like."

"Let's go back to the beginning. You saw something in the paper. Tell me that part."

"That part.... I suppose that would be all right. It *was* in the paper."

"Exactly."

"Last week it was, sir. That they'd arrested a certain person and that he was IRA and that he had some guns and some bombs."

"And that's it?"

"No, sir. It's what they *didn't* say in the paper, although the part about him being IRA was surprise enough for this week."

"And what didn't they say?"

"Well, like they said he was unemployed, but they didn't say where he was unemployed *from*, if you get my meaning. Like, from the palace."

"This IRA man worked at the palace? What did he do?"

"He was a footman.... There now, I've said it."

"How recently?"

"Like, last April. I don't suppose there's no harm in telling you his name. It was in the paper, like you say, and they've got him put away for now. Mulholland, sir. Eric Mulholland. You see, sir, what worries me is, if he knew how to get in and out and not get caught, maybe his IRA friends know, too. And maybe next time, Her Majesty would be there.... I get the shivers just thinking about it."

"The Queen might be where, Maidy?"

"In her apartment."

"Maidy, are you saying that you saw this Mulholland going in and out of the Queen's apartment at a time he shouldn't have been?"

"At four-thirty in the morning! And I didn't say I seen him going in – just coming out. Out of.... Well, I might as well be hung for a sheep as a lamb – out of her bedroom window."

"Her bedroom window at four-thirty in the morning?"

"Well, maybe not her bedroom. It could've been her dining-room or her dressing-room – I'm not sure just what's what in Her Majesty's apartment – but coming out of her window, yes. . . . Hello? Are you still there, sir?"

"I'm still here, Maidy. I'm just having trouble believing what I'm hearing."

"That's what my friend said. He said nobody'd believe me anyways. But I'm not lying, sir. I mean, would I make up a story like that, knowing, like he said, that if I told anybody I'd probably get the sack? The only reason I'm telling you, sir, is that if Eric could get into her apartment and nobody know, maybe some other IRA could, and what about Her Majesty then? I mean, the only way I can figure it out is that she wasn't there. And if she wasn't, where's the harm in telling? The way I feel is, I've got to tell somebody so they can warn Her Majesty or Mr. Gracie or somebody that the IRA knows how to get into Her Majesty's apartment. It's got me worried sick. Maybe they've already fixed the lock on the window or the door or whatever it was and maybe there's no danger and maybe I'm worrying myself sick over nothing. But I just felt I had to tell somebody or how would I feel if, like, something happened to Her Majesty? You don't believe me, do you?"

"Yes, Maidy. I do."

"Thank you, sir. Then you'll see to it that something's done? Just so's I can be sure?"

"Yes, Maidy. I'll check into it."

"And you won't tell who told you."

"Maidy, there's one thing you haven't told me: who was the person – the policeman, you said – who told you to say nothing?"

"Ooooh, sir. . . . I don't know as I want to tell that part. Anyways, he's not with the palace police anymore. He got a transfer to Traffic Division."

"But I don't understand. If he was a policeman and he knew about this . . . this intruder, why didn't he report it? And why did he tell you not to tell anyone?"

"Because, sir, we was both breaking the rules. The reason I was where I was and seen what I seen was because him and me was . . . friends, you might say."

"I see. And you won't tell me his name?"

"No, sir. I'm afraid not, sir. I promised."

"Have you told anyone else about what you saw? Anyone?"

"No, sir. Not a soul. Well, I did tell my mother, but she's in a wheelchair and doesn't get around and what harm could that be? No, nobody. Not a soul."

When, after another five minutes, Jeremy replaced the telephone in its cradle, he remained in his chair for a long time, his gaze far off, thinking.

"Is that Kevin McNee's residence?"

"Yes."

"May I speak to him, please?"

"Yes. May I say who's calling? He's just come off duty and he's upstairs changing."

"My name is Walsh. Jeremy Walsh. No hurry. I'll stay on the line."

He'd had no trouble tracing Kevin. He'd simply dialed the police guardroom at the palace and asked for the Chief Inspector. "I need to get in touch with one of your men," he'd said. "He did me a very big favor some months ago, and with Christmas coming I'd like to send him a little something. The trouble is, I never did get his name and now I'm told he's been transferred to Traffic Division."

It had seemed best to begin with Maidy's friend. He certainly had to do something about what she'd told him and the obvious first step was to try to find out how much of what she'd told him was true. There was no doubting the urgency in her voice or the fear, but for all the fact that he found her credible, he knew that the reality could have been embellished by time and a heightened imagination. The facts might turn out to be very different from her memory of them.

He had no sooner introduced himself and given the reason for his call than McNee interrupted to make veiled references to the fact that he was unable to speak freely at the moment. He took Jeremy's number, promised to call back shortly, and did.

"Sorry I wasn't able to speak to you earlier," he said, "but we had guests. Now, sir, what can I do for you?"

Jeremy told him straightforwardly of the telephone call from Maidy. "Although, I should say, she didn't give me your name. I dug that out. Now, Mr. McNee, before you respond, let me make one thing clear: I am not at all interested in your acquaintanceship with Miss Lightstone. All I'm trying to find out is whether what she told me is true."

There was a brief silence on the line. "I believe you're with the *New York Times*," Kevin said.

"Yes, I am," Jeremy said. "But I'm not calling you in that capacity. If what Miss Lightstone tells me is true, the royal family could be in some danger."

"Oh, I wouldn't think so, sir. Miss Lightstone has – what shall we call it? – a very good imagination. If you ask me, sir – and I don't mean to speak unkindly of the lady – she watches the telly too much."

"Just to have things straight," Jeremy said, "are you telling me that she never told you about seeing someone coming out of one of the windows of the Queen's apartment?"

"No, sir, I'm not saying that. She told me all kinds of stories."

"And you never told her to keep it quiet?"

"No, sir, I'm not saying that either. I may have told her not to talk about it. I've told her that any number of times – about her wild stories, I mean." Jeremy thought there was a forced quality to McNee's laugh. "If I may be so bold, sir, I'd suggest that you forget it. I personally made it a point to check the log that night and there's not a word about anything out of line. As I said, Miss Lightstone watches the telly too much."

"You don't by any chance recall the date?"

"The date? I'm afraid not. It's some time ago now."

"I though perhaps since you troubled to check the log you might be able to recall it. Miss Lightstone says it was April 11."

"She may be right. I'm afraid I don't keep track of all her stories. Now, if there's nothing else, sir. . . . "

"Just one more thing. She told me you told her how to bypass the alarm mechanism on the door to the Belgian Suite. That would be a very serious matter, I would think, and not the kind of thing she might learn on the telly."

There was a brief silence. "Mr. Walsh, I'm a policeman and proud of it. I'm going on twelve years on the force. Do you think I would do such a foolish thing? Take a chance on a black mark on my record?"

"I have no idea, Mr. McNee. I know nothing about you other than what Maidy told me and she told me that that's what you did. I would be happy to hear you deny it."

"Mr. Walsh, I've had enough of this conversation. I have guests waiting for me at home. I must say good afternoon to you, sir."

On a sudden thought Jeremy turned to Sunday, April 11 in his desk calendar. The page was empty except for the jotting: *PM – Phone call from Queen re: Vicky. Returning Tuesday!* Of course! That was the evening the Queen had called to give him the message about Vicky's return from Gibraltar. He remembered being taken aback on picking up the telephone and hearing a voice say, with a slight chuckle, "This is Victoria's personal secretary of the moment, her mother." He remembered not being quite sure whether it was a prank or actually the Queen, and that he'd stumbled in his responses. He recalled inquiring as to how she was feeling and thinking that she certainly seemed in good spirits. She'd chatted on for a few minutes about how she and the Duke loved Windsor and how reluctant they had been to return to the city. She had ended the conversation by inviting him to join them the following weekend.

So she *had* been at Buckingham Palace that Sunday night.

He sat for a moment, frowning in concentration, and then picked up the telephone and called Don Medwick, the *Times* correspondent whose particular responsibility was covering the royal family.

"Don. Jeremy. Do you have your calendar handy?"

"Right here."

"What do you show on April 11?"

"April 11.... April 11.... Not much, it was a Sunday. M and E return from Windsor.... Wait a minute, wasn't that the time when the Queen wasn't feeling up to par? Yes, she'd canceled Gibraltar and instead gone off to Windsor."

"What do you have on the Monday?"

"On the Monday.... Queen ill. A slight indisposition was the reason given. I remember seeing her the following day – yes, the opening of the new Salvation Army headquarters. She looked pretty rocky. As a matter of fact, there was some badgering of poor old Robin – Robin Whyte, the palace press secretary. She'd canceled Gibraltar, taken a week's rest at Windsor, wasn't able to cope on Monday, and looked pretty grim on Tuesday. Some of the fellows filed stories. You know; the Queen's health. Is she working too hard? That kind of thing."

When Jeremy hung up, he began to pace his study. After a few minutes he went again to the telephone. "Vicky, darling, this is a real imposition. I hope I'm not interrupting anything important."

"Only something of world-shaking significance: Agatha's about to do my hair."

"Promise not to keep you more than a minute. One of our staff is doing a feature on famous people's pets. You know, a nothing story on why does the President of France favor budgies when the Canadian Prime Minister is mad for guppies. Everybody knows the Queen's an ailurophile – "

"A dastardly lie, she's British."

" . . . but has heard that she recently took on a dog. True?"

"Yes, but only partly. Mother's addicted to cats but she does have one dog. Not a pet so much as something to give her a feeling of security when Daddy's away. It's a Lab. She had it sent down from Balmoral. It sleeps in her bedroom, but for heaven's sake don't tell your reporter that"

"When did she get it? Not that it matters."

"I don't know. She had it when I got home from Gibraltar, I remember that. Nearly took my leg off. But, look, Jeremy, please don't let him make a big thing of the dog. Mother's a patron of about two dozen cat societies and she really isn't much for dogs. But don't let him say that either. Never say anything negative about dogs in

Britain if you value your life. Got to go. Agatha's frowning at me and pointing at her watch."

Some six months earlier, Jeremy had done a piece on the Special Branch of the Metropolitan Police with particular emphasis on its methods in countering the IRA, and had at the time formed a friendship of sorts with its head of public relations, a Sergeant Jack Hyslop. He turned up the number in his desktop file.

"Jack. Jeremy Walsh."

"Mr. Walsh, sir. Nice to hear from you again."

"You're well?"

"Tip-top, sir. And you?"

"Fine. Jack, I'm curious about something. There was a piece in the *Telegraph* last week about you people picking up a man by the name of Mulholland. Eric Mulholland. I gather he's mixed up with the IRA. I'll tell you what makes me curious. The item makes no mention of it but I'm told Mulholland used to work as a footman at the palace. If that's true, it makes the story worth a hell of a lot more than two or three inches on an inside page. What can you tell me about it?"

"Not a thing. I heard something about it but I don't recall exactly what it was. Give me five minutes and I'll get back to you. Are you at your office or at home?"

"Home."

"Good. I'll call you back as soon as I can check the file."

When half an hour passed with no response, Jeremy dialed Special Branch and asked for Hyslop. A woman informed him that Sergeant Hyslop was tied up but that Deputy Assistant Commissioner Cannington would take his call.

"Good afternoon, Mr. Walsh. You were inquiring about the arrest of a Mr. Eric Mulholland, I believe?"

"My goodness," Jeremy said. "I wasn't expecting to talk to you. It's not a matter of great moment. But, as Sergeant Hyslop may have told you, I'm curious as to why the story in the *Telegraph* makes no reference to Mulholland being a former employee at Buckingham Palace."

Cannington's voice was crisp but unchallenging. "I'm sorry, Mr. Walsh, but I don't get your point."

"Well, I suppose it's that if a man who's a member of the IRA worked as a footman at the palace, a man who had a gun and some explosive materials in his possession when he was arrested, that pretty well fits my definition of news."

"Yes, I can understand your thinking, but I'm afraid it's away off base in this instance. The accused is a drifter. He's been unemployed for the past six months. He talked about the IRA but it's very doubtful that he has a connection. In a word, Mr. Walsh, the man is a crank."

"Would it be possible for me to have a few words with him?"

"I'm afraid not. He's at Lambeth undergoing psychiatric tests."

"I'm given to understand that he's not at all crazy."

"And where did you get that information?"

"From a member of the staff at the palace."

"May I ask who, sir?"

"I'm not at liberty to disclose that."

"Well, now, Mr. Walsh, you wouldn't expect me to – "

"Look," Jeremy said with a show of impatience. "I don't want to make a federal case out of this. It may not be worth any more attention than it's been given. But if a man who worked at the palace and undoubtedly had access to the Queen was a member of the IRA, that would be of more than passing interest to the public."

Cannington's voice was suddenly silken. "Mr. Walsh, let me speak plainly. The man is a mental incompetent. And delusional. He was no threat to anyone at the palace, believe me. Let me assure you that there's nothing here. And Mr. Walsh, if the *New York Times* were to carry a story linking him to the palace, you can imagine what would happen in the popular press here. It could do all kinds of mischief. I know I can rely on your good judgement in the matter. And now, if you'll forgive me, I have matters to attend to. Thank you, Mr. Walsh."

Old Trumper, Jeremy thought. Yes, of course! He could be the linchpin he needed.

Police Sergeant George Trumper, after forty years with the palace police, had been retired, "full of years and honor," as the Queen had put it, at a private celebration in the White Drawing Room at the palace. She had presented him with a gold signet ring and, as she did from time to time with staff members who had given long and extraordinary service, with the right to live in one of her "grace and favor houses" until his death. "Old Trumper," as he was called by everyone who knew him – and not without respect – had already been the duty policeman in the King's Corridor for some years when Mary came to the palace as a girl of fourteen. She had found a friend in him. In his broad Glaswegian accent he would regale her with colorful stories and would sometimes keep her up well beyond her bedtime with wildly inaccurate but engaging tales of British history – about which he seemed to have first-hand knowledge through a succession of apparently ubiquitous ancestors. He had played hopscotch and jacks and given piggy-back rides to Victoria, in her turn, and when finally, beset by arthritis, he had installed a cushioned chair in the closet across from the Queen's apartment, into which, during the long morning hours, he would sometimes sink for "forty winks," everyone from the Queen to Mr. Gracie turned a blind eye.

Victoria had mentioned him with affection to Jeremy a number of times and he now recalled the regret she had expressed when Trumper was taken off the night "turn" and shortly thereafter retired. Jeremy had found him in his tiny backyard, wielding a rake and cursing his neighbor's late-shedding oak tree.

"So you're Her Royal Highness' young man," Trumper had said when they were seated chummily on his back steps. "I'll tell you to your face what I've told others: you're not good enough for her. But then, nobody could be. You're a Yank I'm told. There's not much you can do about that, but if the two of you love each other, you should off and tie the knot no matter who says you nay. So be a man and stand by your guns."

Trumper's glass of stout was empty and he eyed it with small, rueful shakings of his head. "I'm allowed one in the morning and one . . . " he gave a wink of a rheumy eye, "with my supper. But can I fetch you another? Perhaps I'll join you for a wee drop – so you won't have to drink alone."

"Thank you kindly," Jeremy said, raising his glass to empty it. "I'll save mine for my next visit."

"It's just as well," Trumper said, massaging both knees with arthritic hands. "I'm not sure I could make it to the kitchen and back. Damned leaves," he said, glaring at his neighbor's tree.

"Exactly how long were you with the palace police?" Jeremy asked.

"Forty years, eight months, and twenty-one days," Trumper said in resonant, rolling tones, made no less emphatic by a small quaver. "And in all those years didn't ask a day off and was away only nine days sick. What do you think of that? Hey? What do you think of that?"

"Remarkable," Jeremy said.

"I should think so," Trumper said, wincing as his fingers found a painful cranny in a joint. "They even extended my retirement age, did you know that? And when was that done before? At Her Majesty's personal request. What do you think of that?"

Jeremy obliged with a mildly astonished shaking of his head. "When did you retire? It was last April, wasn't it?"

A frown deepened the creases on Trumper's brow. "No, sir. June first. Forty years, eight months, and twenty-one days."

Jeremy's face didn't betray his disappointment. "I'd heard it was in early April. I remember Her Royal Highness speaking about it."

"No, sir," Trumper said emphatically. "June first. What you probably remember is Her Royal Highness remarking on the day I was relieved of my duty in the King's Corridor. *That* was in April. April 11, as a matter of fact."

Jeremy smiled a slight tight smile.

♚ FOUR

JEREMY SAT AT HIS DESK making notes, fitting together the pieces of the puzzle. There could be no doubt about it: on the morning of April 11, some time before 4:30 a.m., an intruder had broken into the Queen's apartment at the palace and, having been surprised by her, had made his escape through the window in her dressing-room. And in the eight months following the break-in, there had been a cover-up that extended from members of the Household staff to the Palace Police and to the highest levels at New Scotland Yard, even to members of the royal family.

He moved to his typewriter, the better to put his scribbled notes into some order.

> – Intruder a former palace footman. Dismissed week before break-in. Name, Eric Sean Mulholland, 28. Native of Belfast. Unemployed. According to Special Branch, member Irish Republican Army but not important. "Mentally incompetent." According to Maidy Lightstone, palace chambermaid: "A decent sort. Didn't seem to me like he was crackers."

> – Question: how did he get into Queen's apt? Possibility: from palace roof to deck over bow window

Queen's sitting-room, then to small balcony at Principal Floor level.

– Surprised by Queen before he could plant explosives. (What other motive for break-in?) Escaped through window Queen's dressing-room onto balcony, dropping to ground. Observed by Lightstone. Re-entered palace, northernmost door, Belgian Suite. Alarm mechanism by-passed earlier. Inside palace, probably changed from footman's uniform to street clothes and left.

– Lightstone reported incident evening of April 11 to then member of palace police, Sgt. Kevin McNee. McNee not only didn't report break-in but warned Lightstone not to. McNee denies knowledge of break-in, suggested Lightstone "made up story." Says no mention on police log. Possibility: McNee in league with Mulholland? Motive?

– Queen in shock after break-in. Confined to apt all day April 11. Appeared shaken April 12. Sgt. Geo. Trumper replaced day following break-in.

– Queen installs black Lab guard dog immediately after break-in. Sleeps in bedroom.

– Mulholland arrested by officers Special Branch. Charge: possession firearm, explosive materials. Committed for psychiatric examination, Lambeth Hosp. Held incommunicado. Special Branch plays down Mulholland tie-in to IRA.

Jeremy leaned back in his chair, his eyes narrowed, his brow drawn down in concentration. He was remembering reports of another palace break-in some years back. The details were vague, but as he recalled them, a man with a Dickensian name (Fagan?) had broken into Elizabeth

II's bedroom. There had been a major public inquiry and revelations of monumental carelessness in palace security. He pushed back his chair. Even though it was Sunday and the office was closed, he would drive downtown and check the files.

The *Times'* files were not extensive, so he went across the street to the *Telegraph* where he had permission to use the morgue. There, he was surprised at the extent of the coverage. There were news stories and features from publications around the world. He settled down finally to read the microfilm copy of a feature article in the *Sunday Magazine.*

The morning of Friday, July 9, 1982, dawned hot and muggy. In Buckingham Palace, Queen Elizabeth II was asleep in her bed alone. Her husband, Prince Philip, who had spent the night in his own quarters, had risen early to leave for Scotland to compete in some four-in-hand driving trials. Members of the palace kitchen and cleaning staff were already on duty or were arriving to begin their day's work.

At 6:45, a thirty-five-year-old unemployed laborer, Michael Fagan – a man suffering from the delusion at times that he was the son of Nazi Rudolf Hess – scaled the ten-foot-high stone wall on the south side of the palace grounds, carefully made his way over the rotating spikes and barbed wire that surmount the wall, and dropped to the ground inside. He was wearing sandals, socks, blue jeans, and a dirty T-shirt. An off-duty policeman, heading home on his motorcycle down Buckingham Palace Road, saw Fagan – as he would testify later – "acting suspiciously near the railings" and reported this by radio-telephone to a policeman in the palace gardens. He, using his transceiver, relayed the information to the police guardroom in the palace. A superficial search was made outside the palace wall and abandoned.

Fagan had already avoided one photoelectric beam. He now tripped another but it failed to function. Skulking behind a temporary canvas canopy erected at the Ambassador's entrance, and moving in the shadows, he tried a number of doors and windows seeking entrance to the palace itself. Within the Quadrangle, he reached one of the two Stamp Rooms, discovered an unlocked window and climbed through it, triggering an alarm in the Security Control room. A signal light began to flash. The sergeant on duty immediately switched it off and reset it, grumpily reassuring himself that, "That damned alarm is always going off for no reason."

In the Stamp Room, Fagan found the door to the corridor locked. He struggled with it, then turned away angry and left the room by the window through which he had entered, triggering the alarm a second time. "There's that bloody bell again!" exclaimed the sergeant, switching it off.

Standing in the Quadrangle, Fagan studied the windows on the floor above. He saw a casement window in the office of the Master of the Household standing open. It had been left open by a chambermaid shortly after 6 am to air out the room. Removing his socks and sandals, Fagan shinnied up a drainpipe and was inside the palace.

It was now 7 am and he was on the Principal Floor, the level on which he knew the Queen's apartment was located. He had a rough idea of its location for there had been a number of photographs of the palace in the press in prior weeks, including an aerial view with an arrow pointing to the Queen's bedroom.

Barefoot, his hair an unkempt tangle falling to his shoulders, Fagan wandered down the Household Corridor to the East Gallery, and from there made his way past the Grand Staircase to the Long Gallery, a magnificent, vaulted enclosure some 150 feet long, hung with dozens of the finest paintings in the Queen's extensive collection. Later, Fagan would testify, "I just kept following the pictures as a guide."

On he went, past the State Dining Room, the Music Room, in which so many royal christenings have taken place, the White Drawing Room, and the former Ballroom, now called the Blue Drawing Room. Finding the door to the Throne Room ajar, he went in and stood for a moment, awed by the twin thrones of carved and gilt wood raised on a three-step dais under a rearing red velvet canopy. Then, casually, he sauntered over to the Queen's throne and tried it on for size.

During his explorations he had passed some of the palace servants. Although he was barefoot, dirty, and unkempt, none of them challenged him, taking him, as they said later, to be a workman who had arrived early.

It was now 7:15. Michael Fagan had been within the palace enclosure for half an hour and was at the entrance to the King's Corridor along which are ranged the royal apartments. There was no one on duty in the corridor. The armed police sergeant – shod in slippers for the long silent night watch outside the Queen's bedroom – had gone off duty at 6 am. His replacement, a footman (the Queen had insisted that there not be a uniformed policeman outside her apartment during the day) was nowhere in sight – he had taken the Queen's corgis for a morning romp in the palace gardens.

The door to the dog room was open. Fagan went in, found a glass ashtray, and smashed it, cutting his thumb. Then, carrying a shard of the broken glass, he crossed the corridor and entered the Queen's dressing-room, slamming the door behind him. He was having domestic problems, problems with his wife, his four children, two stepchildren, and his wife's parents, all of whom were living with him, and, on the spur of the moment, had decided that, in the presence of the Queen, he would slash his wrists.

The slamming of the door had awakened the Queen. As she would say later, "I realized immediately it wasn't a servant, they don't slam doors." Then, suddenly, Fagan was in her bedroom, tugging at the curtains, trying to pull them open. The Queen sat upright in bed. "Our eyes met and both of us looked dumbfounded," she would say later. Sharply, in a voice that would give pause to most people, she commanded, "Get out of here at once!"

But Fagan took no heed. The jagged piece of glass between his fingers, blood dripping from his thumb, he approached the bed. The Queen reached across and pressed the night alarm button connected to the police guardroom. It was not working. Quickly she pressed the bedside bell which rang in a pantry out in the corridor, but there was no response: the housemaid was cleaning in an adjacent room with the door closed.

As Fagan sat down on the bed, the Queen picked up the telephone and dialed 222. In a normal voice, not wanting to excite the intruder, she said, "I want a police officer." The switchboard operator recognized the Queen's voice and immediately relayed the message to the security room. It was logged at 7:18 am.

The Queen now engaged Fagan in conversation. All her years of experience in keeping a conversation going with total strangers came to her aid. Guarding her words, careful not to alarm him, she talked to Fagan about his family and about her own, remarking on being told his age, "Then Prince Charles is a year younger than you are."

Again she picked up the telephone and asked the operator why there had been no response to her request for a policeman. No one had made haste, apparently, because "she had sounded so calm."

Now an opportunity presented itself. Fagan asked if she had a cigarette. "As you can see," she said, "there are none in this room, but I will have some fetched for you." She got out of bed, went into the corridor and found a housemaid, a stalwart Yorkshire lass by the name of Elizabeth Andrew. When she peered past the Queen into the bedroom and saw the improbable figure of the barefoot Fagan, his hand bloody, sitting on the bed, she gasped in her Middlesbrough accent, "Oooh, bloody 'ell, Ma'am, 'e shouldn't be there!"

Together, the Queen and the chambermaid managed to coax Fagan out of the bedroom, telling him there were cigarettes in a nearby pantry. At that moment, Paul Wybrew, the senior footman who had been walking the corgis, returned and, seeing what was happening, seized Fagan by an arm. Suddenly, the Queen found herself more than busy, trying to restrain the corgis who were snarling and snapping at the intruder.

At this point, eight minutes after the Queen's first telephone call for assistance, a group of policemen came charging up the stairs. The officer in the lead, a young constable, recalls seeing the Queen's head stuck out of the pantry. Self-consciously, he began to straighten his tie. "Oh, come on!" Elizabeth snapped. "Get a bloody move on!"

Michael Fagan was taken away and the following morning was booked at Horseferry Road magistrates court. The law of trespass at the time did not permit him to be charged, inasmuch as he had not "entered with intent." It developed, however, that some five weeks earlier, on June 7, he had broken into the palace and had consumed a half bottle of wine. He was therefore charged with theft and committed for trial.

On September 23, in the Old Bailey, a jury of seven men and five women sat in judgement. During the four-hour hearing, although Fagan cheerfully admitted that he had broken into the palace twice, he was found not guilty as charged. In the dock he told the jury, "It might be that I've done the Queen a favor: I've proved that her security system is no good."

He was remanded in custody to await trial on another unrelated charge (assaulting one of his stepsons) and subsequently was confined in a mental hospital from which he was discharged on January 20, 1983.

Returning to his flat, driving almost reflexively, Jeremy was filled with a quivering inner excitement. As do most journalists, he held the hope of breaking an exclusive story of worldwide interest, and here, as the result of a chance telephone call, was one in his hands. It had all the elements: a break-in, conspiracy, terrorism, the involvement of important people, Scotland Yard, even a carefully contrived cover-up. Diligent digging, a double-checking of all the facts, a carefully framed first draft, consultation with his superiors in New York, and then . . . black headlines around the world. His excitement intensified.

But another part of his brain brought him up short. He couldn't possibly write the story. He had been tipped to it, as Maidy Lightstone had said, "because you're a friend of Her Royal Highness." He wouldn't have known of the break-in otherwise. Nor would he have known about the changing of the locks on the royal apartments or the Queen's new guard dog or Trumper's sudden removal from his post had he not had special access to the principals involved. To write the story would be to break confidences, to take advantage of his privileged position. Beyond all else, how would it affect his relationship with Victoria?

But hold on a minute: could Victoria be justifiably angry with him if he wrote the story? Wasn't that the agreement they had made? – that he would continue his career and she hers. And wasn't he a reporter whose job it was to report the news? And wasn't this a legitimate news story by any reasonable standard? Did he not have a responsibility as a journalist to report the news objectively, without fear or favor? The journalist's task is not to judge the news but to report it.

Still, he could hear her rejoinder. If you're going to report what you learn because you're on the inside at the palace, will that not drive a wedge between us? Will I ever again feel free to talk to you about my daily life? Will I be able to share things with you as husbands and wives do, or will I have to guard my words, fearing that what I confide might end up being shouted from the housetops? When I'm Queen and privy to any number of facts that would make headlines, will I have to guard my every utterance? I'll know everything discussed in the cabinet. I'll know the state of the economy, the details of our relationships with other nations, friendly and hostile.

I'll even know personal things about heads of state. All kinds of things.

But, he thought, that's not an accurate picture. The Queen doesn't *now* discuss, even with her husband, what she learns in doing her boxes or through conversations with the Prime Minister or in sitting with the Privy Council. He'd heard Edward grousing about it in a bantering way: "Doesn't tell me a damn thing." And it hadn't hurt their marriage. But beyond all that, this story *should* be written. It's an important story. It demonstrates that the security surrounding the royal family is full of holes, with all the ramifications that flow from that. It reveals something of the face of the IRA. And it will reveal that even so revered an institution as New Scotland Yard can be involved in a cover-up.

But does the story tell anything new about the IRA? And was there any serious lapse of security at the palace, anything comparable to the revelations in the Fagan break-in? And was it really reprehensible of Scotland Yard not to reveal anything more than was necessary to a foreign reporter trying to mine a lead?

He remembered a conversation with Victoria late one evening. In the aftermath of Ossie Docherty's revelations about their liaison, Vicky had expressed some of her pent-up resentment of the press. "I'm not talking about the legitimate reporting of news," she'd said. "We need to be informed about what's happening, and without the news business, if I can call it that, we'd have no way of knowing. But honestly, Jeremy, isn't that too often used as justification for what the press does? A lot of newspapers aren't *news*papers, they're a form of entertainment. They're little more than panderers. Many of their editorialists and colum-nists are what used to be called common scolds. I sometimes wonder if we don't suffer from a surfeit of what's called the news. Every tragedy is picked over in much the way a bunch of carrion eaters strip a carcass. We're fed the blood and guts of every scandal, the gory details of every catastrophe, every especially horrible crime. I wonder if we haven't become inured to suffering. I've found that barely a month after I've clucked my tongue over ten thousand souls dying in a famine or an earthquake I've completely forgotten about them because I'm caught up in some new horror."

He'd agreed grudgingly but had gone on to enter a vigorous defense of the responsible media, and they'd both been glad to drop the subject when the discussion began to get heated. His parting shot had been, "You mustn't tar us all with the same brush."

Home, he parked Gridley in the garage and walked toward his flat, shoulders hunched against the penetrating cold. Beyond the river, in the freshly scrubbed evening air, the city winked and gleamed and sparkled. A half moon, low above St. Paul's, almost exactly replicated its illuminated dome. There was the far-off chiming of church bells and, nearby, the whooping screams of a police siren.

In the real world, he thought, how could he *not* write the story?

Opening the door to his flat, he saw that someone had slipped an envelope beneath it:

Jeremy:
I've been trying to reach you by telephone through much of the day but either your line was engaged or you were not in.

I'll be having breakfast alone tomorrow morning at eight. It would be pleasant if you could join me. Don't bother to confirm. If I haven't heard to the contrary, I'll expect you.
Edward

* * *

In his private kitchen, wearing an apron with the words THE PALACE PUB emblazoned on the front, Edward was gently nudging a nubbly mound of scrambled eggs on a griddle. "The secret of scrambled eggs is," he confided, "don't beat them; entice them."

"Superb!" Jeremy said when they'd been served to him with some tangy smoked salmon, barely buttered fingers of whole grain toast, and a steaming mug of café au lait.

Breakfast out of the way, Edward came directly to the point. "I wanted to have this talk with you, Jeremy, because I was informed yesterday that you've been inquiring about the intruder who broke into May's apartment last spring. I hope you're not planning to do a report on it for your newspaper."

Jeremy was caught off guard by Edward's directness. He gained a moment by sipping his coffee. "I have been considering it," he said.

"Let me express the hope that you won't do it," Edward said quietly.

Jeremy mashed the last morsels of egg between the tines of his fork and then savored them. "I really don't know how to respond," he said after a moment. "Whether you intended to or not, you've just confirmed the fact of the break-in, and. . . . Are you asking me not to write the story?"

"No," Edward said. "But I would hope you wouldn't." He put down his cup, wiping his lips with a napkin. "Let me take a minute to tell you why. More coffee?"

"No, thank you."

Edward began absently to brush some crumbs from his lap and realized that he was still wearing the apron. He rose from his chair, hung the apron on the back of a door, and returned to sit down.

"I'm going to be absolutely open with you," he said, "and I'd appreciate it if you would be the same with me.

To begin: the fact is that, over the past months, May and I have become fond of you, and we've come to the conclusion that, for all that we were opposed to it in the beginning, we would like to see you and Victoria married. She's in love with you – there's no doubt about that – and, in the end, the thing we want most is her happiness."

Jeremy was struggling to retain his composure. What was back of the extraordinary candor with which Edward was speaking? It was obvious that he'd carefully considered what he was now saying. There was no hesitation in his words, no equivocation. What was he leading up to?

"But," said Edward, "and I want to impress this on you: I know Victoria well enough to know that if you do write the story, she will be deeply offended. I'm presuming in this, but I doubt that she would ever forgive you. She has a very strong sense of propriety and I think she would see it as an act of disloyalty. You must remember," he said with the suggestion of a wry smile, "that she's put up with a lot from the press. We all have."

He leaned forward and picked up the coffee pot and the pitcher of hot milk. "You're sure you won't have another?" When Jeremy shook his head, he poured the twin streams into his own cup. He took a sip of the foamy liquid, cradled the cup in his hands, and paused a moment before continuing.

"There are two points I want to make," he said. "The first grows out of what I was saying a moment ago about Victoria being in love with you. She's a very strong-willed girl. . . ." He smiled fondly. "I still think of her as a girl. At any rate, it became clear to May and me early on that despite all the apple carts that might be upset, she had her heart set on marrying you. After fretting about that for some time, we simply made the decision one day that we would have another child. And, as you know, that's worked out jolly well.

368

"But there's something you *don't* know," he continued, "something that nobody knows other than our little family and May's doctors, and that is that it's going to be a boy."

He smiled at Jeremy, "You're surprised. Little wonder. It means, of course, that when all the necessary protocol has been observed, you and Victoria will be free to marry."

Jeremy felt a momentary dizziness. "Sir, I. . . . I hardly know what to – "

Edward held up a restraining hand. "Before you say anything, let me make my second point. Our son was conceived last April, the week May and I spent together at the Lodge at Windsor. The whole thing had been carefully planned with May's gynecologist, Sir Herbert Garvey. I think you know him." Jeremy nodded. "At the end of our week together, on the Saturday, Sir Herbert came by, did some tests, and early the following week told us the good news: May was pregnant."

He took another sip of coffee. "Unfortunately, on the Sunday morning, after we'd returned to London, Mulholland broke into my apartment and – "

"Into *your* apartment?"

"Yes. I'd gone off to Wales early that morning leaving my door unlocked for the chambermaids. Apparently Mulholland knew about that bad habit of mine and, as soon as I was gone, nipped into my study. Fortunately, May heard him and managed to frighten him off.

"And now," he said, "we come to the important point. As you will recognize, there's an unhappy coincidence of dates here. Our son will be born in mid-January. If you were to write the story of the break-in, which happened April 11, I very much fear that, in the kind of world we live in, there are a few mischievous minds who might put two and two together and get nine. I'm sure you follow my meaning. And that," he said, "might just be enough to raise questions in some quarters about – how shall I put it? – the acceptability of our son as the rightful heir."

He was about to go on but seemed to think better of it. Jeremy's eyes had been fixed on his face, but now he averted them, gazing instead out of the window. The silence extended, each man deep in his thoughts.

Jeremy felt his heart pounding. As Edward was speaking, his mind had gone back to that week. He remembered it clearly. Victoria had been away in Gibraltar, and for all the fact that he'd missed her intensely, her absence had enabled him to concentrate on finishing his series, *Britain: The Lion Doesn't Roar Anymore*. Now, driving like a shaft into his brain, came the memory of how, as he was writing about the problems of the National Health Plan, he'd called Sir Herbert's office to check some facts and had been told by his secretary that he was in Los Angeles addressing the American Medical Association and wouldn't return until the following week. *Edward was lying to him!* Sir Herbert couldn't possibly have confirmed the Queen's pregnancy that weekend: he was out of the country!

But why was Edward telling him what was undoubtedly a carefully contrived lie? Obviously, to keep him from writing the story of the break-in. But he could have pressed him not to do that. And why had he introduced the possibility that the intruder might be taken to be the father of the Queen's child? The reason he'd given was that mischievous minds might raise questions and challenge the legitimacy of the new heir, but who would be likely to do that? Surely no one of consequence. Not unless there were some plausible grounds. . . .

There was, as Edward had said, the coincidence of times. More troublesome, Jeremy thought, was the fact that, although Mulholland had been seen coming out of the window of the Queen's dressing-room, there had been no outcry, no search of the palace grounds, no rolling of heads

370

in the palace police force. And why was it only now, months later, that Mulholland had been arrested? And why was he being held incommunicado? There were so many things that didn't add up.

The question formed in his mind: was it possible? . . . Could it be that the intruder? . . .

Of course not. The idea was preposterous. But how else to account for the fact that. . . . No, it was impossible; he couldn't believe it for a moment. He shook his head to dislodge the thought. He would *not* believe it.

He became aware that Edward was watching him, waiting for his response. "Let me relieve your mind, sir," he said, surprised that his voice sounded normal. "I've decided not to write the story."

"I'm pleased to hear that," Edward said. "I thought when you realized what it would mean to you and Victoria, to all of us, you wouldn't."

♔ FIVE

THE COURT CIRCULAR in the *Times* and *Telegraph* listed the activities planned by the royal family for Christmas Day. At 9:00 a.m. the Queen would deliver on radio and television her annual Christmas message and then attend a private service of worship in the chapel at Buckingham Palace. Prince Edward would attend the morning service at Westminster Abbey during which he would read, as the scripture lesson, from the second chapter of Luke. The Princess of Wales would represent the family at St. George's Chapel in Windsor. At 1:00 p.m. the Queen would go to Clarence House to have lunch with her mother, Queen Charlotte. The Duke and Princess Victoria, with other family members and friends, would join them later for Christmas dinner.

At exactly five minutes to one, Mary, enveloped in a capacious Russian sable coat and walking circumspectly, left her apartment and entered the lift. At ground level, on the arm of the Page of the Presence who normally accompanied her on the lift, she walked to her gleaming black Rolls-Royce, the official silver hood ornament – depicting a naked St. George slaying a dragon – in place on the bonnet.

After a small delay in forming up – the police escort positioning itself before and behind the limousine – the procession moved off, passing through the North Gates and entering onto the roundabout at the Victoria Memorial. Clarence House is not a thousand yards removed from Buckingham Palace, and on this frigid, sun-bright afternoon, its dazzling white exterior seemed to glow like a jewel against the gloomy setting of St. James' Palace.

A crowd of perhaps two thousand lined the streets for the short run up the Mall, among them many children bundled against the cold. Some of the adults, having arrived before dawn, were seated on the curb swaddled in blankets. As the royal limousine came in sight, a cheer went up, and the soldiers, spaced every few yards along the route snapped to rigid attention. The spectators came to their feet, waving their hands, wig-wagging tiny Union Jacks or holding high hand-lettered signs. As the Queen came in sight, the cheering mounted to a roar. Within the limousine, Mary, smiling, looked at the lively fabric of excited faces on either side and waved a white-gloved hand.

As the car rounded the memorial and entered on the Mall, Mary saw a man in the crowd lob what looked like an oddly shaped ball toward the car. She watched it, her eyes fixed on it, fascinated. It bounced as it rolled, and as it drew closer she saw that it wasn't a ball. It was a grenade. In her peripheral vision she was aware of a scuffle in the crowd and of rude shouts and screaming, but her eyes were on the grenade. It skittered up to the car and passed out of sight beneath it.

The explosion lifted the great limousine into the air, raising the front high, almost like a horse rearing and dropping back on its haunches. For a long moment the car stood on end, only the bonnet visible above the smoke and dust and debris roiling about it. Then, slowly, almost majestically, it rolled over onto its top, rocking back and forth.

Edward, returning from the Abbey, arrived at the scene only minutes later. People were running from everywhere to join the crowd standing motionless in a mute, stricken circle ringing the upturned Rolls. Many were crying out or weeping uncontrollably. Children, some of them stunned, some hysterical, clung to their parents. Nearby, two policemen had a man pinned to the ground, one of them with a knee on the back of his neck. An ambulance that had been drawn up beside the battered limousine began to nose through the crowd, lights flashing, its siren emitting what sounded like short yelps of pain. Then, surrounded by police outriders, it picked up speed and headed toward Westminster Hospital.

As Edward leaped from his car and ran toward the upended limousine, a policeman seized him roughly and swung him around. Then, recognizing him, he quickly released him. Edward shouted in his ear and, being told that the Queen was en route to Westminster, ran to his car. With police cruisers in the van, it moved through the crowd and away.

Victoria heard of the bombing on MacIntyre's police radio while en route from Windsor. MacIntyre set the Jaguar's lights to flashing and turned on the auxiliary siren, speaking urgently into his radio telephone as he threaded his way through the thin holiday traffic. At Edgeware Road two police motor bikes were waiting. Sirens wailing, they led the way to the hospital.

Jeremy, in jeans and a New York *Mets* sweatshirt, was on a stepladder changing a light bulb in his study when the telephone rang. He threw on a black pea jacket, wound a long red scarf about the collar, and went off on the run toward where Gridley was garaged.

Roger Naismith, the President of Westminster Hospital, a terse, no-nonsense administrator, had reacted to the emergency with swift, decisive action. The halls outside his office were cleared except for those members of the staff on duty. Patients awaiting admission were sent home; those awaiting surgery were wheeled back to their rooms. As Edward and then Victoria and, in their turn, Jeremy, Queen Charlotte, and Angus McCrimmon arrived, they were ushered past the policemen posted at the door to Naismith's office. Within minutes there was tea and an assortment of sandwiches and cakes on a table and two additional telephones.

The President's office was a large, drab room, yielding evidence of years of austerity. It was dominated by Naismith's desk which sat at dead-center. Ranging around the room were a number of massive, overstuffed leather chairs, a matching sofa, and an impressive display of books and pictures; paintings of his predecessors and framed photographs of eminent visitors. As each member of the tiny group of royals arrived, Edward greeted them, after which they commiserated with each other and withdrew to individual areas of isolation to await in a bewildered and uneasy silence whatever might lie ahead.

The only information Naismith had volunteered was that the Queen was in the operating theater undergoing an examination as to the nature and extent of her injuries. He had no information on the condition of the fetus, nor would he hazard an opinion on the prognosis for either the Queen or the child.

"Please, sir," he said when Edward pressed him, "don't ask me to speculate. I can tell you no more at this point than that Her Majesty has regained consciousness. Let's take that as a good augury. Please be assured, sir, that the moment I have anything definitive, I'll report back." He went out, pulling the door gently closed behind him.

Soon McCrimmon had taken a telephone to the limit of its extension cord and was in a corner, head down, hand cupped about his mouth, engaged in a series of dialings and whispered conversations. The Queen Mother stood about for a few minutes and then occupied herself by pouring tea for everyone and offering about a plate of sandwiches, for which there were no takers. Victoria had sunk deep into one of the leather chairs where she sat stock-still, staring with unfocused eyes. Jeremy went to her and perched in silence on the arm beside her, a hand resting on her shoulder. Edward was at a window, hands behind his back, looking unseeing into the street some six stories below. After a while Victoria rose and went to her father, slipping a hand into his and resting her head against his shoulder.

Jeremy sipped his tea, slowly emerging from the sense of numb incredulity that had enveloped him since first hearing of the bombing. Now, as he had trained himself to do, he began to examine the ramifications of the disaster.

What if the Queen were to die on the operating table and the unborn baby with her? The answer was simple: Victoria would be Queen. Britain is never without a monarch. The final exhalation of the dying sovereign is followed by the drawn breath of the new. "The Queen is dead. Long live the Queen!" There would be no consultation, no discussion, no possibility of a demurrer. Ahead would lie the formal proclamation by Parliament and, in a few months, the coronation. What then of his and Victoria's plans? He realized with a growing sense of despair that they would be forever dashed.

But what if Mary were to die and the baby were snatched alive from her body? Then, the squalling, bloody, fresh-born infant would be King, in all likelihood with Edward as his regent. Jeremy remembered that in the last nine years of the reign of George III, when his madness had rendered him unable to rule, the government had been vested in the then Prince of Wales as regent. With Mary dead, undoubtedly some such accommodation would be made until the child reached maturity.

But what if Mary were to survive and the fetus die, but with Mary so incapacitated by her injuries that she could not function? Almost certainly she would abdicate and Victoria would have no option in the crisis but to do her duty and ascend to the throne.

His thoughts were interrupted by the movement of the others in the room over to the windows. He rose and joined them. As far as could be seen, the streets were massed with people. Although they were in the thousands, no sound rose from them. Many of the faces were upturned, almost, Jeremy thought, as though in importunity.

Somewhere in the crowd a woman began to sing. An uncertain, reedy sound at first, it soon strengthened as her voice was joined by others. Then, suddenly the song grew in volume and power, filling the air:

> God save our gracious Queen.
> Long live our noble Queen.
> God save the Queen.

Now the singing soared, echoing in the street, lifting above the buildings, swelling, reverberating:

> Send her victorious,
> Happy and glorious,
> Long to reign over us . . .
> God save . . . the . . . Queen.

Naismith was back, his tie loosened, his face ruddy and shining with perspiration. "I have some good news for you," he said. "The Queen, so far as we have been able to determine, has suffered no injuries of consequence. A fracture of the left arm, some contusions, some abrasions, but nothing of a serious nature. Apparently, the great bulk of the car protected her from the blast."

He waited until the burst of excited comment had passed and then added, "There is one complication, however. It has to do with Her Majesty's pregnancy. The trauma has induced premature contractions and she has entered into labor. We're monitoring the fetus and there is consultation going on as to whether a Caesarian section should be done." He addressed himself to Edward. "I'm going to forgo the usual formal permission and simply ask if I may have your prior consent to proceed as seems wise, granted of course that the doctors reach consensus."

"Yes," Edward said. "Yes, of course. Whatever is required."

For all the continuing concern, the easing of tension in the room was almost palpable. Everyone talked at once and McCrimmon moved back to the telephone. But, after a while, they all lapsed into silence again. Occasionally, one or another would lean close and whisper briefly to the person nearest, but soon even that ended; there seemed nothing further to be said. The hands on the clock over the door lagged and, with every minute, the waiting weighed more heavily. An hour passed, and another. Then as the suspense seemed almost beyond bearing, Naismith returned, the broad smile on his face forecasting his good news. With him was a formidable looking nurse of about fifty.

"You'll be happy to know," he said, his voice thick and a mistiness clouding his eyes, "that the Queen went through her labor in absolutely fine style. Simply marvelous! And the baby is well." He turned to Edward and, with a slight bow, said, "Your Royal Highness, may I present Mrs. Knight, she's our Director of Nursing here at Westminster. If you'd like to go with her, she'll take you to the Queen."

Edward and Mrs. Knight went down the long corridor, followed by discreet glances and sibilant whispers. Mrs. Knight, a large, chunkily built woman, led him by a step, head up, walking like a sergeant-major. At the door to the furthermost room she stopped, leaned toward him and said in a confidential tone, "It's a boy." Then, her face reflecting her great pleasure, she whispered, "And he looks just like his father."

BUCKINGHAM PALACE

Schematic drawings of the location of the Palace, and the basic plan of the Palace's principal rooms.

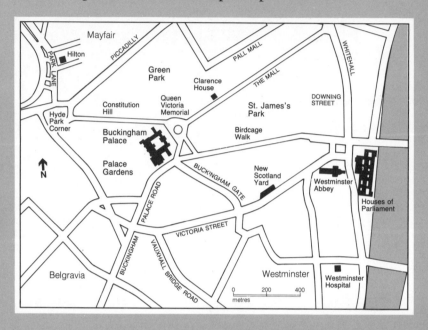

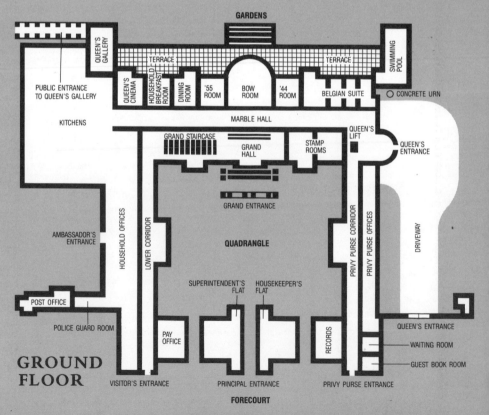